"Translations disrupt the American mind's obsession with its own self-absorbed soul. We are suddenly taken abroad: other voices, soils, and smells. Light falls with another slant and darker shadows. An astonishing range of poets, styles, lands, and centuries is encompassed by Robert Bly's magisterial capacities, opening a Book of the World and giving us a long and lovely read."

—James Hillman, author of *A Terrible Love of War*

"A good translation is an act of friendship. In it, one poet can draw close to another's work without intellectualizing or criticizing. Robert Bly has been engaged in this intimate labor for half a century now, across continents and centuries. He is the greatest literary host America has ever had, and this volume is a twenty-two-course banquet served to celebrate that fact."

—Lewis Hyde, Richard L. Thomas
Professor of Creative Writing, Kenyon College

"Robert Bly lives in the company of poets he translates. He generously introduces his friends. The word spreads. [Bly's] life in poetry has made possible the community of shared delight and compassion that Pablo Neruda and Kenneth Rexroth longed for." —Coleman Barks, author of
Rumi: The Book of Love and *The Drowned Book: Earthy and Ecstatic Reflections of Bahauddin, Rumi's Father*

"[*The Winged Energy of Delight* is] an exceptionally spirited international collection of artful and passionate translations."

—*Booklist*

Jason Langer

About the Author

ROBERT BLY is the author of the bestseller *Iron John*, as well as *The Maiden King* and *The Sibling Society*. He is the editor of *The Fifties, The Sixties, The Seventies,* and *The Thousands,* and the author of many books of poems, most recently *My Sentence Was a Thousand Years of Joy.* His awards include two Guggenheims and the National Book Award. He lives in Minneapolis, Minnesota.

THE WINGED ENERGY
OF DELIGHT

Selected Translations

Robert Bly

Perennial
An Imprint of HarperCollins*Publishers*

A hardcover edition of this book was published in 2004 by HarperCollins Publishers.

HarperCollins books may be purchased for educational, business, or sales promotional use. For information please write: Special Markets Department, HarperCollins Publishers Inc., 10 East 53rd Street, New York, NY 10022.

FIRST PERENNIAL EDITION PUBLISHED 2005.

Designed by Nicola Ferguson

The Library of Congress has catalogued the hardcover edition as follows:

The winged energy of delight: selected translations / [translated by] Robert Bly.—1st ed.
    p. cm.
  ISBN 0-06-057582-4 (alk. paper)
    1. Poetry—Translations into English.   2. Poetry—Collections.
  I. Bly, Robert.

PN6101.W44   2004
808.81—dc22   2003067619

ISBN 0-06-057586-7 (pbk.)

06 07 08 09 ❖/RRD 10 9 8 7 6 5 4 3 2

CONTENTS

SOME WORDS ABOUT THIS BOOK

DURING THE FIFTIES, there was very little sense in the poetry community of contemporary European and South American poetry. While in Norway a few years later I found Paal Brekke's anthology *Modernistisk Lyrikk* (*The Modern Poem*). He included one poem apiece by seven or eight lively poets from each of the major European countries. There was a great freshness in many of these poets. How was it that I had never seen the names of Trakl, Ekelöf, or Vallejo in contemporary American magazines? Many of these poets engaged in an explosive attention to metaphor.

Back in the United States, after driving away one day to a distant library to find a copy of a Tranströmer book called *Den Halvfärdiga Himlen* (*Half-Finished Heaven*), I found on my return a letter from Tranströmer directed to James Wright, a poem of whose he had read in *The Times Literary Supplement*. So some poets in Europe were alert to any movement in the world of the image. I soon translated some of Tomas Tranströmer's poems, and James Wright and I did the first book of Trakl's poems into English. Later we translated Vallejo, Neruda, and Jiménez together. Translating allows one to go deeply into the adventures taking place inside another person's poem; translating with friends is one of the greatest pleasures in the world.

Wright and I depended on Hardie St. Martin, who had a Spanish-speaking mother and an American father, and knew both languages in the cradle. His care and love lie behind all our translations from the Spanish. Tranströmer, whose English is excellent, gave me much help on English versions of his poems. I had no help on Rilke, and depended on my own German, which was probably not good enough. In a little book called *The Eight Stages of Translation,* I follow a single sonnet of Rilke's through the eight stages that I detected from my own practice. This booklet attempts to show how complicated the process of translation is, and how many errors one can fall into. When I have had no help with the language at all, as was the case with my early work on Kabir, I call those poems "versions" instead of translations. My Kabir poems are rewritings of the translations into colonial English made by Rabindranath Tagore in the 1920s. Even in his stodgy English, one could feel the astounding courage and brilliance of Kabir. The Mirabai poems have evolved from word-by-word translations which were given to me by the East Asian Language Department of the University of Chicago. For the Ghalib poems, my son-in-law, Sunil Dutta, made literal translations from the Hindi with elaborate commentaries in English on each line. In my still more recent translations of Hafez, I have had help from an unfailingly fierce and generous scholar of Iranian literature, Leonard Lewisohn.

When Hugh Van Dusen at HarperCollins first suggested that I gather together a large group of my translations in a single book, I was delighted to have the chance. But given that twenty-two poets were to be included, it wasn't at all clear in what order they should come. Arrangement by birthdate didn't seem right, because the book would then begin with Horace, but Horace is most interesting to people familiar with the work done during recent decades on the image and its importance in argument. Arranging the poems by the order in which my translations got published didn't make sense either, because some translations had to wait years. Finally, my daughter, Bridget, said, "Why don't you publish them in the order in which you first loved them?" That idea is the one I settled on for this book.

The most important gift we receive when translating is to see genius—in Mirabai, Rumi, Lorca, Ponge—shine straight through into the world.

TOMAS TRANSTRÖMER

TOMAS TRANSTRÖMER COMES from a long line of ship pilots who worked in and around the Stockholm Archipelago. He is at home on islands. His face is thin and angular, and the swift, spare face reminds one of Hans Christian Andersen's or the younger Kierkegaard's. He has a strange genius for the image — images come up almost effortlessly. The images flow upward like water rising in some lonely place, in the swamps, or deep fir woods.

Swedish poetry tends to be very rational, and therefore open to fads. Tranströmer, simply by publishing his books, leads a movement of poetry in the opposite direction, toward a poetry of silence and depths.

One of the most beautiful qualities in his poems is the space we feel in them. I think one reason for that is that the four or five main images that appear in each of his poems come from widely separated sources in the psyche. His poems are a sort of railway station where trains that have come enormous distances stand briefly in the same building. One train may have some Russian snow still lying on the undercarriage, and another may have Mediterranean flowers still fresh in the compartments, and Ruhr soot on the roofs.

The poems are mysterious because of the distance the images have come to get there. Mallarmé believed there should be mystery in poetry, and urged poets to get it by removing the links that tie the poem to its occasion in the real world. Tranströmer keeps the link to the worldly occasion, and yet the poems have a mystery and surprise that never fade, even on many readings.

Rilke taught that poets should be "bees of the invisible." Making honey for the invisible suggests that the poet remain close to earthly history, but move as well toward the spiritual and the invisible. Tranströmer suspects that as an artist he is merely a way for "the Memory" to get out into the world. Even at seventeen he was aware that the dead "wanted to have their portrait painted." Somehow that cannot be done without making peace with rhetoric. He wants to tell of spiritual matters, but he doesn't want to be a preacher. If rhetoric could kill Christianity in Sweden, maybe it could kill poetry as well. In "From an African Diary," he describes climbing on a canoe hollowed from a log:

> The canoe is incredibly wobbly, even when you sit on your heels. A balancing act. If you have the heart on the left side you have to lean a bit to the right, nothing in the pockets, no big arm movements, please, all rhetoric has to be left behind. Precisely: rhetoric is impossible here. The canoe glides out over the water.

In "The Scattered Congregation," Tranströmer remarks:

> Nicodemus the sleepwalker is on his way
> to the Address. Who's got the Address?
> Don't know. But that's where we're going.

TOMAS TRANSTRÖMER was born in Stockholm on April 15, 1931. His father and mother divorced when he was three; he and his mother lived after that in an apartment in the working-class district of Stockholm. He describes the apartment in the poem called "The Bookcase."

The early fifties were a rather formal time, both here and in Sweden, and Tranströmer began by writing concentrated, highly formal poems, some in iambs and some in the Alcaic meter. His first book, *17 Poems,* published in 1954, glowed with strange baroque elements, and contained only a few poems, but people noticed the power of the book immediately.

For several years, he worked as a psychologist in a boys' prison in Linköping, and then in 1965, he moved with his wife, Monica, and his two daughters, Paula and Emma, to Västerås, a town about forty miles west of Stockholm. He continued to work as a psychologist, this time for a labor organization funded by the State. He helped juvenile delinquents to reenter society and persons with physical disabilities to choose a career, and he counseled parole offenders and those in drug rehabilitation.

Tomas Tranströmer's poems are so luminous that genuine poetry can travel to another language and thrive. His poems have been translated into dozens of European and Asian languages; at this moment, something like thirty-eight.

The praise for his poems has steadily grown both in Europe and in the United States. He has received most of the important poetry prizes in Europe, including the Petrarch Prize in Germany, the Bonnier Award for Poetry, the Pilot Prize in 1988, the Nordic Council Prize in 1990, the Swedish Academy's Nordic Prize in 1991, and the Horst Bieneck Prize in 1992.

The town of Västerås recently had a formal farewell celebration in the old castle for Tomas and Monica, who were moving to Stockholm. A choir sang to him, and presents were piled up five feet high around his chair.

Today, the couple live in an apartment in Stockholm overlooking the harbor, near the old neighborhood where Tomas lived as a boy.

TRACK

2 A.M.: moonlight. The train has stopped
out in a field. Far-off sparks of light from a town,
flickering coldly on the horizon.

As when a man goes so deep into his dream
he will never remember that he was there
when he returns again to his room.

Or when a person goes so deep into a sickness
that his days all become some flickering sparks, a swarm,
feeble and cold on the horizon.

The train is entirely motionless.
2 o'clock: strong moonlight, few stars.

ALLEGRO

After a black day, I play Haydn,
and feel a little warmth in my hands.

The keys are ready. Kind hammers fall.
The sound is spirited, green, and full of silence.

The sound says that freedom exists
and someone pays no taxes to Caesar.

I shove my hands in my haydnpockets
and act like a man who is calm about it all.

I raise my haydnflag. The signal is:
"We do not surrender. But want peace."

The music is a house of glass standing on a slope;
rocks are flying, rocks are rolling.

The rocks roll straight through the house
but every pane of glass is still whole.

MORNING BIRD SONGS

I wake up my car;
pollen covers the windshield.
I put my dark glasses on.
The bird songs all turn dark.

Meanwhile someone is buying a paper
at the railroad station
not far from a big freight car
reddened all over with rust.
It shimmers in the sun.

The whole universe is full.

A cool corridor cuts through the spring warmth;
a man comes hurrying past
describing how someone right up in the main office
has been telling lies about him.

Through a backdoor in the landscape
the magpie arrives,
black and white, bird of the death-goddess.
A blackbird flies back and forth
until the whole scene becomes a charcoal drawing,
except for the white clothes on the line:
a Palestrina choir.

The whole universe is full!

Fantastic to feel how my poem is growing
while I myself am shrinking.
It's getting bigger, it's taking my place,
it's pressing against me.
It has shoved me out of the nest.
The poem is finished.

OUT IN THE OPEN

1

Late autumn labyrinth.
At the entry to the woods a thrown-away bottle.
Go in. Woods are silent abandoned houses this time of year.
Just a few sounds now: as if someone were moving twigs around
    carefully with pincers
or as if an iron hinge were whining feebly inside a thick trunk.
Frost has breathed on the mushrooms and they have shriveled up.
They look like objects and clothing left behind by people who've
    disappeared.
It will be dark soon. The thing to do now is to get out
and find the landmarks again: the rusty machine out in the field
and the house on the other side of the lake, a reddish square intense as
    a bouillon cube.

2

A letter from America drove me out again, started me walking
through the luminous June night in the empty suburban streets
among newborn districts without memories, cool as blueprints.

Letter in my pocket. Half-mad, lost walking, it is a kind of prayer.
Over there evil and good actually have faces.
For the most part with us it's a fight between roots, numbers, shades
    of light.

The people who run death's errands for him don't shy from daylight.
They rule from glass offices. They mill about in the bright sun.
They lean forward over a desk, and throw a look to the side.

Far off I found myself standing in front of one of the new buildings.
Many windows flowed together there into a single window.
In it the luminous nightsky was caught, and the walking trees.
It was a mirrorlike lake with no waves, turned on edge in the
    summer night.

Violence seemed unreal
for a few moments.

3
Sun burning. The plane comes in low
throwing a shadow shaped like a giant cross that rushes over the
    ground.
A man is sitting in the field poking at something.
The shadow arrives.
For a fraction of a second he is right in the center of the cross.

I have seen the cross hanging in the cool church vaults.
At times it resembles a split-second snapshot of something
moving at tremendous speed.

SOLITUDE

1

Right here I was nearly killed one night in February.
My car slewed on the ice, sideways,
into the other lane. The oncoming cars—
their headlights—came nearer.

My name, my daughters, my job
slipped free and fell behind silently,
farther and farther back. I was anonymous,
like a schoolboy in a lot surrounded by enemies.

The approaching traffic had powerful lights.
They shone on me while I turned and turned
the wheel in a transparent fear that moved like eggwhite.
The seconds lengthened out—making more room—
they grew long as hospital buildings.

It felt as if you could just take it easy
and loaf a bit
before the smash came.

Then firm land appeared: a helping sandgrain
or a marvelous gust of wind. The car took hold
and fishtailed back across the road.
A signpost shot up, snapped off—a ringing sound—
tossed into the dark.

Came all quiet. I sat there in my seat belt
and watched someone tramp through the blowing snow
to see what had become of me.

2

I have been walking awhile
on the frozen Swedish fields
and I have seen no one.

In other parts of the world
people are born, live, and die
in a constant human crush.

To be visible all the time — to live
in a swarm of eyes —
surely that leaves its mark on the face.
Features overlaid with clay.

The low voices rise and fall
as they divide up
heaven, shadows, grains of sand.

I have to be by myself
ten minutes every morning,
ten minutes every night,
— and nothing to be done!

We all line up to ask each other for help.

Millions.
One.

THE SCATTERED CONGREGATION

1

We got ready and showed our home.
The visitor thought: you live well.
The slum must be inside you.

2

Inside the church, pillars and vaulting
white as plaster, like the cast
around the broken arm of faith.

3

Inside the church there's a begging bowl
that slowly lifts from the floor
and floats along the pews.

4

But the church bells have gone underground.
They're hanging in the sewage pipes.
Whenever we take a step, they ring.

5

Nicodemus the sleepwalker is on his way
to the Address. Who's got the Address?
Don't know. But that's where we're going.

AT FUNCHAL

(Island of Madeira)

On the beach there's a seafood place, simple, a shack thrown up by survivors of the shipwreck. Many turn back at the door, but not the sea winds. A shadow stands deep inside his smoky hut frying two fish according to an old recipe from Atlantis, tiny garlic explosions, oil running over sliced tomatoes, every morsel says that the ocean wishes us well, a humming from the deep places.

She and I look into each other. It's like climbing the wild-flowered mountain slopes without feeling the least bit tired. We've sided with the animals, they welcome us, we don't age. But we have experienced so much together over the years, including those times when we weren't so good (as when we stood in line to give blood to the healthy giant—he said he wanted a transfusion), incidents which should have separated us if they hadn't united us, and incidents which we've totally forgotten—though they haven't forgotten us! They've turned to stones, dark and light, stones in a scattered mosaic. And now it happens: the pieces move toward each other, the mosaic appears and is whole. It waits for us. It glows down from the hotel-room wall, some figure violent and tender. Perhaps a face, we can't take it all in as we pull off our clothes.

After dusk we go out. The dark powerful paw of the cape lies thrown out into the sea. We walk in swirls of human beings, we are cuffed around kindly, among soft tyrannies, everyone chatters excitedly in the foreign tongue. "No man is an island." We gain strength from *them,* but also from ourselves. From what is inside that the other person can't see. That which can only meet itself. The innermost paradox, the underground garage flowers, the vent toward the good dark. A drink that bubbles in an empty glass. An amplifier that magnifies silence. A path that grows over after every step. A book that can only be read in the dark.

SCHUBERTIANA

1

Outside New York, a high place where with one glance you take in the houses where eight million human beings live.

The giant city over there is a long flimmery drift, a spiral galaxy seen from the side.

Inside the galaxy, coffee cups are being pushed across the desk, department store windows beg, a whirl of shoes that leave no trace behind.

Fire escapes climbing up, elevator doors that silently close, behind triple-locked doors a steady swell of voices.

Slumped-over bodies doze in subway cars, catacombs in motion.

I know also—statistics to the side—that at this instant in some room down there Schubert is being played, and for that person the notes are more real than all the rest.

2

The immense treeless plains of the human brain have gotten folded and refolded 'til they are the size of a fist.

The swallow in April returns to its last year's nest under the eaves in precisely the right barn in precisely the right township.

She flies from the Transvaal, passes the equator, flies for six weeks over two continents, navigates toward precisely this one disappearing dot in the landmass.

And the man who gathers up the signals from a whole lifetime into a few rather ordinary chords for five string musicians

the one who got a river to flow through the eye of a needle

is a plump young man from Vienna, his friends called him "The Mushroom," who slept with his glasses on

and every morning punctually stood at his high writing table.

When he did that the wonderful centipedes started to move on the page.

3

The five instruments play. I go home through warm woods where the earth is springy under my feet,

curl up like someone still unborn, sleep, roll on so weightlessly into the future, suddenly understand that plants are thinking.

How much we have to take on trust every minute we live in order not to drop through the earth!

Take on trust the snow masses clinging to rocksides over the town.

Take on trust the unspoken promises, and the smile of agreement, trust that the telegram does not concern us, and that the sudden ax blow from inside is not coming.

Trust the axles we ride on down the thruway among the swarm of steel bees magnified three hundred times.

But none of that stuff is really worth the trust we have.

The five string instruments say that we can take something else on trust, and they walk with us a bit on the road.

As when the lightbulb goes out on the stair, and the hand follows — trusting it — the blind banister rail that finds its way in the dark.

4

We crowd up onto the piano stool and play four-handed in f-minor, two drivers for the same carriage, it looks a little ridiculous.

It looks as if the hands are moving weights made of sound back and forth, as if we were moving lead weights

in an attempt to alter the big scale's frightening balance: happiness and suffering weigh exactly the same.

Annie said, "This music is so heroic," and she is right.

But those who glance enviously at men of action, people who despise themselves inside for not being murderers,

do not find themselves in this music.

And the people who buy and sell others, and who believe that everyone can be bought, don't find themselves here.

Not their music. The long melody line that remains itself among all its
variations, sometimes shiny and gentle, sometimes rough and
powerful, the snail's trace and steel wire.
The stubborn humming sound that this instant is with us
upward into
the depths.

VERMEER

It's not a sheltered world. The noise begins over there, on the other
    side of the wall
where the alehouse is
with its laughter and quarrels, its rows of teeth, its tears, its chiming of
    clocks,
and the psychotic brother-in-law, the murderer, in whose presence
    everyone feels fear.

The huge explosion and the emergency crew arriving late,
boats showing off on the canals, money slipping down into pockets —
    the wrong man's —
ultimatum piled on ultimatum,
widemouthed red flowers whose sweat reminds us of approaching
    war.

And then straight through the wall — from there — straight into the
    airy studio
and the seconds that have got permission to live for centuries.
Paintings that choose the name: "The Music Lesson"
or "A Woman in Blue Reading a Letter."
She is eight months pregnant, two hearts beating inside her.
The wall behind her holds a crinkly map of Terra Incognita.

Just breathe. An unidentifiable blue fabric has been tacked to the
    chairs.
Gold-headed tacks flew in with astronomical speed
and stopped smack there
as if they had always been stillness and nothing else.

The ears experience a buzz, perhaps it's depth or perhaps height.
It's the pressure from the other side of the wall,
the pressure that makes each fact float
and makes the brushstroke firm.

Passing through walls hurts human beings, they get sick from it,
but we have no choice.
It's all one world. Now to the walls.
The walls are a part of you.
One either knows that, or one doesn't; but it's the same for everyone
except for small children. There aren't any walls for them.

The airy sky has taken its place leaning against the wall.
It is like a prayer to what is empty.
And what is empty turns its face to us
and whispers:
"I am not empty, I am open."

APRIL AND SILENCE

Spring lies abandoned.
A ditch the color of dark violet
moves alongside me
giving no images back.

The only thing that shines
are some yellow flowers.

I am carried inside
my own shadow like a violin
in its black case.

The only thing I want to say
hovers just out of reach
like the family silver
at the pawnbroker's.

DECEMBER EVENING, '72

Here I come the invisible man, perhaps in the employ
of some huge Memory that wants to live at this moment. And I drive by

the white church that's locked up. A saint made of wood is inside,
smiling helplessly, as if someone had taken his glasses.

He's alone. Everything else is now, now, now. Gravity
pulling us toward work in the dark and the bed at night. The war.

MIRABAI

WHEN MIRABAI COMES to meet you, you'll have to be prepared for excess. She formed her opinions in the very teeth of the storm, fighting in her family, and succeeded in establishing her personal life against great odds. Mirabai pushed her way out of her family, out of many social demands, and ignored many commands given to her as a woman of her time. Her religious passion carried her into intensities that make most people turn pale.

> I would like my own body to turn into a heap of incense and
> sandalwood and you set a torch to it.
> When I've fallen down to gray ashes, smear me on your shoulders
> and chest.

We know that hundreds of singers and dancers at that time participated in this sort of excess.

We could say that her poetry brings to us three huge illuminations. First, we get the feeling of what it's like to rebel against entrenched patriarchal interests and a deeply rooted social order. Also, we can sense through her poetry the power of the Krishna movement. Krishna was said to free Indian women from long-standing bonds, and in one story he makes love with a hundred married women at night in the river. Also, we can feel how much Mirabai's poems were like a moving fire — not so friendly to people of wealth, it is a fire from another world.

One has to admire the Indian religious culture for being able to sustain the challenge of such fierce speakers as Kabir, Tulsidas, and Mirabai. We recall that Margaret Porete spoke of similar passions, and she was burned to death in Paris in 1302. Mirabai sustained threats, but she did survive.

When a poem of Mirabai's flows freely, one feels a fast-moving river of thought going in channels of enormous depth, moving and twisting around rocks with quick intelligence. Her river of thought holds the delicate heart of ardor, loverhood, teacher-devotion, Isolde-like intensity, and then mingles that ecstasy with a steely Joan-of-Arc rebelliousness. Her refusal to adjust to a low-spirited social order is so firm and well backed that the order entrenched by men, priests, or angry aunts doesn't have a chance in hell of standing against her. Sarcasm is a fine weapon for her.

> I don't steal money, I don't hit anyone. What will you charge me
>   with?

Krishna has the darker face of people in southern India, and she sometimes calls him the Dark One.

> My friend, I went to the market and bought the Dark One.
> You claim by night, I say by day.
> Actually I was beating a drum all the time I was buying him.
> You say I gave too much; I say too little.
> Actually I put him on a scale before I bought him.

Jane Hirshfield has set down some magnificent lines of Mirabai's about what will happen when you offer the Great One your life:

> Be ready to orbit his lamp like a moth giving in to the light,
> To live in the deer as she runs toward the hunter's call,
> In the partridge that swallows hot coals for love of the moon.

MIRABAI was born in Rajasthan in 1498, while the Hindu Rajputs were still resisting the Muslim domination; they kept their own dreams of family honor and military greatness. Thirty years after Mirabai's birth, the first great Mughal emperor invaded India and established the Mughal Dynasty at Delhi.

Among Rajputs, a family was a feudal patriarchy requiring battle courage in men, chastity and obedience in women.

Mira was born in the village of Kudki. It is said that when she was a tiny girl, she begged from a visiting ascetic a small statue of Krishna that he carried. She refused to eat or drink until she received it. Apparently the ascetic received a dream ordering him to give the statue to Mirabai.

In 1516, she married the son of the Rana Sangha, the leader of the Rajputs. This moment of her life has been decorated with many stories. People say that she insisted on being married to the statuette of Krishna before the marriage to her husband. The marriage did not last long; her husband died after only three years.

It is also said that she had a guru who was an Untouchable, living in the little town near the castle. Her family refused to allow her to make any contact with him, so she would tie her saris together and climb down the castle wall at night. She would wash his old feet with water and then drink it.

Her husband's family failed to control her and apparently tried to kill her several times. In one poem, she mentions the son of Rana Sangha sending her a cup of poison, and later a poisonous snake. She says in a song that she put it around her neck and thanked him for the jewelry. Sometime later, she left the castle and began to travel to Brindavan where Krishna had lived as a youth. Apparently she traveled widely around north India, singing and reciting poems, and arrived at last at the temple at Dwaraka. About 1546, when she would have been forty-eight, it seems a group of Brahmans went to her and staked out the temple, planning to starve to death in such a way that she would seem to be responsible for their death. About this time she wrote a song to Krishna that became a favorite of Mahatma Gandhi centuries later. We don't know when or how she died.

Many versions of her poems exist because different villages she visited kept the songs alive in their own way. Shama Futehally believes that about two hundred poems are authentic among the thousands extant. Most genuine poems exist in a medieval form of the Hindu dialect spoken in Braj. The last line ordinarily includes Mira's name as well as a mention of Krishna, sometimes in a metaphorical way such as The One Who Lifts Mountains. In our time, Subbalakshmi sings Mira's songs all over India, and they still feel fresh and contemporary.

The versions here were done with the help of the East Asian Language Department at the University of Chicago, which gave me originals and word-by-word translations prepared for students in the course on Mirabai.

THE HEAT OF MIDNIGHT TEARS

Listen, my friend, this road is the heart opening,
Kissing his feet, resistance broken, tears all night.

If we could reach the Lord through immersion in water,
I would have asked to be born a fish in this life.
If we could reach Him through nothing but berries and wild nuts,
Then surely the saints would have been monkeys when they came
    from the womb!
If we could reach him by munching lettuce and dry leaves,
Then the goats would surely get to the Holy One before us!

If the worship of stone statues could bring us all the way,
I would have adored a granite mountain years ago.

Mirabai says: The heat of midnight tears will bring you to God.

THE CLOUDS

When I saw the dark clouds, I wept, O Dark One, I wept at the dark
  clouds.
Black clouds soared up, and took some yellow along; rain did fall,
  some rain fell long.
There was water east of the house, west of the house; fields all green.
The one I love lives past those fields; rain has fallen on my body, on
  my hair, as I wait in the open door for him.
The Energy that holds up mountains is the energy Mirabai bows
  down to.
He lives century after century, and the test I set for him he has passed.

THE MUSIC

My friend, the stain of the Great Dancer has penetrated my body.
I drank the cup of music, and I am hopelessly drunk.
Moreover I stay drunk, no matter what I do to become sober.
Rana, who disapproves, gave me one basket with a snake in it.
Mira folded the snake around her neck, it was a lover's necklace, lovely!
Rana's next gift was poison: "This is something for you, Mira."
She repeated the Holy Name in her chest, and drank it, it was good!
Every name He has is praise; that's the cup I like to drink, and only
    that.
"The Great Dancer is my husband," Mira says, "rain washes off all the
    other colors."

DON'T GO, DON'T GO

Don't go, don't go. I touch your soles. I'm sold to you.
No one knows where to find the bhakti path, show me where to go.
I would like my own body to turn into a heap of incense and sandalwood
    and you set a torch to it.
When I've fallen down to gray ashes, smear me on your shoulders and
    chest.
Mira says: You who lift the mountains, I have some light, I want to
    mingle it with yours.

FAITHFULNESS

My friend, he looked, and our eyes met; an arrow came in.

My chest opened; what could it do? His image moved inside.

I've been standing all morning in the door of my house, looking down the road.

The one I love is dark: he is an herb growing in secret places, an herb that heals wounds.

Mira says: The town thinks I am loose, but I am faithful to the Dark One.

ALL I WAS DOING WAS BREATHING

Something has reached out and taken in the beams of my eyes.

There is a longing, it is for his body, for every hair of that dark body.

All I was doing was being, and the Dancing Energy came by my house.

His face looks curiously like the moon, I saw it from the side, smiling.

My family says: "Don't ever see him again!" And imply things in a low voice.

But my eyes have their own life; they laugh at rules, and know whose they are.

I believe I can bear on my shoulders whatever you want to say of me.

Mira says: Without the energy that lifts mountains, how am I to live?

IT'S TRUE I WENT TO THE MARKET

My friend, I went to the market and bought the Dark One.
You claim by night, I say by day.
Actually I was beating a drum all the time I was buying him.
You say I gave too much; I say too little.
Actually I put him on a scale before I bought him.
What I paid was my social body, my town body, my family body, and
    all my inherited jewels.
Mirabai says: The Dark One is my husband now.
Be with me when I lie down; you promised me this in an earlier life.

THE COFFER WITH THE
POISONOUS SNAKE

Rana sent a gold coffer of complicated ivory;
But inside a black and green asp was waiting,
"It is a necklace that belonged to a great Queen!"
I put it around my neck; it fit well.
It became a string of lovely pearls, each with a moon inside.
My room then was full of moonlight as if the full moon
Had found its way in through the open window.

WHERE DID YOU GO?

Where did you go, Holy One, after you left my body?

Your flame jumped to the wick, and then you disappeared and left the lamp alone.

You put the boat into the surf, and then walked inland, leaving the boat in the ocean of parting.

Mira says: Tell me when you will come to meet me.

ANKLE BELLS

Mira dances, how can her ankle bells not dance?
"Mira is insane," strangers say that, "the family's ruined."
Poison came to the door one day; she drank it and laughed.
I am at Hari's feet; I give him body and soul.
A glimpse of him is water: How thirsty I am for that!
Mira's Lord is the one who lifts mountains, he removes evil from
    human life.
Mira's Lord attacks the beings of greed; for safety I go to him.

HIS HAIR

You play the flute well; I love your swing curls and your earlocks.
Jasumati, your mother, wasn't she the one
Who washed and combed your beautiful hair?
If you come anywhere near my house,
I will close my sandalwood doors, and lock you in.

Mira's lord is half lion and half man.
She turns her life over to the midnight of his hair.

WHY MIRA CAN'T COME BACK
TO HER OLD HOUSE

The colors of the Dark One have penetrated Mira's body; all the other
colors washed out.

Making love with the Dark One and eating little, those are my pearls
and my carnelians.

Meditation beads and the forehead streak, those are my scarves and
my rings.

That's enough feminine wiles for me. My teacher taught me this.

Approve me or disapprove me: I praise the Mountain Energy night
and day.

I take the path that ecstatic human beings have taken for centuries.

I don't steal money, I don't hit anyone. What will you charge me
with?

I have felt the swaying of the elephant's shoulders; and now you want
me to climb on a jackass? Try to be serious.

KABIR

FOR THOSE WHO KNOW something of Indian spiritual literature, the word *Kabir* instantly calls up a razor-sharp intellect, an outrageous boldness in speech, inspired scolding of the fuzzy-minded:

> The idea that the soul will join with the ecstatic
> just because the body is rotten—
> that is all fantasy.
> What is found now is found then.
> If you find nothing now,
> you will simply end up with an apartment in the City of Death.

A young poet traveling with me made up a line as we passed through Chicago:

> If you find nothing now,
> you will simply end up with a suite in the Ramada Inn of death.

The change is proper. Kabir never used the elegant language of the Indian upper or middle classes; he wanted his metaphors to awaken the sleepers. His metaphors act like a loose electric wire, or a two-by-four to the head. His contempt for those wishing to be saved by being good is endless. In Kabir's poems, you see an astonishing event—highly religious and intensely spiritual poems written outside of, and in opposition to, the standard Hindu, Mohammedan, or Christian dogmas. Kabir says: "Suppose you scrub your ethical skin until it shines, but inside there is no music, then what?"

His poems are amazing, even from his broad culture, for the way they unite in one body the two traditions—ecstatic Sufism, which is supremely confident, a secretive, desert meditation, utterly opposed to orthodoxy and academics, and given to dancing and weeping—and the Hindu tradition, which is more sober on the surface, coming through the Vedas and Vishnu, Rama, and Krishna.

> Fire, air, earth, water and space—if you don't want the secret one,
>   you can't have these either.

> Kabir will tell you the truth; this is what love is like:
> suppose you had to cut your head off
> and give it to someone else,
> what difference would that make?

In the shortest of his poems, he models the high-spiritedness that he thought is essential for the life we live on this earth.

> The buds are shouting:
> "The Gardener is coming.
> Today he picks the blossoms,
> Tomorrow, us!"

If we cannot recite that last line with joy, then we are probably too gloomy to take Kabir in. He wants us not to worry whether we live or die.

Thought and feeling in most religious poets swim together. In Kabir one leaps ahead of the other, as if jumping out of the sea, and the reader smiles in joy at so much energy. It is as if both thought and feeling feed a third thing, a rebellious originality, and with that tail the poem shoots through the water. We feel that speed sometimes in

Eckhart also. Kabir says that interior work is not done by method, but by intensity. "Look at me, and you will see a slave of that intensity." The word "intensity" widens to its full range here, bringing in intense feeling, thinking, intuition, and intense love of colors and odors and animals. With our good ears, he says, we should hear the sound of "the anklets on the feet of an insect as it walks."

KABIR was born in perhaps 1398, probably into a class of weavers recently converted to Islam. One story of his childhood is told over and over. Ramananda, the Hindu master, would accept only Brahmans as disciples, and refused Kabir. Kabir knew that Ramananda went down the steps of the ghat before dawn every morning at Benares for a bath. In the half-dark, Kabir lay on one of the steps. Ramananda stepped on him and, startled, cried out, "Rama!" Kabir said, "You spoke the name of God in my presence; you initiated me. I am your student." Ramananda accepted him, and Kabir was with him for a long time.

He evidently worked as a weaver himself. He lived as a house-holder, and draws many images from householding or weaving. It is said that he was married, and that he fed every mendicant who came to his house.

Historically, Kabir's life is associated with the gradual rise of "bhakti energy" in India. In the Indian subcontinent, a vast rise of bhakti energy began in the eighth or ninth century A.D., as if ocean water had suddenly reappeared in the center of a continent. Sometime during those centuries, an alternative to the Vedic chanting began. Scholars knew the texts in Sanskrit, and the chanting of the Vedas was done by trained priests in what we might call "religious academics." The new bhakti worship involved the present tense, and contemporary language, more than the old "classical" tongue. Singing and dancing came forward—we see it in Mirabai's poems too—love of color, of intensity, of the male-female poles, of the avoidance of convention.

The poets of India began to write ecstatic poetry in their local languages, and thus refreshed the bhakti experience "from underneath." Some poems were written specifically for the long bhakti sessions, which lasted three or four hours in the middle of the night, and were guided through their stages by chanted and sung poems.

Kabir is thought to have died in Benares, and Bankey Behari estimates the year as 1527, when Kabir would have been 129 years old.

THE CLAY JUG

Inside this clay jug there are canyons and pine mountains, and the
   maker of canyons and pine mountains!
All seven oceans are inside, and hundreds of millions of stars.
The acid that tests gold is there, and the one who judges jewels.
And the music from the strings no one touches, and the source of all
   water.

If you want the truth, I will tell you the truth:
Friend, listen: the God whom I love is inside.

THE OWL AND THE MOON

Why should we two ever want to part?

Just as the leaf of the water rhubarb lives floating on the water,
we live as the great one and the little one.

As the owl opens his eyes all night to the moon,
we live as the great one and the little one.

This love between us goes back to the first humans;
it cannot *be* annihilated.

Here is Kabir's idea: as the river gives itself into the ocean,
what is inside me moves inside you.

THE THIRSTY FISH

I laugh when I hear that the fish in the water is thirsty.

You don't grasp the fact that what is most alive of all is inside your
   own house;
and so you walk from one holy city to the next with a confused look!

Kabir will tell you the truth: go wherever you like, to Calcutta
   or Tibet;
if you can't find where your soul is hidden,
for you the world will never be real!

WHAT MADE KABIR A SERVANT

Between the conscious and the unconscious, the mind has put up a
    swing;
all earth creatures, even the supernovas, sway between these two trees,
and it never winds down.

Angels, animals, humans, insects by the million, also the wheeling sun
    and moon;
ages go by, and it goes on.

Everything is swinging: heaven, earth, water, fire,
and the secret one slowly growing a body.
Kabir saw that for fifteen seconds, and it made him a servant for life.

THE MEETING

When my friend is away from me, I am depressed;
nothing in the daylight delights me,
sleep at night gives no rest,
who can I tell about this?

The night is dark, and long . . . hours go by . . .
because I am alone, I sit up suddenly,
fear goes through me. . . .

Kabir says: Listen, my friend
there is one thing in the world that satisfies,
and that is a meeting with the Guest.

THE ONLY WOMAN AWAKE

Friends, wake up! Why do you go on sleeping?
The night is over—do you want to lose the day the same way?
Other women who managed to get up early have already found an
    elephant or a jewel. . . .
So much was lost already while you slept . . .
and that was so unnecessary!

The one who loves you understood, but you did not.
You forgot to make a place in your bed next to you.
Instead you spent your life playing.
In your twenties you did not grow
because you did not know who your Lord was.
Wake up! Wake up! There's no one in your bed—
He left you during the long night.

Kabir says: The only woman awake is the woman who has heard the
    flute!

THE RADIANCE IN YOUR
MOTHER'S WOMB

I talk to my inner lover, and I say, why such rush?
We sense that there is some sort of spirit that loves birds and animals
    and the ants —
perhaps the same one who gave a radiance to you in your mother's
    womb.
Is it logical you would be walking around entirely orphaned now?
The truth is you turned away yourself,
and decided to go into the dark alone.
Now you are tangled up in others, and have forgotten what you once
    knew,
and that's why everything you do has some weird failure in it.

THINK WHILE YOU ARE ALIVE

Friend, hope for the Guest while you are alive.
Jump into experience while you are alive!
Think . . . and think . . . while you are alive.
What you call "salvation" belongs to the time before death.

If you don't break your ropes while you're alive,
do you think
ghosts will do it after?

The idea that the soul will join with the ecstatic
just because the body is rotten—
that is all fantasy.
What is found now is found then.
If you find nothing now,
you will simply end up with an apartment in the City of Death.
If you make love with the divine now, in the next life you will have the
    face of satisfied desire.
So plunge into the truth, find out who the Teacher is, believe in the
    Great Sound!
Kabir says this: When the Guest is being searched for, it is the intensity
    of the longing for the Guest that does all the work.
Look at me, and you will see a slave of that intensity.

THE LAMP WITHOUT OIL

I know the sound of the ecstatic flute,
but I don't know whose flute it is.

A lamp burns and has neither wick nor oil.

A lily pad blossoms and is not attached to the bottom!

When one flower opens, ordinarily dozens open.

The moon bird's head is filled with nothing but thoughts of the
    moon,
and when the next rain will come is all that the rain bird thinks of.

Who is it we spend our entire life loving?

THE SPIRITUAL ATHLETE IN
AN ORANGE ROBE

The spiritual athlete often changes the color of his clothes,
and his mind remains gray and loveless.

He sits inside a shrine room all day,
so that God has to go outdoors and praise the rocks.

Or he drills holes in his ears, his beard grows enormous and matted,
people mistake him for a goat. . . .
He goes out into wilderness areas, strangles his impulses,
and makes himself neither male nor female. . . .

He shaves his skull, puts his robe in an orange vat,
reads the Bhagavad Gita, and becomes a terrific talker.

Kabir says: Actually you are going in a hearse to the country of death,
bound hand and foot!

ARE YOU LOOKING FOR ME?

Are you looking for me? I am in the next seat.
My shoulder is against yours.
You will not find me in stupas, not in Indian shrine rooms, nor in
synagogues, nor in cathedrals:
not in masses, nor kirtans, not in legs winding around your own neck,
nor in eating nothing but vegetables.
When you really look for me, you will see me instantly—
you will find me in the tiniest house of time.
Kabir says: Student, tell me, what is God?
He is the breath inside the breath.

THE HOLY POOLS HAVE ONLY WATER

There is nothing but water in the holy pools.
I know, I have been swimming in them.
All the gods sculpted of wood and ivory can't say a word.
I know, I have been crying out to them.
The Sacred Books of the East are nothing but words.
I looked through their covers one day sideways.
What Kabir talks of is only what he has lived through.
If you have not lived through something, it is not true.

WHY ARRANGE THE PILLOWS

Oh friend, I love you, think this over
carefully! If you are in love,
then why are you asleep?

If you have found him,
give yourself to him, take him.

Why do you lose track of him again and again?

If you are about to fall into heavy sleep anyway,
why waste time smoothing the bed
and arranging the pillows?

Kabir will tell you the truth; this is what love is like:
suppose you had to cut your head off
and give it to someone else,
what difference would that make?

MY FIRST MARRIAGE

I married my Lord, and meant to live with him.
But I did not live with him, I turned away,
and all at once my twenties were gone.

The night I was married, all my friends sang for me,
and the rice of pleasure and the rice of pain fell on me.

Yet when all those ceremonies were over, I left, I did not go home
     with him,
and my relatives all the way home said, "It's all right."

Kabir says: Now my love energy is actually mine.
This time I will take it with me when I go,
and outside his house I will blow the horn of triumph!

THE MUSIC WITHOUT STRINGS

Have you heard the music that no fingers enter into?
Far inside the house
entangled music—
What is the sense of leaving your house?

Suppose you scrub your ethical skin until it shines,
but inside there is no music,
then what?

Mohammed's son pores over words, and points out this
and that,
but if his chest is not soaked dark with love,
then what?

The Yogi comes along in his famous orange.
But if inside he is colorless, then what?

Kabir says: Every instant that the sun is risen, if I stand in the temple,
   or on a balcony, in the hot fields, or in a walled garden, my own
   Lord is making love with me.

ANTONIO MACHADO

ANTONIO MACHADO WRITES poems that seem, after we know them well, to be words written by a close friend. There is a hidden "we" in his poems:

> Last night, as I was sleeping,
> I dreamt—marvellous error!—
> that I had a beehive
> here inside my heart.
> And the golden bees
> were making white combs
> and sweet honey
> from my old failures.

It doesn't feel confessional; it's not a complaint; we don't sense the self-obsession of so many confessional poems. He dreams that bees were making white combs and sweet honey from his old failures. The image is calm and matter-of-fact, and no one else seems to be able to do that.

So many readers have written to me saying that this poem is the first poem they'd ever memorized.

The important year for Machado and his generation was 1898, the year of the Spanish-American War, when Spain lost the rest of her empire. Machado was twenty-three. It seems clear that the old rhetorical lies of the politicians and the Church had finally come to nothing. It was over. The whole elaborate business of empire had collapsed, and the young ones now had to live with reduced expectations, some sadness and grief. It amounted to a new start in poetry, using a few words that were honest.

It's possible that while we were dreaming
the hand that casts out the stars like seeds
started up the ancient music once more

—like a note from a great harp—
and the frail wave came to our lips
in the form of one or two honest words.

The time for lectures is over. How do we cross over the space between us and another person?

To talk with someone,
ask a question first,
then—listen.

Machado said that if we pay attention exclusively to the inner world, it will dissolve; if we pay attention exclusively to the outer world, it will dissolve. To create art, we have to stitch together both the inner and the outer worlds. How to do that? Machado concludes, Well, we could always use our eyes.

One of his earliest memories, which he published among his notebooks, was this: "I'd like to tell you the most important thing that ever happened to me. One day when I was still quite young, my mother and I went out walking. I had a piece of sugar cane in my hand, I remember—it was in Seville, in some vanished Christmas season. Just ahead of us were another mother and child—he had a stick of sugar cane too. I was sure mine was bigger—I knew it was! Even so, I asked my mother—because children always ask questions they already know the answer to: 'Mine's bigger, isn't it?' And she said, 'No, my boy, it's not. What have you done with your eyes?' I've been asking myself that question ever since."

ANTONIO MACHADO was born on July 26, 1875, in Seville. His father was a teacher and early collector of folk poetry and folk music in Spain. When Antonio was eight, the family moved to Madrid; there Antonio and his brothers attended the Free Institution of Learning, whose founder, Francisco Giner de los Ríos, had a profound effect on two or three generations of Spanish intellectuals and writers. Antonio tended to be torpid and slow; he took ten extra years to get his B.A. Eventually he chose a career as a secondary-school teacher of French, passed the examination, and, when he was thirty-two, got his first job at Soria, a poor and exhausted town in the grazed-out mountain area of Castile. He stayed there five years. During the second year he married the daughter of the family in whose pension he lived, Leonor, then fifteen. They went to Paris for work at the Sorbonne; they lived in poor quarters; she caught tuberculosis and died two years later, in the fall of 1911. "She is always with me," he said; he often addressed her in later poems, and never remarried. He resigned his position at Soria, and transferred to Bacza, in the south, where he stayed seven years. During 1912, his last year in Soria, his second book, *The Countryside of Castile,* came out; and he continued to add poems to it during his years in Baeza. In 1919, he transferred again, this time to Segovia, which is only an hour from Madrid. He was now able to escape on weekends from provincial life, which he complained was boring and deadening; and he began writing plays and taking part in the intellectual life of Madrid. He lived in Segovia from 1919 to 1932, thirteen years, during which time he fell in love with a married woman he called "Guiomar," invented two poet-philosophers named Abel Martín and Juan de Mairena, and published his third book, *Nuevas Canciones (New Poems).* He became more and more active in public life, writing in the papers on political and moral issues during the tense period that led in 1931 to the proclamation of the Second Spanish Republic. He moved to Madrid in 1932 and took a strong part in the defense of the Republic. The civil war began in 1936. Finally, in late January of 1939, moving ahead of Franco's army, he crossed the Pyrenees. In the last picture we have of Antonio, he is a passenger in an old Ford—his manuscripts all lost—holding his mother on his lap, entering France. He died at Collioure, just over the border, on February 22, 1939, and as the gravestones, which I saw, make clear, his mother survived him by only a few days.

MEMORY FROM CHILDHOOD

A chilly and overcast afternoon
of winter. The students
are studying. Steady boredom
of raindrops across the windowpanes.

Recess over. In a poster
Cain is shown running
away, and Abel dead,
not far from a red spot.

The teacher, with a voice husky and hollow,
is thundering. He is an old man badly dressed,
withered and dried up,
holding a book in his hand.

And the whole children's choir
is singing its lesson:
"one thousand times one hundred is one hundred thousand,
one thousand times one thousand is one million."

A chilly and overcast afternoon
of winter. The students
are studying. Steady boredom
of raindrops across the windowpanes.

THE CLOCK STRUCK TWELVE TIMES

The clock struck twelve times . . . and it was a spade
knocked twelve times against the earth.
. . . "It's my turn!" I cried. . . . The silence
answered me: Do not be afraid.
You will never see the last drop fall
that now is trembling in the water clock.

You will still sleep many hours
here on the beach,
and one clear morning you will find
your boat tied to another shore.

CLOSE TO THE ROAD

Close to the road, we sit down one day.
Now our life amounts to time, and our sole concern
the attitudes of despair we adopt
while we wait. But She will not fail to arrive.

THE WATER WHEEL

The afternoon arrived
mournful and dusty.

The water was composing
its countrified poem
in the buckets
of the lazy water wheel.

The mule was dreaming—
old and sad mule!
in time to the darkness
that was talking in the water.

The afternoon arrived
mournful and dusty.

I don't know which noble
and religious poet
joined the anguish
of the endless wheel

to the cheerful music
of the dreaming water,
and bandaged your eyes—
old and sad mule! . . .

But it must have been a noble
and religious poet,
a heart made mature
by darkness and art.

LAST NIGHT, AS I WAS SLEEPING

Last night, as I was sleeping,
I dreamt—marvellous error!—
that a spring was breaking
out in my heart.
I said: Along which secret aqueduct,
Oh water, are you coming to me,
water of a new life
that I have never drunk?

Last night, as I was sleeping,
I dreamt—marvellous error!—
that I had a beehive
here inside my heart.
And the golden bees
were making white combs
and sweet honey
from my old failures.

Last night, as I was sleeping,
I dreamt—marvellous error!—
that a fiery sun was giving
light inside my heart.
It was fiery because I felt
warmth as from a hearth,
and sun because it gave light
and brought tears to my eyes.

Last night, as I slept,
I dreamt—marvellous error!—
that it was God I had
here inside my heart.

IS MY SOUL ASLEEP?

Is my soul asleep?
Have those beehives that labor
at night stopped? And the water
wheel of thought,
is it dry, the cups empty,
wheeling, carrying only shadows?

No my soul is not asleep.
It is awake, wide awake.
It neither sleeps nor dreams, but watches,
its clear eyes open,
far-off things, and listens
at the shores of the great silence.

FROM THE DOORSILL OF A DREAM

From the doorsill of a dream they called my name . . .
It was the good voice, the voice I loved so much.

"Listen: Will you go with me to visit the soul? . . ."
A soft stroke reached up to my heart.

"With you, always . . ." And in my dream I walked
down a long and solitary corridor,
aware of the touching of the pure robe
and the soft beating of blood in the hand that loved me.

THE WIND, ONE BRILLIANT DAY

The wind, one brilliant day, called
to my soul with an aroma of jasmine.

"In return for the odor of my jasmine,
I'd like all the odor of your roses."

"I have no roses; all the flowers
in my garden are dead."

"Well then, I'll take the waters of the fountains,
and the withered petals and the yellow leaves."

The wind left. And I wept. And I said to myself:
"What have you done with the garden that was entrusted to you?"

IT'S POSSIBLE THAT WHILE WE WERE DREAMING

It's possible that while we were dreaming
the hand that casts out the stars like seeds
started up the ancient music once more

— like a note from a great harp —
and the frail wave came to our lips
in the form of one or two honest words.

PORTRAIT

My childhood is memories of a patio in Seville,
and a garden where sunlit lemons are growing yellow;
my youth twenty years on the earth of Castile;
what I lived a few things you'll forgive me for omitting.

A great seducer I was not, nor the lover of Juliet;
—the oafish way I dress is enough to say that—
but the arrow Cupid planned for me I got,
and I loved whenever women found a home in me.

A flow of leftist blood moves through my body,
but my poems rise from a calm and deep spring.
There is a man of rule who behaves as he should, but more
than him, I am, in the good sense of the word, good.

I adore beauty, and following contemporary thought
have cut some old roses from the garden of Ronsard;
but the new lotions and feathers are not for me;
I am not one of the blue jays who sing so well.

I dislike hollow tenors who warble of love,
and the chorus of crickets singing to the moon.
I fall silent so as to separate voices from echoes,
and I listen among the voices to one voice and only one.

Am I classic or Romantic? Who knows. I want to leave
my poetry as a fighter leaves his sword, known
for the masculine hand that closed around it,
not for the coded mark of the proud forger.

I talk always to the man who walks along with me;
—men who talk to themselves hope to talk to God someday—
My soliloquies amount to discussions with this friend,
who taught me the secret of loving human beings.

In the end, I owe you nothing; you owe me what I've written.
I turn to my work; with what I've earned I pay
for my clothes and hat, the house in which I live,
the food that feeds my body, the bed on which I sleep.

And when the day arrives for the last leaving of all,
and the ship that never returns to port is ready to go,
you'll find me on board, light, with few belongings,
almost naked like the children of the sea.

POEMS CHOSEN FROM
MORAL PROVERBS AND FOLK SONGS

(*The Countryside of Castile*)

1

    I love Jesus, who said to us:
Heaven and earth will pass away.
When heaven and earth have passed away,
my word will remain.
What was your word, Jesus?
Love? Affection? Forgiveness?
All your words were
one word: Wakeup.

2

    It is good knowing that glasses
are to drink from;
the bad thing is not to know
what thirst is for.

3

    You say nothing is created new?
Don't worry about it, with the mud
of the earth, make a cup
from which your brother can drink.

4

    All things die and all things live forever;
but our task is to die,
to die making roads,
roads over the sea.

5

    To die . . . To fall like a drop
of water into the big ocean?
Or to be what I've never been:
a man without a shadow, without a dream,
a man all alone, walking,
without a mirror, and with no road?

6

    Mankind owns four things
that are no good at sea:
rudder, anchor, oars,
and the fear of going down.

RAINBOW AT NIGHT

for Don Ramón del Valle-Inclán

The train moves through the Guadarrama
one night on the way to Madrid.
The moon and the fog create
high up a rainbow.
Oh April moon, so calm,
driving the white clouds!

The mother holds her boy
sleeping on her lap.
The boy sleeps, and nevertheless
sees the green fields outside,
and trees lit up by sun,
and the golden butterflies.

The mother, her forehead dark
between a day gone and a day to come,
sees a fire nearly out
and an oven with spiders.

There's a traveler mad with grief,
no doubt seeing odd things;
he talks to himself, and when he looks
wipes us out with his look.

I remember fields under snow,
and pine trees of other mountains.

And you, Lord, through whom we all
have eyes, and who sees souls,
tell us if we all one
day will see your face.

FOURTEEN POEMS CHOSEN FROM
MORAL PROVERBS AND FOLK SONGS
(*Nuevas Canciones*)

Dedicated to José Ortega y Gasset

1

    The eye you see is not
an eye because you see it;
it is an eye because it sees you.

2

    To talk with someone,
ask a question first,
then — listen.

3

    Narcissism
is an ugly fault,
and now it's a boring fault too.

4

    But look in your mirror for the other one,
the other one who walks by your side.

5

    Between living and dreaming
there is a third thing.
Guess it.

6

    Look for your other half
who walks always next to you
and tends to be what you aren't.

7

    In my solitude
I have seen things very clearly
that were not true.

8

    Form your letters slowly and well:
making things well
is more important than making them.

9

    What the poet is searching for
is not the fundamental I
but the deep you.

10

    Beyond living and dreaming
there is something more important:
waking up.

11

    Pay attention now:
a heart that's all by itself
is not a heart.

12

    If it's good to live,
then it's better to be asleep dreaming,
and best of all,
mother, is to awake.

13

    When I am alone
how close my friends are;
when I am with them
how distant they are!

14

    But art?
               It is pure and intense play,
so it is like pure and intense life,
so it is like pure and intense fire.
You'll see the coal burning.

TODAY'S MEDITATION

The fiery palm tree in front of me,
that the setting sun is just now leaving,
this late and silent afternoon,
inside our peaceful garden,
while flowery old Valencia
drinks the Guadalaviar waters —
Valencia of delicate towers,
in the joyful sky of Ausias March,
her river turns entirely into roses
before it arrives at the sea —
I think of the war. The war
is like a tornado moving
through the bleak foothills of the Duero,
through the plains of standing wheat,
from the farmlands of Extremadura
to these gardens with private lemons,
from the gray skies of the north
to these salty marshes full of light.
I think of Spain, all of it sold out,
river by river, mountain by mountain, sea to sea.

JUAN RAMÓN JIMÉNEZ

JIMÉNEZ, ALONG WITH Antonio Machado and Unamuno, led the great and joyful revival of Spanish poetry in the years around 1910. They all dreamed of a new blossoming of Spain. Jiménez was not robust. He was delicate, and slipped off into the sanitorium more than once. Yet his devotion to poetry was healthy and rigorous. He spent years editing poetry magazines and starting publishing ventures to get poets in print, spending endless afternoons poring over young poets' manuscripts. His delight and Machado's stubbornness prepared the way for the great generation of '28: Lorca, Aleixandre, Salinas, Guillén. Lorca's early poems are imitations of Juan Ramón's, who had thrown up light and airy houses made out of willows, and in so many different designs, that all the coming Spanish poets found themselves living in one or another of his willow houses before they moved into their own houses.

He said that poetry is the highest form of speech. Its essence was an inner subtle life; Jiménez added a fierce devotion to craft. "Written poetry continues to seem to me as a form of expression, of that which cannot be said." He asked what sort of life we should have to feel the most poetry. He needed solitude, some distance. When people called at his house, he could reply, "Juan Ramón Jiménez is not home today." Yet his warmth is what first drew people to him. In 1903, he wrote a review praising *Soledades,* the first book of Antonio Machado. His book of prose poems in which he talks to a donkey (*Platero y yo,* — "Platero and Myself," 1917) was immensely popular and is still a book of love to Andalusia.

In 1916, he took a trip to New York, to marry Zenobia Camprubi, whose brother owned a Spanish-language newspaper in New York. His book of poems about that trip, called *Diary of a Poet Recently Married,* is a masterpiece. It includes marvelous prose poems about New York: describing his visit to Whitman's tiny house on Long Island, and about an hour he spent in the Author's Club (which he dreamed of burning down; the club was a hangout of third-rate writers in New York). He took a trip to Boston to admire the lavender windowpanes on Beacon Hill.

He kept changing his poetry toward new styles. He often referred to poetry as a woman. He summed up the whole tale of those changes once in a poem beginning: "At first she came to me pure." He loved the innocence of his early poetry. Then his poems, he said, began to pick up display, ostentation, and affectation, and he began to hate her. After a while, his poetry began to go back toward naiveté, candor, and plainspeaking. She was innocent again, and he fell in love once more. Finally, the poems became severe and naked: "Naked poetry, that I have loved my whole life!"

JUAN RAMÓN JIMÉNEZ was born in 1881 at Moguer in southern Andalusia. From his small town he sent his first poems to newspapers in Seville, and the writers there recognized his talent, and magazines in Madrid published his poetry. He received a letter of invitation signed by several writers, and in 1900, when he was eighteen, he arrived in Madrid to take part in Spanish literary life.

He began publishing books of poetry, and in 1906 started a review, *Renacimiento,* to celebrate the new Spanish poetry. In 1905, he returned to Moguer for seven years. He started then on his astonishing book of prose poems, *Platero y yo.*

When back in Madrid, he and his wife translated the complete works of Rabindranath Tagore, and he continued to work with young poets. He published *Estudiantes,* written in octosyllabic verse. He studied the

English poets, and translated Yeats, while continuing to publish new books of poetry.

In 1936, the Spanish Civil War began. He would have nothing to do with Franco, and went into exile. By the time the Spanish Civil War was over, Lorca was dead; Rafael Alberti, Jorge Guillén, Pedro Salinas, Emilio Prados, Manuel Altolaguirre, and Luis Cernuda were in exile.

Juan Ramón came first to the United States, living in Chevy Chase, Maryland, for a while. But the American literary community ignored him. He then moved to Puerto Rico, where he taught at the University of Puerto Rico until his death.

His love for his wife was one of the greatest devotions of his life, and he wrote many of his poems for her. When he received the Nobel Prize in 1956, his wife was on her deathbed; he told reporters to go away, that he would not go to Stockholm, that his wife should have been given the Nobel Prize, and he was not interested in receiving it. After his wife died, he did not write another poem and died a few months later, in the spring of 1958.

ADOLESCENCE

We were alone together
a moment on the balcony.
Since the lovely morning
of that day, we were sweethearts.

—The drowsy land around
was sleeping its vague colors,
under the gray and rosy
sunset of fall.

I told her I was going to kiss her;
she lowered her eyes calmly
and offered her cheeks to me
like someone losing a treasure.

—The dead leaves were falling
in the windless garden of the house,
and a perfume of heliotrope
was still floating in the air.

She did not dare to look at me;
I told her we would be married,
—and the tears rolled
from her mournful eyes.

FULL MOON

The door is open,
the cricket is singing.
Are you going around naked
in the fields?

Like an immortal water,
going in and out of everything.
Are you going around naked
in the air?

The basil is not asleep,
the ant is busy.
Are you going around naked
in the house?

THE LUMBER WAGONS

The lumber wagons are already there.
—The pines and the wind have told us,
the golden moon has told us,
the smoke and the echo have told us . . .
They are the carts that go by
in these afternoons at dusk,
the lumber wagons carrying
the dead trees down from the mountain.
What a sound of crying from these carts
on the road to Pueblo Nuevo!
The oxen come along
in the starlight, daydreaming
about their warm stalls in the barn
smelling of motherhood and hay.
And behind the lumber wagons
the ox drivers walking,
the ox prod on their shoulders,
and eyes watching the sky.
What a sound of crying from these carts
on the road to Pueblo Nuevo!
The dead trees as they move
through the calm of the fields
leave behind a fresh honest smell
like a heart thrown open.
The Angelus falls
from the steeple of the ancient town
over the stripped fields
which smell like a cemetery.
What a sound of crying from these carts
on the road to Pueblo Nuevo!

WHO KNOWS WHAT IS GOING ON

Who knows what is going on on the other side of each hour?

How many times the sunrise was
there, behind a mountain!

How many times the brilliant cloud piling up far off
was already a golden body full of thunder!

This rose was poison.

That sword gave life.

I was thinking of a flowery meadow
at the end of a road,
and found myself in the slough.

I was thinking of the greatness of what was human,
and found myself in the divine.

THE LAMB WAS BLEATING SOFTLY

The lamb was bleating softly.
The young jackass grew happier
with his excited bray.
The dog barked,
almost talking to the stars.
    I woke up! I went out. I saw the tracks
of the sky on the ground
which had flowered
like a sky
turned upside down.
    A warm and mild haze
hung around the trees;
the moon was going down
in a west of gold and silk
like some full and divine womb . . .
    My chest was thumping
as if my heart were drunk . . .
    I opened the barn door to see if
He was there.
    He was!

"I TOOK OFF PETAL AFTER PETAL"

Birkendene, Caldwell,
   February 20

I took off petal after petal, as if you were a rose,
in order to see your soul,
and I didn't see it.

However, everything around —
horizons of fields and oceans —
everything, even what was infinite,
was filled with a perfume,
immense and living.

NIGHT PIECE

The ship, slow and rushing at the same time, can get ahead of
    the water
but not the sky.
The blue is left behind, opened up in living silver,
and is ahead of us again.
The mast, fixed, swings and constantly returns
—like an hour hand that points
always to the same hour—
to the same stars,
hour after hour black and blue.
The body as it daydreams goes
toward the earth that belongs to it, from the other earth
that does not. The soul stays on board, moving
through the kingdom it has owned from birth.

WALT WHITMAN

"But do you really want to see Whitman's house instead of Roosevelt's? I've never had this request before!"

The house is tiny and yellow, and next to the railroad track, like the hut of a switchman, in a small green patch of grass, marked out with whitewashed stones, beneath a single tree. Around it, the wide meadow area is open to the wind, which sweeps it, and us, and has polished the simple rough piece of marble which announces to the trains:

TO MARK THE BIRTHPLACE OF

WALT WHITMAN

THE GOOD GRAY POET

BORN MAY 31, 1819

ERECTED BY THE COLONIAL SOCIETY

OF HUNTINGTON IN 1905

Since the farmer doesn't seem to be at home, I walk around the house a couple of times, hoping to see something through the windowlets. Suddenly a man, tall, slow-moving, and bearded, wearing a shirt and a wide-brimmed hat—like the early photograph of Whitman—comes, from somewhere, and tells me, leaning on his iron bar, that he doesn't know who Whitman was, that he is Polish, that this house is his, and that he does not intend to show it to anyone. Then pulling himself up, he goes inside, through the little door that looks like a toy door.

Solitude and cold. A train goes by, into the wind. The sun, scarlet for an instant, dies behind the low woods, and in the swamp we walk past, which is green and faintly blood-colored, innumerable toads are croaking in the enormous silence.

AUTHOR'S CLUB

I had always thought perhaps there would be no poets at all in New York. What I had never suspected was that there would be so many bad ones, or a place like this, as dry and dusty as our own Ateneo in Madrid, in spite of its being on the fifteenth floor, almost at the altitude of Parnassus.

Tenth-rate men, all of them, cultivating physical resemblances to Poe, to Walt Whitman, to Stevenson, to Mark Twain, letting their soul be burned up with their free cigar, since the two are the same: bushy-haired men who make fun of Robinson, Frost, Masters, Vachel Lindsay, Amy Lowell and who fail to make fun of Poe, Emily Dickinson, and Whitman only because they are already dead. And they show me wall after wall of portraits and autographs in holograph, of Bryant, of Aldrich, of Lowell, etc., etc., etc . . .

. . . I have taken a cigarette from the fumidor, lighted it, and thrown it into a corner, on the rug, in order to see if the fire will catch and leave behind it, in place of this club of rubbish, a high and empty hole, fresh and deep, with clear stars, in the cloudless sky of this April night.

LAVENDER WINDOWPANES AND
WHITE CURTAINS

Lavender windowpanes! They are like a pedigree of nobility. Boston has many of them and New York has a few, in the old streets around Washington Square, so pleasing, so hospitable, so full of silence! These beautiful panes survive particularly in Boston and are cared for with a haughty, self-interested zeal.

They go back to colonial days. The panes were made with substances which the sunlight over the years has been turning the color of the amethyst, of pansies, of the violet. One feels sure that between the sweet white muslin curtains of those quiet houses, he could glimpse through the violet pane the frail and noble spirit of those days, days of genuine silver and genuine gold, making no hearable sound.

Some of the panes have their violet color almost invisibly, like the flowers and stones I spoke of, and it takes skill simply to see it; others transfer their vague shading to their sister curtains, when the light of the pure sunsets strikes them; finally, by now a few panes are lavender all through, rotten with nobility.

My heart lingers back there with these panes, America, like an amethyst, a pansy, a violet, in the center of the muslin snow. I have been planting that heart for you in the ground beneath the magnolias that the panes reflect, so that each April the pink and white flowers and their odor will surprise the simple puritan women with their plain clothes, their noble look, and their pale gold hair, coming back at evening, quietly returning to their homes here in those calm spring hours that have made them homesick for earth.

OCEANS

I have a feeling that my boat
has struck, down there in the depths,
against a great thing.
                            And nothing
happens! Nothing . . . Silence . . . Waves . . .

—Nothing happens? Or has everything happened,
and are we standing now, quietly, in the new life?

MUSIC

Music—
a naked woman
running mad through the pure night!

ROAD

They are all asleep, below.
                                    Above, awake,
the helmsman and I.

He, watching the compass needle, lord
of the bodies, with their keys turned
in the locks. I, with my eyes
toward the infinite, guiding
the open treasures of the souls.

I AM NOT I

I am not I.
        I am this one
walking beside me whom I do not see,
whom at times I manage to visit,
and whom at other times I forget;
the one who remains silent while I talk,
the one who forgives, sweet, when I hate,
the one who takes a walk when I am indoors,
the one who will remain standing when I die.

AT FIRST SHE CAME TO ME PURE

At first she came to me pure,
dressed only in her innocence;
and I loved her as we love a child.

Then she began putting on
clothes she picked up somewhere;
and I hated her, without knowing it.

She gradually became a queen,
the jewelry was blinding . . .
What bitterness and rage!

. . . She started going back toward nakedness.
And I smiled.

Soon she was back to the single shift
of her old innocence.
I believed in her a second time.

Then she took off the cloth
and was entirely naked . . .

Naked poetry, always mine,
that I have loved my whole life!

FRANCIS PONGE

FRANCIS PONGE is one of the wittiest poets who has ever lived. He is fond of prose poems, and his are unlike anyone else's. He leaps out of the wooden chest of French political verse and academic poetry and, adopting all of the rhetorical power of traditional French prose, begins pointing to objects such as a clump of blackberries, a closed oyster, a dinner plate, a tree losing its leaves in fall. He is the inventor of what we call these days the "thing" poem.

The intense eyes of Daumier have found their way into poetry. About a candle, he says: "Night at times revives a curious plant whose light makes powerfully furnished rooms fall apart into clumps of shadow." The candle "urges the reader on then bends over onto its plate and drowns in what has always fed it." If the reader wants to extend this tiny metaphor into philosophy or religion, that is his job; the poet's job is finished.

About a frog, he says:

When rain like metal tips bounces off the sodden pastures, an amphibious dwarf, an Ophelia with empty sleeves, barely as large as a fist, rises at times from around the poet's feet, and then hurtles herself into the nearest pool.

You'll notice the Greek-based word "amphibious" and the Shakespearean-based "Ophelia" and the common French word for "fist" all brought together in a garden of leafy, grubby, colorful language plants. Even in translation, we can notice acute attention to the history of language. Ponge once said that he doesn't believe in the unconscious. He doesn't study it. Whatever is hidden you can already find in a French dictionary, looking at the history of a given word. If he is in trouble, he's liable to consult a dictionary the way someone else would consult a therapist.

When he turns to the oyster, he notices that the blows that a hungry person gave it leave whitish rings on the shell, "halos of some kind." Once inside, we see a "firmament with the upper heavens approaching the lower heavens." One will find also "a fringe of blackish lace." The pearl itself—should a pearl be present—is called a "beautiful expression." The oyster too is a writer.

And a door! Why not write a poem about a door? Opening it means "holding a door in our arms." Such pleasures that we rarely notice! "The pleasure of grabbing one of those tall barriers to a room abdominally, by its porcelain knot." The door has porcelain at its abdomen. And typically the labor we've gone through with the door moves toward privacy and secrecy as we close it again . . . "which the click of the powerful but well-oiled spring pleasantly confirms."

Many of our enthusiastic prose-poem composers haven't yet learned that the essence of the prose poem is not the absence of lines but the presence of wit.

One of Ponge's masterpieces is his poem about the ordinary dinner plate. The poem is elegant, and yet there are jokes every two seconds. He says: "No poetic leap, no matter how brilliant, can speak in a sufficiently flat way about the lowly interval that porcelain occupies between pure spirit and appetite."

Consulting his French dictionary, he then finds that *porcellana* in Latin means "sow vulva." "Is that good enough for your appetite?"

The plate finds itself compared to Aphrodite, who rose from the sea; suddenly it becomes a round sun; then many plates, all being "multiplied by that free-spirited juggler in the wings," who, as in the circus, replaces "the melancholic old man" who can offer us only one sun per day. The "melancholic old man" is apparently some kind of Jehovah.

FRANCIS PONGE was born in 1899 in Montpellier. As a young man, he moved to Paris. His first book, *Le Parti Pri des Choses,* or *The Side Taken by Things,* was begun around 1922, and he worked on it for close to twenty years before its publication in 1942. Camus came upon the book and wrote a long letter to Ponge. Camus showed the book to Sartre. It was Jean-Paul Sartre who called attention to Ponge's work in a major way. In 1942, Ponge joined the French Resistance and was part of it until the defeat of the Nazis. In ordinary life, he worked at various editorial and teaching jobs. He was a friend of many surrealist poets and painters, particularly Breton, Eluard, Giacometti, and Picasso. In his work, he looked back to Lucretius and Cicero and to the sixteenth-century Malherbe. In 1966, Ponge was a visiting professor at both Barnard College and Columbia University. He was awarded the Neustadt International Prize for Literature in 1974. He died in Paris in 1988.

TREES LOSE PARTS OF THEMSELVES INSIDE A CIRCLE OF FOG

Inside the fog that encloses the trees, they undergo a stripping. . . . Thrown into confusion by a slow oxidation, and humiliated by the sap's withdrawal for the sake of the flowers and fruits, the leaves, following the hot spells of August, cling less anyway.

The up-and-down tunnels inside the bark deepen, and guide the moisture down to earth so as to break off with the more animated parts of the tree.

The flowers are scattered, the fruits brought down. This giving up of their more animated parts, and even of parts of their body, has become, since their earliest days, a familiar pattern for trees.

THE FROG

When rain like metal tips bounces off the sodden pastures, an amphibious dwarf, an Ophelia with empty sleeves, barely as large as a fist, rises at times from around the poet's feet, and then hurtles herself into the nearest pool.

Let this nervous one flee. How beautiful her legs are. A glove impermeable to water envelops her body. Barely flesh at all, her long muscles in their elegance are neither animal nor fish. In order to escape from my fingers, the virtue of fluid allies in her with the battle of the life force. She puffs, widely goitered. . . . And this heart that beats so strongly, the wrinkly eyelids, the old woman's mouth, move me to set her free.

THE END OF FALL

What fall amounts to is really a cold infusion. The dead leaves of all herb species steep in the rain. But no fermenting goes on, no alcohol-making: one has to wait until spring to see the effect a compress has when applied to a wooden leg.

The counting of votes goes on chaotically. All the doors of the polling places fly open and slam shut. Into the wastebasket! Into the wastebasket! Nature rips up her manuscripts, tears down her library, knocks down the last fruits with long poles.

Then she rises crisply from her worktable. Her height all at once seems unusual. Her hair undone, she has her head in the fog. Arms loose, she breathes in with ecstasy the icy wind that makes all her ideas clear. The days are short, the night falls swiftly, who needs comedy.

Earth floating among the other planets regains her serious look. Her sunlit side is narrower, invaded by clefts of shadow. Her shoes, like a hobo's, are great with water, and a source of music.

Inside this frogpond, or energetic amphibiguity, everything regains strength, hops from stone to stone, tries a new field. Streams increase.

Here you see what is called a real soaking, a cleaning that cares nothing for respectability! Dressed as a naked man, soaked to the bone.

And it goes on, doesn't get dry right away. Three months of healthy reflecting goes on in this state; without any circulatory disaster, without bathrobe, without horsehair glove. But her strong constitution can take it.

And so, when the tiny buds begin to point, they know what they are doing and what is going on—and if they come out hesitatingly, numb and flushed, it is in full knowledge of why.

Ah well, but there hangs another tale—that may follow from, but certainly doesn't have the smell of, the black wooden ruler which I will now use to draw my line under this present story.

THE THREE SHOPS

Near the Place Maubert, at the spot where each morning early I wait for the bus, three shops stand side by side: Jewels, Coal and Firewood, Butcher. Observing them in turn, I notice how differently, it seems to me, metal, precious stones, coal, wood chunks, slices of raw meat behave.

We won't linger too long over the metals, which are only the result of man's exploitative or divisive influence on muds or on certain conglomerate rocks that by themselves had no such intentions, nor the precious stones, whose rarity correctly suggests that one give to them only a few exquisite words during a discourse on nature so equitably arranged.

As for the raw meat, a certain shiver as I look, a kind of horror or empathy obliges me to the greatest discretion. Moreover, when freshly sliced, a veil of steam or smoke, sui generis, screens them from the very eyes that would want to reveal certain, one might properly say, cynical thoughts. I will have said all I can say when I have drawn attention for one minute to something *panting* in their appearance.

The contemplation of firewood and coal, however, is a source of delights as immediate as they are sober and certain, which I would be pleased to share. Without doubt, that would require several pages, when in fact I have here only one half of one. That is why I set a limit and propose to you the following subject for your meditations: 1. TIME THAT IS OCCUPIED WITH RADIUSES OF A CIRCLE ALWAYS REVENGES ITSELF, BY DEATH. 2. BECAUSE IT IS BROWN, AND BROWN IS MIDWAY BETWEEN GREEN AND BLACK ON THE ROAD TO CARBON, THE WOOD'S DESTINY INVOLVES—THOUGH IN A SMALL DEGREE—A SERIES OF EXPLOITS; THAT IS TO SAY, ERROR ITSELF, MISTAKES, AND EVERY POSSIBLE MISUNDER-STANDING.

THE DELIGHTS OF THE DOOR

Kings don't touch doors.

They don't know this joy: to push affectionately or fiercely before us one of those huge panels we know so well, then to turn back in order to replace it—holding a door in our arms.

The pleasure of grabbing one of those tall barriers to a room abdominally, by its porcelain knot; of this swift fighting, body-to-body, when, the forward motion for an instant halted, the eye opens and the whole body adjusts to its new surroundings.

But the body still keeps one friendly hand on the door, holding it open, then decisively pushes the door away, closing itself in—which the click of the powerful but well-oiled spring pleasantly confirms.

THE *ASSIETTE* (THE PLATE)

During our consecration here, let's be careful not to make this thing that we use every day too pearly. No poetic leap, no matter how brilliant, can speak in a sufficiently flat way about the lowly interval that porcelain occupies between pure spirit and appetite.

Not without some humor, alas (it fits its animal better), the name for its lovely matter was taken from a mollusc shell. And we, a gypsy species, are not to take a seat there. Its substance has been named porcelain, from the Latin—by analogy—*porcellana,* sow vulva. . . . Is that good enough for your appetite?

But all beauty, which suddenly rises from the restlessness of the waves, has its true place on a seashell. . . . Is that too much for pure spirit?

And the *assiette,* whatever you say, rose in a similar way from the sea, and what's more was multiplied instantly by that free-spirited juggler in the wings who takes the place sometimes of the melancholic old man who tosses us with poor grace one sun per day.

That is why you see the *assiette* here in its numerous incarnations, still vibrating as a skipped stone settles at last on the sacred surface of the tablecloth.

Here you have all that one can say about an object which contributes more for living than it offers for reflection.

THE CANDLE

Night at times revives a curious plant whose light makes powerfully furnished rooms fall apart into clumps of shadow.

Its gold leaf stands unmoved, attached to the hollow of a small column of alabaster by a pure black leafstalk.

The seedy moths attack it rather than attacking the too-high moon that turns the woods to mist. But scorched in an instant or overstrained in the skirmish, they all tremble on the brink of a mania close to stupor.

The candle, meanwhile, by the way its rays flicker on the book as it suddenly discharges its original gases urges the reader on—then bends over onto its plate and drowns in what has always fed it.

BLACKBERRIES

On the typographical bushes that the poem forms along a road that leads neither out of the world of objects nor toward the spirit, certain fruits are composed of a gathering of spheres, filled with a drop of ink.

*   *   *

Blacks, pinks, and khakis all together, they present us with the spectacle of family members of distinct ages more than any strong desire to pick them.

I think the seeds are disproportionately big in comparison with the surrounding flesh; that's why the birds are not so interested. So little after all remains with them once the fruits have traveled through them from the beak to the anus.

*   *   *

But the poet on his professional walk learns something; he takes from the blackberries food for thought: "This is how," he says to himself, "the patient efforts of a flower—a delicate one—succeed, and generously, even though defended by a grim entanglement of brambles. Without many other virtues, they are ripe—yes, they are—they are finished blackberries, in the same way as this poem is now finished."

RAIN

The rain falling in the courtyard where I watch adopts three manners, each distinct. Toward the center it is a delicate netting (or net) often with holes, a determined fall, though somewhat lethargic, the drops light enough, an eternal drizzle with no animal vigor, an obsessed particle of the pure meteor. Near the courtyard walls to the right and left, heavier drops are falling, energetically, less absorbed in the mass. A few seem big as a grain of wheat, others big as a pea, still others big as marbles. Flowing on the cornices and the stone sills, the rain moves horizontally, though underneath these same blocky barriers, raindrops hang upside down shaped like bellied lozenges. Along the plain made by a tiny zinc roof which my position overhangs, the rain makes a frail counterpane, given a silky texture by complicated streams that flow over the faintly visible undulations and humps of the roofing. The flow moves through a raingutter nearby with the difficulty of an insubstantial creek with no slope, then all at once it drops off in a ropelike thread utterly vertical, it has a thick enough weave, drops down to the pavement blocks, where it flies apart; and the fragments leap up, and are the tips of luminous laces.

Each of these presences has its own manner, and each has its own particular sound. The rain, taken all together, runs like some complicated invention, fiercely, unpredictable and precise, a clockwork of which the moving agent is the weight associated with a given mass of water vapor in the process of precipitation.

The bell sounds as the water-threads hit the stones, the gluppy sounds of the rainspouts, the light blows on the gong become complicated and resonate all together in a concerto never boring, never without true feeling.

When the stored energy in the spring is gone, certain wheels keep on running for a while anyway, more and more lethargically, then the whole thing comes to a stop. If the sun should reappear, the entire edifice vanishes, the light-filled device goes into thin air: well, it rained.

PABLO NERUDA

SOME POETS DESCRIBE the light of the sun shining at the center of all things. Neruda instead describes the dense planets. As we read his poems, we suddenly see going around us in circles, like herds of mad buffalo or distracted horses, all sorts of created things: balconies, glacial rocks, lost address books, olive oil, pipe organs, dining room tables, notary publics, pumas, the shoes of the dead. His book *Residencia en la Tierra* (*Living on Earth*—the Spanish title suggests being at home on the earth) contains an astounding variety of earthly things, each with its own private life. The fifty-six poems in *Residencia I* and *II* were written over a period of ten years—roughly from the time Neruda was twenty-one until he was thirty-one—and they are the greatest surrealist poems yet written in a Western language.

Neruda has a gift for breathing in the sorrow that seems to surround all animals and beings. Many surrealist poets are able to throw themselves for minutes backwards into "the unconscious," but Neruda, like a deep-sea crab, all claws and shell, is able to breathe in the heavy substances that lie beneath the daylight consciousness. He stays on the bottom for hours, and moves around calmly and without hysteria.

> There are sulphur-colored birds, and hideous intestines
> hanging over the doors of houses that I hate,
> and there are false teeth forgotten in a coffeepot,
> there are mirrors
> that ought to have wept from shame and terror,
> there are umbrellas everywhere, and venoms, and umbilical cords.

Next he embarked on a long poem, a geological, biological, and political history of South America. He called it *Canto General,* or a poem about everything. James Wright translated some of these poems marvelously:

> It was the twilight of the iguana.
> From the rainbow-arch of the battlements,
> his long tongue like a lance
> sank down in the green leaves,
> and a swarm of ants, monks with feet chanting,
> crawled off into the jungle,
> the guanaco, thin as oxygen
> in the wide peaks of cloud,
> went along, wearing his shoes of gold,
> while the llama opened his honest eyes
> on the breakable neatness
> of a world full of dew.

Canto General is a massive tome, inspired by Whitman, but it includes coal miners, strikes, corrupt conquistadors, people poisoned by sodium nitrate as well. By now, he was a senator in Chile, under a dictator supported by the United States. Neruda said, "I held my hands up and showed them to the generals / and said: 'I am not a part of this crime.' " The government then sent police to arrest him; after a long trip on horseback over mountains, hiding out every night, he finally got to Mexico. He went to France. The first edition of *Canto General* was published in 1950.

During the middle 1950s, he began publishing an entirely new sort of poem, *Odas Elementales,* odes to simple things, love poems to the things of the world, such as salt, wristwatches, a rabbit killed on the road, a watermelon. I've included here his spirited "Ode to My Socks."

He now had a house on the Chilean shore at Isla Negra, which he filled with hundreds of wooden objects, wooden horses and ships' figureheads. In 1966, he gave a reading at the Poetry Center in New York. It began with a poem of Whitman's. He said, "I don't know how many copies of Whitman I've bought in my life." A few years later, he passed through New York again and spoke to a classroom at Columbia. He was now the ambassador to France. He knew the United States government wanted Allende killed. He said to the audience, "I am on my way to Paris to arrange a loan from the World Bank for Chile. I don't think we'll get it. You can bring us down if you want to, and I think you probably will. But please remember the poem by your great poet Coleridge. If you bring us down, we'll be an albatross around your neck."

PABLO NERUDA was born on July 12, 1904, in a small frontier town in southern Chile, the son of a railroad worker. The father was killed in a fall from his train while Neruda was still a boy. Pablo's given name was Neftali Reyes Basoalto, and his pseudonym was taken very young out of admiration for a nineteenth-century Czech writer.

The governments of South America have a tradition of encouraging young poets by offering them consular posts. When Neruda was twenty-three, he was recognized in this way, and the Chilean government gave him a post in the consular service in the Far East. During the next five years, he lived in turn in Burma, Siam, China, Japan, and India.

Neruda came back to South America in 1932 when he was twenty-eight years old. For a while he was consul in Buenos Aires; he met Lorca there, when Lorca came to Argentina on a lecture tour. *Residencia I* was published in 1933. In 1934, he was assigned to the consulate in Spain.

On July 19, 1936, Franco invaded from North Africa. Neruda, overstepping his power a bit, declared Chile on the side of the Spanish Republic. After being retired as consul, he went to Paris, where he raised money for Spanish refugees, helped by Breton and other French poets, and by Vallejo.

In 1944, the workers from Antofagasta, the nitrate mining section of Chile, asked Neruda to run for senator from their district. He did, and was elected, but later barely escaped with his life.

Pinochet, with the help of the American government, succeeded in bringing Allende down. At that time, Neruda was in a hospital, being treated for cancer; the night Pinochet took over, the Chilean doctors were afraid to continue treatment because of Neruda's sentiments, and he died. His wife, Mathilde, has written of that night. Once he was dead, Pinochet's soldiers and supporters ransacked Neruda's Isla Negra house, broke desks and furniture, burned his letters and unpublished poems. So ended this writer's life.

from TWENTY POEMS OF LOVE AND ONE
ODE OF DESPERATION

1

Body of a woman, white hills, white thighs,
when you surrender, you stretch out like the world.
My body, savage and peasant, undermines you
and makes a son leap in the bottom of the earth.

I was lonely as a tunnel. Birds flew from me.
And night invaded me with her powerful army.
Oh the cups of your breasts! Oh your eyes full of absence!
Oh the roses of your mound! Oh your voice slow and sad!

Body of my woman, I will live on through your marvelousness.
My thirst, my desire without end, my wavering road!
Dark river beds down which the eternal thirst is flowing,
and the fatigue is flowing, and the grief without shore.

6

I remember you as you were that ultimate autumn.
You were a gray beret and the whole being at peace.
In your eyes the fires of the evening dusk were battling,
and the leaves were falling in the waters of your soul.

As attached to my arms as a morning glory,
your sad, slow voice was picked up by the leaves.
Bonfire of astonishment in which my thirst was burning.
Soft blue of hyacinth twisting above my soul.

I feel your eyes travel and the autumn is distant:
gray beret, voice of a bird, and heart like a house
toward which my profound desires were emigrating
and my thick kisses were falling like hot coals.

The sky from a ship. The plains from a hill:
your memory is of light, of smoke, of a still pool!
Beyond your eyes the evening dusks were battling.
Dry leaves of autumn were whirling in your soul.

NOTHING BUT DEATH

There are cemeteries that are lonely,
graves full of bones that do not make a sound,
the heart moving through a tunnel,
in it darkness, darkness, darkness,
like a shipwreck we die going into ourselves,
as though we were drowning inside our hearts,
as though we lived falling out of the skin into the soul.

And there are corpses,
feet made of cold and sticky clay,
death is inside the bones,
like a barking where there are no dogs,
coming out from bells somewhere, from graves somewhere,
growing in the damp air like tears or rain.

Sometimes I see alone
coffins under sail,
embarking with the pale dead, with women that have dead hair,
with bakers who are as white as angels,
and pensive young girls married to notary publics,
caskets sailing up the vertical river of the dead,
the river of dark purple,
moving upstream with sails filled out by the sound of death,
filled by the sound of death which is silence.

Death arrives among all that sound
like a shoe with no foot in it, like a suit with no man in it,
comes and knocks, using a ring with no stone in it, with no finger in it,
comes and shouts with no mouth, with no tongue, with no throat.

Nevertheless its steps can be heard
and its clothing makes a hushed sound, like a tree.

I'm not sure, I understand only a little, I can hardly see,
but it seems to me that its singing has the color of damp violets,
of violets that are at home in the earth,
because the face of death is green,
and the look death gives is green,
with the penetrating dampness of a violet leaf
and the somber color of embittered winter.

But death also goes through the world dressed as a broom,
lapping the floor, looking for dead bodies,
death is inside the broom,
the broom is the tongue of death looking for corpses,
it is the needle of death looking for thread.

Death is inside the folding cots:
it spends its life sleeping on the slow mattresses,
in the black blankets, and suddenly breathes out:
it blows out a mournful sound that swells the sheets,
and the beds go sailing toward a port
where death is waiting, dressed like an admiral.

WALKING AROUND

It so happens I am sick of being a man.
And it happens that I walk into tailor shops and movie houses
dried up, waterproof, like a swan made of felt
steering my way in a water of wombs and ashes.

The smell of barbershops makes me break into hoarse sobs.
The only thing I want is to lie still like stones or wool.
The only thing I want is to see no more stores, no gardens,
no more goods, no spectacles, no elevators.

It so happens I am sick of my feet and my nails
and my hair and my shadow.
It so happens I am sick of being a man.

Still it would be marvelous
to terrify a law clerk with a cut lily,
or kill a nun with a blow on the ear.
It would be great
to go through the streets with a green knife,
letting out yells until I died of the cold.

I don't want to go on being a root in the dark,
insecure, stretched out, shivering with sleep,
going on down, into the moist guts of the earth,
taking in and thinking, eating every day.

I don't want so much misery.
I don't want to go on as a root and a tomb,
alone under the ground, a warehouse with corpses,
half frozen, dying of grief.

That's why Monday, when it sees me coming
with my convict face, blazes up like gasoline,
and it howls on its way like a wounded wheel,
and leaves tracks full of warm blood leading toward the night.

And it pushes me into certain corners, into some moist houses,
into hospitals where the bones fly out the window,
into shoe shops that smell like vinegar,
and certain streets hideous as cracks in the skin.

There are sulphur-colored birds, and hideous intestines
hanging over the doors of houses that I hate,
and there are false teeth forgotten in a coffeepot,
there are mirrors
that ought to have wept from shame and terror,
there are umbrellas everywhere, and venoms, and umbilical cords.

I stroll along serenely, with my eyes, my shoes,
my rage, forgetting everything,
I walk by, going through office buildings and orthopedic shops,
and courtyards with washing hanging from the line:
underwear, towels and shirts from which slow
dirty tears are falling.

from LETTER TO MIGUEL OTERO SILVA,
IN CARACAS

When I was writing my love poems, which sprouted out from me
on all sides, and I was dying of depression,
nomadic, abandoned, gnawing on the alphabet,
they said to me: "What a great man you are, Theocritus!"
I am not Theocritus: I took life,
and I faced her and kissed her,
and then went through the tunnels of the mines
to see how other men live.
And when I came out, my hands stained with garbage and sadness,
I held my hands up and showed them to the generals,
and said: "I am not a part of this crime."
They started to cough, showed disgust, left off saying hello,
gave up calling me Theocritus, and ended by insulting me
and assigning the entire police force to arrest me
because I didn't continue to be occupied exclusively with metaphysical
    subjects.
But I had brought joy over to my side.

From then on I started getting up to read the letters
the seabirds bring from so far away,
letters that arrive moist, messages I translate
phrase by phrase, slowly and confidently: I am punctilious
as an engineer in this strange duty.
All at once I go to the window. It is a square
of pure light, there is a clear horizon
of grasses and crags, and I go on working here
among the things I love: waves, rocks, wasps,
with an oceanic and drunken happiness.
But no one likes our being happy, and they cast you

in a genial role: "Now don't exaggerate, don't worry,"
and they wanted to lock me in a cricket cage, where there would be
     tears,
and I would drown, and they could deliver elegies over my grave. . . .

That is why you write your songs, so that someday the disgraced and
     wounded America
can let its butterflies tremble and collect its emeralds
without the terrifying blood of beatings, coagulated
on the hands of the executioners and the businessmen.
I guessed how full of joy you would be, by the Orinoco, singing
probably, or perhaps buying wine for your house,
taking your part in the fight and the exaltation,
with broad shoulders, like the poets of our age—
with light clothes and walking shoes.
Ever since that time, I have been thinking of writing to you,
and when Guillén arrived, running over with stories of you,
which were coming loose everywhere out of his clothes
—they poured out under the chestnuts of my house—
I said to myself: "Now!" and even then I didn't start a letter to you.
But today has been too much for me: not only one seabird,
but thousands have gone past my window,
and I have picked up the letters no one reads, letters they take along
to all the shores of the world until they lose them.
Then in each of those letters I read words of yours,
and they resembled the words I write, and dream of, and put in
     poems,
and so I decided to send this letter to you, which I end here,
so I can watch through the window the world that is ours.

THE UNITED FRUIT CO.

When the trumpet sounded, it was
all prepared on the earth,
and Jehovah parceled out the earth
to Coca-Cola, Inc., Anaconda,
Ford Motors, and other entities:
The Fruit Company, Inc.
reserved for itself the most succulent,
the central coast of my own land,
the delicate waist of America.
It rechristened its territories
as the "Banana Republics"
and over the sleeping dead,
over the restless heroes
who brought about the greatness,
the liberty and the flags,
it established the comic opera:
abolished the independencies,
presented crowns of Caesar,
unsheathed envy, attracted
the dictatorship of the flies,
Trujillo flies, Tacho flies,
Carias flies, Martinez flies,
Ubico flies, damp flies
of modest blood and marmalade,
drunken flies who zoom
over the ordinary graves,
circus flies, wise flies
well trained in tyranny.
Among the bloodthirsty flies
the Fruit Company lands its ships,

taking off the coffee and the fruit;
the treasure of our submerged
territories flow as though
on plates into the ships.

Meanwhile Indians are falling
into the sugared chasms
of the harbors, wrapped
for burial in the mist of the dawn:
a body rolls, a thing
that has no name, a fallen cipher,
a cluster of dead fruit
thrown down on the dump.

MELANCHOLY INSIDE FAMILIES

I keep a blue bottle.
Inside it an ear and a portrait.
When the night dominates
the feathers of the owl,
when the hoarse cherry tree
rips out its lips and makes menacing gestures
with rinds which the ocean wind often perforates —
then I know that there are immense expanses hidden from us,
quartz in slugs,
ooze,
blue waters for a battle,
much silence, many ore-veins
of withdrawals and camphor,
fallen things, medallions, kindnesses,
parachutes, kisses.

It is only the passage from one day to another,
a single bottle moving over the seas,
and a dining room where roses arrive,
a dining room deserted
as a fish bone; I am speaking of
a smashed cup, a curtain, at the end
of a deserted room through which a river passes
dragging along the stones. It is a house
set on the foundations of the rain,
a house of two floors with the required number of windows,
and climbing vines faithful in every particular.

I walk through afternoons, I arrive
full of mud and death,

dragging along the earth and its roots,
and its indistinct stomach in which corpses
are sleeping with wheat,
metals, and pushed-over elephants.

But above all there is a terrifying,
a terrifying deserted dining room,
with its broken olive oil cruets,
and vinegar running under its chairs,
one ray of moonlight tied down,
something dark, and I look
for a companion inside myself:
perhaps it is a grocery store surrounded by the sea
and torn clothing from which sea water is dripping.

It is only a deserted dining room,
and around it there are expanses,
sunken factories, pieces of timber
which I alone know,
because I am sad, and because I travel,
and I know the earth, and I am sad.

Translated by Robert Bly and James Wright

YOUTH

An odor like an acid sword made
of plum branches along the road,
the kisses like sugar in the teeth,
the drops of life slipping on the fingertips,
the sweet sexual fruit,
the yards, the haystacks, the inviting
rooms hidden in the deep houses,
the mattresses sleeping in the past, the savage green valley
seen from above, from the hidden window:
adolescence all sputtering and burning
like a lamp turned over in the rain.

ENIGMAS

You've asked me what the lobster is weaving there with his golden
    feet?
I reply, the ocean knows this.
You say, what is the ascidia waiting for in its transparent bell? What is
    it waiting for?
I tell you it is waiting for time, like you.
You ask me whom the Macrocystis algae hugs in its arms?
Study, study it, at a certain hour, in a certain sea I know.
You question me about the wicked tusk of the narwhal, and I reply by
    describing
how the sea unicorn with a harpoon in it dies.
You inquire about the kingfisher's feathers,
which tremble in the pure strings of the southern tides?
Or you've found in the cards a new question touching on the crystal
    architecture
of the sea anemone, and you'll deal that to me now?
You want to understand the electric nature of the ocean spines?
The armored stalactite that breaks as it walks?
The hook of the angler fish, the music stretched out
in the deep places like a thread in the water?

I want to tell you the ocean knows this, that life in its jewel boxes
is endless as the sand, impossible to count, pure,
and among the blood-colored grapes time has made the petal
hard and shiny, made the jellyfish full of light
and untied its knot, letting its musical threads fall
from a horn of plenty made of infinite mother-of-pearl.
I am nothing but the empty net which has gone on ahead
of human eyes, dead in those darknesses,

of fingers accustomed to the triangle, longitudes
on the timid globe of an orange.

I walked around as you do, investigating
the endless star,
and in my net, during the night, I woke up naked,
the only thing caught, a fish trapped inside the wind.

ODE TO MY SOCKS

Maru Mori brought me
a pair
of socks
which she knitted herself
with her sheepherder's hands,
two socks as soft
as rabbits.
I slipped my feet
into them
as though into
two
cases
knitted
with threads of
twilight
and goatskin.
Violent socks,
my feet were
two fish made
of wool,
two long sharks
sea-blue, shot
through
by one golden thread,
two immense blackbirds,
two cannons:
my feet
were honored
in this way
by

these
heavenly
socks.
They were
so handsome
for the first time
my feet seemed to me
unacceptable,
like two decrepit
firemen, firemen
unworthy
of that woven
fire,
of those glowing
socks.

Nevertheless
I resisted
the sharp temptation
to save them somewhere,
as schoolboys
keep
fireflies,
as learned men
collect
sacred texts,
I resisted
the mad impulse
to put them
into a golden
cage
and each day give them
birdseed

and pieces of pink melon.
Like explorers
in the jungle who hand
over the very rare
green deer
to the spit
and eat it
with remorse,
I stretched out
my feet
and pulled on
the magnificent
socks
and then my shoes.
The moral
of my ode is this:
beauty is twice
beauty
and what is good is doubly
good
when it is a matter of two socks
made of wool
in winter.

ODE TO SALT

I saw the salt
in this shaker
in the salt flats.
I know
you
will never believe me,
but
it sings,
the salt sings, the hide
of the salt plains,
it sings
through a mouth smothered
by earth.
I shuddered in those deep
solitudes
when I heard
the voice
of
the salt
in the desert.
Near Antofagasta
the entire
salt plain
speaks:
it is a
broken
voice,
a song full
of grief.

Then in its own mines
rock salt, a mountain
of buried light,
a cathedral through which light passes,
crystal of the sea, abandoned
by the waves.

And then on every table
on this earth,
salt,
your nimble
body
pouring out
the vigorous light
over
our foods.
Preserver
of the stores
of the ancient ships,
you were
an explorer
in the ocean,
substance
going first
over the unknown, barely open
routes of the sea foam.
Dust of the sea, the tongue
receives a kiss
of the night sea from you:
taste recognizes
the ocean in each salted morsel,
and therefore the smallest,

the tiniest
wave of the shaker
brings home to us
not only your domestic whiteness
but the inward flavor of the infinite.

GEORG TRAKL

IN A TYPICAL Trakl poem, images follow one another in a way that is somehow stately. The rhythm is slow and heavy, like the mood of someone in a dream. Wings of dragonflies, toads, the gravestones of cemeteries, leaves, and war helmets give off strange colors, brilliant and somber colors. Everywhere there is the suggestion of a dark silence:

> The yellow flowers
> Bend without words over the blue pond

The silence is that of things that could speak, but choose not to. As Trakl grew older, more silent creatures agreed to appear in his poems—first it was only wild ducks and dragonflies, but then oak trees, deer, decaying wallpaper, herds of sheep, ponds, and finally steel helmets, armies, wounded men, battlefield nurses, and the blood that had run from the wounds that day.

> Yet a red cloud, in which a furious god,
> The spilled blood itself, has its home, silently
> Gathers, a moonlike coolness in the willow bottoms.

Martin Seymour-Smith has noted that Trakl is not only the visionary poet but the alienated artist as well. His own family equated "poetry" with "failure," and yet his gloom "arose from a consciousness of joy" rather than from decadence. Martin Heidegger showed in his essay on Trakl that "green" is the green both of spring and of decay.

Trakl was influenced by Rimbaud and by Nietzsche, but more deeply by Hölderlin, who was opposed to orthodox religion but was profoundly religious. Austrian culture was in decay in Trakl's time, but he retained great integrity in the midst of that decay. He has many images of a decline going steeply into death or sleep.

Rilke said of him: "Trakl's poetry is to me an object of sublime existence. . . . It occurs to me that his whole work has a parallel in the aspiration of a Li Po: in both, falling is the pretext for the most continuous ascension."

GEORG TRAKL was born in Salzburg in 1887, the son of an ironmonger. The family was partially Czech, but spoke German. While still at school, he began to inhale chloroform and drank heavily. He took a degree in pharmacology in Vienna, and entered military service for a year. He then returned to Salzburg. His sister Margareta, who appears often in his poems, was a concert pianist; she committed suicide. The theme of incest often appears in his poems.

Trakl had a deep commitment to the life of the artist and the work of writing poetry. Some of his letters about that commitment influenced Rilke. Rilke, for his part, never touched drugs, but Trakl could not go on living without them. Ludwig Wittgenstein knew that Trakl was a genius, and he set aside money for Trakl through a patron, Ludwig von Ficker, who published Trakl's poetry in the magazine *Der Brenner.* Only one book of Trakl's poems appeared in his lifetime, a selection made by Franz Werfel, published in 1913. In August of 1914, he was called up as a lieutenant in the Austrian medical corps. He served in the field near Galizia.

After the battle of Grodek, ninety badly wounded men were left in a barn for him to care for. He had no supplies and was not a doctor. That night he attempted to kill himself, but was prevented by friends. The last poems in this selection were written during this time, and the sense of his own approaching death is clear, and set down with astonishing courage. His poem called "Grodek," which is thought to be his last work, is a ferocious poem. It is constructed with great care. A short passage suggesting the whole of German Romantic poetry of the nineteenth century appears, and is followed instantly by a passage evoking the mechanical violence of the German twentieth century. This alternation, so strong that it can even be felt slightly in the translation, gives the poem great strength and fiber.

> At evening the woods of autumn are full of the sound
> Of the weapons of death, golden fields
> And blue lakes, over which the darkening sun
> Rolls down.

After the crisis at Grodek, Trakl went on serving in his post for several months, meanwhile using the drugs obtained from his pharmacy supplies. He was transferred to the hospital at Kraków and assigned, to his surprise, not as a corpsman, but as a patient. He developed a delusion that he would be executed as a deserter. No one was near to help, and he died in November 1914 of an overdose of cocaine, probably unintentionally.

THE SUN

Each day the gold sun comes over the hill.
The woods are beautiful, also the dark animals,
Also man; hunter or farmer.

The fish rises with a red body in the green pond.
Under the arch of heaven
The fisherman travels smoothly in his blue skiff.

The grain, the cluster of grapes, ripen slowly.
When the still day comes to an end,
Both evil and good have been prepared.

When the night has come,
Easily the pilgrim lifts his heavy eyelids;
The sun breaks from gloomy ravines.

SUMMER

At evening the complaint of the cuckoo
Grows still in the wood.
The grain bends its head deeper,
The red poppy.

Darkening thunder drives
Over the hill.
The old song of the cricket
Dies in the field.

The leaves of the chestnut tree
Stir no more.
Your clothes rustle
On the winding stair.

The candle gleams silently
In the dark room,
A silver hand
Puts the light out;

Windless, starless night.

ON THE MARSHY PASTURES

A man who walks in the black wind; the dry reeds rustle quietly
Through the silence of the marshy pastures. In the gray skies
A migration of wild birds moves in ranks
Catty-corner over dark waters.

Insurgence. In the collapsing houses
Decay is fluttering out with black wings;
Crippled-up birches breathe heavily in the wind.

Evening in empty roadhouses. The longing for home settles about
The delicate despair of the grazing flocks,
Vision of the night: toads plunge from silver waters.

SONG OF THE WESTERN COUNTRIES

Oh the nighttime beating of the soul's wings:
Herders of sheep once, we walked along the forests that were
    growing dark,
And the red deer, the green flower and the speaking river followed us
In humility. Oh the old old note of the cricket,
Blood blooming on the altarstone,
And the cry of the lonely bird over the green silence of the pool.

And you Crusades, and glowing punishment
Of the flesh, purple fruits that fell to earth
In the garden at dusk, where young and holy men walked,
Enlisted men of war now, waking up out of wounds and
    dreams about stars.
Oh the soft cornflowers of the night.

And you long ages of tranquillity and golden harvests,
When as peaceful monks we pressed out the purple grapes;
And around us the hill and forest shone strangely.
The hunts for wild beasts, the castles, and at night, the rest,
When a man in his room sat thinking justice,
And in noiseless prayer fought for the living head of God.

And this bitter hour of defeat,
When we behold a stony face in the black waters.
But radiating light, the lovers lift their silver eyelids:
They are one body. Incense streams from rose-colored pillows
And the sweet song of those risen from the dead.

IN HELLBRUNN

Once more following the blue grief of the evening
Down the hill, to the springtime fishpond —
As if the shadows of those dead for a long time were hovering above,
The shadows of church dignitaries, of noble ladies —
Their flowers bloom so soon, the earnest violets
In the earth at evening, and the clear water washes
From the blue spring. The oaks turn green
In such a ghostly way over the forgotten footsteps of the dead,
The golden clouds over the fishpond.

BIRTH

These mountains: blackness, silence, and snow.
The red hunter climbs down from the forest;
Oh the mossy gaze of the wild thing.

The peace of the mother: under black firs
The sleeping hands open by themselves
When the cold moon seems ready to fall.

The birth of man. Each night
Blue water washes over the rockbase of the cliff;
The fallen angel stares at his reflection with sighs,

Something pale wakes up in a suffocating room.
The eyes
Of the stony old woman shine, two moons.

The cry of the woman in labor. The night troubles
The boy's sleep with black wings,
With snow, which falls with ease out of the purple clouds.

THE HEART

The wild heart grew white in the forest;
Dark anxiety
Of death, as when the gold
Died in the gray cloud.
An evening in November.
A crowd of needy women stood at the bare gate
Of the slaughterhouse;
Rotten meat and guts fell
Into every basket;
Horrible food.

The blue dove of the evening
Brought no forgiveness.
The dark cry of trumpets
Traveled in the golden branches
Of the soaked elms,
A frayed flag
Smoking with blood,
To which a man listens
In wild despair.
All your days of nobility, buried
In that red evening!

Out of the dark entrance hall
The golden shape
Of the young girl steps
Surrounded by the pale moon,
The prince's court of autumn,
Black fir trees broken
In the night's storm,
The steep fortress.
O heart
Glittering above in the snowy cold.

DESCENT AND DEFEAT
To Karl Borromäus Heinrich

Over the white fishpond
The wild birds have blown away.
An icy wind drifts from our stars at evening.

Over our graves
The broken forehead of the night is bending.
Under the oaks we veer in a silver skiff.

The white walls of the city are always giving off sound.
Under arching thorns
O my brother blind minute hands we are climbing toward midnight.

THE MOOD OF DEPRESSION

You dark mouth inside me,
You are strong, shape
Composed of autumn cloud,
And golden evening stillness;
In the shadows thrown
By the broken pine trees
A mountain stream turns dark in the green light;
A little town
That piously dies away into brown pictures.

Now the black horses rear
In the foggy pasture.
I think of soldiers!
Down the hill, where the dying sun lumbers,
The laughing blood plunges,
Speechless
Under the oak trees! Oh the hopeless depression
Of an army; a blazing steel helmet
Fell with a clatter from purpled foreheads.

The autumn night comes down so coolly.
With her white habit glittering like the stars
Over the broken human bodies
The convent nurse is silent.

THE EVENING

With the ghostly shapes of dead heroes
Moon, you fill
The growing silence of the forest,
Sickle moon—
With the gentle embraces
Of lovers,
And with ghosts of famous ages
All around the crumbling rocks;
The moon shines with such blue light
Upon the city,
Where a decaying generation
Lives, cold and evil—
A dark future prepared
For the pale grandchild.
Your shadows swallowed by the moon
Sighing upward in the empty goblet
Of the mountain lake.

ON THE EASTERN FRONT

The ominous anger of masses of men
Is like the wild organ of the winter storm,
The purple surge of battle,
Leafless stars.

With broken eyebrows and silver arms
The night waves to dying soldiers.
In the shade of the ash tree of autumn
The souls of the slain are sighing.

A thorny desert surrounds the city.
The moon chases the shocked women
From the bleeding stairways.
Wild wolves have broken through the door.

MOURNING

The dark eagles, sleep and death,
Rustle all night around my head:
The golden statue of man
Is swallowed by the icy comber
Of eternity. On the frightening reef
The purple remains go to pieces,
And the dark voice mourns
Over the sea.
Sister in my wild despair
Look, a precarious skiff is sinking
Under the stars,
The face of night whose voice is fading.

GRODEK

At evening the woods of autumn are full of the sound
Of the weapons of death, golden fields
And blue lakes, over which the darkening sun
Rolls down; night gathers in
Dying recruits, the animal cries
Of their burst mouths.
Yet a red cloud, in which a furious god,
The spilled blood itself, has its home, silently
Gathers, a moonlike coolness in the willow bottoms;
All the roads spread out into the black mold.
Under the gold branches of the night and stars
The sister's shadow falters through the diminishing grove,
To greet the ghosts of the heroes, bleeding heads;
And from the reeds the sound of the dark flutes of autumn rises.
O prouder grief! you bronze altars,
The hot flame of the spirit is fed today by a more monstrous pain,
The unborn grandchildren

RAINER MARIA RILKE

RILKE HAS FOR hundreds of readers been their first introduction
to poetry that goes steeply and unapologetically up with the spirit.
One could say that when a young man or woman encounters him, he
will slip his hand under the elbow and guide the person on to some
small house that stands nearby, perhaps a hut where the railway
switchman lives. Once inside, the young person notices that the ceil-
ing is higher than one would have thought. In fact, the hut is a cathe-
dral, with immensely high vaults, like Chartres, with deep shadows.
Meanwhile, Rilke pretends that nothing unusual has happened.

Rilke, when in Paris, often lived in a rented room, sometimes one
where a lonely violinist who is staying next door plays all night.
Something about that lonely music coming through the wall is right
for Rilke's life. He writes magnificently about nature, especially the
fall, and he's a great love poet; but in the end he loves great works of
art more than nature or human life. Looking at a statue of Buddha he
notices that

[S]omething has already started to live
in you that will live longer than the sun.

He is an acute observer of human beings; for example, the way a
blind woman walks across a room. He does that well, but when he is
really concentrated, he describes—as no one else can—a stone statue
of Apollo. If a work of art is true, he says,

There is no place at all
that isn't looking at you. You'll have to change your life.

Poets like to write about what the world is like after a hurricane, or after a rainstorm, but Rilke likes to write about what the world is like after a great work of art has been created. That work of art changes the normal world. He wants you to give up all the miscellaneous collection of memories that the poetry workshops encourage, and become serious—move toward great art. His emphasis on great art offends many critics so much, they don't even mention it. What's more, Rilke doesn't say art is born out of life; he says art gives birth to art, and you need to study great artists if you want to write. What is music? Great music doesn't depend on human life, but on music itself. Music is "a statue breathing." Music doesn't give "impressions" of a landscape. It is a "countryside we can hear. . . . The deepest thing in us, that forces its way out . . . as the other side of the air."

We know that in ancient Greece, when a road forked, someone often built a temple there, so that the traveler could decide which way to go. Today, we are in trouble, Rilke says, because where two roads fork "no one has built Apollo's temple." Poetry doesn't mean talking well, but being truly alive. Poetry is "a god breathing." This is highly offensive to many people, and they often refuse to read him. He doesn't care.

Those who attack Rilke for being too "aesthetic" or spiritual miss the point. Neruda and he were opposites, and Neruda once wrote a poem attacking Rilke for being too "celestial." But they are both great artists and both are warriors. Rilke takes "the way less traveled." He urges you to change your life in such a way that you can actually take in the Buddhist art, the art of Greeks, "the deepest thing in us."

RAINER MARIA RILKE was born on December 4, 1875, in Prague, and baptized René Karl Wilhelm Johann Josef Maria Rilke. The many names became suggestive of the various personalities that he carried all his life. His father, after a brief career as a gunner, became a civil servant in the North Bohemian Railway. His mother, who had once lived in a large mansion which belonged to an old Prague family, didn't accept reality well. She refused to acknowledge that Rainer was a boy; she actually put him in dresses and sent him out in the hall to knock on the door. He had to give a girl's name to get in. He describes his mother in *"Aus Einer Kindheit."* In his twenties, he became friends with a group of painters living at Worpswede. He fell in love with one of them, and married another, Clara Westhoff. The couple, who had a daughter named Ruth, did not live together after 1902, though they wrote elaborate letters to each other year after year, often astonishing ones.

He accepted an offer from Rodin in 1906 to be his secretary, and he moved to Meudon near Paris. His close connection to Rodin lasted two years. He remarked that Rodin's influence made him see more. Rodin actually told him if he couldn't write he should go to the zoo and look at a panther. Out of this exercise came *New Poems,* published in 1908, great poems on the movement of a swan in water, on the way a panther walks in a cage, and the like. In 1915, the German government drafted him into the army, and he worked during 1916 as an archivist in Vienna. A long fallow period followed. All at once, in a huge burst of energy, he wrote both the *Duino Elegies* and the *Sonnets to Orpheus.* In his view of his own life, he had now done his work. As it turned out, he had only three more years to live. During this time he stayed in a small tower in Switzerland where he continued to write astonishing poems. His leukemia was not diagnosed correctly for two years, and he died at Muzot in 1926 at the age of fifty-one.

THE MAN WATCHING

I can tell by the way the trees beat, after
so many dull days, on my worried windowpanes
that a storm is coming,
and I hear the far-off fields saying things
I can't bear without a friend,
I can't love without a sister.

The storm, the shifter of shapes, drives on
across the woods and across time,
and the world looks as if it had no age:
the landscape, like a line in the psalm book,
is seriousness and weight and eternity.

What we choose to fight is so tiny!
What fights with us is so great!
If only we would let ourselves be dominated
as things do by some immense storm,
we would become strong too, and not need names.

When we win it's with small things,
and the triumph itself makes us small.
What is extraordinary and eternal
does not *want* to be bent by us.
I mean the Angel who appeared
to the wrestlers of the Old Testament:
when the wrestlers' sinews
grew long like metal strings,
he felt them under his fingers
like chords of deep music.

Whoever was beaten by this Angel
(who often simply declined the fight)
went away proud and strengthened
and great from that harsh hand,
that kneaded him as if to change his shape.
Winning does not tempt that man.
This is how he grows: by being defeated, decisively,
by constantly greater beings.

I LIVE MY LIFE IN GROWING ORBITS

I live my life in growing orbits
which move out over the things of the world.
Perhaps I can never achieve the last,
but that will be my attempt.

I am circling around God, around the ancient tower,
and I have been circling for a thousand years,
and I still don't know if I am a falcon, or a storm,
or a great song.

SOMETIMES A MAN STANDS UP DURING SUPPER

Sometimes a man stands up during supper
and walks outdoors, and keeps on walking,
because of a church that stands somewhere in the East.

And his children say blessings on him as if he were dead.

And another man, who remains inside his own house,
dies there, inside the dishes and in the glasses,
so that his children have to go far out into the world
toward that same church, which he forgot.

I AM TOO ALONE IN THE WORLD

I am too alone in the world, and not alone enough
to make every minute holy.
I am too tiny in this world, and not tiny enough
just to lie before you like a thing,
shrewd and secretive.
I want my own will, and I want simply to be with my will,
as it goes toward action,
and in the silent, sometimes hardly moving times
when something is coming nearer,
I want to be with those who know secret things
or else alone.
I want to be a mirror for your whole body,
and I never want to be blind, or to be too old
to hold up your heavy and swaying picture.
I want to unfold.
I don't want to stay folded anywhere,
because where I am folded, there I am a lie.
And I want my grasp of things
true before you. I want to describe myself
like a painting that I looked at
closely for a long time,
like a saying that I finally understood,
like the pitcher I use every day,
like the face of my mother,
like a ship
that took me safely
through the wildest storm of all.

SONNETS TO ORPHEUS, VII

To praise is the whole thing! A man who can praise
comes toward us like ore out of the silences
of rock. His heart, that dies, presses out
for others a wine that is fresh forever.

When the god's energy takes hold of him,
his voice never collapses in the dust.
Everything turns to vineyards, everything turns to grapes,
made ready for harvest by his powerful south.

The mold in the catacomb of the king
does not suggest that his praising is lies, nor
the fact that the gods cast shadows.

He is one of the servants who does not go away,
who still holds through the doors
of the tomb trays of shining fruit.

THE SWAN

This clumsy living that moves lumbering
as if in ropes through what is not done
reminds us of the awkward way the swan walks.

And to die, which is a letting go
of the ground we stand on and cling to every day,
is like the swan when he nervously lets himself down

into the water, which receives him gaily
and which flows joyfully under
and after him, wave after wave,
while the swan, unmoving and marvelously calm,
is pleased to be carried, each minute more fully grown,
more like a king, composed, farther and farther on.

ARCHAIC TORSO OF APOLLO

We have no idea what his fantastic head
was like, where the eyeballs were slowly swelling. But
his body now is glowing like a gas lamp,
whose inner eyes, only turned down a little,

hold their flame, shine. If there weren't light, the curve
of the breast wouldn't blind you, and in the swerve
of the thighs a smile wouldn't keep on going
toward the place where the seeds are.

If there weren't light, this stone would look cut off
where it drops clearly from the shoulders,
its skin wouldn't gleam like the fur of a wild animal,

and the body wouldn't send out light from every edge
as a star does . . . for there is no place at all
that isn't looking at you. You'll have to change your life.

DAY IN OCTOBER

Lord, the time has come. The summer was immense.
Lay down your shadow on the sundials,
and on the open places let the winds go free.

Give the tardy fruits the hint to fill;
give them two more Mediterranean days,
drive them on into their greatness, and press
the final sweetness into the heavy wine.

Whoever has no house by now will not build one.
Whoever is alone will be a long time alone,
will stay up, read, write long letters,
and then in the wide avenues drift restlessly
here and there, as the withered leaves blow by.

I FIND YOU

I find you in all these things of the world
that I love calmly, like a brother;
in things no one cares for you brood like a seed;
and to powerful things you give an immense power.

Strength plays such a marvelous game—
it moves through the things of the world like a servant,
groping out in roots, tapering in trunks,
and in the treetops like a rising from the dead.

"WE MUST DIE BECAUSE WE HAVE KNOWN THEM"

*from Papyrus Prisse. From the sayings of Ptah-Hotep, 6th Dynasty
    (2300–1650 BCE)*

"We must die because we have known them." Die
of the unbelievable flower of their smile. Die
of their delicate hands. Die of women.

The adolescent boy praises the death-givers,
when they float magnificently through his
heart halls. From his blossoming body
he cries out to them:
impossible to reach. Oh, how strange they are.
They go swiftly over
the peaks of his emotions and pour down
the marvelously altered night into his deserted
arm valley. The wind that rises
in their dawn makes his body leaves rustle. His brooks
glisten away in the sun.

But the grown man
shivers and says nothing. The man
who blundered around all night
on the mountains of his feelings remains
silent.

As the old sailor remains silent,
and the terrors
he's experienced leap about in him as if in rocking cages.

PARIS, JULY 1914

BUDDHA INSIDE THE LIGHT

The core of every core, the kernel of every kernel,
an almond! held in itself, deepening in sweetness:
all of this, everything, right up to the stars,
is the meat around your stone. Accept my bow.

Oh, yes, you feel it, how the weights on you are gone!
Your husk has reached into what has no end,
and that is where the great saps are brewing now.
On the outside a warmth is helping,

for, high, high above, your own suns are growing
immense and they glow as they wheel around.
Yet something has already started to live
in you that will live longer than the sun.

from THE LIFE OF THE
VIRGIN MARY

1. The Birth of Mary

Oh what it must have cost the angels
Not to break out singing (as we burst in tears),
For they knew well that this night was the Night
Of the Mother's birth . . . whose son would soon be here.

In their silence the angels pointed out from the air
Where Joachim's farm stood by itself in the field.
They could feel the Great Descending all around
And in their beings, but no descending was allowed.

The farm couple were already half out of it.
A neighbor woman came and talked and knew nothing;
And the old man went out and consciously
Quieted a dark cow. Nothing like this ever.

2. Mary Presented at the Temple

In order to understand how Mary was at that
Moment, you'd have to find some place inside you
Where pillars hold you up, where you can feel
Stairways, where arches give support to
A perilous bridge over some deep space which
Endured in you simply because it was built up
Out of rocks that you couldn't possibly lift
Now out of yourself or you would bring yourself down.
If you're so far along that everything in you is stone,
Great walls, ascending stairs, views, domes — then try
To pull aside with both hands that great hanging cloth
Just in front of your face, a little at least.

The light of glory shines down from the high things
More powerful than your breath or your feelings.
One palace over another palace, from below, from above,
Parapets rise out of deeper parapets
Finally emerging so high up that you, if
You took it in, would be afraid of falling.
Meanwhile, clouds of incense from the burners
Trouble the air around you, but the most distinct things
Aim straight at you with their steady beam.
And when next the clear flames of the burning lamps
Play over the elaborate robes that are approaching
Could you endure this?
But she did come, and lifted her
Eyes and addressed the whole scene.
(A child, a half-grown girl among grown women)
She mounted the stair calmly, knowing who she was,
Toward this great extravagance which shifted to meet her.
Everything that people have built was already
Deeply outweighed by the praise that remained
In her heart. And by the urge
To give herself over to the inner presence.
Her parents' plan was just to bring her there, present her.
The scary man with his chest of jewels
Seemed to receive her. But she went on through,
Small as she was, past every hand
On into her destiny which is now complete,
Higher than the building, heavier than the whole temple.

4. Mary's Visit with Elizabeth

It all went well from the very start,
Although sometimes when climbing she was aware
Of the amazing thing far inside her body.
Then she would stop, and breathe, on the top of a high

Hill in Judea. It wasn't the land around her,
It was her own abundance that surrounded her.
As she walked she felt: No woman will ever
Have any more largeness than I have now.

And she recognized a longing to place her hand
On her cousin's big belly, farther along toward birth.
The two women bent toward each other;
Each touched the other's dress and touched the hair.

Each one, full of her own holy treasure,
Found a safe place at the side of her kin.
Ah, the Savior in Mary was only a blossom
But the joy of it roused the little Baptist
In the womb to hop and leap about.

5. The Suspicions of Joseph

And the Angel spoke, not without carefully hearing
This man who stood there with his fists tightened.
"But isn't it clear from every fold of her dress
That she is as cool as the morning mist?"

The man however looked suspiciously back
And said, "I want to know how this happened."
The Angel spoke louder: "You woodworker,
Don't you see any mark of God at all in this?

"Just because you know how to make planks
Out of tree trunks, are you unable to imagine
One who can bring forth leaves
And pregnant buds out of the same wood?"

He got it. And the instant he lifted
His deeply shocked eyes to the Angel,
The Angel was gone. He took hold of his cap
And pulled it off slowly. And what he sang was a hymn.

12. The Quiet Mary Knew with the Risen Christ

What they felt was this: Isn't it
Fantastically sweet beyond all other mysteries,
And yet immensely earthbound:
That he, slightly pale still from the grave,
Walked light as air toward her,
Risen in every particle of his being.
Oh it was to her first. Far beyond speech
They felt that healing.
Yes, healing was what it was
And there was no need for firm touch.
He laid for a second only
His hand, about to be
Eternal, on her woman's shoulder
And they began
As quietly as trees in April,
Wholly mingled,
The new season
Of their deepest union.

PALM

Palm of the hand. Sole, that walks now
only on feeling. The hand turns over
and in its mirror
shows heavenly roads, that themselves are
walking.
It has learned to stroll on water
when it dips down,
walks on top of fountains,
causes all roads to fork.
It steps forward into another's hand,
changes its doubles
into a countryside,
travels into them and arrives,
fills them with having arrived.

MUZOT, OCTOBER 1924

ON MUSIC

Music: the breathing of statues. Perhaps:
the silence of paintings. Language where
language ends. Time
that stands head-up in the direction
        of hearts that wear out.

Feeling . . . for whom? Place where feeling is
transformed . . . into what? Into a countryside we can hear.
Music: you stranger. You feeling space, growing
away from us. The deepest thing in us, that,
rising above us, forces its way out . . .
a holy goodbye:
when the innermost point in us stands
outside, as amazing space, as the other
side of the air:
pure,
immense,
not for us to live in now.

MUNICH, JANUARY 1918

A WALK

My eyes already touch the sunny hill,
going far ahead of the road I have begun.
So we are grasped by what we cannot grasp;
it has its inner light, even from a distance—

and changes us, even if we do not reach it,
into something else, which, hardly sensing it, we already are;
a gesture waves us on, answering our own wave . . .
but what we feel is the wind in our faces.

MUZOT, MARCH 1924

JUST AS THE WINGED ENERGY
OF DELIGHT

Just as the winged energy of delight
carried you over many chasms early on,
now raise the daringly imagined arch
holding up the astounding bridges.

Miracle doesn't lie only in the amazing
living through and defeat of danger;
miracles become miracles in the clear
achievement that is earned.

To work with things is not hubris
when building the association beyond words;
denser and denser the pattern becomes —
being carried along is not enough.

Take your well-disciplined strengths
and stretch them between two
opposing poles. Because inside human beings
is where God learns.

MUZOT, FEBRUARY 1924

BASHO

FOR THE HAIKU poets, the cry of a mosquito is just as important as a general's hat or a storm. Basho, in his poems, reaches out to a time before birth and after death as well. Observing an autumn evening, he remarks that, "Hades must be a little like this." He often feels Buddha's presence, and the old monks who were masters of meditation. He remarks:

> Dried salmon
> and Kuya's breakthrough into the spirit—both
> belong to the cold time of the year!

A simple walk can be—and he likes it to be—a meditation:

> It's fall and a full moon.
> I walked around the shore
> of the pond all night.

He wrote apparently a thousand haiku. His task was to revive the power of the haiku at a time when the form had become academic and conceptual. He took long walks often in wild weather so he could register every tiny event; but it's always as if some spiritual master were looking over the shoulder of the poem. He is aware of how long the spiritual road is, the Road to the Deep North. Dogen wrote poems but thought of himself more as a teacher of enlightenment than as a poet, but Basho always stayed in nature. Lucien Stryk remarked that he "strove to place his reader within an experience whose unfolding might lead to revelation."

In *Records of a Worn-Out Knapsack,* he said something like this:

Inside this pitiful body which has one hundred bones and nine holes, there is something called spirit, which is like a flowing curtain easily blown around by wind. It was spirit that got me to writing poetry, at first for amusement, later as a way of life. At times, my spirit has been brought down so low that I almost quit writing, and at other times the spirit became proud and powerful. It's been like that from the start: the spirit never is at peace, always in doubt of the value of what it does. Sometimes it has been attracted to life at court, at another time it's been leaning toward the dangerous life of a scholar. But the spirit would not allow either route; it stuck to haiku. Artists who have achieved greatness—Saigyon in poetry, Sogi in linked verse, Sesshu in painting, Rikyu in tea ceremony—each of them obeys the spirit. They all possess one thing in common. Each remains through the four seasons at one with nature.

Basho warned readers about the animalistic—or "barbarian"—heart and mind. He asked for haiku poets to adopt elegance and "lightness," which results from the well-known quality of "nonattachment":

Skylark in the waste fields—
one sweet cry
of nonattachment.

BASHO was born Matsuo Munefusa in 1644 in a small town named Ueno, some thirty miles southeast of Kyoto. His father died when he was twelve. Basho entered the service of a local feudal lord at that time. When the lord died ten years later, Basho left his hometown and traveled, perhaps to Kyoto, for the first time. He then studied with a well-known priest, and edited a collection of haiku, to which thirty poets contributed poems. In 1680, when he was thirty-six, his students built a hut for him on the Sumita River, near a large banana tree, or *basho*. He took that name for himself. As the hut would burn down, a new one would be built. He lived sparsely, and believed that nature is what is important. When he was about forty, he began a series of wanderings or long walks. Taking only his knapsack and a stick, he would walk for miles and miles, writing haiku on what he saw. He described his first trip in *Travel Diary of Weathered Bones*. He also published accounts of a trip to Kenshin Shrine, and to Sarashao, and another long trip to various places, which resulted in *Records of a Worn-Out Knapsack*. Finally, when he was forty-five, he journeyed north to the provinces of Honshu. From that came *The Narrow Road to the Deep North,* probably his most famous book.

In the five years that he still had left to live, he suffered often from headaches and fevers. He built a hut for the third time, and wrote *Commentaries on an Autumn Night.* He constantly helped others with their haiku, and always complained that he had too much social life and not enough solitude. At one point he closed his gate and refused to see visitors. He took one more walking trip and then died in Osaka when he was fifty years old.

Spider, if you had a voice,
what would you sing,
swaying in the fall wind?

It's fall and dusk.
And no one is walking
along the road.

The temple bell stops —
but the sound keeps coming
out of the flowers.

It's late fall.
I wonder how the man
next door lives.

It's fall and a full moon.
I walked around the shore
of the pond all night.

Dried salmon
and Kuya's breakthrough into the spirit—both
belong to the cold time of the year!

Storm on Mount Asama!
Wind blowing
out of the stones!

Give your longing to wound
and to own more things
away to the willow.

The sea grows rough.
The Milky Way reaches past
the islands of Sado!

How marvelous the man is
who can see a lightning flash
and not think, "Life is short!"

It's spring, all right;
that hill we never named
is hidden in the mist.

The sea grows dark.
The voices of wild ducks
turn white.

It's quiet, all right.
The cries of the cicadas
sink into the rocks.

Octopuses caught in floating pots,
dreams that are not eternal
under the summer moon.

ROLF JACOBSEN

IN SOME WAYS, Rolf Jacobsen was the first "modern" poet in Norway. He began writing poems in the thirties. By then cars were becoming common, and their tires were softer than they are now. He noticed that the *F* of Firestone was pressed into the sand of a forest road going along between pines.

> [A] car had passed by on the dusty road
> where an ant was out with his pine needle working
> he was wandering around in the huge *F* of Firestone
> that had been pressed into the sandy earth
> for a hundred and twenty kilometers.

We too have been pressed into the sandy earth. We too are wandering around in the *F* of Firestone.

Even in the thirties, some people in Norway did feel abandoned in the cities. He mentions a street lamp in the city that holds up its light umbrella over the paving stones "so that the wicked dark will not come near." The street lamp speaks:

> It says: We are all far from home.
> There's no hope anymore.

In the old Norway of the deep forests, there was always hope. If you walked long enough you'd come to a well-built group of farm buildings, perhaps with a lame old man out in front, chopping wood. He'd invite you in for dinner. But in the city—in Oslo—that did not happen.

> Let the young rain of tears come.
> Let the calm hands of grief come.
> It's not all as evil as you think.

So we have a poet who is sensitive to contemporary loneliness; and yet he is able to produce exquisitely tender riffs almost like Mozart in their elegance. He is a willing participant in the invisible world. He refuses to be a pedestrian; he does not complain; he is not elsewhere. He is willing to go to that bodiless world where the invisibles live above us or below us, unusual for a poet of his generation.

So we have something remarkable in Jacobsen—someone who lives in the same disappointing world in which we all live, and yet is willing to imagine glory: he is willing to praise the beauty of this populated earth. He sees a lot of things wrong with human beings, and yet he is willing to look at people almost without judgment, like a Buddhist:

> Some people
> ascend out of our life, some people
> enter our life,
> uninvited and sit down . . .
>   some people
> eat asparagus, some people
> are children,
> some people climb up on the roof,
> sit down at table,

lie around in hammocks . . . some people
want to take your hand, some people
die during the night,
some people are other people, some people are you, some people
don't exist,
some people do.

ROLF JACOBSEN was born in Oslo, March 8, 1907. For most of his
life, he lived in Hamar, north and east of Oslo. He worked as an editor
for the local newspaper, many times taking the night shift. In his first
book, *Earth and Iron,* he took on himself the task of writing about
iron, as well as about the old Norwegian poetic subject, the earth itself.
To the astonishment of many readers, a number of the poems were in
free verse, and were not rhymed. He brought trains in, gaslights, tele-
phone poles, telescopes, advertisements for scotch whisky, steam shov-
els, as well as the stave churches and the old forests. He remarked on
interesting developments as well, noticing that the age of the great
symphonies was now over, but the magnificent sound continues to
"pour down like rain" into the farmer's living room, "a sack of noise."
After World War II, he became more skeptical of technology's
promise, and of the consumer society. Altogether he produced twelve
books of poems, and he received the Norwegian Critics' Prize in 1960,
the Aschehoug Prize in 1986, the Bergen Prize in 1968, and the "little
Nobel Prize," the Grand Nordic Prize from the Swedish Academy in
1989. He went on a reading tour of the United States during the
eighties. When his wife, Petra, to whom he had been married for
forty-three years, became ill and died in 1983, he wrote a sequence of
poems for her that was published in his last book, *Night Watch,* in
1985. These poems have been beautifully translated by Roger
Greenwald. Even though Norway is a small country, 15,000 copies of

that book were sold, more than are sold for most poets in the United States.

During the last years of his life, he became friends with Olav H. Hauge. Jacobsen's poems were translated into more than twenty languages. He died when he was eighty-seven years old, in 1994.

COUNTRY ROADS

A pale morning in June, 4 A.M.
the country roads still grayish and moist
tunneling endlessly through pines
a car had passed by on the dusty road
where an ant was out with his pine needle working
he was wandering around in the huge *F* of Firestone
that had been pressed into the sandy earth
for a hundred and twenty kilometers.
Fir needles are heavy.
Time after time he slipped back with his badly
    balanced
    load
and worked it up again
and skidded back again
traveling over the great and luminous Sahara lit by clouds.

MOON AND APPLE

When the apple tree blooms,
the moon comes often like a blossom,
paler than any of them,
shining over the tree.

It is the ghost of the summer,
the white sister of the blossoms who returns
to drop in on us,
and radiate peace with her hands
so that you shouldn't feel too bad when the hard times come.
For the Earth itself is a blossom, she says,
on the star tree,
pale and with luminous
ocean leaves.

THE AGE OF THE GREAT SYMPHONIES

The age of the great symphonies
is over now.

The symphonies rose toward heaven with real magnificence —
sunlit clouds with thunder in
over the brilliant centuries.
Cumulus under blue skies. Coriolanus.

Now they are coming back down again in the form of rain,
a banded, stone-colored rain on all the wavelengths and programs
covering earth like a wet overcoat, a sack of noise.

Now they are coming back down from the sky,
they bounce off the skyscrapers like electric hail
and seep down into farmers' living rooms
and roll over the suburbs and brick-oceans
as immortal sound.
A rain of sound,
"You millions of this earth, embrace,"
so as to deaden screams

every day, every day
on this earth which is thirsty and takes them back into itself again.

SUNFLOWER

What sower walked over earth,
which hands sowed
our inward seeds of fire?
They went out from his fists like rainbow curves
to frozen earth, young loam, hot sand,
they will sleep there
greedily, and drink up our lives
and explode it into pieces
for the sake of a sunflower that you haven't seen
or a thistle head or a chrysanthemum.

Let the young rain of tears come.
Let the calm hands of grief come.
It's not all as evil as you think.

LIGHT POLE

My street lamp is so glacially alone in the night.
The small paving stones lay their heads down all around
where it holds up its lightumbrella over them
so that the wicked dark will not come near.

It says: We are all far from home.
There's no hope anymore.

ROAD'S END

The roads have come to their end now,
they don't go any farther, they turn here,
over on the earth there.
You can't go any farther if you don't want
to go to the moon or the planets. Stop now
in time, and turn to a wasp's nest or a cow track,
a volcano opening or a clatter of stones in the woods —
it's all the same. Something else.

They won't go any farther as I've said
without changing, the engine to horseshoes,
the gear shift to a fir branch
    which you hold loose in your hand
—what the hell is this?

THE OLD WOMEN

The girls whose feet moved so fast, where did they go?
Those with knees like small kisses and sleeping hair?

In the far reaches of time when they've become silent,
old women with narrow hands climb up stairs slowly

with huge keys in their bags and they look around
and chat with small children at cemetery gates.

In that big and bewildering country where winters are so long
and no one understands their expressions anymore.

Bow clearly to them and greet them with respect
because they still carry everything with them, like a fragrance,

a secret bite-mark on the cheek, a nerve deep in
the palm of the hand somewhere betraying who they are.

GUARDIAN ANGEL

I am the bird that flutters against your window in the morning,
and your closest friend, whom you can never know,
blossoms that light up for the blind.

I am the glacier shining over the woods, so pale,
and heavy voices from the cathedral tower.
The thought that suddenly hits you in the middle of the day
and makes you feel so fantastically happy.

I am the one you have loved for many years.
I walk beside you all day and look intently at you
and put my mouth against your heart
though you're not aware of it.

I am your third arm, and your second
shadow, the white one,
whom you cannot accept,
and who can never forget you.

OLD AGE

I put a lot of stock in the old.
They sit looking at us and don't see us,
and have plenty with their own,
like fishermen along big rivers,
motionless as a stone
in the summer night.

I put a lot of stock in fishermen along rivers
and old people and those who appear after a long illness.
They have something in their eyes
that you don't see much anymore
the old, like convalescents
whose feet are not very sturdy under them
and pale foreheads as if after a fever.

The old
who so gradually become themselves once more
and so gradually break up
like smoke, no one notices it, they are gone
into sleep
and light.

MEMORIES OF HORSES

The lines in the hands of old people
gradually curve over and will point soon toward earth.
They take with them their secret language,
cloud-words and wind-letters,
all the signs the heart gathers up in the lean year.

Sorrow bleaches out and turns to face the stars
but memories of horses, women's feet, children
flow from their old people's faces down to the grass kingdom.

In huge trees we can often see
images of the peace in the sides of animals,
and the wind sketches in the grass, if you are happy,
running children and horses.

THE OLD CLOCKS

The old clocks often have encouraging faces.
They are like those farmers in the big woods or in the mountains
Whose whole being contains some calm acceptance
As if they belonged to some other race than ours.
A race that has fought its way through its time down here
And has seen its unhappiness shrink back like grass
During that earlier period when the Earth was earth.

They are guests with us this time and they nod in tune to our distress
Next to our bed with their mild wisdom: it's OK,
Oh yes, oh yes, it's OK, it's OK.

THE SILENCE AFTERWARDS

Try to be done now
with deliberately provocative actions and sales statistics,
brunches and gas ovens,
be done with fashion shows and horoscopes,
military parades, architectural contests,
and the rows of triple traffic lights.
Come through all that and be through
with getting ready for parties and eight possibilities
of winning on the numbers,
cost of living indexes and stock market analyses,
because it is too late,
it is way too late,
get through with and come home
to the silence afterwards
that meets you like warm blood hitting your forehead
and like thunder on the way
and the sound of great clocks striking
that make the eardrums quiver,
because words don't exist any longer,
there are no more words,
from now on all talk will take place
with the voices stones and trees have.

The silence that lives in the grass
on the underside of every blade
and in the blue spaces between the stones.
The silence
that follows shots and birdsong.
The silence

that pulls a blanket over the dead body
and waits in the stairs until everyone is gone.
The silence
that lies like a small bird between your hands,
the only friend you have.

SOME PEOPLE

Some people
ascend out of our life, some people
enter our life,
uninvited and sit down,
some people
calmly walk by, some people
give you a rose,
or buy you a new car,
some people
stand so close to you, some people
you've entirely forgotten,
some people, some people
are actually you,
some people
you've never seen at all, some people
eat asparagus, some people
are children,
some people climb up on the roof,
sit down at table,
lie around in hammocks, take walks with their red
umbrella,
some people look at you,
some people have never noticed you at all, some people
want to take your hand, some people
die during the night,
some people are other people, some people are you, some people
don't exist,
some people do.

GUNNAR EKELÖF

GUNNAR EKELÖF IS not a well-adjusted writer, happy to be living on earth. His work makes people uncomfortable; he tries to make the reader conscious of lies, and of the unstable and shifty nature of human perception. He doesn't particularly bother about how many readers like his poems. When he says something which he knows is too difficult for the reader to understand, he looks back and laughs. Sometimes he veers off mischievously into a side path that is too narrow anyway. His intelligence is awake all through the poem, cutting away nonsense, like a swift knife thin as gold leaf, cutting away soft and pulpy egoism. He cuts away egoism because he knows that if the Westerner can cut down the pride of his well-fed ego, if the self-contentments can be swept away, he stands some chance of experiencing the floating state the Eastern meditators value so much.

Ask for a filter for all these things that separate us from one another
a filter for life
You say you can hardly breathe?
Well, who do you think *can* breathe?
For the most part we take it however with equanimity
A wise man has said:
"It was so dark I could barely see the stars"
He just meant that it was night.

He is an oblique, arrogant, nervous, witty poet of the European city, a sort of poet known in all Western countries. Yet early on, he reached out to two sources which were outside the Scandinavian tradition: to the mystical poetry of Persia and to French poetry, especially the surrealist poetry of the late twenties.

At the same time, curious images slip into Ekelöf's poems from the North. These other images have risen from the heathen Swedish ground, from old Finnish swamps and that part of the Northern unconscious still obsessed by shamanic hallucinations, changing of bodies, journeys of souls during trance.

I heard wild geese over the hospital grounds
one autumnlike spring morning
I heard wild geese one morning
one springautumn morning
trumpeting—

To the north? To the south?
To the north! To the north!
Far from here—

A freshness lives deep in me
which no one can take from me
not even I myself—

GUNNAR EKELÖF was born in 1907 in Stockholm to a wealthy family. His father contracted syphilis and died, after years of insanity, in 1916. Ekelöf and his mother were not close, and he left home soon after passing his high school examinations. He studied at the School of Oriental Studies in London, and read Persian and Sanskrit in Uppsala. He moved to Paris at the end of the 1920s, and intended to become a musician. However, it was French painting and poetry, especially Desnos and Breton, which attracted him. His first book of poetry, *Late Arrival on Earth,* in 1932, is thought of as the first book of surrealist poetry in Sweden.

He began to admire T. S. Eliot, and translated "East Coker." He thought of poetry as giving off waves of meaning, almost like a radioactive bit of matter; he preferred that to identifiable content. In 1934, he published *Dedication,* which included a quotation from Rimbaud, and several elegies to Stagnelius. Two years later he published *Sorrow and the Star,* and two years after that, *Buy the Blind Man's Song.* He is speaking of the yellow-and-black armband worn by blind persons. His World War II book was called *Non Serviam.* He hated the Swedish welfare state. In general, he thought social movements were meaningless. He said, "When you have come as far as I have in meaninglessness / every word becomes interesting again."

Ekelöf loved seclusion. Apparently he bought a fine house for his wife in a well-developed park, but he himself lived in a tiny trailer house parked near the main door. During the last ten years of his life, he received many prizes and honorary awards. He died in Stockholm in 1968.

QUESTIONNAIRE

What do you consider your mission in life?
I am an absolutely useless human being.
What are your political convictions?
What we have now is fine. The opposition
to what we have now is fine. One ought to be
able to imagine a third — but what?
Your opinion on religion, if any?
The same as my opinion on music, namely only
he who is truly unmusical can be musical.
What do you look for in people? My relationships
have unfortunately little or no constancy.
What do you look for in literature? Philosophic depth?
Breadth or height? Epic? Lyric?
I look for the perfect circle.
What is the most beautiful thing you know of?
Birds in the cemeteries, butterflies on battlefields,
something in between. I really don't know.
Your favorite hobby? I have no hobby.
Your favorite sin? Onanism.
And to conclude (as briefly as possible):
Why do you write?
I have nothing else to do. Emma Wright?
You make puns, also?
I do make puns, yes.

from ÉTUDES

3

Each person is a world, peopled
by blind creatures in dim revolt
against the I, the king, who rules them.
In each soul thousands of souls are imprisoned,
in each world thousands of worlds are hidden
and these blind and lower worlds
are real and living, though not full-born,
as truly as I am real. And we kings
and barons of the thousand potential creatures within us
are citizens ourselves, imprisoned
in some larger creature, whose ego and nature
we understand as little as our master
his master. From their death and their love
our own feelings have received a coloring.

As when a great liner passes by
far out below the horizon where the sea lies
so still at dusk. And we know nothing of it
until a swell reaches us on the shore,
first one, then one more, and then many
washing and breaking until it all goes back
as before. Yet it is all changed.

So we shadows are seized by a strange unrest
when something tells us that people have left,
that some of the possible creatures have gotten free.

MONOLOGUE WITH ITS WIFE

Take two extra-old cabinet ministers and overtake them on the
    North Sea
Provide each of them with a comet in the rear
Seven comets each!
Send a wire:
If the city of Trondheim takes them in it will be bombed
If the suet field allows them to escape it will be bombed
Now you have to signal:
Larger ships approaching
Don't you see, there in the radio! Larger ships
in converging path. Send a warning!
All small strawberry boats shall be ordered to go into the shore and
    lie down

— Come and help me. I am disappearing.
The god is in the process of transforming me, the one in the corner
    over there (whispering)

from VARIATIONS

5

I believe in the solitary person,
in the man who walks about alone,
and does not run like a dog back to his own scent,
and does not run like a wolf away from human scent:
At once human and anti-human.

How to reach community?
Avoid the upper and the outer road:
What is herdlike in others is herdlike also in you.
Take the lower and inward road!
What is ground in you is ground also in others.

Hard to get into the habit of yourself.
Hard to get out of the habit of yourself.

He who does it shall never be deserted anyway.
He who does it shall remain loyal anyway.
The impractical is the only thing practical
in the long run.

6

There exists something that fits nowhere
and yet is in no way remarkable
and yet is decisive
and yet is outside it all.
There exists something which is noticed just when it is not noticeable
(like silence)
and is not noticed just when it becomes noticeable
for then it is mistaken (like silence) for something else.

See the waves under the sky. Storm is surface
and storm our way of seeing.
(What do I care for the waves or the seventh wave.)
There is an emptiness between the waves:
Look at the sea. Look at the stones of the field.
There is an emptiness between the stones:
They did not break loose—they did not throw themselves here,
They lie there and exist—a part of the rock sheath.
So make yourself heavy—make use of your dead weight,
let it break you, let it throw you, fall down,
let it leave you shipwrecked on the rock!
(What do I care about the rock.)

There are universes, suns, and atoms.
There is a knowledge, carefully built on strong points.
There is a knowledge, unprotected, built on insecure emptiness.
There is an emptiness between universes, suns, and atoms.
(What do I care about universes, suns, and atoms.)
There is an odd viewpoint on everything
in this double life.

There is peace beyond all.
There is peace behind all.
There is peace inside all.

Concealed in the hand.
Concealed in the pen.
Concealed in the ink.
I feel peace everywhere.
I smell peace behind everything.
I see and hear peace inside everything,
monotonous peace beyond everything.
(What do I care about peace.)

from THE SWAN

1

I heard wild geese over the hospital grounds
where many pale people walk back and forth
— one morning in a daze
I heard them! I hear them!
I dreamt I heard —

And nevertheless I did hear them!

Here endless walks circle about
around bottomless dams
Here the days all reflect
one monotonous day
at the slightest touch
beautiful blossoms close
their strange petals —

The woman on a nurse's arm
she screams incessantly:
Hell Devil Hell
— is led home
hurriedly . . .
Dusk has come
over the salmon-colored buildings
and outside the wall
an anemic blush over endless suburbs
of identical houses
with some vegetable beds steaming as if in spring between . . .

They are burning twigs and leaves:
It is fall
and the vegetable beds are attacked by worm-eaten cabbages
and bare flowers —

I heard wild geese over the hospital grounds
one autumnlike spring morning
I heard wild geese one morning
one springautumn morning
trumpeting —

To the north? To the south?
To the north! To the north!
Far from here —

A freshness lives deep in me
which no one can take from me
not even I myself —

IF YOU ASK ME WHERE I LIVE

If you ask me where I live
I live right here behind the mountain
It's a long way off but I am near
I live in another world
but you live there also
That world is everywhere even if it is as rare as helium
Why do you ask for an airship to bear you off?
Ask instead for a filter for carbon dioxide
a filter for hydrogen, for nitrogen, and other gases
Ask for a filter for all these things that separate us from one another
a filter for life
You say you can hardly breathe?
Well, who do you think *can* breathe?
For the most part we take it however with equanimity
A wise man has said:
"It was so dark I could barely see the stars"
He just meant that it was night

ISSA

ISSA IS THE most playful of the haiku poets. He is always making jokes with frogs, speaking to crickets he notices in bed with him: "Cricket, be careful. I am rolling over." Early in his life, he became a Pure Land Buddhist. The Pure Land group was created as a kind of alternative or rebuke to Rinzai Zen, for mentorship in which a rich cultural training was required. Many intricate disciplines around warriorhood came into Rinzai as well. When the Pure Land Buddhist sect was developed in the eleventh century, ordinary farmers could join it, as well as tradespeople and thieves. The sect fit Issa perfectly. At that time, windowpanes were made of paper. Issa notices a tear in his window paper. He says, "It's true I have a tear—but through it I can see the Milky Way." He stood up for or with the poor. He said, "Sparrows, look out! Big-ass horse is coming through!" His poems are wonderfully lighthearted. They show that astonishing observation of details of nature that we associate with Thoreau in his best prose or Tu Fu in his description of the battle between chickens and ants, or William Carlos Williams in some of his spring and fall poems.

Issa's task was to return the haiku to the rich outdoor place where Basho had left it a hundred years earlier. Basho said, "You can learn about the pine only from the pine, and about bamboo only from bamboo." It's not that Basho wanted more pine and less self, but he wanted more pine and more pine-self. Tiny details seen with a high and serious intent was an ideal for both poets.

———

ISSA was born Yatoro Kobayashi in 1763 in a small mountain village in central Japan, the eldest son of a farm family. His father evidently loved writing haiku, and left several good haiku behind. When Issa was two, his mother died, but he always felt near to her. One of his poems could be translated as: "Whenever I see the ocean, I see my mother's face." His grandfather brought Issa up, and he apparently received some schooling from a haiku poet in the neighborhood. When he was seven, his father married again, and now he fell on hard times. The son of the new marriage was favored, and Issa was apparently whipped a hundred times a day.

When he was thirteen, he left home and went to live in what is now Tokyo. There he joined a group of poets who were trying to revive the sober, moving style in which Basho wrote. When he was twenty-seven he went back to his village and was reconciled with his father. Two years later, he adopted the pen name Issa, which means "a cup of tea." This simple pen name fit well with the Pure Land school.

He soon began to take a series of long walking trips, much as Basho had done a century earlier, and he kept up this habit for the next ten years. He would write haiku about what happened each day. The most famous of those collections is *The Year of My Life,* which was well translated a few years ago by Nobuyuki Yuasa, who was aware that a walking trip for Basho was a discipline in solitude and a mode of renunciation. But for Issa, this tended to bond him more closely to human beings than he might have in everyday life.

After his father died, Issa returned and settled in his native village — in fact in the house in which he was born. By then he was fifty-one. He married a young woman who was about twenty-seven, and they had a child who died shortly after birth. The next child died as well. At last a daughter, Sato, was born. Issa had a great love for her, though he recognized that this attachment was not quite in line with Buddhism. When she died, he said,

I know this world
is a drop of dew—
and still . . . still . . .

Some months later, he wrote another haiku about her:

Last night I dreamt
my daughter lifted
a melon to her cheek.

Several of the poems that are included here are from *The Year of My Life,* which is set in 1819. He faced many griefs that year, and after that, other disasters followed. Two more babies died, then his wife. He married two more times; nothing worked. And in 1827, his house burned down. By that time Issa was ill, and the next day he was moved to a kind of granary in which snow came in through the cracks in the wall. When he died, his death poem was found under his pillow:

This snow on the bed quilt—
this too
is from the Pure Land.

Insects, why cry?
We all go
that way.

Now listen, you watermelons —
if any thieves come —
turn into frogs!

Leaping for the river, the frog
said, "Excuse
me for going first!"

The night is so long,
Yes, the night is so long;
Buddha is great!

Morning glories, yes —
but in the faces of men
there are flaws.

Lanky frog, hold
your ground! Issa
is coming!

This line of black ants —
Maybe it goes all the way back
to that white cloud!

The old dog bends his head listening . . .
I guess the singing
of the earthworms gets to him.

Cricket, be
careful! I'm rolling
over!

THE PIGEON MAKES HIS REQUEST

Since it's spring and raining,
could we have a little different expression,
oh owl?

FEDERICO GARCÍA LORCA

LORCA IS THE genius of geniuses: no one like him has ever been born, and no one like him will ever be born again. He arrives in the world with the full knowledge that every particle in the universe is searching:

> The rose
> was not searching for the sunrise:
> almost eternal on its branch,
> it was searching for something else.

Those readers whose soul can vibrate like an instrument made of old wood fall in love with him during the first poem, and become faithful lovers.

> The rose
> was not searching for darkness or science:
> borderline of flesh and dream,
> it was searching for something else.

Even a genius is not searching for genius.

> The rose
> was not searching for the rose.
> Motionless in the sky
> it was searching for something else.

Lorca's poetry inherited much delicacy from medieval Arabic-Andalusian poetry, but his immediate spiritual father was Juan Ramón Jiménez. Jiménez's love of silence, his love of perfection, his gaiety of soul was famous in Madrid.

If we read Lorca and Jiménez carefully, we can sense the subtle nature of the soul ground from which prophetic poetry rises. It is a ground cultivated in silence behind garden walls, shrewdly protected, loving the perfections of high art, an art that fights for the values of the feminine and reverie and the soul:

> When the moon sails out
> the sea covers the earth
> and the heart feels it is
> a little island in the infinite.

He says that everyone is looking for his or her voice, because only your own voice can do it.

> The small boy is looking for his voice.
> (The King of the Crickets had it.)
> The boy was looking
> in a drop of water for his voice.

I follow Lorca's images with amazement; and as soon as I have caught up to one of them and taken it in, I see only his coattails. He was not waiting for us; he has gone on far ahead.

> All I want is a single hand,
> A wounded hand if that is possible.
> All I want is a single hand
> Even if I have no bed for a thousand nights.

He inherited from the gypsy flamenco singers, whom he loved, the delicate dance before pure death that a bullfighter dances. He loved the taunting of death by those who had lost much to him already, and would soon lose more, lose all, as Mary did, as Joseph and Jesus did.

FEDERICO GARCÍA LORCA was born in 1898 in a small Andalusian town west of Granada. The family established a house in the city itself when Federico was eleven. You can still see that house in Granada, in the center of a grove of trees; you can still see the piano on which he left his music when he was taken off to be shot. How near was the house, and often the grove is filled with schoolchildren come to visit that sweet place!

As an adolescent, he participated in the rich cultural life around the Café Alameda in Granada. When he was twenty, his parents agreed to enroll him in the famous Residence de Estudiantes in Madrid, a place modeled on Oxford and Cambridge, based on liberal ideas. There he heard Claudel, Valéry, Cendrars, Marinetti, Wanda Landowska, and became close friends with Rafael Alberti, Salvador Dalí, and Luis Buñuel. Juan Ramón Jiménez became a sort of mentor to him. Lorca published *Book of Poems* in 1921, along with other early books, and the *Gypsy Ballads* in 1927.

He loved flamenco or Cante Jondo music; he also wrote puppet plays and farces. Becoming a bit tired of his reputation as a "gypsy poet," he left Spain. With a friend he traveled to New York in June of 1929, where he took some English classes at Columbia University. There he saw the full power of the Depression. He saw the full collision of the feeling life of provincial Granada and the brutality of what would become global capitalism. His response was the book he wrote, later printed as *Poet in New York*, still the greatest poem about New York. After he returned to Spain, he wrote a number of ghazals giving honor to the love poetry of the Arabs. He also organized a traveling theater troupe, so as to be closer to the Spanish people. He was fearful of attack because of his homosexuality, and his fears turned out to be justified. In August of 1936, the fascists had become active in Granada, and he was taken from his house and shot. So his life ended at thirty-eight.

QUESTIONS

A parliament of grasshoppers is in the field.
What do you say, Marcus Aurelius,
about these old philosophers of the prairie?
Your thought is so full of poverty!

The waters of the river move slowly.
Oh Socrates! What do you see
in the water moving toward its bitter death?
Your faith is full of poverty and sad!

The leaves of the roses fall in the mud.
Oh sweet John of God!
What do you see in these magnificent petals?
Your heart is tiny!

THE BOY UNABLE TO SPEAK

    The small boy is looking for his voice.
(The King of the Crickets had it.)
The boy was looking
in a drop of water for his voice.

    I don't want the voice to speak with;
I will make a ring from it
that my silence will wear
on its little finger.

    The small boy was looking
in a drop of water for his voice.

    (Far away the captured voice
was getting dressed up like a cricket.)

SONG OF THE RIDER

Córdoba.
Distant and alone.

Black pony, full moon,
and olives inside my saddlebag.
Though I know the roads well,
I will never arrive at Córdoba.

Over the low plains, over the winds,
black pony, red moon.
Death is looking down at me
from the towers of Córdoba.

What a long road this is!
What a brave horse I have!
Death is looking for me
before I get to Córdoba!

Córdoba.
Distant and alone.

MALAGUENA

Death
is entering and leaving
the tavern.

Black horses and sinister
people are riding
over the deep roads
of the guitar.

There is an odor of salt
and the blood of women
in the feverish spice-plants
by the sea.

Death
is entering and leaving
the tavern,
death
leaving and entering.

THE QUARREL
For Rafael Méndez

The Albacete knives, magnificent
with stranger-blood,
flash like fishes
on the gully slope.
Light crisp as a playing
card snips out of bitter
green the profiles of riders
and maddened horses.
Two old women in an olive
tree are sobbing.
The bull of the quarrel
is rising up the walls.
Black angels arrived
with handkerchiefs and snow water.
Angels with immense wings
like Albacete knives.
Juan Antonio from Montilla
rolls dead down the hill,
his body covered with lilies,
a pomegranate on his temples.
He is riding now on the cross of fire,
on the highway of death.

*

The State Police and the judge
come along through the olive grove.
From the earth loosed blood moans
the silent folk song of the snake.
"Well, Your Honor, you see,

it's the same old business—
four Romans are dead
and five Carthaginians."

*

   Dusk that the fig trees and the
hot whispers have made hysterical
faints and falls on the bloody
thighs of the riders,
and black angels went on flying
through the failing light,
angels with long hair,
and hearts of olive oil.

THAMAR AND AMNON
For Alfonso García-Valdecasas

The moon turns in the sky
above the dry fields
and the summer plants
rumors of tiger and flame.
Nerves of metal
resonated over the roofs.
Bleatings made of wool
arrived on curly winds.
The earth lies covered
with scarred-over wounds,
or shaken by the sharp
burnings of white stars.

*

Thamar was dreaming of
birds in her throat.
She heard frost tambourines
and moon-covered zithers.
Her nakedness on the roof,
a palm pointing north,
asks for snowflakes at her stomach,
and hailstones at her shoulders.
Thamar was there singing
naked on the rooftop.

*

Huddled near her feet
five frozen doves.
Amnon, lithe and firm,
watched her from his tower.
His genitals were like surf,

and his beard swaying.
Her luminous nakedness
stretched out on the terrace,
her teeth sound like an arrow
that has just hit its mark.
Amnon was looking over
at the round and heavy moon,
and he saw there the hard
breasts of his sister.

*

    At three-thirty Amnon
threw himself on his bed.
The hundred wings in his eyes
disturbed the whole room.
The moonlight, massive, buries
towns under dark sand,
or opens a mortal coral
of dahlias and roses.
Underground water oppressed
breaks its silence in jars.
The cobra is singing on the tree,
stretched out on the mosses.
Amnon groans from the fresh
sheets of his bed.
An ivy of icy fever
covers his burning body.
Thamar walked silently
into the silence of his bedroom,
the color of blood and Danube
troubled with far-off footprints.
"Thamar, put out my eyes
with your piercing dawn.
The threads of my blood

are weaving the folds on your dress."
"Leave me be, brother.
Your kisses are wasps
on my shoulder, and winds blowing
in a double twirling of flutes."
"Thamar, I hear two fishes
calling me from your steep breasts,
and the sound of closed rosebuds
in the tips of your fingers."

*

The hundred horses of the king
neigh together in the courtyard.
The sun in buckets fought
the slenderness of the vine.
Now he takes her by the hair,
now he rips her dress.
Warm corals start drawing
rivulets on a blond country.

*

What screams are heard now
lifting above the houses!
What a thicket of knives,
and cloaks torn up!
Slaves keep going up
the sad stairs and back down.
Pistons and thighs play
under the motionless clouds.
Standing around Thamar
gypsy virgins give cries,
others gather up the drops
of her murdered flower.
White fabrics slowly turn red
in the locked bedrooms.

At first whisper of warm dawn
fish turn back into tendrils.

*

The raper, Amnon, flees,
wild, on his horse.
Negroes shoot arrows
at him from the parapets.
When the beat of the four hoofs
became four fading chords,
David took a scissors
and cut the strings of his harp.

from POET IN NEW YORK

While the Chinaman was crying on the roof
without finding the nakedness of his wife,
and the bank president was watching the pressure gauge
that measures the remorseless silence of money,
the black mask was arriving at Wall Street.

This vault that makes the eyes turn yellow
is not an odd place for dancing.
There is a wire stretched from the Sphinx to the safety deposit box
that passes through the heart of all poor children.
The primitive energy is dancing with the machine energy,
in their frenzy wholly ignorant of the original light.
Because if the wheel forgets its formula,
it might as well sing naked with the herds of horses;
and if a flame burns up the frozen plains
the sky will have to run away from the roar of the windows.

This place is a good place for dancing, I say this truth,
the black mask will dance between columns of blood and numbers,
between downpours of gold and groans of unemployed workers
who will go howling, dark night, through your time without stars.
O savage North America! shameless! savage,
stretched out on the frontier of the snow!

RUN-DOWN CHURCH
(Ballad of the First World War)

I had a son and his name was John.
I had a son.
He disappeared into the arches one Friday of All Souls.
I saw him playing on the highest steps of the Mass
throwing a little tin pail at the heart of the priest.
I knocked on the coffin. My son! My son! My son!
I drew out a chicken foot from behind the moon and then
I understood that my daughter was a fish
down which the carts vanish.
I had a daughter.
I had a fish dead under the ashes of the incense burner.
I had an ocean. Of what? Good Lord! An ocean!
I went up to ring the bells but the fruit was all wormy
and the blackened match-ends
were eating the spring wheat.
I saw a stork of alcohol you could see through
shaving the black heads of the dying soldiers
and I saw the rubber booths
where the goblets full of tears were whirling.
In the anemones of the offertory I will find you, my love!
when the priest with his strong arms raises up the mule and the ox
to scare the nighttime toads that roam in the icy landscapes of the
     chalice.
I had a son who was a giant,
but the dead are stronger and know how to gobble down pieces of
     the sky.
If my son had only been a bear,
I wouldn't fear the secrecy of the crocodiles
and I wouldn't have seen the ocean roped to the trees

to be raped and wounded by the mobs from the regiment.
If my son had only been a bear!
I'll roll myself in this rough canvas so as not to feel the chill of the
    mosses.
I know very well they will give me a sleeve or a necktie,
but in the innermost part of the Mass I'll smash the rudder and then
the insanity of the penguins and seagulls will come to the rock
and then they will make the people sleeping and the people singing on
    the street corners say:
he had a son.
A son! A son! A son
and it was no one else's, because it was his son!
His son! His son! His son!

LITTLE INFINITE POEM
For Luis Cardoza y Aragón

To take the wrong road
is to arrive at the snow
and to arrive at the snow
is to get down on all fours for twenty centuries and eat the grasses of
the cemeteries.

To take the wrong road
is to arrive at a woman,
woman who isn't afraid of light,
woman who murders two roosters in one second,
light which isn't afraid of roosters,
and roosters who don't know how to sing on top of the snow.

But if the snow truly takes the wrong road,
then it might meet the southern wind,
and since the air cares nothing for groans,
we will have to get down on all fours again and eat the grasses of the
cemeteries.

I saw two mournful wheatheads made of wax
burying a countryside of volcanoes;
and I saw two insane little boys who wept as they leaned on a mur-
derer's eyeballs.

But two has never been a number—
because it's only an anguish and its shadow,
it's only a guitar where love feels how hopeless it is,
it's the proof of someone else's infinity,
and the walls around a dead man,

and the scourging of a new resurrection that will never end.
Dead people hate the number two,
but the number two makes women drop off to sleep,
and since women are afraid of light,
light shudders when it has to face the roosters,
and since all roosters know is how to fly over the snow
we will have to get down on all fours and eat the grasses of the cemeteries forever.

JANUARY 10, 1930. NEW YORK.

NEW YORK
(*Office and Attack*)

To Fernando Vela

Beneath all the statistics
there is a drop of duck's blood.
Beneath all the columns
there is a drop of sailor's blood.
Beneath all the totals, a river of warm blood;
a river that goes singing
past the bedrooms of the suburbs,
and the river is silver, cement, or wind
in the lying daybreak of New York.
The mountains exist, I know that.
And the lenses ground for wisdom,
I know that. But I have not come to see the sky.
I have come to see the stormy blood,
the blood that sweeps the machines to the waterfalls,
and the spirit on the cobra's tongue.
Every day they kill in New York
ducks, four million,
pigs, five million,
pigeons, two thousand, for the enjoyment of dying men,
cows, one million,
lambs, one million,
roosters, two million
who turn the sky to small splinters.
You may as well sob filing a razor blade
or assassinate dogs in the hallucinated foxhunts,
as try to stop in the dawnlight
the endless trains carrying milk,

the endless trains carrying blood,
and the trains carrying roses in chains
for those in the field of perfume.
The ducks and the pigeons
and the hogs and the lambs
lay their drops of blood down
underneath all the statistics;
and the terrible bawling of the packed-in cattle
fills the valley with suffering
where the Hudson is getting drunk on its oil.
I attack all those persons
who know nothing of the other half,
the half who cannot be saved,
who raise their cement mountains
in which the hearts of the small
animals no one thinks of are beating,
and from which we will all fall
during the final holiday of the drills.
I spit in your face.
The other half hears me,
as they go on eating, urinating, flying in their purity
like the children of the janitors
who carry delicate sticks
to the holes where the antennas
of the insects are rusting.
This is not hell, it is a street.
This is not death, it is a fruit stand.
There is a whole world of crushed rivers and unachievable distances
in the paw of a cat crushed by a car,
and I hear the song of the worm
in the heart of so many girls.
Rust, rotting, trembling earth.
And you are earth, swimming through the figures of the office.

What shall I do, set my landscapes in order?
Set in place the lovers who will afterwards be photographs,
who will be bits of wood and mouthfuls of blood?
No, I won't; I attack,
I attack the conspiring
of these empty offices
that will not broadcast the sufferings,
that rub out the plans of the forest,
and I offer myself to be eaten by the packed-up cattle
when their mooing fills the valley
where the Hudson is getting drunk on its oil.

SONG OF THE CUBAN BLACKS

When the full moon comes
I'll go to Santiago in Cuba.
I'll go to Santiago
in a carriage of black water.
I'll go to Santiago.
Palm-thatching will start to sing.
I'll go to Santiago.
When the palm trees want to turn into storks,
I'll go to Santiago.
When the banana trees want to turn into jellyfish,
I'll go to Santiago.
With the golden head of Fonseca.
I'll go to Santiago.
And with the rose of Romeo and Juliet
I'll go to Santiago.
Oh Cuba! Oh rhythm of dry seeds!
I'll go to Santiago.
Oh warm waist, and a drop of wood!
I'll go to Santiago.
Harp of living trees. Crocodile. Tobacco blossom!
I'll go to Santiago.
I always said I would go to Santiago
in a carriage of black water.
I'll go to Santiago.
Wind and alcohol in the wheels,
I'll go to Santiago.
My coral in the darkness,
I'll go to Santiago.
The ocean drowned in the sand,

I'll go to Santiago.
White head and dead fruit,
I'll go to Santiago.
Oh wonderful freshness of the cane fields!
Oh Cuba! Arc of sighs and mud!
I'll go to Santiago.

GHAZAL OF THE DARK DEATH

I want to sleep the sleep of the apples,
I want to get far away from the busyness of the cemeteries.
I want to sleep the sleep of that child
who longed to cut his heart open far out at sea.

I don't want them to tell me again how the corpse keeps all its blood,
how the decaying mouth goes on begging for water.
I'd rather not hear about the torture sessions the grass arranges for
nor about how the moon does all its work before dawn
with its snakelike nose.

I want to sleep for half a second,
a second, a minute, a century,
but I want everyone to know that I am still alive,
that I have a golden manger inside my lips,
that I am the little friend of the west wind,
that I am the elephantine shadow of my own tears.

When it's dawn just throw some sort of cloth over me
because I know dawn will toss fistfuls of ants at me,
and pour a little hard water over my shoes
so that the scorpion claws of the dawn will slip off.

Because I want to sleep the sleep of the apples,
and learn a mournful song that will clean all earth away from me,
because I want to live with that shadowy child
who longed to cut his heart open far out at sea.

GHAZAL OF THE TERRIFYING PRESENCE

I want the water to go on without its bed.
And the wind to go on without its mountain passes.

I want the night to go on without its eyes
and my heart without its golden petals;

If the oxen could only talk with the big leaves
and the angleworm would die from too much darkness;

I want the teeth in the skull to shine
and the yellowish tints to drown the silk.

I can see the night in its duel, wounded
and wrestling, tangled with noon.

I fight against a sunset of green poison,
and those broken arches where time is suffering.

But don't let the light fall on your clear and naked body
like a cactus black and open in the reeds.

Leave me in the anguish of the darkened planets,
but do not let me see your pure waist.

CASIDA OF THE ROSE

The rose
was not searching for the sunrise:
almost eternal on its branch,
it was searching for something else.

The rose
was not searching for darkness or science:
borderline of flesh and dream,
it was searching for something else.

The rose
was not searching for the rose.
Motionless in the sky
it was searching for something else.

OLAV H. HAUGE

OLAV H. HAUGE's flavor is persistent, like the taste of persimmons which we can never forget. His poems are as nourishing as an old apple that a goat has found in the orchard. He has much to give, and he gives it in small spoonfuls, as nurses give medicine. Everywhere in the daylight of his work, you see tiny experiences being valued.

> Midwinter. Snow.
> I gave the birds a piece of bread.
> And it didn't affect my sleep.

He loved to honor culture, and he honored it more than many classics professors do. People in his neighborhood felt a little fear when they entered his small, book-filled house. He was liable to pull down a fat volume, printed in Oxford, and say, "No doubt you've read this?" Very few people in town had read it, but there wasn't a trace of scorn in his question. He loved the book so much he thought it quite possible that you knew it too.

What is it like to spend your whole life on a farm with no support from your family or from the community? It would be lonely, something like walking in a marsh in the middle of the woods.

> It is the roots from all the trees that have died
> out here, that's how you can walk
> safely over the soft places.

One would have to realize that the old Chinese poets have lived this sort of life before you; they wrote poems; they didn't die of fear. Hauge was able to compare himself to a drowned person he once heard about.

>   That cold person
> who drowned himself here once
> helps hold up your frail boat.
> He, really crazy, trusted his life
> to water and eternity.

If you have a tiny farm, you need to love poetry more than the farm. If you sell apples, you need to love poetry more than the apples. It's good to settle down somewhere and to love poetry more than that.

Lewis Hyde in his great book called *The Gift* discusses the nature of the old pre-commercial gift-giving society. The economy of scarcity, he says, is always associated with gift-giving. Olav H. Hauge lived in a gift-giving, pre-communal society all of his life. The richness in his small house lay in the handmade spoons and bowls, the wooden reading chair, and the bookcases to which the best poetry from many continents had found its way.

OLAV H. HAUGE was born in 1908 in Ulvik, a tiny settlement in Hardanger north of Utne, and he died there eighty years later. As a typical younger son in a traditional Norwegian family, he received virtually no land. The older brother gets the main farm, and Olav lived all his life on what he could produce from three acres of ground. During his late twenties, he spent some time in a mental institution. He married for the first time at sixty-five, to the Norwegian artist Bodil Cappelen, who had met him at one of his rare poetry readings. He settled into married life very well, and his house became considerably cheerier. He died in the old way; no real evidence of disease was present. He simply didn't eat for ten days and so he died. People who attended his funeral, which took place at a church down in the valley where he had been baptized as a child, described a service full of feeling and gratitude. A horse-drawn wagon carried his body back up the mountain after the service. Everyone noticed a small colt that ran happily alongside its mother and the coffin all the way back up.

MIDWINTER. SNOW.

Midwinter. Snow.
I gave the birds a piece of bread.
And it didn't affect my sleep.

LOOKING AT AN OLD MIRROR

The front a mirror.
The back a picture of the Garden of Eden.

A strange find
of the old master of glass.

DON'T COME TO ME
WITH THE ENTIRE TRUTH

Don't come to me with the entire truth.
Don't bring the ocean if I feel thirsty,
nor heaven if I ask for light;
but bring a hint, some dew, a particle,
as birds carry only drops away from water,
and the wind a grain of salt.

HARVEST TIME

These calm days of September with their sun.
It's time to harvest. There are still clumps
of cranberries in the woods, reddening rosehips
by the stone walls, hazelnuts coming loose,
and clusters of black berries shine in the bushes;
thrushes look around for the last currants
and wasps fasten on to the sweetening plums.
I set the ladder aside at dusk, and hang
my basket up in the shed. The glaciers
all have a thin sprinkling of new snow. In bed
I hear the brisling fishermen start their motors
and go out. They'll pass the whole night
gliding over the fjord behind their powerful searchlights.

LEAF HUTS AND SNOW HOUSES

These poems don't amount
to much, just
some words thrown together
at random.
And still
to me
there's something good
in making them, it's
as if I have in them for a little
while a house.
I think of playhouses
made of branches we built
when we were children:
to crawl into them, sit
listening to the rain,
in a wild place alone,
feel the drops of rain on your nose
and in your hair—
or snow houses at Christmas,
crawl in and close it after
with a sack,
light a candle, be there
through the long chill evenings.

EVENING CLOUDS

Clouds are arriving now
With greetings from
Distant coasts;
It's been a while since
They sent a message to me.
You shy pink
High on the evening sky—
It's probably for
Someone else.
Well, there's still
Some hope left
In the world.

ACROSS THE SWAMP

It is the roots from all the trees that have died
out here, that's how you can walk
safely over the soft places.
Roots like these keep their firmness, it's possible
they've lain here for centuries.
And there is still some dark remains
of them under the moss.
They are still in the world and hold
you up so you can make it over.
And when you push out into the mountain lake, high
up, you feel how the memory
of that cold person
who drowned himself here once
helps hold up your frail boat.
He, really crazy, trusted his life
to water and eternity.

I STAND HERE, D'YA UNDERSTAND

I stand here, d'ya understand.
I stood here last year too, d'ya understand.
I am going to stand here too, d'ya understand.
I take it too, d'ya understand.
There's something you don't know, d'ya understand.
You just got here, d'ya understand.
How long are we to stand here?
We have to eat too, d'ya understand.
I stand when I eat too, I do that, d'ya understand,
and throw the plates at the wall.
We have to rest too, d'ya understand.
We have to piss and shit too, d'ya understand.
How long are we to stand here?
I stand all right, d'ya understand.
I take it too, d'ya understand.
I'm going to stand here, d'ya understand.

THE BIG SCALES

It is the old-time weights
That are the significant things
In the weighing room
(Along with myself).
That's why they've gotten their spot
In the middle of the floor—it is
They who
Weigh and decide
What the freight charge will be.
I have a good sense
When I handle sacks and crates of apples
How heavy they are,
But they have to go onto the scales
So the scales can have their opinion.
We bargain—the two of us;
I add weights;
We mostly reach
Agreement—they tip,
I nod,
And we both say,
"That's it."—We
Don't bother much with ounces.
The scales are rusted, and I
Am stiff in my back
And that's OK, the weights are lighter
Than the thoughts I am weighing.
Sometimes I notice that people have doubts
If my figures are right.
People are odd.
If they sell something

They want it heavy;
If they ship it
They want it light.
A judge came here one day;
He also brooded about scales, probably
Thinking what things he
Has to weigh.
"These aren't pharmacist's scales," I said,
But I really was remembering scales I once
Saw at a goldsmith shop.
He weighed gold dust
Using tweezers.
I've thoughts also of what
A judge has to weigh:
Right and wrong,
Sentences and fines,
Life and destiny.
Who checks over
Those weights,
And those scales?

IT IS THAT DREAM

It's that dream we carry with us
That something wonderful will happen,
That it has to happen,
That time will open,
That the heart will open,
That doors will open,
That the mountains will open,
That wells will leap up,
That the dream will open,
That one morning we'll slip in
To a harbor that we've never known.

THE DREAM

Let us slip into
Sleep, into
The calm dream,
Just slip in—two bits
Of raw dough in the
Good oven
That we call night,
And so to awake
In the morning as
Two sound
Golden loaves!

THE CARPET

Weave a carpet for me, Bodil,
weave it from dreams and visions,
weave it out of wind,
so that I, like a Bedouin, can
roll it out when I pray,
pull it around me
when I sleep,
and then every morning cry out,
"Table, set yourself!"
Weave it
for a cape in the cold weather,
and a sail
for my boat!
One day I will sit down on the carpet
and sail away on it
to another world.

HARRY MARTINSON

HARRY MARTINSON BELONGS to the generation of John Steinbeck, Tillie Olsen, and Kenneth Rexroth. He was brought up in the Swedish southeast, and remembers how that childhood was:

> And other insignificant things happened at the same time.
> The kicksled broke a thin leg
> and we rolled around like food baskets in snow on the zinc-gray ice.
>
> Clary—you and I.
> We sat down deep in the snowy bushes by the shore,
> we pissed in the snow,
> and laughed like mad about it, as children do.
> There was a starvation winter, with rickets,
> and epidemics going all around the lake.

It's clear from the nakedness of his poems that for years he walked around the world in charge of his own skin, and of little more.

His poems have a curious and luminous grace of language. The poems slip on through their own words like a ship cutting through a quiet sea. Everything feels alive, fragrant, resilient, like seaweed underwater. In Swedish his poems feel a little like Lawrence in "Bavarian Gentians." A good Martinson poem never closes with a snap. It is like a tunnel that is open at both ends.

His poems have something that Lawrence's do not, as well. We feel in his work an experience of modern commerce possible only to one who has made his living in it. Martinson's work as a seaman brought him in touch not only with the romantic body of the sea, as similar work did for Gary Snyder, but also with the stiff skeletal will of commerce. When Martinson talks of trade, he drops all thought of brotherhood; he knows it cannot be reformed. Meeting Ogden Armour's yacht is like shaking hands with a rock.

> In the latitude of the Balearic Islands
> we sighted Ogden Armour's yacht.
> This cargo ship is part of his fleet, as you know,
> he has five slaughterhouses in Chicago,
> and eight packing plants near La Plata.
> He put his telescope to his eye and no doubt said,
> "Oh Christ! It's nothing but my old cattleboat, the *Chattanooga*."
> We dipped the flag and all the cows started in mooing
> like a thousand hoarse sirens over the endless ocean.

Often Martinson's poems, by their sheer grace, shoot into the future and become prophetic. He begins to become aware of a certain flatness becoming prevalent in the West. What will happen when there is no more "undiscovered" wilderness? The world will gradually lose its inwardness; people will cry out for new worlds, they will look for a new world in the stars. The old Scandinavians found something wild in their trolls, in "the weird people" who would occasionally steal a daughter or a son. All that will be gone. We'll have flatness, a form of forgetfulness that is associated with repetitive motions. Even the demons will be flat. It is already happening:

> Demons flatter than stingrays
> swept above the plains of death,
> flock after flock of demons went abreast, in ranks, and parallel
>   through Hades.

And the dead who are victims of flat evil—what will their afterlife be like? They will be received after death

> with no comfort from a high place
> or support from a low place,
> received without dignity,
> received without a rising,
> received without any of the standards of eternity.
> Their cries are met only by mockery
> on the flat fields of evil.

HARRY MARTINSON was born in 1904 in southeastern Sweden. His father died when he was six, and his mother emigrated to the United States, leaving the children in the parish. Martinson ran away from various schools, and finally signed on as a seaman when he was sixteen. He spent six years working as a deckhand or stoker on fourteen different ships, visiting many ports of the world. He returned home in 1926, published his first collection of poems, soon married, and established his credentials as a travel writer through two books of prose. He published three books of essays in the thirties. He was invited in 1934 to the Soviet Writers' Congress in Moscow, and was appalled by its motto: "The writer is the engineer of the human soul." A few years later, he took part as a volunteer in the Finnish war against the Russians.

In his novel *The Road to Klockrike* in 1948, he praises the life of tramps, he encourages indolence. It reminds us of John Steinbeck's California stories. Later, he began a large cycle of poems, which was published at last in 1956 as *Aniara*. Its story takes place after the earth has become hopelessly ruined by radiation; the giant spaceship *Aniara* takes off for Mars; but after four years, all the passengers die, and the spaceship continues on. This epic fantasy had an enormous effect in

Sweden; it was made into an opera, etc. It has been translated several times into English. Meanwhile, his nature poems remained as fresh as the earliest ones.

In 1974, Martinson received the Nobel Prize. It turned out to be an unhappy event. Swedish critics felt ashamed of his countrified poems. They tended to disdain all nature poetry, and in newspapers, attacked him on all fronts. He called off the publication of a book of nature poems, and died in 1978.

NO NAME FOR IT

It's marvellous in winter to dance on the ice—
and to carry memories of the torches
that threw light on us so long ago
as they swayed back and forth in the north wind.

And other insignificant things happened at the same time.
The kicksled broke a thin leg
and we rolled around like food baskets in snow on the zinc-gray ice.

Clary—you and I.
We sat down deep in the snowy bushes by the shore,
we pissed in the snow,
and laughed like mad about it, as children do.
There was a starvation winter, with rickets,
and epidemics going all around the lake.

Clary—you had such impudent, beautiful eyes—
and you died before your breasts had begun to grow.

CREATION NIGHT

We met on the stone bridge,
the birches stood watch for us,
the river gleaming like an eel wound toward the sea.
We twisted together in order to create God,
there was a rustling in the grain,
and a wave shot out of the rye.

LIGHTHOUSE KEEPER

In the puffing gusty nights,
when the lighthouse sways under storm clouds,
and the sea with its burning eyes climbs on the rocks,
you sit silently, thinking—
about Liz—who betrayed you that time—
and the fated, howling longing that exiled you out here
in the storm-beaten Scilly Islands.
And you mumble something to yourself
during the long watches on stormy nights
while the beacon throws its light a hundred miles out in the storm.

MARCH EVENING

Winterspring, nightfall, thawing.
Boys have lit a candle in a snowball house.
For the man in the evening train that rattles past,
it is a red memory surrounded by gray time,
calling, calling, out of stark woods just waking up.
And the man who was traveling never got home,
his life stayed behind, held by that lantern and that hour.

THE CABLE SHIP

We fished up the Atlantic Cable one day between the Barbados and
    the Tortugas,
held up our lanterns
and put some rubber over the wound in its back,
latitude 15 degrees north, longitude 61 degrees west.
When we laid our ear down to the gnawed place
we could hear something humming inside the cable.

"It's some millionaires in Montreal and St. John
talking over the price of Cuban sugar, and ways to
reduce our wages," one of us said.

For a long time we stood there thinking, in a circle of lanterns,
we're all patient fishermen,
then we let the coated cable fall back
to its place in the sea.

COTTON

The day they strung the cable from America to Europe
they did a lot of singing.
The cable, the huge singing cable was put in use
and Europe said to America:
Give me three million tons of cotton!
And three million tons of cotton wandered over the ocean
and turned to cloth:
cloth with which one fascinated the savages of Senegambia,
and cotton wads, with which one killed them.
Raise your voice in song, sing
on all the Senegambic trading routes!
sing cotton!
cotton!

Yes, cotton, your descent on the earth like snow!
Your white peace for our dead bodies!
Your while anklelength gowns when we wander into heaven
saved in all the world's harbors by Booth's Jesus-like face.

Cotton, cotton, your snowfall:
wrapping the world in the fur of new necessities,
you shut us in, you blinded our eyes with your cloud.
At the mouth of the Trade River,
and on the wide oceans of markets and fairs,
cotton, we have met there
the laws of your flood,
the threat of your flood.

LETTER FROM A CATTLEBOAT

In the latitude of the Balearic Islands
we sighted Ogden Armour's yacht.
This cargo ship is part of his fleet, as you know,
he has five slaughterhouses in Chicago,
and eight packing plants near La Plata.
He put his telescope to his eye and no doubt said,
"Oh Christ! It's nothing but my old cattleboat, the *Chattanooga.*"

We dipped the flag and all the cows started in mooing
like a thousand hoarse sirens over the endless ocean.
It was depressing,
and I felt like writing the whole thing off as: flesh praising flesh.

Shortly after we hit a heavy storm
and the cows, that have four stomachs, as you know,
had a bad time with seasickness.

ON THE CONGO

Our ship, the *Sea Smithy,* swerved out of the tradewinds
and began to creep up the Congo River.
Vines trailed along the deck like ropes.
We met the famous iron barges of the Congo,
whose hot steeldecks swarmed with Negroes from the tributaries.

They put their hands to their mouths
and shouted, "Go to hell" in a Bantu language.
We slid marveling and depressed through the tunnels of vegetation
and cook in his galley thought:
"now I am peeling potatoes in the middle of the Congo."

At night the *Sea Smithy*
goggled with its red eyes into the jungle,
an animal roared, a jungle rat plopped into the water,
a millet mortar coughed sharply,
and a drum was beating softly in a village somewhere where the rubber
    Negroes were going on with their slave lives.

THE SEA WIND

The sea wind sways on over the endless oceans —
spreads its wings night and day
rises and sinks again
over the desolate swaying floor of the immortal ocean.
Now it is nearly morning
or it is nearly evening
and the ocean wind feels in its face — the land wind.

Clockbuoys toll morning and evening psalms,
the smoke of a coalboat
or the smoke of a tar-burning Phoenician ship fades away at the
    horizons.
The lonely jellyfish who has no history rocks around with burning
    blue feet.
It's nearly evening now or morning.

DUSK IN THE COUNTRY

The riddle silently sees its image. It spins evening
among the motionless reeds.
There is a frailty no one notices
there, in the web of grass.

Silent cattle stare with green eyes.
They mosey in evening calm down to the water.
And the lake holds its immense spoon
up to all the mouths.

FROM HADES AND EUCLID
(*first version*)

1

When Euclid started out to measure Hades,
he found it had neither depth nor height.
Demons flatter than stingrays
swept above the plains of death,
their barks had no echoes as they ran
along the fire frontiers and the ice frontiers,
along the lines laid down in Hades.

Along the lines that fell apart
and joined again as lines
flock after flock of demons went abreast, in ranks, and parallel through
    Hades.

There were only waves, no hills, no chasms or valleys.
Only lines, parallel happenings, angles lying prone.
Demons shot along like elliptical plates;
they covered an endless field in Hades as though with moving
    dragonscales.

On the smoothed-over burial mounds that forgetfulness had destroyed
    with its flatness,
snakes were crawling—they were merely heavy lines:
lashed, crawled, stung their way
along the flowing lines.

A raging grassfire in roaring flatflight
rushed over the round like a carpenter's plane of fire.
It shot over the evil prairies, over the evil steppes, over the flat evil
    pusta
back and forth, ignited again and again by heat
on the flat fields in Hades.

2

The ovens of Hell lay close to the ground
on the flat fields.
There the capriciously damned were burned
in the brick rooms —
near the surface as graves are —
victims of flat evil,
with no comfort from a high place
or support from a low place,
received without dignity,
received without a rising,
received without any of the standards of eternity.
Their cries are met only by mockery
on the flat fields of evil.

And Euclid, the king of measurement, cried
and his cry went looking for Kronus, the god of spheres.

HENHOUSE

The hens drift in early from the day's pecking.
They take a few turns about the henhouse floor
and arrange themselves according to who's the favorite.
Then, when all that is clear,
the leaping up to the roost begins.
Soon they're all sitting in rows and the rooster is present.
He tests out sleep
but there is to be no sleep right away.
The hens shove to the side and cause trouble.
He has to straighten them out, with his beak and a cawkle.
Now it's shifting and settling down.
One of the hens tries to remember the last worm
she caught today.
But the memory is already gone down,
on its way through the crop.
Another hen, just before she falls asleep, recalls
the way the rooster looked, the white of her eyeballs fluttering,
her shutterlike lids closing out the world.

CÉSAR VALLEJO

THIS MAN IS so far out that he is only an inch away from his own face. Some poets may say that they don't feel well. Vallejo tells you that he is afraid that he is really an animal made of white snow. He creates in his poems paintings in words that suggest frightful things, and we do feel frightened, and wonder why the rest of the painters are painting flowers.

When I asked Neruda once about Vallejo, whom he knew well, he said that Vallejo was Peruvian, while he was merely Castillian: he implied that he saw things straight on, but Vallejo took things in from the side, in an Indian way. Vallejo, he said, has "a subtle way of thought, a way of expression that is not direct but oblique. I don't have it."

César Vallejo is not a poet of the partially authentic feeling, but a poet of the absolutely authentic. He does not hide part of his life, and describe only the more "poetic" parts. He lived a difficult life, full of fight, and in describing it never panders to a love of pleasantries nor a love of vulgarity. He had a tremendous feeling for, and love of, his family—his father, his mother, and his brothers—which he expresses with simple images of great resonance. His wildness and savagery exist side by side with a tenderness. The wildness and savagery rest on a clear compassion for others, and a clear intuition into his own inward path. He sees roads inside himself. In the remarkable intensity with which he follows a thought or an image, there is a kind of heroism. He follows the poem wherever it goes, even into the sea.

Vallejo's art is not in recapturing ideas but in actually thinking. We feel the flow of thought, its power like an underground river finding its way for the first time through some shifted ground—even he doesn't know where it will come out.

César Vallejo embodies the history of mankind, as Jung and Freud do, not by sprinkling the dust of the past on his words, but by thinking his way backward and forward through it.

He loves thinkers and refers to Marx, Feuerbach, Freud, Socrates, Aristotle again and again. At the same time he respects human suffering so much he is afraid all thought might be beside the point.

In *Poemas Humanas* especially, Vallejo suggests so well the incredible weight of daily life, how it pulls men and women down; carrying a day is like carrying a mountain. And what the weight of daily life wants to pull us down to is mediocrity. He hates it. Vallejo wants life and literature to be intense or not at all.

> And what if after so many wings of birds
> the stopped bird doesn't survive!
> It would be better then, really,
> if it were all swallowed up, and let's end it!

It is this marvelous intensity that is his mark. We all know poets who are able to make quick associations when there are not many mammal emotions around, but when anger or anguish enters the poem, they become tongue-tied, or lapse into clichés. Vallejo does just the opposite. Under the pressure of powerful human feeling, he leaps about wildly, each leap throwing him further out onto the edges of consciousness, and at the same time deeper into the "depths."

CÉSAR VALLEJO was born March 15, 1892, in a small mining town, Santiago de Chuco, in northern Peru; his family were Indians. The Indians worked on haciendas with little pay, and terrible housing. His brother worked in the office of a tungsten mine. Vallejo's father was governor of the town; César had eight brothers and sisters. He received a bachelor's degree at the University of Trujillo in 1916, and belonged to a lively group of students and writers who wanted revolution. They read Ruben Dario, Walt Whitman, and many French poets. César became a schoolmaster, and apparently a good one. Some of his early poems written during this period were later collected in *Los Heraldos Negros*.

Vallejo moved to Lima, and there joined an active group of bohemian writers. When he returned one day to his hometown for a visit, a political quarrel broke out and a friend was killed by the police; Vallejo was put in jail for three months. There he wrote some of the poems that would appear in *Trilce*.

In 1923, he left South America for Paris, but his life there became a disaster. He slept at times in parks or the Paris Metro; he lived without warm clothes, and sometimes ate only potatoes. He often had no food at all. He developed elaborate theories such as how to step out of the Metro without wearing out your shoes, how to cross your legs without wearing out your trousers. One French woman from across the courtyard saw him sitting in a chair for thirty-six hours without moving; she went over to him. In January of 1929, they were married. The couple moved to Spain, and Vallejo wrote stories for Madrid newspapers. On their return to France, they were arrested and expelled for radical activity. Back in Spain, he met García Lorca, Alberti, and Salinas. It was there his book *Trilce* was published. In 1932, the couple were given permission to return to Paris. But he wrote few poems, and it was a time of great poverty again.

He went to Spain once more in 1937, for a congress of revolutionary writers. The Spanish Civil War spurred him to write poems once more. The poems were collected as *Poemas Humanas*. In the early months of 1938, he became sick, lived with a high fever for months, and died on April 15 on a rainy day.

THE BLACK RIDERS

There are blows in life so violent—don't ask me!
Blows as if from the hatred of God; as if before them,
the deep waters of everything lived through
were backed up in the soul. . . . Don't ask me!

Not many; but they exist. . . . They open dark ravines
in the most ferocious face and in the most bull-like back.
Perhaps they are the horses of that heathen Attila,
or the black riders sent to us by Death.

They are slips backward made by the Christs of the soul,
away from some holy faith that is sneered at by Events.
These blows that are bloody are the crackling sounds
from some bread that burns at the oven door.

And man . . . poor man! . . . poor man! He swings his eyes, as
when a man behind us calls us by clapping his hands;
swings his crazy eyes, and everything alive
is backed up, like a pool of guilt, in that glance.

There are blows in life so violent. . . . Don't ask me!

THE SPIDER

It is a huge spider, which can no longer move;
a spider which is colorless, whose body,
a head and an abdomen, is bleeding.

Today I watched it with great care. With what tremendous energy
to every side
it was stretching out its many feet.
And I have been thinking of its invisible eyes,
the death-bringing pilots of the spider.

It is a spider which was shivering, fixed
on the sharp ridge of a stone;
the abdomen on one side,
and on the other, the head.

With so many feet, the poor thing, and still it cannot
solve it! And seeing it
confused in such great danger,
what a strange pain that traveler has given me today!

It is a huge spider, whose abdomen
prevents him from following his head.
And I have been thinking of his eyes
and of his many, many feet . . .
And what a strange pain that traveler has given me!

GOD

I feel that God is traveling
so much in me, with the dusk and the sea.
With him we go along together. It is getting dark.
With him we get dark. All orphans . . .

But I feel God. And it seems
that he sets aside some good color for me.
He is kind and sad, like those who care for the sick;
he whispers with sweet contempt like a lover's:
his heart must give him great pain.

Oh, my God, I've only just come to you,
today I love so much in this twilight; today
that in the false balance of some breasts
I weigh and weep for a frail Creation.

And you, what do you weep for . . . you, in love
with such an immense and whirling breast. . . .
I consecrate you, God, because you love so much;
because you never smile; because your heart
must all the time give you great pain.

THE MULE DRIVERS

Mule driver, you walk along fantastically glazed with sweat.
The Menocucho ranch charges
daily one thousand troubles for life.
Twelve noon. We've arrived at the waist of the day.
The sun that hurts so much.

Mule driver, you gradually vanish with your red poncho,
enjoying the Peruvian folk song of your coca leaves.
And I, from a hammock,
from a century of irresolution,
brood over your horizon, mourned for
by mosquitoes, and by the delicate
and feeble song of a paca-paca bird.
In the end you'll arrive where you are supposed to arrive,
mule driver, behind your saintly burro, going
away . . .
away . . .

You are lucky then, in this heat in which
all our desires and all our intentions rear up;
when the spirit that hardly rouses the body
walks without coca, and does not succeed in pulling
its brute toward the western
Andes of Eternity.

THE RIGHT MEANING

"Mother, you know there is a place somewhere called Paris. It's a huge place and a long way off and it really is huge."

My mother turns up my coat collar, not because it's starting to snow, but in order that it may start.

My father's wife is in love with me, walking up, always keeping her back to my birth, and her face toward my death. Because I am hers twice: by my good-bye and by my coming home. When I return home, I close her. That is why her eyes gave me so much, pronounced innocent of me, caught in the act of me, everything occurs through finished arrangements, through covenants carried out.

Has my mother confessed me, has she been named publicly? Why doesn't she give so much to my other brothers? To Victor, for example, the oldest, who is so old now that people say, "He looks like his father's youngest brother!" It must be because I have traveled so much! It must be because I have lived more!

My mother gives me illuminated permissions to explore my coming-home tales. Face-to-face with my returning-home life, remembering that I journeyed for two whole hearts through her womb, she blushes and goes deathly pale when I say in the discourse of the soul: "That night I was happy!" But she grows more sad, she grew more sad.

"How old you're getting, son!"

And she walks firmly through the color yellow to cry, because I seem to her to be getting old, on the blade of the sword, in the delta of my face. Weeps with me, grows sad with me. Why should my youth be necessary, if I will always be her son? Why do mothers feel pain when their sons get old, if their age will never equal anyway the age of the mothers? And why, if the sons, the more they get on, merely come nearer to the age of the fathers? My mother cries because I am old in my time and because I will never get old enough to be old in hers!

My good-byes left from a point in her being more toward the outside than the point in her being to which I come back. I am, because I am so overdue coming back, more the man to my mother than the son to my mother. The purity that lights us both now with three flames lies precisely in that. I say then until I finally fall silent:

"Mother, you know there's a place somewhere called Paris. It's a huge place and a long way off and it really is huge."

The wife of my father, hearing my voice, goes on eating her lunch, and her eyes that will die descend gently along my arms.

I AM GOING TO TALK ABOUT HOPE

I do not feel this suffering as César Vallejo. I am not suffering now as a creative person, nor as a man, nor even as a simple living being. I don't feel this pain as a Catholic, or as a Mohammedan, or as an atheist. Today I am simply in pain. If my name weren't César Vallejo, I'd still feel it. If I weren't an artist, I'd still feel it. If I weren't a man, or even a living being, I'd still feel it. If I weren't a Catholic, or an atheist, or a Mohammedan, I'd still feel it. Today I am in pain from further down. Today I am simply in pain.

The pain I have has no explanations. My pain is so deep that it never had a cause, and has no need of a cause. What could its cause have been? Where is that thing so important that it stopped being its cause? Its cause is nothing, and nothing could have stopped being its cause. Why has this pain been born all on its own? My pain comes from the north wind and from the south wind, like those hermaphrodite eggs that some rare birds lay conceived of the wind. If my bride were dead, my suffering would still be the same. If they had slashed my throat all the way through, my suffering would still be the same. If life, in other words, were different, my suffering would still be the same. Today I am in pain from higher up. Today I am simply in pain.

I look at the hungry man's pain, and I see that his hunger walks somewhere so far from my pain that if I fasted until death, one blade of grass at least would always sprout from my grave. And the same with the lover! His blood is too fertile for mine, which has no source and no one to drink it.

I always believed up till now that all things in the world had to be either fathers or sons. But here is my pain that has neither a father nor a son. It hasn't any back to get dark, and it has too bold a front for dawning, and if they put it into some dark room, it wouldn't give light, and if they put it into some brightly lit room, it wouldn't cast a shadow. Today I am in pain, no matter what happens. Today I am simply in pain.

POEM TO BE READ AND SUNG

I know there is someone
looking for me day and night inside her hand,
and coming upon me, each moment, in her shoes.
Doesn't she know the night is buried
with spurs behind the kitchen?

I know there is someone composed of my pieces,
whom I complete when my waist
goes galloping on her precise little stone.
Doesn't she know that money once out for her likeness
never returns to her trunk?

I know the day,
but the sun has escaped from me;
I know the universal act she performed in her bed
with some other woman's bravery and warm water, whose
shallow recurrence is a mine.
Is it possible this being is so small
even her own feet walk on her that way?

A cat is the border between us two,
right there beside her bowl of water.
I see her on the corners, her dress — once
an inquiring palm tree — opens and closes. . . .
What can she do but change her style of weeping?

But she does look and look for me. This is a real story!

Translated by Robert Bly and James Wright

BLACK STONE LYING ON A WHITE STONE

I will die in Paris, on a rainy day,
on some day I can already remember.
I will die in Paris — and I don't step aside —
perhaps on a Thursday, as today is Thursday, in autumn.

It will be a Thursday, because today, Thursday, setting down
these lines, I have put my upper arm bones on
wrong, and never so much as today have I found myself
with all the road ahead of me, alone.

César Vallejo is dead. Everyone beat him,
although he never does anything to them;
they beat him hard with a stick and hard also

with a rope. These are the witnesses:
the Thursdays, and the bones of my arms,
the solitude, and the rain, and the roads . . .

Translated by Robert Bly and John Knoepfle

THE ROLL CALL OF BONES

They demanded in loud voices:
"We want him to show both hands at the same time."
And that simply couldn't be done.
"We want them to check the length of his steps while he cries."
And that simply couldn't be done.
"We want him to think one identical thought during the time a zero
goes on being useless."
And that simply couldn't be done.
"We want him to do something crazy."
And that simply couldn't be done.
"We want a mass of men like him to stand in between him and another
man just like him."
And that simply couldn't be done.
"We want him to compare him with himself."
And that simply couldn't be done.
"We want them to call him finally by his own name."
And that simply couldn't be done.

IN THE MOMENT

In the moment the tennis player majestically launches
his ball, he possesses the rare innocence of an animal;
in the moment
the philosopher catches a new truth by surprise
he is a beast through and through.
Anatole France is very clear
that the religious impulse is produced by a bodily organ totally dedicated
and never before noticed,
in fact, we can go farther and state categorically
that in the very instant in which this organ is working at full power,
the man of faith is so empty of malice
as to be virtually a rutabaga.
Oh soul! Oh thought! Oh Marx! Oh Feuerbach!

I HAVE A TERRIBLE FEAR

I have a terrible fear of being an animal
of white snow, who has kept his father and mother
alive with his solitary circulation through the veins,
and a fear that on this day which is so marvellous, sunny,
    archbishoprical,
(a day that stands so for night)
this animal, like a straight line,
will manage not to be happy, or to breathe,
or to turn into something else, or to get money.

It would be a terrible thing
if I were a lot of man up to that point.
Unthinkable nonsense . . . an overfertile assumption
to whose accidental yoke the spiritual
hinge in my waist succumbs.
Unthinkable . . . Meanwhile
that's how it is on this side of God's head,
in the tabula of Locke, and of Bacon, in the pale neck
of the beast, in the snout of the soul.

And, in fragrant logic,
I do have that practical fear, this marvellous
moony day, of being that one, this one maybe,
to whose nose the ground smells like a corpse,
the unthinkable alive and the unthinkable dead.

Oh to roll on the ground, to be there, to cough, to wrap oneself,
to wrap the doctrine, the temple, from shoulder to shoulder,
to go away, to cry, to let it go for eight
or for seven or for six, for five, or let it go
for life with its three possibilities!

AND WHAT IF AFTER

And what if after so many words,
the word itself doesn't survive!
And what if after so many wings of birds
the stopped bird doesn't survive!
It would be better then, really,
if it were all swallowed up, and let's end it!

To have been born only to live off our own death!
To raise ourselves from the heavens toward the earth
carried up by our own bad luck,
always watching for the moment to put out our darkness with our
    shadow!
It would be better, frankly,
if it were all swallowed up, and the hell with it!

And what if after so much history, we succumb,
not to eternity,
but to these simple things, like being
at home, or starting to brood!
What if we discover later
all of a sudden, that we are living
to judge by the height of the stars
off a comb and off stains on a handkerchief!
It would be better, really,
if it were all swallowed up, right now!

They'll say we have a lot
of grief in one eye, and a lot of grief
in the other also, and when they look
a lot of grief in both. . . .
So then! . . . Naturally! . . . So! . . . Don't say a word!

THE ANGER THAT BREAKS A MAN DOWN INTO BOYS

The anger that breaks a man down into boys,
that breaks the boy down into equal birds,
and the bird, then, into tiny eggs;
the anger of the poor
owns one smooth oil against two vinegars.

The anger that breaks the tree down into leaves,
and the leaf down into different-sized buds,
and the buds into infinitely fine grooves;
the anger of the poor
owns two rivers against a number of seas.

The anger that breaks the good down into doubts,
and doubt down into three matching arcs,
and the arc, then, into unimaginable tombs;
the anger of the poor
owns one piece of steel against two daggers.

The anger that breaks the soul down into bodies,
the body down into different organs,
and the organ into reverberating octaves of thought;
the anger of the poor
owns one deep fire against two craters.

MASSES

When the battle was over,
and the fighter was dead, a man came toward him
and said to him: "Do not die; I love you so!"
But the corpse, it was sad! went on dying.

And two came near, and told him again and again:
"Do not leave us! Courage! Return to life!"
But the corpse, it was sad! went on dying.

Twenty arrived, a hundred, a thousand, five hundred thousand,
shouting: "So much love, and it can do nothing against death!"
But the corpse, it was sad! went on dying.

Millions of persons stood around him,
all speaking the same thing: "Stay here, brother!"
But the corpse, it was sad! went on dying.

Then all the men on the earth
stood around him; the corpse looked at them sadly, deeply moved;
he sat up slowly,
put his arms around the first man; started to walk . . .

NOVEMBER 10, 1937

MIGUEL HERNANDEZ

MIGUEL HERNANDEZ WAS a fierce fighter in words. He was born in the province of Alicante, and he wrote his first poems in the Gongora style of elaborate images, a practice in which the poet keeps from the reader the secret of what the poem is actually about. Here is a sample:

> For pulling the feathers from icy archangels,
> the lilylike snowstorm of slender teeth
> is condemned to the weeping of the fountains
> and the desolation of the running springs.

He published his first book, *Perito en Lunas* (*Expert in Moons*) in 1933 and sent copies to all the major poets of the day. When he gave readings, audiences could not solve the riddles. It took years before critics realized his "white narcissus" poem was not about the moon but a poem on shaving.

In April of 1933, he wrote to Federico García Lorca, whom he had met in Madrid, and complained. Lorca in his reply told him not to despair about the silence surrounding his first book.

> Your book stands deep in silence, like all first books, like my first, which had so much delight and strength. Write, read, study, and FIGHT! Don't be vain about your work. Your book is strong, it has many interesting things, and to eyes that can see makes clear *the passion of man,* but it doesn't, as you say, have more *cojones* than

those of the most established poets. Take it easy. Europe's most beautiful poetry is being written in Spain today. . . . Books of poetry, my dear Miguel, catch on very slowly.

I know perfectly well what you are like, and I send you my embrace like a brother, full of affection and friendship. (Write to me.)—Federico

Lorca returned to Madrid in 1934, and this time he met Neruda, who was a consul from Chile to Spain. Hernandez was tired of his own precious style, and in a famous review that he wrote of Neruda's *Residencia en la Tierra*, he said:

> I am sick of so much pure and minor art. I like the disordered and chaotic confusion of the Bible, where I see spectacular events, disasters, misfortunes, worlds turned over, and I hear outcries and explosions of blood.
>
> *(translated by Timothy Baland)*

Neruda mentioned that Miguel had a face like "a potato just lifted from the earth." He remembered Miguel's occasional visits to his house, his face and body still shining from his swim in the river.

On July 18, 1936, the Spanish Civil War officially began. On August 19, the Francoists killed Lorca. In September, Hernandez joined the Republican army. There's a photograph of him passionately reading to men with helmets on. His poems have changed:

> Today I am, I don't know how,
> today all I am ready for is suffering,
> today I have no friends,
> today the only thing I have is the desire
> to rip out my heart by the roots
> and stick it underneath a shoe

Today my destiny is too much for me.
And I'm looking for death down by my hands,
looking at knives with affection,
and I remember that friendly ax,
and all I think about is the tallest steeples
and making a fatal leap serenely.

The passage above is from some uncollected poems written by
Hernandez in 1936. The rest of his life, he was deeply connected to
the war, and he died in a Franco prison.

MIGUEL HERNANDEZ was born on October 30, 1910, in the vil-
lage of Orihuela in Alicante Province. The family were goatherders.
He had somewhere between two and seven years of school. In 1916,
Miguel had to leave school at his father's insistence and join his
brother and father herding goats and sheep.

The Canon of the cathedral at Orihuela took an interest in
Hernandez and gave him the old classical Spanish literature of
Cervantes, Lope de Vega, St. John of the Cross, and Frey Luis de
Leon. Miguel especially loved the elaborate Gongora style and he
wrote beautifully incomprehensible poems in this style. He met two
poets of the neighborhood, Manon and Gabriel Sijé. They helped
Miguel with early publications, but Miguel did not want to be type-
cast as a shepherd poet, and, against much advice, moved to Madrid
in December of 1931 to get acquainted with the literary world. He
met a few poets devoted to the Gongora style, but not much hap-
pened; after six months there, he returned to Orihuela.

Hernandez met and fell in love with Josefina Manresa, whose father
belonged to the Guardia Civil. In 1934, he moved to Madrid again, but
on a return visit to his hometown in January of 1936, he was arrested by
the Guardia, beaten, and held in the barracks. Neruda, as the Chilean

consul, arranged for Hernandez's release. A letter of protest against the arrest was signed by Lorca, Neruda, Alberti, and many others.

In August 1936, Manuel Manresa, the father of Josefina, was killed by leftists. In the same month, the Franco police shot García Lorca. After some months spent digging trenches around Madrid, he was sent to give readings to the men at the front and on radio stations.

In March of 1937, he and Josefina were married, and in June he helped organize the Second International Conference of Anti-Fascist Writers, attended by Auden, Neruda, Spender, Vallejo, and many others. In October, he was sent back to the front lines. On March 29, 1938, the war ended with the leftists defeated. Hernandez fled to Portugal, but was turned back at the border. There he was arrested by the Guardia Civil and beaten. He was held in Torrijos Prison in Madrid. Neruda worked furiously to get him released and a cardinal petitioned Franco for Hernandez's release. Against the warnings of friends, he returned to Orihuela, but two weeks later he was rearrested and taken to prison in Orihuela and then to a prison in Madrid. With twenty others, he was charged and sentenced to death. The government issued a flyer:

Miguel Hernandez, condemned to death.
Crime: Poet and soldier of the mother country.
Aggravating, intelligentsia.
Death to the intelligentsia.

His sentence was later commuted to thirty years in prison, but Hernandez died of tuberculosis on March 28, 1942.

YOU THREW ME A LEMON

You threw me a lemon, oh it was sour,
with a warm hand, that was so pure
it never damaged the lemon's architecture.
I tasted the sourness anyway.

With that yellow blow, my blood moved
from a gentle laziness into an anguished
fever, for my blood felt the bite
from a long and firm tip of a breast.

Yet glancing at you and seeing the smile
which that lemon-colored event drew from you,
so far from my dishonorable fierceness,

my blood went to sleep in my shirt,
and the soft and golden breast turned
to a baffling pain with a long break.

FOR PULLING THE FEATHERS
FROM ICY ARCHANGELS

For pulling the feathers from icy archangels
the lilylike snowstorm of slender teeth
is condemned to the weeping of the fountains
and the desolation of the running springs.

For diffusing its soul into metals,
for abandoning the sunrises to the iron,
the stormy blacksmiths drag away the fire
to the anguish of the brutal anvils.

I see myself rushing recklessly toward the painful
retribution of the thorn, to the fatal
discouragement of the rose, and the aciduous

power of death, and so much ruin
is not for any sin or any other thing
except loving you, only for loving you.

YOUR HEART? — IT IS A FROZEN ORANGE

Your heart? — it is a frozen orange,
inside it has juniper oil but no light
and a porous look like gold: an outside
promising risks to the man who looks.

My heart is a fiery pomegranate,
its scarlets clustered, and its wax opened,
which could offer you its tender beads
with the stubbornness of a man in love.

Yes, what an experience of sorrow it is
to go to your heart and find a frost
made of primitive and terrifying snow!

A thirsty handkerchief flies through the air
along the shores of my weeping,
hoping that he can drink in my tears.

I HAVE PLENTY OF HEART

Today I am, I don't know how,
today all I am ready for is suffering,
today I have no friends,
today the only thing I have is the desire
to rip out my heart by the roots
and stick it underneath a shoe.

Today that dry thorn is growing strong again,
today is the day of crying in my kingdom,
depression unloads today in my chest
a depressed heavy metal.

Today my destiny is too much for me.
And I'm looking for death down by my hands,
looking at knives with affection,
and I remember that friendly ax,
and all I think about is the tallest steeples
and making a fatal leap serenely.

If it weren't for . . . I don't know what,
my heart would write a suicide note,
a note I carry hidden there,
I would make an inkwell out of my heart,
a fountain of syllables, and goodbyes and gifts,
and *you stay here* I'd say to the world.

I was born under a rotten star.
My grief is that I have only one grief
and it weighs more than all the joys together.

A love affair has left me with my arms hanging down
and I can't lift them anymore.
Don't you see how disillusioned my mouth is?
How unsatisfied my eyes are?

The more I look inward the more I mourn!
Cut off this pain? —who has the scissors?

Yesterday, tomorrow, today
suffering for everything,
my heart is a sad goldfish bowl,
a pen of dying nightingales.

I have plenty of heart.

Today to rip out my heart,
I who have a bigger heart than anyone,
and having that, I am the bitterest also.

I don't know why, I don't know how or why
I let my life keep on going every day.

SITTING ON TOP OF CORPSES

Sitting on top of corpses
fallen silent over the last two months,
I kiss empty shoes
and take hold wildly
of the heart's hand
and the soul that keeps it going.

I want my voice to climb mountains,
descend to earth, and give out thunder:
this is what my throat wants
from now on, and always has.

Come near to my loud voice,
nation of the same mother,
tree whose roots hold
me as in a jail.
I am here to love you,
I am here to fight for you,
with my mouth and blood
as with two faithful rifles.

If I came out of the dirt
and was born from a womb
with no luck and no money,
it was only that I might become
the nightingale of sadness,
an echo chamber for disaster,
that I could sing and keep singing
for the men who ought to hear it

everything that has to do with suffering,
with poverty, with earth.

Yesterday the people woke
naked, with nothing to pull on,
hungry, with nothing to eat,
and now another day has come
dangerous, as expected,
bloody, as expected.
In their hands, rifles
long to become lions
to finish off the animals
who have been so often animals.

Although you have so few weapons,
nation with a million strengths,
don't let your bones collapse:
as long as you have fists,
fingernails, spit, courage,
insides, guts, balls, and teeth,
attack those who would wound us.
Stiff as the stiff wind,
gentle as the gentle air,
kill those who kill,
loathe those who loathe
the peace inside you
and the womb of your women.
Don't let them stab you in the back;
live face-to-face and die
with your chest open to the bullets
and wide as the walls.

I sing with a griever's voice,
my people, for all your heroes,
your anxieties like mine,
your setbacks whose tears were drawn
from the same metal as mine,
suffering of the same mettle,
your thinking and my brain,
your courage and my blood,
your anguish and my honors,
all made of the same timber.
To me this life is like
a rampart in front of emptiness.

I am here in order to live
as long as my soul is alive,
and I am here to die
when that time comes,
deep in the roots of the nation,
as I will be and always have been.
Life is a lot of hard gulps,
but death is only one.

LETTER

The pigeon-house of letters
opens its impossible flight
from the trembling tables
on which memory leans,
the weight of absence,
the heart, the silence.

I hear the wingbeat of letters
sailing toward their center.
Wherever I go I meet
men and women badly
wounded by absence,
wasted by time.

Letters, descriptions, letters,
postcards, dreams,
bits of tenderness
planned in the sky,
sent from blood to blood,
from one longing to another.

Even though my loving body
lies under the earth now,
write to me here on earth
so I can write to you.

Old letters, old envelopes,
grow taciturn in the corner,
and the color of time pressed
down on the writing.

The letters slowly perish there
full of tiny shudders.
The ink feels death agony,
the loose sheets begin to fail,
and the paper fills with holes
like a diminutive cemetery
of emotions now gone,
of loves to come later.

Even though my loving body
lies under the earth now,
write to me here on earth
so I can write to you.

When I'm about to write you
even the inkwells get excited:
those black and frozen wells
blush and start quivering,
and a transparent human warmth
rises from the black deeps.
When I start to write you
my bones are ready to do it:
I write you with the permanent
ink of my love.

There goes my warm letter,
a dove forged in the fire,
its two wings folded down
and the address in the center.
A bird that only wants
your body, your hands, your eyes
and the space around your breath

for a nest of air and heaven.
And you will stay there naked
inside of your emotions,
without clothes, so you can feel
it wholly against your breast.

Even though my loving body
lies under the earth now,
write to me here on earth
so I can write to you.

Yesterday a letter was left
unclaimed, without an owner:
flying over the eyes
of someone who had lost his body.
Letters that stay alive
and talk for the dead:
wistful paper, human,
without eyes to look at it.

As the eyeteeth keep growing,
I feel the gentle voice
of your letter closer each time
like a great shout.
It will come to me asleep
if I can't manage to be awake.
And my wounds will become
the spilt inkwells,
the mouths that quiver,
remembering your kisses,
and they will repeat
in a voice no one has heard: I love you.

LULLABY OF THE ONION

(Lines for his son, after receiving a letter from his wife in which she said that all she had to eat was bread and onions.)

An onion is frost
shut in and poor.
Frost of your days
and of my nights.
Hunger and onion,
black ice and frost
huge and round.

My son is lying now
in the cradle of hunger.
The blood of an onion
is what he lives on.
But it is your blood,
with sugar on it like frost,
onion and hunger.

A dark woman
turned into moonlight
pours herself down thread
by thread over your cradle.
My son, laugh,
because you can swallow the moon
when you want to.

Lark of my house,
laugh often.
Your laugh is in your eyes
the light of the world.
Laugh so much
that my soul, hearing you,
will beat wildly in space.

Your laugh unlocks doors for me,
it gives me wings.
It drives my solitudes off,
pulls away my jail.
Mouth that can fly,
heart that turns to
lightning on your lips.

Your laugh is the sword
that won all the wars,
it defeats the flowers
and the larks,
challenges the sun.
Future of my bones
and of my love.

The body with wings beating,
the eyelash so quick,
life is full of color
as it never was.
How many linnets
climb with wings beating
out of your body!

I woke up and was an adult:
don't wake up.
My mouth is sad:
you go on laughing.
In your cradle, forever,
defending your laughter
feather by feather.

Your being has a flying range
so high and so wide
that your body is a newly
born sky.
I wish I could climb
back to the starting point
of your travel!

You laugh, eight months old,
with five orange blossoms.
You have five tiny
ferocities.
You have five teeth
like five new
jasmine blossoms.

They will be the frontier
of kisses tomorrow,
when you feel your rows
of teeth are a weapon.
You will feel a flame
run along under your teeth
looking for the center.

My son, fly away, into the
two moons of the breast:
the breast, onion-
sad, but you, content.
Stay on your feet.
Stay ignorant of what's happening,
and what is going on.

RUMI

As American readers have learned recently, Rumi is astounding, fertile, abundant, almost more an excitable library of poetry than a person. In his poems, Rumi often adopts the transparent "you," using it so beautifully that each of us feels as if we too were being spoken to. Coleman Barks has echoed that tender "you" so brilliantly in his translations that we will never get over our gratitude to him.

His *Mathnawi* is as complicated as Shakespeare's works in its self-contradicting, high-spirited, chaotic, indulgent, loving, gossiping, outrageous, obscene, passionate, witty poetry, which is immensely learned. His poetry in its abundance seems to be a gift presented by half-mad lovers who have been doing the same work for hundreds of years.

When I started reading Rumi, all at once I felt at home. I think many readers of his work have that feeling. It's almost as if his poems resonate in some echo chamber that we retain only in memory. Some people say we once had that ecstatic love poetry in the religious culture around the Albigensians in southern France in the thirteenth and fourteenth centuries. The Albigensians brought to the troubadours the concept of *amor.* That teaching was hated by the more dogmatic and rigid fathers at Rome. In fact, one joke at that time, which was discussed in public meetings, was that *amor* is *roma* spelled backward. The Catholics held, for example, that real love was only possible inside marriage, the Albigensians that real love was only possible outside of marriage. All that ended when Simon de Montfort, supported by the Church, invaded southern France and destroyed the culture utterly.

Orthodox Islam, on its side, has always been uneasy as well about the ecstatic tradition of the Sufis and the lovers. The orthodox Muslims murdered several Sufis, among them Al-Hallaj, but they never undertook the wholesale murder of the ecstatic culture in the way the Christians did. Though often threatened, the Sufi culture survived in a number of Middle Eastern cities, among them Konya. It was there, with the help of Shams, that Rumi wrote the poems that still seem so amazing.

RUMI was born in what is now Afghanistan, in Balkh on September 30, 1204. His father was a well-known theologian. It is said that the Prophet gave him a special title in a dream which all the scholars in Balkh experienced on the same night. Balkh was at that time one of the centers of Islamic learning, as it had earlier been a center of Buddhism. Rumi inherited from his own father doubts about the dominant place of intellect in religion. Because the Mongols were approaching from the north, Rumi left with his family in 1218. It was a wise move. In 1220, thousands of people in Balkh were killed and the city entirely destroyed.

There's a story that in the travelings of Rumi's family, they visited the great poet Attar in Nishapur. Attar apparently sensed the genius of the young Rumi and gave him a copy of his book. Rumi's family then made a pilgrimage to Mecca, afterwards visiting Damascus. Finally, around 1125, they reached central Anatolia, in the area known as Rum. So "Rumi" means "from Rum."

Rumi's father was called to the city of Konya by Sultan Kaykobed, who gathered scholars and mystics from many countries. The father became an important teacher, and when he died in 1231, his son Jalaluddin was appointed to his place. A favorite discipline of Sufis was the chilla, that is, a period of solitude and prayer that lasts forty days. Jalaluddin apparently experienced a number of these chillas.

By 1242, the Mongol armies were coming close. The rulers of Konya paid heavy tributes to them and so the city was saved. In late October 1244, a strange event occurred. Shams, who was a wandering ascetic, stopped Rumi's donkey as Rumi was returning from a lecture, and threw him a difficult question about the difference between Mohammed and Bayazid. The two masters recognized the genius in each other, and Rumi decided to remain in seclusion with Shams for six months, abandoning his classes and family. The two of them talked "without eating, drinking or any human needs." When Shams disappeared, Rumi felt all the anguish of the abandoned lover. He had not paid much attention to Persian poetry and music, but he began now to write poems and sing them, as well as to dance. After a long search, Shams was finally located in Damascus, and Rumi brought him back to Konya, had him move in, and married him to one of Rumi's adopted daughters. The time of ecstasy between the two men resumed, but there was enormous jealousy. On December 5, 1248, when Rumi and Shams were talking late at night, someone knocked at the door. Shams went out and was killed, perhaps with the help of Rumi's second son, Alludin. No one was sure what had happened, and Rumi himself went out this time searching for Shams, but Shams was not found. Rumi wrote and named his collection of ecstatic poems *The Works of Shams of Tabriz.*

Rumi later became fond of several other confidants, to whom he dictated more poems, as well as the fables and jokes that make up the *Mathnawi,* which is an enormous work of more than 50,000 lines. Rumi died on December 17, 1273, at sunset. His tomb still stands in Konya, and hundreds visit it each day.

THE CAPTAIN WHO WALKS ON HIS DECK

The dictionaries have no entry for the sort of love we praise.
If you can define a road, it's not the Lover's road.
The high branches of love shoot into the air that existed before eternity.
And the roots grow down into the earth that exists after eternity.
This branch of love is beyond the divine throne and beyond the
    Pleiades.
We have pulled reason down from his throne.
We've broken up all the set rules for animal desire and instinctual life.
The kind of love that we know of is too great for sober reason
And too great for this simple instinctual life.
Now if you believe that your need can be met by something on the
    outside,
And your wanting satisfied from the outside,
You are really a tiger or a cougar.
Are you praying any longer to wooden idols? If not,
Then why do you keep praying to your desire?
If you become the one you long for, what will you do with your longing?
The Captain stalks on the deck of his ship. The planks are his fears
Of the bad things that may happen, and the joists
Are his longing for the marvellous things that may happen.
When the planks and the joists both go, nothing remains but the
    drowning.
Shams al Tabriz is the ocean, and also the pearl deep in the ocean.
His personality is the one secret the Holy One never gave away.

LOVE AND SILENCE

Love cuts a lot of arguments short.
It helps when you're with intellectuals.
The lover decides he won't say any more,
Afraid the pearl may fall out of his mouth.
As when Mohammed recited parts of the Koran,
Think how still and alert his companions became,
As when a bird lights on your head, and you barely breathe.
You don't cough or sneeze, lest it fly away.
If anyone speaks, whether sweet or sour, you say, "Shhh . . ."
Awe resembles the bird that makes you quiet.
Awe and wonder put a lid on the kettle as soon as your love inside is
    boiling.

EATING POETRY

My poems resemble the bread of Egypt—one night
Passes over the bread, and you can't eat it anymore.

So gobble my poems down now, while they're still fresh,
Before the dust of the world settles on them.

Where a poem belongs is here, in the warmth of the chest;
Out in the world it dies of cold.

You've seen a fish—put him on dry land,
He quivers for a few minutes, and then is still.

And even if you eat my poems while they're still fresh,
You still have to bring forward many images yourself.

Actually, friend, what you're eating is your own imagination.
These poems are not just some bare statements and old proverbs.

WALKING WITH OTHERS

It's important to join the crowds of those traveling.
You know, even Mohammed's horse ascended
In the throngs of meditators.
Such a lifting doesn't resemble a man rising to the moon,
It's more like grapes being lifted up into wine.
Mist rises when water boils, but that's not it. It's more like
An embryo changing into a person capable of thought.

THE EDGE OF THE ROOF

I don't like it here, I want to go back.
According to the old Knowers
If you're absent from the one you love
Even for one second that ruins the whole thing!

There must be someone . . . just to find
One *sign* of the other world in this town
Would be helpful.

You know the great Chinese Simurgh bird
Got caught in this net . . .
And what can I do? I'm only a wren.

My desire-body, don't come
Strolling over this way.
Sit where you are, that's a good place.

When you want dessert, you choose something rich.
In wine, you look for what is clear and firm.
What is the rest? The rest is mirages,
And blurry pictures, and milk mixed with water.
The rest is self-hatred, and mocking other people, and bombing.

So just be quiet and sit down.
The reason is: you are drunk,
And this is the edge of the roof.

TELL ME, WHAT HAVE I LOST?

I lived for thousands and thousands of years as a mineral and then I
    died and became a plant.
And I lived for thousands and thousands of years as a plant and then
    I died and became an animal.
And I lived for thousands and thousands of years as an animal and
    then I died and became a human being.
Tell me, what have I ever lost by dying?

ECSTATIC LOVE IS AN OCEAN

Ecstatic love is an ocean, and the Milky Way is a flake of foam
  floating on that ocean.
The stars wheel around the North Pole, and ecstatic love, running in
  a wheel, turns the stars.
If there were no ecstatic love, the whole world would stop.
Do you think that a piece of flint would change into a plant
  otherwise?
Grass agrees to die so that it can rise up and receive a little of the
  animal's enthusiasm.
And the animal soul, in turn, sacrifices itself. For what?
To help that wind, through one light waft
Of which Mary became with child. Without that wind,
All creatures on Earth would be stiff as a glacier,
Instead of being as they are,
Locustlike, searching night and day for green things, flying.
Every bit of dust climbs toward the Secret One like a sapling.
It climbs and says nothing; and that silence is a wild praise of the
  Secret One.

THAT JOURNEYS ARE GOOD

If a fir tree had a foot or two like a turtle, or a wing,
Do you think it would just wait for the saw to enter?

You know the sun journeys all night under the Earth;
If it didn't, how could it throw up its flood of light in the east?

And salt water climbs with such marvellous swiftness to the sky.
If it didn't, how would the cabbages be fed with the rain?

Have you thought of Joseph lately? Didn't he leave his father in tears,
    going?
Didn't he then learn how to understand dreams, and give away grain?

And you, if you can't leave your country, you could go into yourself,
And become a ruby mine, open to the gifts of the sun.

You could travel from your manhood into the inner man, or from
    your womanhood into the inner woman —
By a journey of that sort Earth became a place where you find gold.

So leave your complaints and self-pity and internalized death-energy.
Don't you realize how many fruits have already escaped out of
    sourness into sweetness?

A good source of sweetness is a teacher; mine is named Shams.
You know every fruit grows more handsome in the light of the sun.

PRAISING MANNERS

We should ask God
To help us toward manners. Inner gifts
Do not find their way
To creatures without just respect.

If a man or woman flails about, he not only
Smashes his house,
He burns the whole world down.

Your depression is connected to your insolence
And your refusal to praise. If a man or woman is
On the path, and refuses to praise—that man or woman
Steals from others every day—in fact is a shoplifter!

The sun became full of light when it got hold of itself.
Angels began shining when they achieved discipline.
The sun goes out whenever the cloud of not-praising comes near.
The moment that foolish angel felt insolent, he heard the door close.

THE DRUNKARDS

The drunkards are rolling in slowly, those who hold to wine are
approaching.
The lovers come, singing, from the garden, the ones with brilliant
eyes.

The I-don't-want-to-lives are leaving, and the I-want-to-lives are arriving.
They have gold sewn into their clothes, sewn in for those who have
none.

Those with ribs showing who have been grazing in the old pasture
of love
Are turning up fat and frisky.

The souls of pure teachers are arriving like rays of sunlight
From so far up to the ground-huggers.

How marvellous is that garden, where apples and pears, both for
the sake of the two Marys,
Are arriving even in winter.

Those apples grow from the Gift, and they sink back into the Gift.
It must be that they are coming from the garden to the garden.

THE MILL, THE STONE,
AND THE WATER

All our desire is a grain of wheat.
Our whole personality is the milling-building.
But this mill grinds without knowing about it.

The mill stone is your heavy body.
What makes the stone turn is your thought-river.
The stone says: I don't know why we all do this, but the river has
    knowledge!

If you ask the river, it says,
I don't know why I flow.
All I know is that a human opened the gate!

And if you ask the person, he says:
All I know, oh gobbler of bread, is that if this stone
Stops going around, there'll be no bread for your bread-soup!

All this grinding goes on, and no one has any knowledge!
So just be quiet, and one day turn
To God, and say: "What is this about bread-making?"

THE HAWK

We are a little crazier now, and less sober, and some joy has risen out of us . . . it was so glad to be gone . . .

When it noticed the sober water no longer was holding its leg, it flew—

It is not in the mountains nor the marshes, it has sent itself to be with the Holy One who is alone.

Don't look here and there in the house, it belongs to air, it is made of air, and has gone into air.

This is a white hawk that belongs to Gawain's master; it belongs to him and has gone to him.

THE TWELVE LIES

People say, "The one you love is unfaithful."
That's the first lie.

They say, "Your night will never end in dawn."
Did you hear that lie?

They say, "Why give up sleep and die for love? Once in the grave,
All that is forgotten; it's over."
That's the third lie.

Some thinkers say, "Once you leave our time system,
The spirit stops moving; in fact, it goes backwards."
People love to tell lies!

Daydreamers with sluggish eyes say,
"Your poems and your teaching stories are nothing but daydreams."
I heard that lie.

People running around in the underbrush say,
"There's no path to the mountain and no mountain either."
That's the sixth lie!

They say, "The keeper of secrets never tells
A single secret except to an intermediary."
People love that lie.

They say, "If you're a worker, you'll never receive the key;
The master alone goes to heaven."
That's the eighth lie.

They go on: "If you have too much earth in your chart,
You'll never grasp what angels are."
Another lie!

They like to say, "You'll never get out of this nest
With your stubby love wings; you'll drop like a stone."
Did you hear that lie?

They maintain, "What human beings do is insignificant anyway.
Stones weigh more than our evil. God cares nothing about it."
That's a big lie.

So just keep silent, and if anyone says to you,
"No communion takes place without words," just say to him,
"I heard that lie."

TWO KINDS OF MIRACLES

Miracles secret and open flow from the teacher.
That's reasonable—it's not unusual at all.
And the tiniest of these miracles
Is this: Everyone near a saint gets drunk with God.

When a spiritual man lets the water hold up his feet
We are moved, because by ways we cannot see
The sight of that links
The soul back to the source of all lightness.

Of course a saint can move a mountain!
But who cares about that? How marvellous is the bread
Made without dough, the dishes of food
That are invisible, Mary's grapes that never saw the vine!

HORACE

HORACE IS A cagey bringer of bad news. The reader needs to gain an appreciation of his tartness. He refers again and again to death coming toward us, using images as flavorful as those of Trakl or Vallejo.

When he's lying on the grass, drinking some old wine, he doesn't feel we should just relax:

> Why do the darkling pines and the white
> Delicate poplars weave their shady
> Branches together, and the excited water
> Work to curl itself around us?

There's something ominous in the whole afternoon:

> Bring some roses, already turning dark,
> And cardamom and wines; being rich
> And young, we have to trust the dark threads
> Of the Three Sisters are still unbroken.

The English used him for years to educate young men toward an even temperament. But here we're not in a typical Oxford mood; we're really in the mood of some Russian story with Baba Yaga in it. The boat can sink. The ground can open up any second.

You'll soon lose your cunningly acquired
Strips of woods, the estate by the yellow
Tiber, the Roman house, its silver and gold,
To some miserable heir, and it's over.

He's alert to the way human beings keep animals about to be sacrificed inside fences. How does the sky look to them? What is this huge force that prepares them for sacrifice?

Whether we descend from the great houses,
Or drift unprotected under the naked
Sky, it's all one; we are sacrifices
To Death, not well known for compassion.

Someone or something is keeping us, as humans keep herds.

We are obliged and herded. The lot is
Inside the urn; the ball with our number
Will roll out. And what we'll get
Is an everlasting absence from home.

There are hundreds of ways to translate his disturbing, understated, ominous poems; I prefer the way in which we can feel fear.

You know that what most disturbs the soul
Is not Dindymene, nor that one who lives
With the Great Snake, nor the half-
Mad dancers with their crying metals,

It is grim-faced anger.

We don't feel Marvell here nor Whittier nor Alexander Pope; it's more like Robinson Jeffers:

> The Noric swords
> Cannot dissolve it, nor the ship-
> Swallowing sea, nor greedy fire, nor
> God himself when he comes roaring down.

HORACE was born on December 8, 65 B.C. His father was a freed slave who worked as an auctioneer in Apulia, near the heel of Italy, in a town founded by ex-soldiers. His father took him to Rome in order to find a good education for his son. Horace studied Greek in Rome and then in Athens. He was in his early twenties when Julius Caesar was murdered, and Brutus recruited him as a young regiment officer. He fought in the battle at Philippi, where he felt he was fighting for the old liberty against the fascism of Julius Caesar. After Brutus was killed in battle, Horace decided to throw down his shield and run. Once back in Italy, he found that his father's house had been confiscated. Three years later, many soldiers, Horace among them, received amnesty, and he apparently took a job in a treasury records office. By then, he was publishing poems.

Virgil noticed the poet, and asked the cultural lord, Maecenas, to help him. Maecenas did. Horace received a small farm in the Sabine Hills, where he lived the rest of his life.

One could say that his greatest gift was as a musician; he was a genius in sound. He managed to break up old sound habits so that Latin words fit into the old Greek song patterns, particularly the Alcaic pattern, which fixed all the short and long syllables for its four-lined form. (Tomas Tranströmer as a young man adapted the same Alcaic form to Swedish.) We know that both Alcaeus and Sappho sang their poems to stringed instruments, but there is no evidence that Horace did that. His odes in the Alcaic meter were not well received, and for six years, he gave up writing these concentrated, emotional poems. But the emperor Augustus admired Horace, and enticed him back to the Greek form, this time to Sappho's meter, by commissioning a triumphal ode. Horace died when he was fifty-six years old in 8 B.C. He was buried on a hill along with other famous Roman writers near the grave of Maecenas.

THE ANGER POEM

About my angry lines, burn them, do
Whatever you wish, or dip them
In the Adriatic Ocean; do this, hear me,
Handsome mother of a still more handsome daughter.

You know that what most disturbs the soul
Is not Dindymene, nor that one who lives
With the Great Snake, nor the half-
Mad dancers with their crying metals,

It is grim-faced anger. The Noric swords
Cannot dissolve it, nor the ship-
Swallowing sea, nor greedy fire, nor
God himself when he comes roaring down. . . .

Prometheus did what he did, he added a bit
To us from seals and orioles, dropped
Those bits into our clay, and had no choice
But to put into us the lion's mad angers.

Anger is what broke Thyeste's life,
And many shining cities went down brick
By brick before anger, and aggressive
Battalions ran their ploughs in great

Delight over ground covering those walls.
Calm your mind. Heat tempted
Me in my sweet early days, and sent
Me deeply mad to one-sided poems. Now

I want to replace those sour lines with
Sweet lines; now, having sworn off harsh
Attacks, I want you to become
My friend, and give me back my heart.

Book 1, Number 16

BRING ROSES AND CARDAMOM

To keep the soul serene even when the way is
Arduous, and to remain moderately unmoved
When gifts roll in, well, that's my advice for you,
Friend Dellius, for you are mortal too.

Evenness is best, whether disasters make
Everything crooked, or whether you can
Enjoy sipping, while you lie on your back
In the grass, the host's hidden-away wine.

Why do the darkling pines and the white
Delicate poplars weave their shady
Branches together, and the excited water
Work to curl itself around us?

Bring some roses, already turning dark,
And cardamom and wines; being rich
And young, we have to trust the dark threads
Of the Three Sisters are still unbroken.

You'll soon lose your cunningly acquired
Strips of woods, the estate by the yellow
Tiber, the Roman house, its silver and gold,
To some miserable heir, and it's over.

Whether we descend from the great houses,
Or drift unprotected under the naked
Sky, it's all one; we are sacrifices
To Death, not well known for compassion.

We are obliged and herded. The lot is
Inside the urn; the ball with our number
Will roll out. And what we'll get
Is an everlasting absence from home.

Book 2, Number 3

POEM FOR ARTEMIS

Doorkeeper of mountains and oak groves,
You who, when girls call three
Times to you as they are about to
Give birth, slip them past death.

A great mountain pine shades my roof; I give
This tree to you, and joyfully each November
I'll pour blood from a young boar on its ground,
A boar just learning to thrust his tusks to the side.

Book 3, Number 22

GRIEVING TOO LONG

Clouds do not send their rain down endlessly
On the rough-whiskered fields, and obstinate
Gales do not work up the Caspian Sea
The whole winter, nor in Armenia, dear friend,

Do glaciers remain there inert month
After month, and those oak-forested headlands
Facing the Adriatic don't have winds
Stripping leaves from branches all winter.

But you still weepily carry on about
The initiate in love you lost; your moans do
Not end even when the Western Star rises,
Nor when the Morning Star hurries away at dawn.

And yet that old man Nestor, who had lived three
Lives, did not mourn his son forever;
When they lost Troilus the lovable, his
Phrygian sisters and parents did not go on

And on. So it's good to check your endless
Lamentations; instead, let's take note of the gains
That our Caesar, called the Augustus, has
Made in the world—some Turkish peaks

Are lower now, the Euphrates waters are
A bit more constrained, the Medes are part
Of the Empire these days, and the Scythians riding
Over the steppes are, in fact, no longer nomads.

Book 2, Number 9

LET'S DO THIS POEM

Being a big favorite of the Muses, I'll appeal to
The winds to carry my depression off
To the seas of Crete. Which bearded German king,
Looking up at the Great Bear, worries us, or what disaster

Threatens Tiridatias in Persia, it's all
One with me. Giver of new poems,
Lover of the clear springs, weave some
Ornate lines as a gift for Lucius.

If you don't come, none of my honoring
Will take hold. Let's do this in Alcaic meter,
With its sonorities; you and your sisters, do
Come, let's make this boy immortal.

Book 1, Number 26

GHALIB

GHALIB IS IMPISH, reckless, obsessed with titles and distinctions, roguish, a breaker of religious norms, a connoisseur of sorrow, and a genius. He knows all the old poems of love and says:

> While telling the story, if each eyelash does not drip with blood
> You're not telling a love story, but a tale made for the kids.

Delhi, in his time (the mid-nineteenth century), had a lively culture and a vigorous tradition of poetry recitals, or mushiras, sponsored by the Mughal emperor. Ghalib's poems veered away from the traditional poetics clichés of the time, and were thought to be difficult.

> I have to write what's difficult; otherwise it's difficult to write.

Ghalib was a Muslim, and yet the wine he drank was not symbolic:

> Just put a wineglass and some wine in front of me;
> Words will fall out of my mouth like apple blossoms.

Ghalib's lines, so elegant and sparse, stretch the muscles that we use for truth, muscles we rarely use:

> My destiny did not include reunion with my Friend.
> Even if I lived a hundred years this failure would be the same.

It is as though when Kabir writes a letter to God, God always answers. We could say that when Ghalib writes a letter to God, God doesn't answer. Ghalib says:

> When I look out, I see no hope for change.
> I don't see how anything in my life can end well.

Ghalib's tart, spicy declaration of defeated expectations ranges over many subjects:

> Heart-sorrow eventually kills us, but that's the way the heart is.
> If there were no love, life would have done the trick.

This shift from the buoyant confidence of Kabir, Rumi, and Mirabai to the disappointment of Ghalib: what could it mean? Perhaps the turn to failure is natural six centuries after Rumi and four centuries after Kabir. Perhaps spiritual achievement involves more difficulty now than it did in the thirteenth century, or perhaps this change in tone has nothing to do with history at all. Perhaps Ghalib writes only six letters a day to God, instead of forty; perhaps he's distracted from the Road by the very love affairs that are to him the essence of the Road. He is a truth-teller around losing the Road. Awareness of this change was my first surprise.

We might look at the amazing way that Ghalib's ghazals are put together. No clear thread unites all the couplets. For example, if we return to the poem mentioned above, "My Spiritual State," which begins:

> When I look out, I see no hope for change.
> I don't see how anything in my life can end well.

we see a statement of theme. But a fresh theme, a little explosion of humor and sadness, arrives in the next stanza:

Their funeral date is already decided, but still
People complain that they can't sleep.

The third couplet, or *sher,* embarks on a third theme:

When I was young, my love-disasters made me burst out laughing.
Now even funny things seem sober to me.

It slowly becomes clear that we are dealing with a way of adventuring one's way through a poem utterly distinct from our habit of textual consistency in theme. Most of the poems we know, whether written in English, French, German, or Hausa, tend to follow from an idea clearly announced at the start. "Something there is that doesn't love a wall." The poet then fulfills the theme, often brilliantly, by drawing on personal experience, and by offering anecdotes, dreams, other voices: "Good fences make good neighbors." By the end, the theme is fulfilled. The ghazal form does not do that. It invites the reader to discover the hidden center of the poem or the hidden thought that ties it all together, a hidden center unexpressed by the poet himself or herself. I find this delicious. Moreover, when we arrive at the final *sher,* where, according to our typical expectations, the poet should clinch his argument, Ghalib often does exactly the opposite. He confounds everyone by making a personal remark:

Your talk about spiritual matters is great, O Ghalib.
You could have been thought of as a sage if you didn't drink all the
time.

GHALIB was born in Agra on December 27, 1797. His grandfather, who was Turkish, had come to India from Samarkand as a military mercenary, working for the governor of Punjab and other emperors. His two sons continued in this profession, which was a dangerous one. Ghalib's father died when he was four. His mother belonged to an affluent family in Agra, and Ghalib lived in that house with his maternal relatives. He began writing poems in Persian when he was nine; all his life he loved the Persian language best, but wrote hundreds of poems in Urdu as well. Ghalib was married at thirteen and, shortly after, moved to Delhi where he remained the rest of his life. Delhi was the capital of the Mughal Empire; the emperor, Bahadur Shah, was of course subordinate to the British at that time. Inside the palace, however, called the Red Fort, the emperor was the Majesty, the Shadow of God, the Refuge of the World. The emperor held elaborate poetry readings twice a month in the palace. Ghalib became immensely famous as a poet in Delhi, even though his poems were considered very difficult.

He led a rather rakish life. He had many debts with wine sellers. For making poetry and drinking wine, he best loved "cloudy days and moonlit nights." Late at night when he was writing, with the help of wine, he would tie a knot in his long sash each time he finished a stanza. Finally he would go to bed, and in the morning, as he untied each knot, he would recall the stanza and write it down. He got into a lot of trouble with the Islamic authorities, and was arrested for gambling as well. A pension had been awarded to Ghalib's father, and that pension came down to him; Ghalib spent much time over the years making sure this pension continued.

In 1857, all that period of poetry readings and social lightheartedness came crashing down. The Delhi revolt against the British started in May of 1857. The rebels invaded the city, killed many English soldiers and officials, and razed their houses. The English took up position outside the city and four months later recaptured it with great brutality. They retook the Red Fort, flattening houses in a wide area around it in order to have the space clear for cannon. They began hanging Indians suspected of treason and ultimately hanged over 20,000 people. At one point, Colonel Brown began to call in persons of importance and question them. Most arrived dressed very soberly.

Ghalib arrived wearing red and yellow clothes and a conical hat. Colonel Brown asked, "Are you a Muslim?" "I'm half a Muslim." "How can that be?" "I don't eat pork, but I do drink." Colonel Brown was apparently amazed at this sort of reply, and questioned him no further.

Ghalib remained inside his own house, living very cautiously: "Death is cheap," he said, "and food expensive." During this time, he was often ill, had severe depressions, and was eventually bedridden with sores and swelling all over his body. Many of his poems had been lost. The poetry readings and the "exciting life" ended, and he still had twelve more years to live. But everything had changed. Nonetheless he went on writing his poems and continued to become embroiled in literary controversies. Ghalib died in 1869 and was given an official Sunni burial. His wife died exactly a year later.

My last breath is ready to go, is leaving.
And now, friends, God, only God exists.

All of the following translations of Ghalib have been done with the generous collaboration of Sunil Dutta.

WHEN THE DAY COMES

One can sigh, but a lifetime is needed to finish it.
We'll die before we see the tangles in your hair loosened.

There are dangers in waves, in all those crocodiles with their
    jaws open.
The drop of water goes through many difficulties before it becomes
    a pearl.

Love requires waiting, but desire doesn't want to wait.
The heart has no patience; it would rather bleed to death.

I know you will respond when you understand the state of my soul,
But I'll probably become earth before all that is clear to you.

When the sun arrives the dew on the petal passes through existence.
I am also me until your kind eye catches sight of me.

How long is our life? How long does an eyelash flutter?
The warmth of a poetry gathering is like a single spark.

O Ghalib, the sorrows of existence, what can cure them but death?
There are so many colors in the candle flame, and then the day comes.

THE CLAY CUP

If King Jamshid's diamond cup breaks, that's it.
But my clay cup I can easily replace, so it's better.

The delight of giving is deeper when the gift hasn't been demanded.
I like the God-seeker who doesn't make a profession of begging.

When I see God, color comes into my cheeks.
God thinks—this is a bad mistake—that I'm in good shape.

When a drop falls in the river, it becomes the river.
When a deed is done well, it becomes the future.

I know that Heaven doesn't exist, but the idea
Is one of Ghalib's favorite fantasies.

LEFTOVERS IN THE CUP

For my weak heart this living in the sorrow house is more than
     enough.
The shortage of rose-colored wine is also more than enough.

I'm embarrassed, otherwise I'd tell the wine server
That even the leftovers in the cup are, for me, enough.

No arrow comes flying in; I am safe from hunters.
The comfort level I experience in this cage is more than enough.

I don't see why the so-called elite people are so proud
When the ropes of custom that tie them down are clear enough.

It's hard for me to distinguish sacrifice from hypocrisy,
When the greed for reward in pious actions is obvious enough.

Leave me alone at the Zam Zam Well; I won't circle the Kaaba.
The wine stains on my robe are already numerous enough.

If we can't resolve this, today will be like the Last Day.
She is not willing and my desire is more than strong enough.

The blood of my heart has not completely exited through my eyes.
O death, let me stay awhile, the work we have to do is abundant
     enough.

It's difficult to find a person who has no opinion about Ghalib.
He is a good poet, but the dark rumors about him are more than
     enough.

MY DESTINY

My destiny did not include reunion with my Friend.
Even if I lived a hundred years this failure would be the same.

Your promise determined my life; but it was not believable.
If I had believed it, I would have died of joy anyway.

What kind of friendship is this when friends give advice?
I wish they knew healing or simple, ordinary sympathy.

Heart-sorrow eventually kills us, but that's the way the heart is.
If there were no love, life would have done the trick.

This night of separation, whom can I tell about it?
I think death would be better, because at least it doesn't repeat.

Your hesitation indicates that the thread you had tied is weak;
You would never have broken the thread had it been strong.

Ask my heart sometime about your arrow shot from a loose bow.
It would not have hurt so much if it had actually gone through.

Rocks are hard, so they don't cry, but if your pain
Were genuine, Ghalib, it would make even rocks cry.

After my death, my reputation worsened. Maybe if I had just
    drowned
In a river, and had no tomb, they would have let Ghalib alone.

This great one, who can possibly see her? She is this One.
With just a hint of two, we might have achieved a meeting.

Your talk about spiritual matters is great, O Ghalib.
You could have been thought of as a sage if you didn't drink all
the time.

QUESTIONS

Since nothing actually exists except You,
Then why do I keep hearing all this noise?

These magnificent women with their beauty astound me.
Their side glances, their eyebrows, how does all that work? What is it?

These palm trees and these tulips, where did they come from?
What purpose do they serve? What are clouds and wind?

We hope for faithfulness and loyalty from people.
But people don't have the faintest idea what loyalty is.

Good rises from good actions, and that is good.
Beyond that, what else do saints and good people say?

I am willing to give up my breath and my life for You,
Even though I don't know the first thing about sacrifice.

The abundant objects of the world mean nothing at all!
But if the wine is free, how could Ghalib hang back?

DON'T SKIMP WITH ME TODAY

For tomorrow's sake, don't skimp with me on wine today.
A stingy portion implies a suspicion of heaven's abundance.

The horse of life is galloping; we'll never know the stopping place.
Our hands are not touching the reins nor our feet the stirrups.

I keep a certain distance from the reality of things.
It's the same distance between me and utter confusion.

The scene, the one looking and the ability to see are all the same.
If that is so, why am I confused about what is in front of me?

The greatness of a river depends on what it shows to us.
If we separate it into bubbles and waves, we are lost.

She is not free from her ways to increase her beauty.
The mirror she sees is on the inside of her veil.

What we think is obvious is so far beyond our comprehension.
We are still dreaming even when we dream we are awake.

From the smell of my friend's friend I get the smell of my friend.
Listen, Ghalib, you are busy worshiping God's friend.

MY SPIRITUAL STATE

When I look out, I see no hope for change.
I don't see how anything in my life can end well.

Their funeral date is already decided, but still
People complain that they can't sleep.

When I was young, my love disasters made me burst out laughing.
Now even funny things seem sober to me.

I know the answer—that's what keeps me quiet.
Beyond that it's clear I know how to speak.

Why shouldn't I scream? I can stop. Perhaps
The Great One notices Ghalib only when he stops screaming.

This is the spiritual state I am in:
About myself, there isn't any news.

I do die; the longing for death is so strong it's killing me.
Such a death comes, but the other death doesn't come.

What face will you wear when you visit the Kaaba?
Ghalib, you are shameless even to think of that.

MY HEAD AND MY KNEES

If I didn't cry all the time, my house would still be desolate.
The ocean is huge and empty, just like the desert.

Am I to complain about the narrowness of my heart?
It's unbelieving; no matter what happened, it would have been confused.

If I were patient for a lifetime, the Doorkeeper would surely let me in.
The doorkeeper of your house could model itself on such a heart.

Before anything, there was God; had there been nothing, there would
    have been God.
It was because I lived that I died. If I had never lived, what would
    have become of me?

Sorrow stunned my head; so why should I feel bad about my beheading?
If it hadn't been detached, it would be resting on my knees anyway.

Ghalib died centuries ago. But we still remember his little questions:
"What is before God?" "If I had never been born, how would that be?"

SOME EXAGGERATIONS

The world I see looks to me like a game of children.
Strange performances and plays go on night and day.

King Solomon's throne is not a big thing to me.
I hear Jesus performed miracles, but I'm not interested.

The idea that the world exists is not acceptable to me.
Illusion is real, but not the things of the world.

The desert covers its head with sand when I appear with my troubles.
The river rubs its forehead in the mud when it sees me.

Don't ask me how I am when I am parted from you.
I notice that your face turns a little pale when you're near me.

People are right to say that I love looking at myself, but sitting
In front of me is a beauty whose face is bright as a mirror.

Just put a wineglass and some wine in front of me;
Words will fall out of my mouth like apple blossoms.

People imagine that I hate, but it's merely jealousy.
That's why I scream: "Don't say her name in my presence!"

Faith pulls me in one direction, but disbelief pulls me in another.
The Kaaba stands far behind me, and the Church stands next to me.

I am a lover; therefore, charming a woman is my work.
When she is near me, Laila makes fun of Majnoon.

The time of reunion brings happiness rather than death.
When reunion came, I remembered the night of parting.

We have a sea of blood now with large waves.
I am content with it; I know worse could happen.

My hands move with difficulty, but at least my eyes are lively.
Just leave the glass and the wine jug standing where they are.

Ghalib is a Muslim also, so we know a lot of each other's secrets.
Please don't speak badly of Ghalib when I'm around.

HAFEZ

As we read a Hafez poem, we are tasting some sweetness that has been preserved by lovers and poets for a thousand years. Hafez's poetry is so amazing that some Persians consider it another thing entirely—something more complicated than poetry. He achieves drunkenness through sobriety, and a wildness through perfect form. Hafez often stretches his poem far back into time, into "Pre-Eternity."

> I have dropped in a heap on the earth, crying,
> In the hope that I will feel a touch of His hand . . .
>
> How blessed is the man who, like Hafez,
> Has tasted in his heart the wine made before Adam.

A poem of Hafez's moves steadily forward, somewhat like a Bach prelude; it reaches into the invisible world with its first note, and the low notes bring up the endless sorrow of life on earth. The left hand goes on talking of failure and repentance, and the light, quick right hand talks about the magnificence of poetry and religion, of the side glances given to us by God. Both hands together move toward a perfection that belongs more to angels than to human beings.

> Your perch is on the lote tree in Paradise,
> Oh wide-seeing hawk. What are you doing
> Crouching in this mop closet of calamity?

Hafez wrote about 480 ghazals. Inside them, he sometimes converses with other poets of his time, embedding phrases from another person's poem. In that way he honors other poets, and the poets could be said to be working on some huge poem together. It is as if Blake had found a community of forty other poets in England, who also worked on the poems of Eternity. Such was the immense spiritual culture of Persia in the fourteenth century.

Anne Marie Schimmel mentions that we can feel in each stanza of Hafez the smoke of this world and the clarity of the spiritual world. He is fond of the resources of the Islamic creation myth. A Hafez stanza may contain one elaborate Islamic doctrine after another, summed up swiftly like crystals formed under great pressure. He adopts the metaphors of the old Zoroastrian religion:

Last night I heard angels pounding on the door
Of the tavern. They had been kneading clay and they
Threw the clay of Adam in the shape of a wine cup.

Priests of the Zoroastrian religion sold wine at the temple, and so the words *tavern* and *wine* in his work delicately refer to the esoteric religion of love that we know in Western culture from the troubadours. He won't accept the fear of women that is such a striking tone of the Islamic mullahs. He reports in one poem that a "wild daughter has shown up missing."

Reason is lost with her . . . beware, your sleep may not be safe.
She is a night-woman of sharp taste, delicate, rosy . . .
If you should happen to find her, please bring her to Hafez's house.

HAFEZ was born in Shiraz, southwest of Tehran, probably in A.D. 1320 (the year before Dante died). His father, who was a coal merchant, read the Koran to him, and the boy began to memorize it and many poems of earlier poets as well. His pen name was Hafez, which means someone who has memorized the Koran. He had to leave school in order to help support the family, working in a drapery shop and a bakery. He probably worked as a copyist too. The library in Tashkent has a copy of Amir Khusrau's *Kamsa* in Hafez's hand, dated February 9, 1355. He learned mathematics and astronomy, as well as Arabic and Turkish.

The story goes that one day he fell in love with the daughter of a wealthy man when delivering bread to their house. It wasn't a successful courtship, but he began to write poems at this time. Eventually his poetry became very famous. Several kings, including the emperor of the Bahmanid kingdom in south India, invited him to live there, but he accepted none of the invitations. We do know that he was married, that he had children; he wrote an elegy for his son who died in 1362.

During his lifetime, Tamburlane's invasion from the north was proceeding. He reached Shiraz in 1387, the same year in which he and his army massacred 70,000 people in Isfahan. Tamburlane stayed for two months in Shiraz. A well-known stanza of Hafez went:

For the Hindu mole of that Shirazy Turk who attracts
Our hearts, I would give all of Samarkand and Bokhara.

Tamburlane called for Hafez and said something like: "Do you realize how much wealth and effort I have spent in order to make Bokhara and Samarkand magnificent cities, and you're going to give all that away for a mole?"

Hafez was clearly in danger. He said, "Well, it's by generosity of that sort that I've been reduced to the state that you see me in now." The wit of the answer pleased Tamburlane, and he said something like, "Send this man home with an escort."

Hafez's grasp of metaphor is so delicate and sure that several points of view exist together within a single stanza. He wove the many threads of the Persian poetic tradition into a continuous fabric. Most houses in Iran today will have the collected poems of Hafez on the dining room table. In some families, it is treated as the Chinese used to treat the I Ching; when a family has a problem, they open Hafez's poems at random and see what the ghazal says.

He was an enemy of the mullahs and the ascetics; he makes that clear in virtually every poem. He declares himself on the side of the *rends,* the wild ones or the reprobates, those who wanted to avoid praise for their goodness. He also leaned toward the *malamats,* who would attract public blame in order to lessen self-esteem.

The best supposition is that Hafez died in Shiraz in 1389. At that time there was a serious question as to whether the religious authorities would allow his body to be buried in a Muslim graveyard. It is told that the main mullah of Shiraz had several hundred stanzas of Hafez copied out on small pieces of paper, which were then put into an urn; he ordered a small boy to pick one of them out. The boy picked out this one:

When Hafez's coffin comes by, it'll be all right
To follow behind. Although he is
A captive of sin, he's on his way to the Garden.

That settled it.

All the following ghazals have been done with the generous help of Leonard Lewisohn.

AS RICH AS SOLOMON

Don't expect obedience, promise-keeping, or rectitude
From me; I'm drunk. I have been famous for carrying
A wine pitcher around since the First Covenant with Adam.

That very moment when I cleansed myself in the Spring
Of Love, that very day I said four times
Over the world, as over a corpse, "God is great!"

Give me some wine so I can pass on news of the mystery
Of Fate, and whose face it is with whom I have fallen
In love, and whose fragrance has made me drunk.

The mountain's withers are actually tinier than
The withers of an ant. You who love the fragrance of wine,
Don't lose hope about the door of mercy being open.

Except for the nodding narcissus blossom — may no
Evil eye touch it — no creature has ever been
Really comfortable beneath this turquoise dome.

May my soul be sacrificed to your mouth, because
In the Garden of Contemplation, no bud has ever
Been created by the Gardener of the World sweeter than yours.

Purely because of his love for you, Hafez became
As rich as Solomon; and from his union with you,
Like Solomon, he has nothing but wind in his hands.

#21

THE CRIES WE MAKE

No one has seen your face, and yet a thousand
Doorkeepers have been appointed. You are a closed rose,
And yet a hundred nightingales have arrived.

I may be a long way from you. Let's pray to God
That no human being may be far! But I know
Hope is at hand for a close union with you.

If I should find myself in your neighborhood one day,
That's not strange. For there are in this country,
Thousands of people like me who are strangers.

Is there any lover whose darling never threw
A fond look at his face? There is no pain in you.
With enough pain, the doctor would be here.

In the business of love, there's no great distinction between
The Sufi house and the tavern; in every spot of the universe,
Light shines out from the face of the Friend.

There where the work of the Muslim cloister
Is celebrated, one finds as well the bell
Of the monk's cell and the name of the Cross.

The cries that Hafez has made all of his life
Have not gone to waste; a strange story has emerged
Inside those cries, and a marvelous way of saying.

#64

SITTING IN THE GRIEF HOUSE

Joseph the lost will return, Jacob should not
Sink into sadness; those who sit in the Grief
House will eventually sit in the Garden.

The grieving chest will find honey; do not let
The heart rot. The manic hysterical head
Will find peace—do not sink into sadness.

If the way the Milky Way revolves ignores
Your desires for one or two days, do not
Sink into sadness: all turning goes as it will.

I say to the bird: "As long as Spring
Baptizes the grass, the immense scarlet blossoms
Will continue to sway over your head."

Even if the flood of materialism
Drowns everything, do not sink into
Sadness, because Noah is your captain.

Do not sink into sadness, even though the mysteries
Of the other world slip past you entirely.
There are plays within plays that you cannot see.

When you are far out into the desert, longing
For the Kaaba, and the Arabian thornbush
Pierces your feet, do not sink into sadness.

Although the way station you want to reach
Is dangerous and the goal distant, do not
Sink into sadness: all roads have an end.

God knows our true spiritual state: separated
From Him and punished by rivals. Still do not
Sink into sadness. God is the one who changes conditions.

Oh Hafez in the darkness of poverty and in
The solitude of the night, as long as you can sing
And study the Koran, do not sink into sadness.

#250

THE FIVE DAYS REMAINING

The goods produced in the factories of space and time
Are not all that great. Bring some wine,
Because the desirables of this world are not all that great.

Heart and soul are born for ecstatic conversation
With the soul of souls. That's it. If that fails,
Heart and soul are not in the end that great.

Don't become indebted to the Tuba and Sidra trees
Just to have some shade in heaven. When you look closely,
My flowering cypress friend, you'll see that these trees are not all
    that great.

The true kingdom comes to you without any breaking
Of bones. If that weren't so, achieving the Garden
Through your own labors wouldn't be all that great.

In the five days remaining to you in this rest stop
Before you go to the grave, take it easy, give
Yourself time, because time is not all that great.

You who offer wine, we are waiting on the lip
Of the ocean of ruin. Take this moment as a gift; for the distance
Between the lip and the mouth is not all that great.

The state of my being—miserable and burnt
To a crisp—is proof enough that my need
To put it into words is not all that great.

You ascetic on the cold stone, you are not safe
From the tricks of God's zeal: the distance between the cloister
And the Zoroastrian tavern is not after all that great.

The name of Hafez has been well inscribed in the books,
But in our clan of disreputables, the difference
Between profit and loss is not all that great.

#75

THE STAIN OF THE SEA

Last night I walked sleep-stained to the door
Of the tavern. My prayer rug
And my patched cloak were both stained with wine.

A young Zoroastrian boy stepped tauntingly
From the door; "Wanderer, wake up!"
He said, "The way you walk has the stain of sleep."

Our place is a tavern of ruin, so
Wash in clear water, so that you
Will not leave stains on this holy house.

You are yearning for sweet ruby lips; but
How long will you stain your spiritual
Substance with this sort of ruby?

The way station of old age is one
To pass cleanly; don't let the urgencies
Of youth stain the whiteness of your hair.

The great lovers have found their way
Into the deep ocean, and drowned
Without ever taking one stain from the sea.

Become clean and pure; come up
Out of nature's well! How could
Mud-stained water ever clean your face?

I said to the Soul of the World: "In springtime
Roses are red and drunk. Is there a big problem
Then if my book of roses is stained with wine?"

He replied: "Just cut out selling your friends
These subtle ideas." "Hafez," I said,
"The grace of the teacher is often stained with rebukes."

#414

THE LOST DAUGHTER

Listen to the cry going on at the marketplace
Where lovers lose their souls. All of you who live
In the alley and veer into sin, listen to the cry!

For several days now, the wild daughter has shown
Up missing. She's turned to her own
Affairs; no one knows where. Be alert!

She has a flowing, ruby-colored dress, and bubbles
In her hair. Reason is lost with her, so is learning.
Be careful, beware, your sleep may not be safe.

Whoever brings this bitter one to me, I'll
Repay with halvah as exquisite as your life.
Even though she's gone into the dark, go into hell after her.

She's a night-woman of sharp taste, delicate rosy
Color, and wild and drunk. If you should happen
To find her, please bring her to Hafez's house.

Fragment 19

GABRIEL'S NEWS

Come, come, this Parthenon of desire is set
On wobbly stones. Bring some wine,
For the joists of life are laid on the winds.

The man who can walk beneath the blue wheeling
Heavens and keep his clothes free of the dark
Of attachment—I'll agree to be the slave of his high will.

What can I tell you? Last night at the tavern,
When I was drunk and ruined, what glad news
Did Gabriel bring from the invisible world?

"Your perch is on the lote tree in Paradise,
Oh wide-seeing hawk, what are you doing
Crouching in this mop closet of calamity?

"People on the battlements of heaven are
Blowing a whistle to bring you back.
How does it happen that you tripped the noose?

"I'll give you this advice: Please learn it
And practice it well. These few words
Were given to me by my teacher on the Path.

"Don't expect this rotten world to be faithful
To you. The world we know is a hag
Who has known a thousand husbands.

"Don't let the sorrow of the world bite your soul.
Don't forget what I say. A traveler walking
The road taught me this subtlety about love:

"Be content with what you have now;
Smooth out your forehead. The door of free will
Has never been open for you or for me.

"The smile you see on the face of the rose implies
No promise has been given or kept. Let the nightingale
Lover cry. Cry on. This is a place of wailing."

You writers who write such bad poems, why
Do you envy Hafez so much? His grace of speech
That people love comes entirely from God.

#37

DECIDING NOT TO GO TO INDIA

To spend even one moment grieving about this world
Is a waste of time. Let's go and sell our holy
Robes for wine. A robe does not make one more holy.

It's impossible to buy in the crooked alleys where
The wine sellers hang out even one glass of wine
For a prayer mat. Even a master wouldn't take that deal.

The Zoroastrian tavern keeper says, "You're not worthy
To put your head down on the doorsill." What sort of view of heads
    is this
If the dust on a doorsill is worth more than a head?

Hidden inside the glory of kingship is always
The fear of assassination; a crown is a stylish hat,
But a head is too much to pay for it.

It seemed quite easy to put up with the ocean
And its torments, to receive a profit, but I was wrong;
A hurricane is too much to pay for a hundred pearls.

It's better if you turn your face away from your
Admirers; the joy the general receives from dominating
The world is not worth the suffering of the army.

It's best to aim—as Hafez does—for contentment and abandon
What everyone else wants; one grain of indebtedness
To the base life weighs more than a hundred bushels of gold.

#147

THE FISH IN DEEP WATER

When the one I love takes the cup of wine,
Then the shop of the idols falls to the ground.

I have dropped in a heap on the earth, crying,
In the hope that I will feel a touch of His hand.

I have fallen like a fish into deep water
In the hope that he will throw His net.

Whoever looks into His luminous eyes cries:
"Someone will soon be drunk, get the police!"

How blessèd is the man who, like Hafez,
Has tasted in his heart the wine made before Adam.

#144

THE NIGHT VISIT

Her hair was still tangled, her mouth still drunk
And laughing, her shoulders sweaty, the blouse
Torn open, singing love songs, her wine cup full.

Her eyes were looking for a drunken brawl, her lips
Ready for jibes. She sat down
Last night at midnight on my bed.

She put her lips close to my ear and said
In a whisper these words: "What is this?
Aren't you my old lover—Are you asleep?"

The friend of wisdom who receives
This wine that steals sleep is a traitor to love
If he doesn't worship that same wine.

Oh ascetics, go away. Stop arguing with those
Who drink the bitter stuff, because it was precisely
This gift the divine ones gave us in Pre-Eternity.

Whatever God poured into our goblet
We drank, whether it was the wine
Of heaven or the wine of drunkenness.

The laughter of the wine, and the disheveled curls
Of the Beloved—Oh how many nights of repentance—like
Hafez's—have been broken by moments like this?

#22

NIGHT AND DAWN

Human beings and spirits all take their sustenance
From the existence of love. The practice of devotion
Is a good way to arrive at happiness in both worlds.

Since you aren't worthy of the side glance
She gives, don't try for union. Looking directly
Into Jamshid's cup doesn't work for the blind.

Make an effort, oh Lordly Person, don't miss out
On getting a share of love. No one buys a slave
Who hasn't a single accomplishment of art or grace.

How long will you gobble down the wine of sunrise
And the sugar of dawn sleep? Ask for forgiveness
In the middle of the night and cry when dawn comes.

Come! And with the cash provided by your beauty
Buy the kingdom from us. Don't let this
Slip away; you will regret it if you do.

The prayers of the people who live in corners
Keep disaster away. Why don't you help us
With one single glance out of the corner of your eye?

Both union with you and separation from you
Confuse me. What can I do? You are not present
Nor are you utterly absent from my sight.

A thousand holy souls have been burned up
By this jealousy: you are every dawn and dusk
The candle that's lit in the center of a different group.

Since every bit of news I hear opens a different
Door to bewilderment, from now on I'll take
The road of drunkenness and the path of knowing nothing.

Come, come — the condition of the world as I see it
Is such that if you checked up on it,
You'd sip wine rather than the water of grief.

Because of the good offices of Hafez, we can
Still hope that on some moonlit night we'll
Be able to enjoy our love conversation once more.

ON THE WAY TO THE GARDEN

The garden is breathing out the air of Paradise today;
I sense this friend of heavenly
Nature, and myself, and the genius of the wine.

It's all right if the beggar claims to be a King
Today. His tent is a shadow thrown by a cloud;
The sown field is his room for receiving guests.

The meadow is composing a story of a spring day
In May; the person who knows lets the future
And its profits go and accepts the cash now.

Please don't imagine that your enemy will
Be faithful to you. The candle that stays lit
In the hermit's hut flickers out in the worldly church.

Make your soul strong then by letting it drink
The secret wine. You know that once we're dead,
This rotten world will press our dust into bricks.

My life is a black book. But don't rebuke
Me too much. No one can ever read
The words written on his own forehead.

When Hafez's coffin comes by, it'll be all right
To follow behind. Although he is
A captive of sin, he is on his way to the Garden.

#77

PERMISSIONS

Many of these translations originally appeared in the following books:

Basho: *Basho* (illustrated by Arthur Okamura) (San Francisco: Mudra, 1972).

Gunnar Ekelöf: *Friends, You Drank Some Darkness: Three Swedish Poets: Martinson, Ekelöf, and Tranströmer* (Boston: Beacan Press, 1975); *I Do Best Alone at Night* (with Christina Paulston) (Washington, D.C.: The Charioteer Press, 1968); *Late Arrival on Earth: Selected Poems of Gunnar Ekelöf* (with Christina Paulston) (London: Rapp & Carroll, 1967).

Ghalib: *The Lightning Should Have Fallen on Ghalib: Selected Poems of Ghalib* (with Sunil Dutta) (New York: Ecco Press, 1999).

Hafez: *The Soul Is Here for Its Own Joy: Sacred Poems from Many Cultures* (New York: Ecco Press, 1995).

Olav H. Hauge: *Trusting Your Life to Water and Eternity* (Minneapolis: Milkweed Editions, 1987).

Miguel Hernandez: *Miguel Hernandez and Blas de Otero: Selected Poems,* ed. Timothy Baland and Hardie St. Martin (Boston: Beacon Press, 1972).

Horace: *Horace, the Odes: New Translations by Contemporary Poets,* ed. J. D. McClatchy (Princeton, N.J.: Princeton University Press, 2002); *Horace's Poem on Anger* (Red Wing, Minn.: Red Dragonfly Press, 2000).

Issa: *Ten Poems by Issa* (illustrated by Arthur Okamura) (Point Reyes Station, Calif.: Floating Island Publications, 1992).

Rolf Jacobsen: *The Roads Have Come to an End Now: Selected and Last Poems of Rolf Jacobsen* (with Roger Greenwald and Robert Hedin) (Port Townsend, Wash.: Copper Canyon Press, 2001); *Twenty Poems of Rolf Jacobsen* (Madison, Minn.: Seventies Press, 1977).

Juan Ramón Jiménez: *Lorca and Jiménez: Selected Poems* (Boston: Beacon Press, 1973); *Forty Poems of Juan Ramón Jiménez* (Madison, Minn.: The Sixties Press, 1967).

Kabir: *The Kabir Book* (Boston: Beacon Press, 1977); *Try to Live to See This* (Denver: The Ally Press, 1976); *28 Poems* (New York: Siddha Yoga Dham, 1975); *The Fish in the Sea Is Not Thirsty* (Northwood Narrows, N.H.: Lillabulero Press, 1971).

Federico García Lorca: *Lorca and Jiménez: Selected Poems* (Boston: Beacon Press, 1973).

Antonio Machado: *Times Alone: Selected Poems of Antonio Machado* (Middletown, Conn.: Wesleyan University Press, 1983); *Times Alone* (Port Townsend, Wash.: Graywolf Press, 1982); *Twenty Proverbs* (Marshall, Minn.: Ox Head Press, 1981); *Canciones* (West Branch, Ia.: The Toothpaste Press, 1980); *I Never Wanted Fame* (St. Paul, Minn.: Ally Press, 1979).

Harry Martinson: *Friends, You Drank Some Darkness: Three Swedish Poets: Martinson, Ekelöf, and Tranströmer* (Boston: Beacon Press, 1975).

Mirabai: *Versions* (Penland, N.C.: Squid Ink, 1993); *Mirabai Versions* (The Red Ozier Press, 1980).

Pablo Neruda: *Neruda and Vallejo: Selected Poems* (with John Knoepfle and James Wright) (Boston: Beacon Press, 1971); *Twenty Poems of Pablo Neruda* (with James Wright) (Madison, Minn.: The Sixties Press, 1967).

Francis Ponge: *Ten Poems of Francis Ponge Translated by Robert Bly and Ten Poems of Robert Bly Inspired by the Poems of Francis Ponge* (Riverview, New Brunswick: Owl's Head Press, 1990).

Rainer Maria Rilke: *Selected Poems of Rainer Maria Rilke* (New York: Harper and Row, 1981); *October Day and Other Poems*

(Sebastopol, Calif.: Calliopea Press, 1981); *I Am Too Alone in the World* (New York: The Silver Hands Press, 1980); *The Voices* (Denver: The Ally Press, 1977); *Ten Sonnets to Orpheus,* printed in *Zephyrus Image Magazine* (1), 1972.

Rumi: *Night and Sleep* (with Coleman Barks) (Cambridge, Mass.: Yellow Moon Press, 1981); *When Grapes Turn to Wine* (Cambridge, Mass.: Yellow Moon Press, 1986).

Georg Trakl: *Twenty Poems of George Trakl* (with James Wright) (Madison, Minn.: The Sixties Press, 1961).

Tomas Tranströmer: *The Half-Finished Heaven: The Best Poems of Tomas Tranströmer* (St. Paul, Minn.: Graywolf Press, 2001); *Truth Barriers* (San Francisco: Sierra Club Books, 1980); *Friends, You Drank Some Darkness: Three Swedish Poets: Martinson, Ekelöf, and Tranströmer* (Boston: Beacon Press, 1975); *Night Vision* (Northwoods Narrows, N.H.: Lillabulero Press, 1971); *Twenty Poems of Tomas Tranströmer* (Madison, Minn.: The Seventies Press, 1970).

Cesar Vallejo: *Neruda and Vallejo: Selected Poems* (with John Knoepfle and James Wright) (Boston: Beacon Press, 1971); *Twenty Poems of Cesar Vallejo* (with John Knoepfle and James Wright) (Madison, Minn.: The Sixties Press, 1962).

We are grateful to these publishers and editors for permission to publish translations here.

INDEX

WALTER
PAYTON

GREAT AMERICAN SPORTS LEGENDS

WALTER PAYTON

◇

FOOTBALL'S SWEETEST SUPERSTAR

MIKE TOWLE

CUMBERLAND HOUSE
NASHVILLE, TENNESSEE

WALTER PAYTON: FOOTBALL'S SWEETEST SUPERSTAR
PUBLISHED BY CUMBERLAND HOUSE PUBLISHING
431 Harding Industrial Drive
Nashville, TN 37211

Copyright © 2000, 2005 by Mike Towle

This book was previously published as *I Remember Walter Payton.*

Cover design: Gore Studio, Inc.

Library of Congress Cataloging-in-Publication Data
Towle, Mike.
    Walter Payton : football's sweetest superstar / Mike Towle.
        p. cm. — (Great American sports legends)
    Includes bibliographical references and index.
    ISBN 1-58182-476-9 (pbk. : alk. paper)
    1.   Payton, Walter, 1954-1999—Juvenile literature. 2.   Football players—United States—Biography—Juvenile literature.   I. Title. II. Series.
    GV939.P39T695 2005
    796.332'092—dc22

                                                                                          2005018421

Printed in the United States of America
1 2 3 4 5 6 7—11 10 09 08 07 06 05

To Roy

CONTENTS

◇

ACKNOWLEDGMENTS

Many people went the extra yard in helping me to make this book a reality by opening doors that had appeared to be closed. First and foremost, my wife, Holley, and son, Andrew, posted their share of two-hundred-yard games in waiting patiently and being supportive while the midnight oil burned as I sequestered myself dozens of times to complete this book in a timely fashion. Thanks for standing by me, guys, and for giving me another chance to make up the lost family time.

Ron Pitkin, my publisher, and Mary Sanford, my editor, and all the gang at Cumberland House played a winning role, sometimes cheering me on from the sidelines and other times joining me in the huddle.

Thanks to all the folks who returned the phone calls and consented to interviews for this book, many of whom graciously allowed me to visit them in their offices or homes so I could take a good chunk out of their day or evening. A book like this depends heavily on networking. A number of the people I interviewed were instrumental in helping me to break the ice with others subsequently interviewed for this book. In that regard, special thanks go to Quin Breland, Gil Brandt, Don Pierson, Michael Silverman, Robert Brazile, Clyde Emrich, and Hub Arkush. Michael Arkush, one of my "writing partners in crime,"

was instrumental in helping me get in contact with Hub. Phil
Theobald opened up his book of contacts as well. Charles Boston,
Payton's first high school football coach, also led me in the right
directions.

Ken Valdiserri, former Bears director of marketing and broad-
casting, was a huge help during what for him was a turbulent
time that ultimately ended with the sun shining. Ken's dad, Roger
Valdiserri, was a mentor of mine at Notre Dame, and the entire
Valdiserri family is a class act. Bryan Harlan and Scott Hagel of
the Bears were a big help in digging out historical facts and tele-
phone numbers. Rich Dalrymple of the Dallas Cowboys and
Paula Martin and John Biolo of the Green Bay Packers helped put
me in touch with a number of players who played against Payton
in the National Football League.

Dan Barile and Greg Miller at WFLD Fox Television in
Chicago were kind enough to accommodate me for a few hours
while I reviewed videotape of the memorial service for Payton
held at Soldier Field.

Harold Bryant, mayor of Columbia, Mississippi, regaled me
with a bit of local knowledge of Payton's hometown and sur-
rounding area, as did Breland. At Jackson State University, Sam
Johnson and Patsy Johnson of the alumni office helped me track
down some of Payton's former college teammates. One of Payton's
high school teammates, Forrest Dantin, dug out his high school
yearbook for me. Bill Magrane of the Bears gave me a copy of the
book *The Bears: A 75-Year Celebration*. Thanks, Bill.

Nothing in my life worth talking about would be possible
without the intervention of Jesus Christ in my life. If you don't
know the Lord and are willing to spend only five minutes giving
Him a shot, please use that time to read 1 John 2. It could change
your life.

INTRODUCTION

Walter Payton passed away in 1999, on November 1. That's All Saints' Day on the Christian calendar, and Payton was seen as somewhat of a saint in the eyes of most people whose lives brushed his.

Payton's death at the ripe young age of forty-five wasn't sudden. It came at the end of a months-long battle with his health. The first public sign of trouble came late in 1998 when Payton was becoming noticeably thinner to family and friends, and the whites of his eyes were turning to yellow. On February 2, 1999, Payton finally went public with the bad news no one had ever expected, or wanted, to hear: He announced he had primary sclerosing cholangitis (PSC), a rare progressive disorder that affects about three in one hundred thousand adults. PSC involves the accumulation of bile resulting from the narrowing of inflamed and scarred bile ducts. It often leads to cirrhosis and liver failure, although it is not caused by alcohol consumption, viral hepatitis, or the use of anabolic steroids.

Eleven years removed from his last game as a Chicago Bear, Walter "Sweetness" Payton was playing in a Super Bowl of his own, with his life on the line. A liver transplant was needed to save his life, and to everyone but his closest confidants, it would

only be a matter of time before Payton would get a new liver and bounce back to become the same ol' zestful, caring, considerate, fun-loving Walter, up to his old jokes and back out enthusiastically taking care of all his obligations and meeting new friends all along the way. But what few people knew in the last few months, and what Payton zealously guarded from public consumption, was that he was dying. No turning or running back. A visit in May to the Mayo Clinic for an exam to determine his suitability for a new liver turned up a malignant tumor on his bile duct. His cancer took him off the list for eligible liver recipients, and without a new liver he was too weak to undergo chemotherapy. It was the classic Catch-22 scenario, and it had caught No. 34 from behind. No stiff-arm, stutter step, or flying leap over the goal-line defense was going to bail him out of this one.

There's nothing like a death to bring out the best in what is remembered and said about the deceased. That's when a person's stock goes up, when all the warts and waywardness of a person's past are forgotten, to be replaced for posterity's sake by glowing faux testimonials and fudged praises. A celebrity who is a five on the overall popularity scale of one to ten becomes a seven, or even an eight, in dying. Death can do more for a person's reputation than the best PR flack in the world could possibly manufacture.

Then there's Walter Payton. He was a man extremely generous with his time and affection, and this was a reality when he was alive. He lived and accepted his life as a genuine role model, whether it meant taking the time to help a friend in need or giving his best to his team, the Chicago Bears, through thirteen seasons and about two hundred games. Payton was the people's superstar, a touchable icon who would often stop and chat with fans at his restaurant, in a Chicago mall, or in the pits at an auto race. He was serious about the game and in honoring his commitments, but he never took himself seriously and was usually the first with a laugh, joke, or prank in a group of three, thirty, or

three thousand. We knew and acknowledged all this and so much more when he was still alive. So, in death, we remember Walter Payton for how he lived his life, and the ways in which he triumphed, without need for any hyperbole or fudge. This guy was the real deal, a ten in life as well as a ten in heaven.

WALTER
PAYTON

OUT OF MISSISSIPPI

COLUMBIA IS A QUIET KIND of backwoods town in south-central Mississippi, but not backwoods in the sense of being a hick town. Literally, it is backwoods, surrounded by thousands of acres of timber, which is the source of one of the area's biggest industries—logging. Columbia's population hovers at around eight thousand, and downtown is a quaint reminder of small-town Americana. A stately courthouse occupies one end of a main street lined with family-owned businesses, retail shops, and tidy bank buildings, and where diagonal parking along the street is an everyday convenience.

Columbia is the state's fourth-oldest municipality, founded in 1819. It is part of Marion County, which touts itself as a place "where history meets the future." One of the local department stores lives up to that motto, retaining a piece of history with its pneumatic money tubes. The owner of one of the state's oldest hardware stores, situated in Columbia, says, "If we ain't got it, you probably don't need it." The cost of living here is cheap, and the people are friendly, although if you occasionally need a quick-

oned pace of life, Jackson is only about ninety miles away to the north, with New Orleans less than two hours away to the south.

This is where Walter Payton grew up in the sixties and early seventies, at a time and in a place where racial unrest was almost every bit as hot as it was elsewhere in Mississippi. This isn't exactly Mississippi Burning a generation and a half removed, but embers warm to the touch still lurk beneath the surface. A shopping center on the southern outskirts of town is right across the highway from where Ku Klux Klan meetings attended by hundreds were held in a field now occupied by various establishments that include a Comfort Inn and gas station/convenience store. Over the years Mississippi's state capital has twice made temporary stops in Columbia, where whites to blacks number about 60-40, and where perhaps the greatest football player in National Football League history was born.

Payton was the youngest of Peter and Alyne Payton's three children, four years junior to Eddie and three years younger than sister Pam. As everyone in Columbia knows, Walter—or "Spider Man" as he called himself in his youth—played in the band before he played organized football. Drums; bass, snare, bongo—he loved them all. It wasn't until he got to all-black Jefferson High School that he began playing football alongside the likes of good chum Edward "Sugar Man" Moses and under the tutelage of head coach Charles Boston. Payton switched schools midway through his junior year, moving on to Columbia High School, which in October 1969 was court-ordered to integrate. Jefferson's students and faculty were absorbed into Columbia High in January 1970 in a move that went rather smoothly, disappointing the many media and their cameras that had parked outside the school in anticipation of unrest giving way to action. Payton quickly made friends with his new schoolmates, a process quickened that spring when his new teammates saw in practice what "Spider Man" could do with a football, or even just a stiff forearm.

Payton played one season at Columbia before graduating in 1971 and moving on to Jackson State. Let the record show that he was one of three Paytons who graduated from Columbia that spring, although twin brothers Eli and Levi Payton were supposedly not related to Walter, according to one of his high school teammates. Of course, Payton was a man among boys on the football field for Columbia, leading the Wildcats to an 8-2 record in 1970. Payton also played basketball at Columbia, although, interestingly, he wasn't voted Most Athletic by classmates. That honor went to Steve Stewart, one of two all-state players on the football team (yes, Payton was the other and, yes, Stewart is white). Among Payton's other high school activities listed in the Cohian 1971 (Columbia's yearbook) were choir, science club, French club, Hi-Y, baseball, and track.

Major-college coaches didn't flock to Columbia to scout Payton. Few had even heard of him, mostly because media attention accorded the Wildcats was scant. Payton shared much of Columbia's ball-toting duties with Moses and quarterback Archie Johnson, while head coach Tommy Davis fiddled with his offense so as to feature a different threat each week to keep opponents off-balance. The near-obscurity factor followed Payton to Jackson State, one of a number of all-black football programs like Grambling State, rich in talent and long on style, that played beneath the radar of the Notre Dames, Alabamas, Southern Cals, and Nebraskas of the world.

By the time Walter was a senior at Columbia, older brother Eddie was already firmly entrenched up the road at Jackson State, although it was never a given that his younger brother would follow him there. Ultimately, however, he did, along with the likes of his good friend Sugar Man. At Jackson State, Walter Payton met up with the future-NFL likes of Robert Brazile, Jerome Barkham, Vernon Perry, Ricky Young, and Jackie Slater. Payton finished his Jackson State career with 3,563 rushing yards, averaging 6.1 yards a carry, and he scored

sixty five touchdowns. He merited serious Heisman Trophy consideration in 1974, his senior season, although he never really had a chance considering the backdrop against which he played.

◇

One of Payton's best friends growing up in Columbia, Mississippi, was **EDWARD "SUGAR MAN" MOSES,** who now pastors a Methodist church in Biloxi. Moses was Payton's backfieldmate in high school, although they had known each other long before they got to high school.

When I met Walter and his family, we were about five or six years old, and we went through school together. We lived in an area called Smith Quarters in Columbia, and they lived down the street from us. They moved over around Jefferson High School and so did we, but about two miles from them.

I had always been one of the fastest kids in class, and I always had to race him. Later on we used to play football at Jefferson High School—it contained all the grades. He was one of the good players, and I was one of the good players. We knew he was a strong guy, but he was sort of a home person in a close-knit family. I was, too, but I got out into the community and played more. Then he got started playing in the band. He played drums and bongo. He also played the piano because they had one at home, and he learned to play some songs there.

The guy was always quiet and reserved, sort of living as the second brother behind an older brother who's famous, and I would imagine in his mind he was going to go beyond Eddie's achievements. When we got into high school, we took shop and a lot of other classes together. We were both playful and would do some pranks. When we got to be juniors in high school, he had pumped iron throughout the summer while the rest of us were playing baseball. He played some baseball, but he spent a lot of time pumping iron because his brother was doing a lot of that in

college, and he was bringing back a higher-scale athletic life to him. When the rest of us were getting high school-type training, he was getting college-type training. And he was keeping it to himself. He got really big and strong. When we got back to school that fall, where you had those hydraulic things that open the doors to the main building, those things sticking out, he would say, "Man, I can knock that thing off," and I said, "Don't do that!" We looked around and he hit it, boom, with his hand, and those things jumped out of it. Then we had to run and hide. We were good kids, but we would do some mischievous things, too.

◇

Moses and Payton did a lot of other things together with their friends, such as joining the Boy Scouts for several years and camping out on the outskirts of Columbia, sometimes with a scoutmaster present and sometimes without, as **MOSES** elaborates:

We went camping sometimes up in Harmony, on some of the people's property in the woods up there. We also went to the riverbank, to what we called the sandbar, just down from Smith Quarter. One time on the banks, we could hear the dogs at night, and, just for a sense of intrigue, we proclaimed that they were wild dogs or wolves coming after us. We had to have at least one weapon, and I happened to have a pistol with me. So we were all walking toward the sounds of the dogs, and what it was was someone training their hunting dogs. Everybody in our little group was behind me, and all of a sudden the dog could see us or smell us fifty yards away, and he let out with one of those yips, like "Wooof, wooof, wooof," and everyone turned around. I started shooting in the air, and we ran all the way back to the camp and lay down. We were really scared, because there really were some wild dogs out there.

When we were camping in the woods, there was stuff we liked to do, like knowing where Mr. Wilson kept his bootleg

beer it wasn't illegal in those days. He knew people were watching him, so he would hide it in a different place every time to keep you off-balance. One time, we found where he hid it and we were talking about it in school on Monday. So me and another guy went to get it. I don't know why we thought we could sneak it into school. We never thought about the fact that this beer had a pretty strong aroma. We ran out during lunchtime, I think, to get it and bring it back. When we got back, the students were lined up going back into the rooms. We went around to a window in the room where Walter was, this big window, and we reached in through the window to give Walter this big cup of bootleg beer. While handing it through we spilled it all over the window. Me and this other guy ended up getting a whupping about it. Those were good days back in the old school.

◇

Payton and Moses both belonged to faithful, churchgoing families, **MOSES** said, and that's a part of themselves they always kept close by, even at football games:

We always had our Bibles with us before the game in the bag that we carried. We would open it up and read during quiet time. His had a white cover and mine a black cover. Imitation leather, with zippers. They were both King James Bibles.

◇

FORREST DANTIN, an attorney who still lives in Columbia, was one of Payton's classmates and teammates at Columbia High School, which integrated in 1970, halfway through Payton's junior year, and, in so doing, attracted its share of media attention, with racial strife still lurking beneath the surface in a South that had been embroiled in racial controversy through the sixties:

The only thing that happened the first day of school that year was when five guys stood outside for about an hour or two and protested, and they weren't even students of Columbia High at that time. And that's the story Newsweek ran. I think they had actually gone to private schools themselves. This actually happened in January because the order to integrate had come down in October.

Before we were integrated, we hadn't really heard much about Walter. We'd heard that they had a really good running back coming over from Jefferson, and I actually knew Eddie Payton. I didn't know him well, but he came down from Jackson State a couple of days before we started spring practice. I guess he was there to run on the track or the field, and he wound up in a game of touch football with us. Nobody could catch him. He was so much faster than anybody else on our team and so much quicker. It was unbelievable. And if you've seen Eddie now, he's not a really big guy but back then he was just as muscled up as Walter. He just wasn't real tall.

◇

QUIN BRELAND has lived in Columbia, Mississippi, most of his life. He became one of Payton's football teammates when Columbia High School was integrated in January 1970 and Payton and other African Americans made the move from old Jefferson High School to Columbia High:

It was an interesting time in a lot of people's lives. All the national news media was here because we were one of the first schools in this area to integrate, and they thought there was going to be a lot of trouble. In fact, I think they were hoping there would be some trouble. People would ask me what I thought about it, what change I thought would come about, and I said I thought we would have a better football team, now that we're integrated. It was no big deal. People get along pretty

much in these little towns, and there wasn't anything to it. So the media packed up and left town because there were no confrontations.

It was a special time playing with Walter Payton, and I think we knew it at the time to some extent. I hadn't heard much about Walter before we were integrated, and recruiters didn't come here to look at us. I think Jackson State was the only school to offer him a full scholarship. Pearl River Junior College offered him a half-scholarship and I went down there and played, and I told the coach there, "Why in the world didn't you offer Walter a full scholarship?" and he said, "Well, I already have a running back." Imagine that.

We had a black quarterback (Archie Johnson), and I was the center. I was always glad to be on Walter's side in practice because it meant I wouldn't have to tackle him. He was a one-man show; you didn't have to do much; just snap the ball, and it would be handed off to Walter, and then you could just stand around and watch him run. He was that good, that much above everyone else. He was a natural. There was no weight-training program in those days, but he looked as though he had been working out his whole life. One rumor was that after he got to Jackson State, they put him on a weight program and his thighs got so big that he couldn't cross his legs.

◇

Payton and Moses started their high school football days at all-black Jefferson High School and then moved over to previously all-white Columbia when it was integrated halfway through their junior year. The two good buddies and running-back companions had little trouble proving their merits as starters when they got to Columbia, although, as **MOSES** remembers, some changes were still in store:

He was a bigger back, stronger and with more power, and geared toward college and professional ball. By the time he played his

first year in high school, I was playing, too. They had some really good halfbacks, and he was one of them. Even though I was the smallest guy there, they stuck me at fullback. They did it because I could block real well. But I didn't get a chance to play at Jefferson very much. This was in the tenth grade. Then I started the next year. We played out of the T formation. Coach (Charles) Boston was confident in my blocking, and I did block. We did well, but we didn't win any championships or anything like that.

Then we went to Columbia and we thought Mr. Boston should have been the head coach, but they hired another white coach, Tommy Davis, so Walter and I boycotted. We just stayed out all the summer. Meanwhile, Coach Boston had been telling Coach Davis about these two backs, Walter Payton and "Sugar Man," all that time, but the boycott was the only thing we could do to draw attention to the fact that we thought Coach Boston should have gotten the head coach's job. Finally, after we had made our point, we decided it was time to join the team before things got too far along.

We ran from a split backfield, which allowed both of us to have halfback-type plays. That first game he was featured in was against Prentiss. I was upset because I hadn't run much, hadn't scored. Then the next game I got my chance, rushing eight times for something like 140 yards, and the competition was on. He and I were both wanting the ball, just like that bottle of wine, and the competition was on. I got thrown out of the Hazelhurst game for throwing an elbow on defense, and that was it for me. It was before the half, so Walter had the whole second half to move ahead of me, and he was getting better and better. Growing up with him, we didn't have any idea that he was that Walter Payton. He just kept growing right before your eyes.

◇

Spring football of 1970 brought players from the all-black Jefferson High School together with their white comrades at Columbia High for

the first time, and **DANTIN,** a tackle for Columbia High, said it didn't take long for everyone to make one another's acquaintance on the practice field:

In the first scrimmage we had, Walter just plowed over a guy we considered our best tackler—the guy was playing middle line-backer. He hit Walter like a ton of bricks and wrapped him up, and then the next thing everybody knew, Walter was gone. Right then we knew this guy was good.

We took advantage of Walter's size. People think of him as not being big, but in high school at that point in time he weighed 195 and the biggest guy on our team weighed 225. We had two guys that weighed about 225, and the rest of the tackles weighed maybe 200 tops. So, you know, being 195 was like a tackle going through a line. And he was undoubtedly the strongest guy on the team.

The game in which everybody knew for sure that he was good was when we played Prentiss, just up the highway. It's a big rivalry. Two different times in that game Walter just blew through a hole and was gone. One time it was about seventy yards and the other eighty-something yards. After that game Coach (Tommy) Davis came back and said, "Okay, fellows, everybody is going to be keyed on Walter next week. So, this coming week, we're going to work, it's going to be Sugar Man's (backfieldmate Edward Moses's) week." So we ran tailback plays all week to get ready for Tylertown, and Sugar Man ran all over them.

So then the next week, if I remember right, we played Warren Central, which is now a 5A school, and we were a 4A school—and probably ought to be a 3A school. Warren Central could have been a 5A school back then. They had beaten us a lot, including 38-0 the year before. This time Coach Davis said, "Okay, fellows, they're going to be looking for Walter and they're going to be looking for Sugar Man, so we're going to put Archie Johnson on them this week." Archie Johnson was our quarterback, and on the first play from scrimmage he ran all the way. After that nobody

knew what to expect from us. It was great. We had a ball. It was always fun. We'd go to away games and sing on the way back, mostly the Temptations as I remember.

It came down to where if we were to win our last game of the season, against Monticello, we would have won the South Little Dixie Conference title. But we lost in the last two minutes. We actually scored the winning touchdown, by Walter, but there was a late-hit penalty that called it back. We drove it back down to about the two, by which time Walter had gained something like 165 yards. After he pounded it back down to around the two, Coach Davis, who had been making great play-making decisions all year long—and this would have been one of them if it had worked out right—called a pass. We hadn't thrown the ball all night, even though Archie was a good passer. He got intercepted and that was it.

Sports coverage then wasn't what it is now. Out of curiosity I went back a year or two ago to look through the old newspapers from those years and I found where they had skipped two games. They didn't even put an article in there. People in town were really excited about us and everything, but Walter never got the attention he deserved. We had two guys on that team who made All-State that year. One was Walter and the other was Steve Stewart, who's now a golf coach in Texas.

◇

L. E. DANIELS was one of Walter Payton's teachers at both Jefferson and Columbia High Schools and probably knew the future football Hall of Famer as well as or better than any of the schools' teachers. Daniels coached Payton in basketball back at Jefferson and also taught classes such as civics, Mississippi history, government, and economics down through the years:

I knew Walter quite well. He had a great personality, and I never saw him angry. And he would never give up. In basketball, we

could be down ten or twenty points with two minutes to go, and he would still be fighting as hard as he could. I used to call him the big-eyed boy. Look at the pictures of him from high school, and you can see how there was so much white visible in his eyes.

He was an exciting ballplayer. He had good stiff-arms to ward people off and good speed. Pound for pound, though, I used to think Moses was the better player, but Walter was big for high school in those days, and Moses was just quick and could get knocked off his rocker a little easier.

Walter was quiet, shy, but would talk to you if you talked to him. And he called himself Spider Man because I think that was his favorite comic book. Classmates liked him. He took all his success well. It never went to his head. I never saw him critical of anybody. He would always praise somebody else. He'd always give someone else credit, such as his offensive linemen, and I noticed he kind of continued with that through to the pros. Walter didn't really develop until his brother, Eddie, got off the scene. He respected his brother, who was shorter. His brother helped him some, but Walter would go out and do a lot of things on his own to get better as a football player, and you don't see a lot of kids doing that.

Fine kid. Listened. A little above average for his grades. Asked questions. Would respond if you called on him. Completed his assignments and turned them in on time. Never disruptive. I might have had to chew him out a few times, but never had to send him home or give him detention. If you had tried to keep him after school, he probably would have ended up cracking you up.

◈

Count Columbia High School classmate and teammate **DANTIN** among those who, as it turns out, didn't know Walter as well as he thought he did. Not that Payton harbored any deep, dark secrets, only

that as friendly and outgoing as Payton was, he usually held a part of himself back, and sometimes it was hard to keep track of his whereabouts, as Dantin explains:

I had Walter in two or three classes—actually two classes and a library, but no one studied in the library. Walter was a real personable guy, and we liked sitting around talking to him. I'd be lying if I said we were close friends. I always kind of wondered who Walter's friends were. He was as friendly and upbeat as you'd want somebody to be, but he never seemed real close to anyone. He was bound to have had a girlfriend, big football star and nice-looking guy and all, but I never saw him with a steady girlfriend, although he may have had one. Walter told me one time he wasn't able to stay in shape because he was always going from one sport to another, but later I found out he used to go running in the woods up behind his house. He and Eddie used to do that for fun.

Part of the deal during high school was that while we had integrated schools, socially things were still pretty separate. That's one of the reasons I didn't see Walter much. What my friends and I did was hang out at a little drive-in place called Cook's Dairy Light. That's where you went if you wanted to find somebody. One of the few times I saw Walter away from school was down there. He had a little scooter, which I had never seen before or since. One night he came riding up and everybody was glad to see him, and we sat around talking with him. Same old Walter, cutting up and having fun. Saw him once or twice that summer, and when I left here going to college the last thing I heard was that he was going to college in Kansas or at Kansas State. After that I watched the box scores for Jackson State.

Because we got cable and had WGN, my son became a big Cubs fan. We actually went to a couple of Cub games, and the second time we went the only thing available was standing room only, where you couldn't see anything. My dad, through some business connections, was real good friends with Bud Holmes

(Payton's agent). Either Bud or my dad called Walter's office and arranged for us to have good seats right behind home plate. That was really nice, and my son got a big kick out of that.

◇

Payton had a social life growing up that included girls, and he and **MOSES** would often double-date. Both had female friends in another community a few miles away, and they obviously had no qualms about "territorial rights" when it came to whom they could date and where they happened to live:

He and I would date some girls down from another school, which wasn't good because it meant you had to go around the other guys from that school. They had the girls we liked. My girlfriend was about three miles from where he had to go. Sometimes when he went down there, guys would gang around him and want to fight, but he would manage to get out of it, get his daddy's truck, and come back and get me. I would go down there sometimes, too, but they never bothered me, and they knew I dated one of their girls, too. They really had a beef with Walter, maybe because his brother was a big name playing sports. And they knew me from playing baseball in the summer. His girlfriend lived down from a little store where they hung out, so that created some dynamics to that.

Sometimes on Sunday after church, while his father was resting, we would push his father's truck around the corner, and then we'd crank it up and go down to those houses to see those girls. That was fun. His mother let him use her car periodically, but we liked his father's truck because it was good and strong. We would go swimming sometimes. We might be driving around and stop by a field with pear trees or watermelon, and raid the field and jump back in the truck and get out of there. We would also go swimming or ride our bicycles. We had fun times. We were churchgoers. He went to the Baptist Church in the city, and I went to another one.

There came a time when we wanted to try some particular kind of wine that wasn't sold in our area. We had a friend, Charles "Heavy" Virgil, who worked selling fish and often went outside the area, and finally he brought some back. And we took it into the woods and we were all standing there—Charles, Archie (Johnson), me, Walter, Michael Woodson—with one bottle between us. The worst problem was deciding who was going to drink first. Walter and I were both the babies of the group, and Archie was the oldest. With Walter and I being the babies, we had first rights. Everyone kept saying, "Okay, who's going to drink first?" and we couldn't settle on it. So we did something like flipping for it and I won, so Walter didn't want to drink it. He was the baby. We always had to compete like that.

◇

The teenage Payton's girlfriend was **JILL BREWER,** who was two years younger than him and lived about nine miles from Walter's house, south of town. Brewer and Payton went to rival schools from different school districts, with Brewer attending Marian Central High School while Payton went, first, to Jefferson and then on to Columbia. Brewer describes her relationship with the teenage Payton as more of a friendship than a romance, although Payton would buy her gifts on occasions such as Christmas and her birthday. He was more likely to take her for a ride in his truck than to buy her flowers and candlelight dinners. Brewer today lives in Jackson, Mississippi, where she works as a senior planner for housing for the city's Department of Planning and Community Development:

We met when I was in junior high. We were introduced to each other by a mutual friend at a football game—not one in which he was playing, but I think it was a semiprofessional game that we both happened to be attending. This was before he had even started playing football. At that point, he was in the band at his school, and I was in the band at my school—I played saxophone

and he played drums. He was a very nice, sweet guy, kind of shy. He was also very caring and kind of a jokester, although I did not have that kind of jokester relationship with him. He was just a fun-loving person.

What mattered most to me was that he was very respectful. He was caring and protective. We went to the movies a couple of times, and he used to visit me at school when he shouldn't have. He would also visit me at my home. My parents ran a teen center near where I lived, and he would come there on weekends, too, sometimes with a friend. Quite often Sugar Man and several other of his friends would accompany him. He loved to dance, and this was a great place to dance and play games. Walter was known to kind of steal his dad's truck, and then he would come by my house. As you know, he got into (auto) racing, and it was always in his blood. I don't know exactly how fast he drove in that truck, but I know he would exceed the speed limit, even though it wasn't the kind of truck you would do any racing in. He could be somewhat of a daredevil, but he never did anything like that with me in the vehicle.

We didn't exchange any rings or anything like that. I was a bit young to be accepting things like that at that point. But I was his girlfriend for a while. He was my first boyfriend and was unforgettable in that he was a fine young man and a nice person. I consider myself lucky for having known him. He was always very kind, and I miss him very much. We maintained a lifelong friendship and were always able to talk to each other and share things. He was never Walter the superstar, he was just Walter Jerry. Even if a year went by without my speaking with him, we could just pick up and catch up on each other's experiences. When Walter died, Sugar Man and I went to the memorial for him that was held in Jackson, Mississippi. My thoughts then were of the Walter I had always known as a person. I wondered in going to the service how many people were there just because he played football instead of because of the wonderful person he was.

◇

As much as Payton worked out to further develop his physique, there's no question that genes had played a big role in giving him a head start on his football-playing career. **BRELAND** can vouch for the genetic angle:

One summer I was working at a warehouse, where the cotton gin was. I was in there loading some stuff for a Dollar General store, and I saw this older black man walking by with a two-wheeled buggy with a bale of cotton on it, and those things were heavy. As he walked by, I could see he had a tight-fitting T-shirt on and that he was built like Schwarzenegger. I figured I had to see what the deal was, so I spoke to him, told him who I was, and he told me who he was. He said his name was Payton, and I asked him if he was any kin to Walter, and he said, "Walter's my nephew." This guy was at least sixty years old, but I swear he looked like he could be playing professional football right then. He was ready to rip out of that T-shirt. It made an impression on me.

◇

Coming out of high school, neither Payton nor Moses was getting a lot of attention from college coaches because as good as they both were, **MOSES** realized they were playing great football but with little media attention. Even after they got to Jackson State for summer workouts, the school came very close to losing the services of Payton:

Walter had more notoriety than me. My desire was to go to Jackson State, so I was ready to sign. Walter had some other offers, so when the coach and Eddie (Payton, who was already playing at Jackson State) came by, Eddie was glad to see me signing with Jackson State; he knew Walter and I were close friends and would probably go to the same school. Walter held out until the end, then finally consented to go to Jackson State. By the time we got there for the summer, they had a new coach, Bob Hill.

Taskmaster. He was very old school, and we were not used to that. By the time we finished that second summer session of workouts and started home, Walter didn't want to go back. Bob Hill thought I was trying to pull Walter away, but Walter insisted on going to Pearl River Junior College.

So we're getting ready to go home around the Fourth of July, and Pearl River had just started to dress out its players. Walter talked me into going, so I went down there with him, and we went into their dressing room to try out. They knew he was Walter Payton, but they had a guy named Willie Heidleberg out of some place, it might have been Hattiesburg, and the coach told us Willie was his running back. I don't remember the coach's name, but here he was with a shot at Walter Payton, and he told us point-blank he didn't have anything to dress us out in.

Bob Hill found out about all this, and that severed my relationship with him. He blamed me, and that ended my football career, although I stayed at Jackson State and got my degree in speech and theater arts.

Later in life Walter and I sometimes talked, but never about ministry or football. We talked about high school. We'd pull out the annual, and he'd start pointing at people's pictures and remembering all this stuff about them. He had his own world of being a professional football player in Chicago and held that together, but when he came back where his home is, he went back right to where we had left off. At a memorial we had for him down here, I spoke and said, "There was a Columbia Walter, and a Columbia–Jackson State Walter, and then there's a Chicago Walter," and all these people had demands on his life, and they were unrealistic demands. But he would try and do what he could.

◇

One of Payton's teammates at Jackson State was center **DOUGLAS BAKER,** who was a year ahead of Payton but was redshirted and ended up leaving school the same time as Payton:

We knew he was going to be a great player from the first day. The first look we got of him in pads in practice we knew that. He was an all-around good guy, a clean-cut guy. He didn't do any drugs and drank so little that if he had a half-can of beer, he'd be as high as a kite, and we'd be laughing at him. He worked out year-round and was stronger than some of the linemen we had. I never worked out with him because it would have killed me. I couldn't hang with that guy.

We had good teams. The talent was there. In some areas, we could have played some of the teams in Division 1-A, at least as far as the skills position and the guys on the line were concerned—guys like Leon Gray, Manuel Sanders, Edgar Hardy, Jackie Slater. . . . Those are four guys off the line I can recall right away who went on to play in the pros. But we didn't have enough money to get the publicity we needed. Walter was up for the Heisman the last two years and Archie Griffin got it. We all thought Walter was going to get drafted by Dallas, but they drafted Randy White, and it worked out for both teams. They could have flipped a coin and still it would have come out all right. As an offensive lineman working in front of Walter, we didn't have to give him but a few inches. He had deceptive speed in college. In the pros you had all these guys running 9.2 and 9.3 in the hundred, and Walter ran something like a 9.7 or 9.8, so he had some speed, although it wasn't the real sprinter's speed.

Coach Bob Hill taught us in practice to deliver blows when getting tackled because that had been his style in college, where he had been a running back. "Don't let them just take you down," he would say. "Punish them and make them pay, so that next time you come at them it will make them cringe." Walter took those lessons to heart, and when defenders got right up on him, you could see him burst right into them. You could see him take that little hop-step that he does and next thing they knew, instead of them coming into him, he was bursting into them. We had a lot of hitting in our practices. Our practices were harder than our

games. We had more people hurt in practice than got hurt in the game.

His freshman year we played Grambling, and they had all these all-American guys like (defensive lineman) John Mendenhall. We beat them something like 13-7, and Walter kicked a field goal. It was Walter's first big game, and as a freshman he played with all kinds of class. It showed that he could play under pressure because Grambling State was ranked No. 1 among the black colleges back then. We were ranked something like seventh, eighth, or ninth. That guy could do it all. He could punt, kick off, kick field goals, and he could pass. He could stand flat-footed and dunk a basketball. The strength in this guy's legs was awesome. We had a really deep backfield—it also included Ricky Young, who went on to play in the NFL, too, and everyone figured there was no way a freshman was going to start in the backfield, but Eddie said, "You just watch." And Walter ended up starting in the backfield alongside Ricky Young.

◈

When Payton arrived at Jackson State, he was already one of the most highly touted players in school history, but that didn't preclude him from having to earn a new level of respect from his new teammates, who had been told of Walter's incredible talents by older brother, Eddie, who had preceded Walter to Jackson State. **BAKER** remembers:

At first we thought his brother, Eddie, had just been bragging on him. The first day of practice in pads, we had a defensive back who was about six-foot-four, 220 pounds. Walter took a quick pitch around the corner, and this defensive back come up to hit him, but Walter spun into him and hit him with that stiff-arm and just drove him back. And everybody went "Wooooooooooo." Right then we knew what was happening. You could really hear those pads hitting, and the guy never did bring him down. The

best he could do was ride him out of bounds. It was awesome. Even when Walter went down, he would spring right back up like a monkey, and that's why we started calling him "Monkey." He wasn't ever going to stay down to let anybody think they had gotten the better of him. It was funny. Usually, it was hard to get respect until you started getting into some big games. Where you get respect is in practice. Your teammates you practice with every day know if you're scared and if you are what everyone is saying you are. We find out in practice. You weed out the weak in practice. And Coach Hill was a military coach. Some drills he wouldn't let you out of until he saw blood. You know how Bobby Knight coaches? Coach Hill was that kind of coach. Coaches like that become obsolete, but a coach like that would bring out the best in you.

◈

Linebacker **ROBERT BRAZILE** was one of a number of Payton's teammates at Jackson State who successfully made it to the National Football League. Brazile was drafted out of college by the Houston Oilers, and by then he had formed a strong bond with Payton and other members of the Jackson State team, such as Ricky Young and Vernon Perry. Those four ended up hanging together at school while developing a friendship that went well beyond football:

The biggest thing I could remember about Walter was his smile. He also had a frown, but the thing that was behind that was a deep, loving, caring smile. That was one of the best things you wanted to see. If he was frowning, it meant he was pouting.

He had great influence on a lot of people. He brought the scouts, he brought the press, he brought the fans to my four years of collegiate football, and that helped me go high in the draft. The team we had during those four years could have competed against any Division 1 team. And I'm not talking about our winning by one point; I'm talking about, literally, taking the heads off of some of these major-college teams. I remember telling Bo

Schembechler one year, "If you had played us, you wouldn't have been drinking champagne on New Year's Eve." I think he understood where I was coming from because he had to coach me and Walter in the East-West Shrine Game, and he admitted he never knew before then that we had such ability.

Telling someone who doesn't know football about what it was like to play football at Jackson State under Bob Hill is difficult. The analogy I use, if it's your wife, you could compare it to getting to Hawaii by a boat ride; once you got there, you understand why it was worth the rough trip. I think I was ready for professional football by my sophomore or junior year because of what we endured under Coach Hill, with all the workouts that we had. If somebody else was doing twenty of something, we'd do sixty; if they did sixty, we did 120. We were workaholics.

◇

Defensive back **VERNON PERRY** was another of Payton's Jackson State teammates who formed the core of a close friendship in which football was only part of the equation. Perry was a year behind Payton, Brazile, and Ricky Young, but he quickly endeared himself to his older teammates by, literally, butting helmeted heads with Young during an early practice in 1972:

I first met Walter in the dormitory. How you met him was that he played a trick on you. He walked up behind me and scared me. I started hanging with him and Ricky Young and Robert Brazile. I was about the only freshman that hung with them. I guess there was something they liked about me because I was cuckoo, too. Walter was the kind of guy who liked to have fun. He wasn't a dull person. He might walk up to you and bite you in the shoulder or come up behind you and just holler real loud. He would always do some kind of prank or joke to get your attention.

One time, Brazile had gotten this mask—the ugliest monster mask you've ever seen. He put the monster mask on, and it could look just like a real person. Walter would put it on sometime, too,

and we'd go around scaring people. I mean, people would really be scared by that mask. Walter put it on one time and we were in the car, and this little kid was looking at us, trying not to look at Walter, and all of a sudden this little kid started crying. Guys would be sitting in the park with their girlfriends, and whoever had the mask on would jump out from the bushes, and people would start running because of that mask. You had to be there to see how really afraid those people were.

One night we all broke curfew, and at two o'clock in the morning Bob Hill made all of us get up out of bed and go out to the practice field and run and run, and crawl, and bark like a dog until like four o'clock in the morning. It tickled Walter to death. To him, it was a big joke, and the rest of us were dying out there. At football games, Walter and Ricky Young would be sitting by each other in the locker room at halftime, and Bob Hill would walk into the dressing room and he couldn't figure out why everybody in the room had their helmets on. Coach Hill would often walk in and be mad at Walter for fumbling the ball or whatever, and he would take his clipboard and hit everybody sitting by Walter upside the head, so no one would sit by Walter. He would be mad at Walter and pop somebody else upside the head, and Walter thought that was pretty funny. Coach Hill was a discipline coach. He would just make Walter run and run and run. And he was also Coach Hill's pet. You couldn't touch Walter in practice. He'd say, "Don't touch Walter; just let him run."

You had to be with us to see how much fun we had. Sometimes Walter would go with me to my mom's house to get something to eat. She always fried fish, and she loved cooking for him. She lived one street behind Jackson State. And oh, man, Walter would eat. She had something he loved that she would always cook for him, it was either greens or black-eyed peas, I don't remember.

How good was Walter? Mannnnnnn, let me tell you something: When Walter was in the game, if you were sitting on the sideline, you didn't go get water because you didn't want to miss

any time he put his hands on that ball, because you would miss something good. I saw times where Walter would run right over someone. He would take that forearm and run right into them. You want to know something? I used to hate to play against him. I was glad I was on his side in college. I played against him one time when he was in Chicago and I was with the Oilers, a teammate of Brazile's, and I knew if I had to come one on one to try to tackle Walter, he was going to run over me.

◇

Payton wasn't all business at Jackson State. Teammates not only respected him; they genuinely liked him because he knew how to have fun. But exhibiting a playful side was not the same as revealing his innermost self, and as teammate **BAKER** found out, there was a limit to how well someone got to know Payton:

Walter was a super athlete because he was super dedicated and wanted to make something out of himself. I talked to Walter a lot while we were there, but he was the kind of guy who pretty much kept his emotions in. He would play around some and have fun on the bus and stuff like that, but as far as really letting you in on his personal life, he wouldn't do that. You'd go in to talk to him, and he would be playing his stereo.

My mother would cook cakes and send them down to me from Tupelo, Mississippi, and he would eat some of them, and she would love to tell her friends that Walter Payton was eating her cooking. Everybody came by the room trying to get what they called sweet bread, although she called it pumpkin bread. It was like family. By the time Walter found out I had gotten some, they were already about gone. He stayed at the other end of the hall. I had them right there in my foot locker. We hardly ever talked about football—just life, and he would always want to show you his big stereo system. He would blast that hallway and would do all kinds of stuff like that with jazz and the popular music of the

day. Some Teddy Pendergrass stuff. The Whispers. Earth, Wind, and Fire. He liked to dance, and even went on Soul Train. His dying early makes me cherish my time with him all the more. I didn't get much of a chance to talk to him late in his life, but he was a great guy.

◇

Chances are that New York Times sports columnist **WILLIAM H. RHODEN** is the one true sports scribe who can say he went head-to-head with Payton on the football field. That occurred in November 1971, when Rhoden was playing senior defensive back for Morgan State and Payton was a freshman at Jackson State, as Rhoden recalled in a tribute he wrote in the Times following Payton's death, part of which follows:

I was not close to Walter Payton, but rather attached to him. We first met twenty-eight years ago this month. This was the sort of one-on-one introduction that defensive backs dread and out-standing running backs love. We met at the ten-yard line in Mississippi Memorial Stadium. This was before Payton became Sweetness; before he became a Chicago Bear; before we were paid for plying our particular crafts. We met in the rarified atmosphere of black college football.

My recollection of the game is reduced to one poignant frame—that first meeting at the ten-yard line. A sweep with Payton slicing past the line, over the linebackers, and finally into the secondary. There was Payton, there was me; I attempted a tackle and felt solid contact, then felt him bounce back to the outside. What I remember thinking at the moment was that he had great balance, like a gyroscope, when he was nearly horizon-tal, legs still churning. He was rushing toward the National Football League; I was not doing such a good job of tackling but was recording the moment.[1]

◇

Offensive tackle **JACKIE SLATER,** a Jackson State teammate of Payton's who went on to star with the Rams, on Payton's selflessness:

A lot of times in college I'd do half my job and Walter would break a long run anyway. Then he'd tell the press it was my block that sprang him loose, when all the time I knew the block could have been a whole lot better. That kind of thing builds. You start to get confidence in yourself. Now the linemen say to themselves, "Hey, we've got an all-pro back there—we've got to block all-pro to keep him going."[2]

◇

One of the many legacies Payton left behind at his untimely death was the quality of play at black colleges such as Jackson State and

Payton signs autographs during a July workout at Northwestern University's Dyche Stadium in Evanston, Illinois, prior to the 1975 College All-Stars' game against the reigning world champion Pittsburgh Steelers. Payton, fresh out of Jackson State, had just signed his first contract to play for the Chicago Bears.

Grambling State, both of which have sent dozens of great players to the NFL over the last forty years. Perry points out that the NFL record holders for career rushing yards (Walter Payton), career receiving yards (Jerry Rice), and single-game interceptions (Perry) all came out of all-black schools. So did, among others, one-time Super Bowl MVP quarterback **DOUG WILLIAMS:**

If Walter had been at one of those big schools like UCLA, he would have won the Heisman. But the bad thing about that is then I wouldn't have known him. That was my buddy, man. I called him just before he passed away and said, "Why don't you just let me come get with you?" Nobody would tell me how sick he was. His brother (Eddie Payton) wouldn't tell me. I didn't even know he had cancer. If I had known he was that sick, I would have gone and just picked him up and taken him somewhere for a while. They just kept saying he was waiting on a liver. When I heard about his death, I was driving down the street in my car, crying like a baby and mad at the world. I shut myself off from people for about two or three hours. I didn't want to talk to nobody.

When Walter set his record for most career yards, he did it against the Saints and I was with the Saints, and one of my best friends, Whitney Paul, made the tackle on the play where Walter broke the record. Was I excited to be playing in that game? More like scared, afraid that Walter would run over me at some time.

◇

BILL TOBIN joined the Bears in 1975 as the director of pro scouting and eventually left the team in the early nineties with the title of vice president and director of player personnel. Tobin, who had been with the Green Bay Packers before Jim Finks hired him to join the Bears, hit the ground running when he joined the Bears, coming along just as the Bears were in the process of piecing together one of the best drafts in franchise history:

The first time I saw Walter was when he was out at an All-Star game in Lubbock, Texas, as a junior. A Jackson State offensive lineman who was a senior—it might have been Jackie Slater, I'm not sure—was playing in the game, which benefited college coaches and lasted about three or four years. Apparently, the NFL flew Walter out there to get him exposed to the NFL atmosphere and scouts and because he was such a highly sought-after guy and, besides, there was a new league starting (the World Football League). Walter would have been a junior, which is why he wasn't playing in the game. I was working for the Green Bay Packers at the time. That was my first exposure to him, and I remember some scout from down south standing next to me and saying, "That's that junior running back at Jackson State that everyone is talking about."

When he was drafted by the Bears as the fourth player taken, it wasn't like he was an unknown subject to other NFL teams. The scouting report on him: Tough, hard-nosed, durable, productive, quality person—just about all that he turned out to be with us in Chicago. Determined. One thing about him is that he was not as fast as he always thought he was. He always thought he was a 4.4 guy, and he wasn't a 4.4 guy. He was more like a 4.6 guy or a 4.55 guy, but that was plenty fast. He had very few negatives, or things that I used to call hickeys. There were no hickeys on him. The only negative, maybe, was his coming from a small school and wondering how he would be able to cope in the big city, which obviously he did quite well. They don't pick their competition. They have to play who their schedule says they play against. At that particular time in the early seventies, there were a lot of kids coming from what they then called the black colleges that were playing and playing quite well.

I shared my information with Jim Finks prior to the draft, but the day of the draft I was not in the room because he didn't think it would be ethical to be in the room, even though I was a free agent, having been fired by Bart Starr, who was taking over at Green Bay. It was a surprise when Payton was still available

for the fourth pick, but remember this was a time when everyone did their own work and you didn't talk to the press and you didn't talk to other teams, so there wasn't a big brouhaha over who teams did take and who they didn't take. There was no live television saying "That was a mistake" and all of a sudden it's branded as a mistake. Everyone just did their work and went on about their business. It was a surprise to us that they took Huff, but at the time Joe Thomas of the Colts was recognized as the top personnel guy and if that's who they wanted, that's who they should take. We thought it might come down to between Randy White and Walter, and we would have taken either one of them, gladly.

◇

Speaking at her late husband's memorial service held at Soldier Field, **CONNIE PAYTON,** Walter's widow, remembers some genuine concern over the prospect of leaving the South and moving to Chicago, also known as the Windy City:

I've got to admit that when Walter was first drafted by the Bears, being the young person I was, I sort of felt sorry for him, I thought, Boy, it's blowing and it's freezing, and some of the other guys from Jackson State have been drafted, like Robert Brazile by Houston and Ricky Young by San Diego, and at least they're going to where it's warm. But little did I know that Walter was was coming to Chicago to be part of one of the best, best football families of all times. And it didn't take me long to realize that, and Walter and I truly, truly felt glad to have been a part of the Chicago Bear tradition, and we're so thankful that the Halas family took us in and just loved us and cared for us, and I'm still sort of over-whelmed by everything, because I know Walter just came out and did what he loved, and sometimes it's a little hard for me to understand because he was just my husband and Jarrett and Brittany's father, and he loved football. So it was what he wanted to do.[3]

◇

Even after Payton had left Jackson State to begin a stellar career with the Bears, he didn't really leave his friends behind. Loyalties ran deep with Payton, and one of those loyalties was to **PERRY,** who was a year younger than Payton and didn't get drafted by the NFL coming out of Jackson State:

I didn't get drafted out of Jackson State, and Walter was in Chicago, and of all the people that helped me try to get in the pros, I give Walter all the credit for my playing pro ball. Walter got me a tryout with the Chicago Bears. He picked me up and took me to their training camp. If it hadn't been for Walter, I never would have gotten a shot. He took me to the Chicago Bears, and the only reason I got cut was because I got caught in that numbers game—too many DBs and too many corners. He got my foot in the door.

Walter had this little gold 280Z, and we could go from Jackson, Mississippi, to Chicago in like seven and a half hours. He used to be driving ninety or a hundred all the way, and that's usually a twelve-hour drive. I would be scared, but I'd go with him. He had everything in that Z, and he would run. He had the cams, he had it all, and he would be flying.

THE BAD NEWS BEARS

WHEN THE CHICAGO BEARS DRAFTED Walter Payton with the overall No. 4 pick in 1975, they were sticking with familiar selection criteria. In each of their three previous drafts, their first picks had been players from small schools (1972—Lionel Antoine, Southern Illinois; 1973—Wally Chambers, Eastern Kentucky; and 1974—Waymond Bryant, Tennessee State). Second, they were a ground-oriented team interested in finding a great runner to finally replace the long-departed (and even longer-injured) Gale Sayers, whose sixty-eight-game career ended in 1971 following an unmendable knee injury.

Payton's arrival coincided with the departure of rotund, old-school Abe Gibron, whose three-year rain (yes, rain) as Bears head coach had produced all of eleven victories against thirty losses and a tie. Those truly black-and-blue Bears of Gibron's had beaten up more opponents than they had actually beaten, and that wasn't good. In those three seasons of lean and mean, the team's leading rusher had been quarterback Bobby Douglass, with 968 yards; Carl Garrett, 655 yards; and some guy named Ken

Grandberry, 475 yards. The path was wide open for Payton, although it would mean joining a team down in the dumps with a playoff berth likely light-years away. Chicago had no other offensive weapons worth noting, meaning Sweetness would be carrying a city's hopes on his shoulders.

But Payton wasn't alone. He joined the Bears at the same time they had brought in a new general manager (Jim Finks) and a new head coach (Jack Pardee). At the time, Mike Ditka was an assistant coach under Tom Landry with the Dallas Cowboys, and the Cowboys were picking second in the 1975 draft behind the Atlanta Falcons. Atlanta took California quarterback Steve Bartkowski at No. 1, leaving it to the Cowboys to choose between Maryland defensive tackle Randy White and Payton. Cowboys coaches debated the merits of White and Payton up until the last minute before choosing to go with defense. Then came the Baltimore Colts, who already had a promising running back in Lydell Mitchell and decided to go with North Carolina guard Ken Huff. Within seconds, the Bears grabbed Payton, only twenty years old, at No. 4 and signed him to a three-year contract that, with incentives, was worth nearly $500,000. Included was a $126,000 signing bonus.

That first year certainly wasn't smooth for Payton. He arrived at the Bears' training camp nursing a sore elbow and then rushed for zero yards in the season opener, a 35-7 loss to Huff and the Colts. On the bright side, Payton established himself as the Bears' starting halfback and finished his first season with 679 rushing yards, averaging 3.5 a carry, and led the league in kickoff returns with an average of 31.7. The Bears matched their 4-10 record of a year earlier, but improved to 7-7 in 1976 and then in 1977 made the playoffs for the first time since the 1963 league championship season. Even then, it was a long, bumpy ride, as in Payton's first eight seasons the Bears posted an aggregate sub-.500 record and made the playoffs just twice, and those ended up in first-round exits.

◇

Again, the Bears were not a good team when they drafted Payton with the NFL's No. 4 pick in 1975, as *Chicago Tribune* sportswriter **DON PIERSON** remembers, oh, so well:

Gibron's teams were really awful. They were tough teams and played hard—Butkus was on that team—and they played hard, but they were terrible and didn't really have much of a chance. They had Continental League players playing for them. When it came to the '75 draft, Payton wasn't nearly as familiar a name as someone like Archie Griffin or Randy White. But he was well enough known that nobody said, "Why in the hell are they taking him, a kid from an unknown school?" That's one element. The other is that it wouldn't have mattered who they took, they could have sold him to this town because the Bears were so awful. They would have been happy no matter who came in with the fourth pick.

When they picked him, we all went down to a TV station to see him interviewed. He wasn't very polished, although no one really is when coming out of college. In fact, we probably expected him to be less polished than he was. You could tell he had that twinkle in his eye. He wasn't a shy kid, but he wasn't real confident. I think he was confident in how he could do on the field, but he didn't seem real confident in how he presented himself. He went to the College All-Star camp and got hurt, hurt his elbow. And when he reported to the Bears he was hurt. His arm was really swollen, so he never got off to the kind of start that he expected or anyone else expected. Still, he gained something like 675 yards. O. J. Simpson had had about the same number of yards his first year, so that says something.

This also happened to be (Jack) Pardee's first year as coach. The team was probably as bad as any of Gibron's teams, but people were so happy that they were finally starting to do something—a new coach, a top player—someone to hang their hats

on. Initially, there was a hope that he would be a franchise player, but I don't remember any time during that first year where he really flashed that kind of effect. A story in *Sports Illustrated* early in his career—maybe it was when he was a rookie, but I'm not sure—painted him with one brush as just another small-black-college running back who liked to play the drums—it was almost a racist comment—but they just kind of wrote him off as just another guy coming along. Of course, that was premature, but the point is there was no reason for the guy to write anything else at that point. Only in his second year did you start seeing the stats, even though the Bears weren't winning. He was carrying twenty-five or thirty times a game and gaining 100 to 125 yards and you went, "Holy smoke, this guy is pretty good."

◇

Quarterback **BOB AVELLINI** joined the Bears in 1975, the same year Payton came along. They were the new generation that was going to be saviors for a lousy team:

We all came up together—guys like Roland Harper, Payton, and me. A lot of our offensive line was brand-new, too. It was a very young team. It was Jim Finks's first draft, and he brought us all in because there was going to be a change in the Bears. It was one of those things where we were in the right place at the right time, although, yeah, Walter would have cracked the lineup regardless of who was there.

At the time we not only had to adapt to the NFL, but we were adapting to a new team of new players. Walter came from a small school. You've also got to remember that in 1975 things were a lot different. This was before ESPN and cable TV, when all you really had was the local news, although Chicago was a pretty big city and the Bears were big. But in those days it wasn't like it is now, where you can't go out and have a drink. We used to go out after a Monday practice—me, Walter, Matt Suhey—and no one would

bother us. No one even knew us. Times were a little bit different. I mean, here's a guy like Walter Payton coming out of Jackson State and people were raising their eyebrows, wondering, Who is Walter Payton? They had never heard of him. I was a (college) senior at the same time. I went to the Senior Bowl and was chosen to quarterback and captain the South team. I was told to just get the ball to this one guy, and I said, "Well, who is he?" And they said, "It's Walter Payton." I had never heard of him. In today's world, can you imagine someone being a college senior at the same time he was and never hearing of him?

At our first Senior Bowl practice, I turned to hand the ball off to him, and he was so quick that I missed the handoff. I had never seen anything like that, and I had played with a pretty good tailback at Maryland. But Walter was just at another level. Even if we were in just shorts and shoulder pads, he was so much quicker. I wouldn't say he was overly fast, but he was quick. He could cut on a dime and then get back to full speed real fast. This was before we were even drafted, and then we ended up together. Can you imagine something like that today, not hearing of someone like Randy Moss? Randy Moss played at a small school (Marshall), but everybody had heard of him, and he was right up there in the running for the Heisman. Nobody heard of Walter Payton, although I'm sure the scouts did.

◇

DAN JIGGETTS, a popular Chicago sportscaster, joined the Bears in 1976, a year later than Payton did, and he knew from day one who the team's main man was:

That was a time of very serious transition. A lot of the veterans who had been around for four or five years were a little leery because they knew Jim Finks was taking the team in a completely different direction, and a lot of those guys weren't going to be along for the ride. It was an opportunity to come in as a young

player and feel pretty comfortable. It was somewhat like two teams, the guys who had been around and the new group.

When Walter walked in the door, it was magic. Certainly, by his second year, everyone knew exactly what they had gotten with that fourth pick in the draft. Everyone says that in those early days it was Walter right, Walter left, and Walter up the middle . . . and they were right. You don't get style points for saying, "Well we've decided to throw the ball a lot to give Walter a rest." He didn't want a rest. The time he was the happiest was the games where you ran him thirty-five or forty times. Of course, he also wanted to throw the ball or kick the ball, too, and he could do these things about as well as anyone else on the team.

◈

For more than two decades, **GIL BRANDT** was a key component of the brain trust that deftly turned the Dallas Cowboys into America's team. Brandt was the Cowboys' director of player personnel, an astute and savvy personnel expert whose scouting and networking techniques were years ahead of their time. When it came to trades and especially the NFL draft, Brandt was at the top of his game, even in 1975 when the Cowboys passed up the chance to draft Walter Payton with the No. 2 pick and instead went with another future All-Pro in the person of defensive tackle Randy White. Brandt left the Cowboys around the time the franchise's regime switched from the Tex Schramm–Tom Landry era to the one with Jerry Jones and Jimmy Johnson. To this day, Brandt remains one of the most informed and active football experts in the world, and he remembers the 1975 draft almost as if it were yesterday:

Going back to that 1975 draft, you first need to remember what happened with the first pick. Atlanta made a trade with Baltimore that gave the Falcons the No. 1 pick, and they used it to take quarterback Steve Bartkowski, as expected. We had the second pick, and we came right down to the morning of the draft not knowing whether we were going to take Payton or Randy White. The feeling

Chicago Bears training camp in the summer of 1977 has just opened, and a still-young-looking Walter looks ahead to his third season. It would turn out to be his best season ever yardage-wise, as he went on to rush for more than 1,800 yards.

AP/WIDE WORLD PHOTOS

at the time was that White would probably have more longevity than a running back because in those days people didn't have as good off-season programs and so forth, and a running back's longevity was shorter than it is today. That consideration probably more than anything tilted our decision to take White over Payton.

I think the draft started at noon, and on the morning of the draft we were so torn as to what we were going to do, as if any one little thing one way or the other was going to change our attitude on something. But we had had tremendous success with black college players such as Jethro Pugh from Elizabeth City Teachers College and Ed Jones from Tennessee State, and Jones had been the first pick taken in a draft.

I had spent a great deal of time studying both of them. They both played in the East-West game, and they both had good—not

was flanker **JOHNNY MORRIS,** who played for the Bears from 1958 through 1967, along the way setting the team record for pass receptions in one season (ninety-three), a record that still stands. After his playing days ended, Morris completed a transition into television sportscasting and for about thirty years became a fixture on Chicago TV as Channel 2's sports anchor. Morris played with Sayers, covered Payton, and commiserated with Michael Jordan, giving him a rare perspective on how Payton ultimately fit into the Chicago sports scene:

Walter was kind of like the epitome of Chicago in that he had big shoulders and played in a working man's town. He always showed up for work, and he missed only one game in his entire career. To me, he was the greatest running back that ever played the game, and for a lot of reasons. He was a great blocker. He had great hands, was quick, and was a power runner who was also an elusive-type runner—he could do whichever was needed. He could also throw the ball—he threw a number of touchdown passes in his career—and all that makes him the greatest.

Believe it or not, a lot of people didn't really start watching Payton until later in his career, in the eighties, because if you will recall, in the seventies, when he came up, the Bears were a bad team. He had to, literally, carry that team, and he was much quicker in those days. He had pretty good break-away speed, but people around the nation didn't really know about any of it. All they would see were a few highlights because a lot of the Bears games weren't nationally televised. So a lot of people around the country never really saw Payton consistently game after game at his best until he was past his prime. Even the highlights shows like they have now on ESPN didn't come along until the early eighties.

I think if the nation had gotten to see Payton play starting in the seventies, there would have been a consensus that he was the greatest running back ever. Believe me, he was better than Jimmy Brown and better than O. J., and he was so much more durable than Gale Sayers. The two greatest running backs that ever played

the game were Barry Sanders and Walter Payton. But if I wanted somebody for one play, I would probably take Gale Sayers. If I wanted somebody for a game or for a season or a career, I'd take Payton. I mean, he was a good blocker . . . a great blocker . . . a devastating blocker. Nobody, nobody, can ever tell me that Jimmy Brown or Barry Sanders or O. J. Simpson or whoever was a great blocker.

He had amazing strength. I mean, he was a perfect specimen for pro football. And he wasn't that big, as you know. He weighed about 205 or something like that. The other thing I would probably tell you is that he perfected himself as a football player. He really worked to dedicate himself to improve himself. When Walter first came to Chicago, he was shy and had trouble expressing himself. And he didn't like giving speeches because he was so shy and just not worldly. But he worked on that. He forced himself when he first came into the league to do things, things that he didn't necessarily want to do as far as getting out in public and giving speeches and learning what the world's all about and stuff like that. He managed to make himself into a well-rounded individual by the time he retired from football.

◈

BILL MAGRANE, the Bears' director of administration, joined the team in 1975 along with general manager Jim Finks, the same year that Payton came to the Bears in the NFL draft. Magrane was Payton's unofficial first host upon the rookie's arrival in Chicago. First up on the itinerary was a night out for dinner in Chicago with Finks, Payton, and Payton's agent, Bud Holmes:

He was shy that night. We were in a real fancy French restaurant with a menu this tall and everything in French. Walter looked at the menu and looked and looked, and the waiter finally came around, and Walter said, "You got anything that's, you know, like, just a piece of meat with nothing on it?"

The first game he played was against Baltimore, and they were pretty good. That's when Bert Jones was playing quarterback for the Colts. Walter carried the ball I don't how many times that day, and he gained zero yards. Afterwards, coming out of Soldier Field, I was walking out with my wife and here came Walter walking along. And he's walking along with me and my wife and it wasn't prearranged, we were just walking out. I started to introduce him to my wife, and then I noticed he was crying. He had some tears running down his cheeks, and my wife saw him and you know she reached over and patted him on the arm and she said things will get better. And of course things did get better. The next week he rushed for a hundred yards and that was that.

◇

Bears linebacker **DOUG BUFFONE** played fourteen seasons with the Bears, including five with Payton as the last remaining holdover from the old school George Halas era. Buffone came to the NFL too late to get a taste of the last remnants of the Halas success years and left a few years too early to have a chance to enjoy the success of the Ditka years, but the time in between was not a total waste. He got to crack skulls alongside the likes of Dick Butkus and got to play alongside two of the game's greatest running backs—first Sayers, and then Payton:

Jim Finks basically took over the team in 1975. Basically, we hadn't had a running back since Sayers. So when Payton came in, he made a tremendous difference right away.

The first time I hit him in practice, I thought I had hit a brick wall. I had been around a while, but as I kept playing against him I realized this guy was something special because he just wasn't going down. You could tell he had a lot of determination when he ran the ball. A lot of guys coming up, when they get to the hole will tiptoe where Walter would be going through at a hundred miles an hour. I had played with Sayers, and he was just phenomenal, one of the greatest running backs I ever saw. Then there's

Walter. Not only does he run, but now he's picking up blitzes. Then he's catching passes out of the backfield.

◈

A twenty-twenty hindsight retrospective of Payton's incredible career with the Bears could suggest the whole plot played out as expected. Here was Payton, setting all kinds of records at Jackson State, generating tremendous word of mouth and being drafted as the fourth player picked in 1975—when you take all that into consideration along with his physical assets of strength and speed, a Hall of Fame career seems inevitable. But that's the beauty of hindsight. It doesn't tell the whole truth, and one truth in 1975, as seen by **MAGRANE,** is that the Bears, while they knew who they were getting, found out they really didn't know who they had more than sixteen thousand yards later:

I don't think anybody had a clue as to what was going to happen. Finks was very enthusiastic about him. Finks said, in effect, that he's the total package: "He's what we want. If he stays healthy, he should be a great back." And of course that was the key—staying healthy. That was the thing that made Walter different. And all of these guys (running backs) who chased Walter (his career rushing record), like the guy at Dallas (Emmitt Smith) has said, "As I get older, it dawns on me what's involved in trying to break this guy's record. You just get so beat up and you're playing in so much pain," and Walter would play in pain. You'd see Walter on Wednesday, and he might have his arm beat up or his knee or whatever—something where you didn't think he was going to play. But he just overcame injuries mentally. He overcame them. That's the only explanation of Walter.

The day he set the single-game rushing record, he was puking in the locker room before the game. He had the stomach flu. And he was shivering and shaking, and he went out and ran for 275 yards on a cold, wet day. We went to Minnesota once and I think his knee was swollen up. Fred Caito was the trainer, and he

said, "There's no way he can play." And Walter said, "Let me go out for a while and run beforehand." And Fred said, "Well, I'll take a look at him," and even then he still wasn't real comfortable with it. But they let him play, and he gave them a hundred and something yards. What they had done was drain his knee, and he went out and played. Another time he had turf toe really bad down in Tampa Bay. And you know turf toe is really painful to the touch and everything. And he went ahead and played, and there was one play in there where he was tiptoeing along the sidelines to keep from going out of bounds and obviously he was right up on his toes. He never complained about it. And he was tough. He was just a tough guy. It's like Matt said—he said, "I hear about all these guys, this guy and that guy, and I know there's none like Walter. Nobody was as tough as Walter was."

◇

Trainer **FRED CAITO** was one of the first members of the Bears team who made Payton's acquaintance when the latter was drafted in 1975, although not necessarily for the right reason. Payton had hurt his elbow in that summer's College Football All-Star game and came to the Bears nursing a bruised limb. Enter Caito:

The elbow was very inflamed and infected. He came right from the All-Star game to our training camp and missed the first three weeks of the camp. We put him in the hospital in Evanston because the doctors who were treating him were over there. So right away Walter and I started going back and forth every day in my car, and we got to know each other. It was about a twenty-minute drive, and we just got to talking. He was very shy and it took a while for him to open up, but when he started you saw that bubbly personality right away. On one trip he said, "Hey, wanna stop and get an ice cream cone?" and I said, "Yeah." Here I've got the No. 1 rookie with me, and he wants to go to the ice cream parlor. I paid. And I thought, Jeez, this guy just got this big

signing bonus. But right away we developed a friendship and camaraderie. And I had no idea that it would go on for thirteen years—that he would play that long.

We became good friends over the years. I could call him with a personal issue and he'd listen, he'd talk, where you couldn't do that with a lot of people. I could talk to him about anything like a brother. There were some issues in my family life that didn't go good for me, and I would talk to him about it. I could talk to him, and he would listen. We shared a lot of conversations on the airplane because we sat next to each other for fourteen years. We wouldn't talk about football but about life, different issues and things, while everybody would be sleeping. He never slept much on the plane.

◇

Placekicker **BOB THOMAS** and Payton arrived at the Bears in the same year, both having been taken in the 1975 draft. They came from contrasting backgrounds, Thomas having spent four years in the media spotlight at Notre Dame and Payton practically hidden from the rest of the world as an incredible achiever at Jackson State. When Payton got to the Bears, Thomas was among those who thought that the Jackson State star still had a few rough edges to work off when it came to dealing with the big time:

I think there he had a reliance upon his agent (Mississippi-based Bud Holmes) at the time in terms of what he was going to talk about, and he would refer a number of things to his agent. But even in his first year you could see a genuine humility that was part of the equation. It didn't take him very long to get acclimated. Even up by the time of his second year, it seemed he felt a little bit more sure of himself. He was no longer in a new situation, and he was aware that he was the guy. A lot of his personality came out—the humorous side of him.

God broke the mold when He created a superstar like Walter, because I look back at those interviews and listen to them, and

after a while you come to realize that the humility wasn't an act. That's just part of who he is—that he knew he had been blessed with God-given talent and was just a consummate team player. I remember Walter, when on the sidelines when a guy would either miss a kick, drop an interception, or fumble the ball, would be the first one over there picking those guys up and telling them, "Don't worry, you'll get the next one." In today's world, that's the exception rather than the rule.

◇

Payton's thirteen-year career with the Bears actually consisted of three eras—the remnants of the pitiful years, the building years with the occasional playoff fling, and, finally, the teams of Super Bowl caliber. *Chicago Tribune* football writer **DON PIERSON** remembers:

His career had three parts, and they coincided with the coaches. First the Pardee years, which was the start. But there was the question of whether the Bears would be able to put a team around a running back who would then be able to carry the team to a championship. You know, Jim Brown had won a championship. Finks went out and traded for a Phipps.

The second phase of Payton's career was the (Neill) Armstrong years, which I would describe as the really frustrating years. You knew the guy was in his prime, but they were still spinning their wheels, unable to make much progress or a break-through. They squeaked into the playoffs in 1977 and 1979, but there never was really any progress in terms of carryover. By 1982 (Mike) Ditka came in, and (George) Halas put his foot down and changed everything, even though Finks was still here and didn't want Ditka. Yet everyone was on the same page, knowing that they needed a quarterback. They decided on (Jim) McMahon rather than Art Schlichter. That was the turnaround. At that point, they became a different team. That was the strike year. Then the next year they got Willie Gault and were finally ready to

join the twentieth century, putting together some sort of play-action game to complement the running game.

Then there's the misconception that by 1984 and 1985 Payton was just along for the ride, which isn't true at all. Just look at the stats. You might say, "Well now they had the great defense and McMahon at quarterback, and that's why they were winning." But Payton was still the nucleus of the team. He was the fulcrum that defenses still had to focus on. He had excellent stats in 1985—he had a hell of a season and he sort of got lost in the shuffle, literally ("The Super Bowl Shuffle"), with Perry, McMahon, and the way the defense was playing. Payton had a good year in '86, too, but by '87 they were trying to phase in Neal Anderson. By then Payton was thirty-two and had a hell of a lot of mileage on him, and you could tell it was getting tough for him. He could have probably gone another year or two, but by then the handwriting was on the wall.

◇

Before Payton came along in 1975, the Bears weren't exactly the laughingstock of the NFL—they bruised opponents too much to elicit that kind of response—but they were bad, and **BUFFONE** remembers the before and after:

Phase One was like the Old Testament: the old Bears—grizzly, tough, and no-nonsense. Under Abe Gibron, we could play the Detroit Lions, lose the game, and I would come into the locker room really dejected, and Abe would say, "Great game." And I say, "But we lost." And he says, "Yeah, but we put out fourteen Lions." That was the mental philosophy of the Bears in those days. We would just beat people up, but we didn't win. Everyone hated playing the Bears because they knew they could beat us eventually, but they would have to pay a tremendous price.

After '75, however, it was "Let's win some games," and I didn't care if it meant having to play like a ballet dancer once in a while.

That's what Finks brought in. Before, we would always beat our selves eventually. Finks changed things around, brought in some new players, and brought a new philosophy. Thing about Sayers and Butkus is that I don't think they ever went to a playoff game. I did. That was because of Finks. If I had been able to keep playing, I could have gone to the Super Bowl, but I just couldn't hang on that long, even though they wanted me to stay longer. Finks never got rid of that physical toughness, but they added on to it. It was having more skill-oriented stuff that made the difference between winning and losing. The forward pass was one thing. They brought in (Bob) Avellini and then (Mike) Phipps and started doing a little more with the pass and that kind of stuff.

There were something like thirty-three players gone when I came back the next year. They chopped everybody, including management, and changed how they handled the training room, how they handled the players. Everything. They were better organized, and they were scouting well. Jim Finks to me was a genius. He should have been the commissioner of football. The guy was just phenomenal with what he did and how he did it.

I was the last of the Mohicans. There was a separation there. I was the last player playing who had ever played for George Halas. I hung on. I could see it coming, and I wanted to play some more. But I could see where it was taking me ten days to recover, so they told me to slip into another role.

◈

Long before the Bears won their Super Bowl after the 1985 season, they had established themselves as a team of split personalities—a ground-oriented offense built around Walter and a rugged defense that still at times hinted of the days of the Monsters of the Midway. As the *Chicago Sun-Times*'s **BRIAN HEWITT** saw it, it was two teams rolled into one, and that wasn't necessarily a good thing:

Defenses and offenses on the same NFL teams don't ordinarily like each other, but on the Bears they hated each other. Part of the reason for that was that the offense was so bad and the defense was decent and tough with guys like Doug Plank and Doug Buffone. There was antagonism on the practice field all the time between the offense and the defense. Sometimes Walter would come out there with this sort of pranksterish way about him, and a lot of the guys in practice weren't very amused by it. Walter would do something kind of goofy, some typical Walter thing where he would run into somebody in some sort of half-contact drill and then he would kiss the guy or something like that—and the guys on defense never thought much of that. Plank would call him Wally. On some days Walter would get preferential treatment because he had taken such a pounding on Sunday, and they sometimes wouldn't ask him to do much until Wednesday or Thursday because his body was recovering. And Plank and these other guys would be, "Oh, Wally (which we think Walter hated), can Wally come out and play today?" and stuff like that. They were all over him, even though they realized how good he was. Walter could be a little bit of a pain in the neck.

◇

Even with a stellar draft in 1975 that yielded a number of eventual starters in addition to Payton, the Bears were in for a long and slow improvement from 1975 on. There were years there that they took a step back, but one thing was certain in those days and that was that Walter was going to get the ball a lot. Quarterback **BOB AVELLINI** offers a scouting report on Payton and those up-and-down Bears teams of the late seventies:

If anybody is going to break Walter Payton's record, it will be tough in this day and age because everyone passes the ball more. We were basically a running team and a defensive team in those days. We could have had Joe Namath here, and we still would

have run the ball. It was one of those things. For as great as Walter was, we relied too heavily on him. It seemed like the only time we would throw the ball was on third and long, and everyone knows you can't make a living throwing on third and long. We had coaches with the philosophy that "well, if he averages four and a half yards a carry, and we give the ball to him on first down and second down, then we've got third and one." With a bad philosophy like that, that's why they are ex-coaches. It was very difficult to play quarterback that way, but great for a running back.

Walter played at a time when we were just getting into the media age, when now we make a superstar out of a guy who has one good game, or based on what a guy did in college. There were many years where we weren't even on TV, and when I say TV I mean national TV. I grew up in New York and I never saw Gale Sayers play. I very seldom saw Jim Brown play. We saw the Giants, and we saw the Rams. We saw either an East Coast team or a West Coast team. Nowadays, if you want to watch the Chicago Bears on TV, you can do it with a satellite dish. But back in the seventies and eighties, there was no such thing. Things have changed. Just like Butkus. I saw him when he came to Yankee Stadium in an exhibition game, and he was on one knee and he was making tackles all over the place, and you could see how good a player he was. But otherwise I didn't get to see him play.

◇

Of course there was no way to predict in 1975 that Payton would emerge as perhaps the greatest NFL running back of all time, or even that Randy White would be an All-Pro player numerous times over. **BRANDT** of the Cowboys didn't have a crystal ball, and he knew that Payton was good, but even he couldn't anticipate what was to transpire:

Oh, I guess his success early on surprised me a little bit because the Bears were not a very good football team at the time. This guy played on some teams that were very, very average teams. And they really didn't have a quarterback. We thought he was going to be a Pro Bowl player, but if we knew he was going to be the lead ground gainer of all times, we'd have probably drafted him.

THE GOLDEN BEARS

IN THE B.D. (BEFORE DITKA) years of the Bears, there had been glimmers of hope. In 1977 Payton and Pardee led the Bears to a 9-5 season and a playoff spot, but Pardee was gone by 1978. Then under Neill Armstrong, the Bears bounced back in 1979 to go 10-6 and return to the playoffs. But then came 7-9 and 6-10 seasons, and Armstrong was jettisoned, replaced in 1982 by Mike Ditka. Things didn't immediately improve. Ditka's first Bears team suffered through a strike-shortened 3-6 season, although on the bright side the three losses over their last four games had been by a total of only twelve points.

The two constants in all this were Payton and general manager Jim Finks. Payton had averaged more than fourteen hundred rushing yards over the previous six seasons, and Finks was finding his groove in building through the NFL draft. By trading away thirteen of the team's first- through fifth-round picks between 1976 and 1979, Finks was able to further stock his cabinet for future picks that, between 1980 and 1983, brought into the fold linebackers Otis Wilson, Mike Singletary, and

Wilbur Marshall, defensive end Richard Dent, fullback Matt
Suhey, tackles Keith Van Horne and Jimbo Covert, quarterback
Jim McMahon, wide receiver Willie Gault, defensive backs Mike
Richardson and Dave Duerson, and offensive linemen Mark
Bortz and Tom Thayer.

Those drafts and Payton became the nucleus of a power-
house team that started to jell in 1983, Ditka's second season,
with a deceptively strong 8-8 record that ended with victories in
five of their last six games, including an impressive 13-3 defeat
of the San Francisco 49ers. The only loss in that stretch was by
three points to the Green Bay Packers—the same team the Bears
defeated two weeks later, 23-21, to complete their impressive
climb to .500. A year later, Chicago improved to 10-6 and won
the NFC Central, finally bowing out in the NFC title game to
the 49ers. In 1985 it was the Bears' turn, as they routed the
49ers, 26-10, in Week Six en route to a 12-0 start, a 15-1 regu-
lar-season finish, and a 46-10 Super Bowl victory over the New
England Patriots.

By now a thirty-year-old veteran in his eleventh NFL sea-
son, Payton had established himself as the league's premier
superstar and most dependable rusher with the ball. He had
persevered through nine mostly mediocre seasons with the
Bears and escaped the dubious category of great players who
never won a championship. The mid-eighties were the golden
years for Payton and the Bears, even though they might have
fallen short of expectations by winning "only" one Super Bowl
when history and circumstances—they were one of the league's
youngest teams in their Super Bowl season—suggested they
were capable of winning two or three in the second half of that
decade. As amazing as it seems, Payton was overshadowed dur-
ing the Bears' Super Bowl season by defensive coordinator
Buddy Ryan's incredible Forty-six Defense and even the three-
hundred-pound-plus phenomenon known as "the Fridge"
(rookie defensive tackle/occasional goal-line ballcarrier William
"Refrigerator" Perry). Meanwhile, Sweetness had the fourth-best

rushing season of his career, gaining 1,551 yards while averaging 4.8 yards a carry and scoring eleven touchdowns (including two on pass receptions).

◇

When offensive tackle **KEITH VAN HORNE** arrived on the Bears scene in 1981, he discovered a team that was a lot Walter Payton and a bit in turmoil:

The Bears' defense was their strong point, although Walter certainly could run, so they must have been doing something right. But there were 10-7 games in which he ran for over two hundred yards, and that kind of thing proves how impotent the offense was. When I got there, the team was truly divided. It was like the defense against the offense. They weren't playing together as a team; they were playing against each other. From what I could tell, they truly didn't like each other. Then we started getting some good players for each of the next several drafts, guys like Jim McMahon, Richard Dent, Otis Wilson, Jimbo Covert. . . . From 1980 through 1983, those drafts were really the backbone of the team that went on to go to the Super Bowl. We matured and built up a groove offensively. McMahon came in and provided another point of leadership, which was good for Walter because it took much of the load off of him. It allowed him to have more fun, and now we had a quarterback who was a leader and knew the game and could motivate guys. This is where I give Mike Ditka the credit. He came in and got rid of anybody that didn't want to toe the team line, and he brought that team together. He finally got us all on the same page and playing together, and we went on to the Super Bowl. And we should have won two more at least, but we didn't, unfortunately. I feel bad for Walter for that—not only for Walter but for Chicago, too, because we had the youngest team and the best team, but some management decisions and some injuries and some egos all got in the

way and, unfortunately, we didn't win anymore. But that '85 season was something special.

Even when Walter wasn't getting the ball, he was always looking to see if he could block somebody. He took more pleasure in that than in running the ball. There were times in meetings where we were watching films that he would get all excited, saying, "Watch this! Watch this!" and he wouldn't even have the ball. He was going right through defenders to knock some linebacker on his butt . . . Bam!! He was a devastating blocker. He would just level people.

◇

By the time lineman **MARK BORTZ** was drafted by the Bears in 1983, Payton had already logged eight seasons and surpassed ten thousand yards rushing. But although he already was past the median average length of a running back's career, Payton was still at full throttle by the time Bortz arrived, and the rookie saw more of the best of Payton yet to come:

One football player that everybody respected was Walter Payton. The thing about our club in those days was that we always seemed to have a really good defense, and yet he was the Chicago Bears for many years. The biggest thing about Walter was the way he punished people, would-be tacklers, whether they were trying to push him out of bounds or tackle him out on the field. Actually, he beat the crap out of a lot of people trying to tackle him. He was a very physical player and always in great shape.

I got to start on offense in 1984 and it was really something to be in the huddle with him, looking up and seeing those eyes. No matter what else happened or didn't happen on offense, we always knew that with Walter we could get those three, four, or five yards at a time to keep things going. In those years at least, we built the offense around Walter, and with his running ability and stuff we just couldn't be denied. He gave us an opportunity

to be whatever we could be as a team. With our great defense, a lot of times it would be three and out for our opponents, then we would take the ball and control the clock real well because we had such a good running game. I think we were first or second in the league in rushing some of those years.

◈

JEFF FISHER, head coach of the 2000 Super Bowl runner-up Tennessee Titans and a Payton teammate from 1981 through 1984, said he eventually coached against Payton as secondary coach under Buddy Ryan after Ryan moved on to Philadelphia to become the Eagles' head coach. At Tennessee Fisher coaches one of Payton's biggest fans, Titans star running back Eddie George, a Heisman Trophy winner out of Ohio State. Fisher says Payton has had a big impact on George's life, so much so that George occasionally will visit Fisher in his office and plop down in his chair to hear the coach regale him with Payton stories. "Eddie wants to be the best running back ever," Fisher says, "so who better to pattern yourself after than the guy who now ranks as the best ever?" Here's a sampling of some of the things Fisher has to say about his former Bears teammate and, later, on-field adversary:

There are so many things about Walter that always stick out in my mind, not just one thing in particular. I refer to him probably three or four times a year to my players, usually when it's right before a game and a player is knocked down with something like the flu or food poisoning. That's when I tell them about the time Walter set the NFL single-game rushing mark (275 yards vs. the Vikings) with a temperature of more than 102 and being sick to his stomach. When I bring that up, I always get a smile from the player I'm telling this to, letting him know that it's possible to play when you're sick.

I've got a Super Bowl ring from that 1985 team, although I would have to say that the experience of playing on the same team with Walter and watching him from the sidelines every Sunday for five years and then having that friendship was better

to me than winning the world championship. I got plenty of chances to see him in practice every day because it was usually the backup defense playing against the first-team offense. It wasn't played at full speed, but when I first got there (in 1981) I quickly discovered that the first rule in practice was that you didn't hit Walter, and it wasn't just because indirectly Walter was signing your paycheck. I later found out that you didn't hit Walter in practice because it really hurts—not Walter—you. I can remember one of my first days in practice when I was covering him on a swing pass. I collided with him just as the ball got to him, jarring it loose. He just looked at me kind of funny, but didn't say anything. The next day we were in shorts and jerseys doing a walk-through at three-quarters speed. At one point I was in position to take his block, and he just knocked me flat to the ground. He got me back.

After I became the secondary coach for the Philadelphia Eagles, we played the Bears a couple of times in there. Before each of those games, I made it very clear in the meeting room to all of my defensive backs that "you had better be careful when going for Walter near the sidelines because I've seen him knock out defensive backs with a forearm, and he's not going to go out of bounds. Better take him low, and good luck." They really respected him.

Just as the Bears were hitting their stride as a team nearing the mid-eighties, Payton wasn't looking too good under close observation, with good friend and trainer **FRED CAITO** among a select few who knew just how badly Payton's body was hurting:

Halfway through his career, we took Walter up to East Lansing (Michigan) to have both of his knees checked out. Bud Holmes, his agent, and I took him up there. He went up with the intention of scoping his left knee, which had really been bothering him.

Here's a familiar scene experienced by multitudes of defensive backs, linebackers, and even a few defensive linemen over the years—Payton delivering a brutal stiff-arm to a would-be tackler. It certainly wasn't impossible to tackle Payton, but quite often there was a price to be paid—in pain.

The doctor examined him the night before the surgery, and he asked about the right knee. Walter didn't want him to mess with that right knee. But the right knee had also been a problem. And the doctor said, "I think you need to scope them both." And this was Walter's contract year. He had played seven or eight years, and this was the big one, this was going to be the big contract. And we knew we were going to have a good team.

So the next morning we scoped both knees, and they were in bad shape. I was shocked because I've seen a lot of scopes, and when I saw these and how bad the knees were, I go, "Wow how did this guy do it?" I had to make a phone call back to the Bears management. Jim Finks wanted to know right away what condition Walter was in. I said, "Well, Jim, we scoped them both, not just one, and they're pretty beat up. And he's still out and I

haven't been able to talk to him." When he woke up, the doctor was there and I was there and his agent was there, and Walter said, "Well, can I play?" And the doctor said, "I'm not saying you can't, but it's going to be a tough road. Your knees were pretty beat up." So we left, and the Bears ended up signing him to a big contract. We started rehabbing at his house at Arlington Heights.

By the time we went to training camp, he had just started doing a little bit of running on the hill—just a little, not a lot. It got down to the week before the season started, and I remember Coach Ditka getting a little irritated, wondering if this guy was going to play or not. And Walter would say, "I'll be ready. I'm going to play." And he started doing some strides. His strength was back, and the knees were feeling good. They were a little puffy, but they were feeling better. And it came right down to where the coach said that if he didn't practice by Friday, he wasn't going to play him. And Walter didn't practice Friday. On Sunday, of course, Ditka said, "Well, what's he going to do?" And I said, "He says he's going to play." So he said, "Well, tell him I'll give him one series, the first series. We don't want him to hurt himself, but if we've got to wait two weeks, well, let's wait two weeks." No big deal.

So Ditka, myself, and Walter went into a room and Walter said, "Coach, I'm ready. I want to play." And he had that look, you could tell, and that was the old look, but I could also sense an urgency about him. It was kind of agreed that he'd go the first series, as Coach Ditka said, "I'm going to call your number the first play, and we'll see how you do." We had to kick off, and then when we got the ball, the offense trotted out to the field. I don't know the play, but they pitched him the ball wide, and he was running around the corner, and he went about sixty yards for a touchdown. I looked at Ditka and I said, "Well, he's ready." He went on to gain eighteen hundred yards that season. He led the league in rushing and did it on two knees that I knew were hurting.

◇

DON PIERSON missed only one of Payton's games over thirteen years, although he found a Payton performance in practice almost as exciting:

He played hard every single week and he was the best football player I ever saw because he could do everything and was there every week. I loved to watch him practice. I always told (Jim) Finks that he should charge to watch practice, and I'm sure if Finks had stuck around for another twenty years he would have. They could have charged to watch this guy practice because he was so phenomenal.

The one game that sticks out the most in my mind was the '85 game in Green Bay, during the height of the Ditka-Gregg feud. Anticipation and tempers were running short. Before the game the Bears found a sack of manure in the locker room with a card on it from a radio station that said something about the Bears stinking. Early in the game, Kenny Still, a safety for Green Bay, lit up Matt Suhey so long after the play was over that he got penalized. On another play Payton was running down the sidelines when a defensive back hit Payton out of bounds—and Payton was sort of pulling him out of bounds—but the guy rode Payton so far out of bounds that he got kicked out. And the game sort of deteriorated into a slugfest and a very dirty game, one of the dirtiest I ever saw. I think the Fridge scored a TD on a pass from McMahon, and McMahon ran past the Green Bay bench and gave Gregg the finger right in front of everybody at Lambeau Field. It wasn't a very high-scoring game, just an ugly game (Chicago won, 16-10). Payton took the game completely into his hands and ended up gaining something like two hundred yards. He just took the game over.

◇

HUB ARKUSH started in 1979 as publisher and editor of *Pro Football Weekly*, which is based in Chicago. He later started doing some radio work for the Bears in 1985, working with the pregame, halftime, and postgame shows. In 1986, Payton's next-to-last year as a player, Arkush started doing color commentary on the Bears radio network. Arkush interviewed Payton a number of times over the years and continued to see him after his retirement through some charity work and other similar circumstances:

I remember 1985, the Super Bowl year, as definitely a year in which he was as focused and dedicated as anyone I've ever seen. The Bears got off to a great start in '85. Week Three was the Thursday night game in Minnesota, where McMahon came off the bench to—what everyone said—was win the game for Chicago, but in fact it was a block that Walter threw that made the difference. It was on the very first play where McMahon audibled at the line of scrimmage and they had Willie Gault running a fly. Walter read the blitz and just annihilated the linebacker. They proceeded to score three touchdowns in five minutes and turn that game around. Against San Francisco that year, something like Game Five or Game Seven (they had lost to the 49ers in the NFC Championship game the year before), they went out to San Francisco, and that was the game Walter had been pointing to since the offseason. I believe it was on the Bears' final possession that they drove for a touchdown. It was something like twelve plays for seventy-some yards, and Walter carried the ball ten or eleven times for almost all of those yards, and he really put the game on his back as if to say, "This is it. We're going to put this game away."

He had always been a great leader, more by example than vocal. But he became a little more of a vocal leader when it was necessary, because people sometimes forget that this was the youngest team in the NFL. Walter knew he was already in the Hall of Fame but that it wouldn't mean anything if he didn't have a ring to go with it. I think he may have had his best season that year even though he had better numbers in other years. In the national perspective, I think he was overshadowed a

bit, mainly because of things like the Forty-six Defense, McMahon's being so obnoxious, and then the whole Fridge phenomenon. But in Chicago there was no question that it was Walter first and then everybody else. Matter of fact, *Time* magazine got caught up in the whole thing, and their cover shot was Ditka, the Fridge, and Walter, even though the defense seemed to be the story.

◇

Payton's dream came true after the 1985 season when the Bears won the Super Bowl in dominating fashion, although it had a bittersweet feel to it, as placekicker **BOB THOMAS** points out:

By 1984, when we went to the NFC Championship against the 49ers, the talk was starting about how Walter was getting toward the end of his career, and the feeling on the team at this point was how few years he had left and that he deserves to win a Super Bowl. So it went from where he was the entire team and the goal was to be a better team, to where we had more weapons and the thinking is he is entitled to a Super Bowl. That's why people were so up in arms when he didn't score a touchdown in that game because by that time the focus was on Walter and how he needed a Super Bowl, which is so important in defining a career when you consider how stars like Dan Fouts and Dan Marino ended up never winning a Super Bowl.

◇

ESPN reporter **ED WERDER** has covered NFL football for more than a decade, and his interest in the game dates back much farther, giving him a credible perspective when it comes to ranking Payton among football's greatest players:

He was a very competitive guy who came from a small school, and that didn't happen all that often. Everyone will remember the

grace with which he ran and his incredible ability to change directions. But I think it was his strength as a player that most surprised people because it escaped their notice. Just the number of times he was able to shed tacklers; his trademark stiff-arm. Then in the twilight of his career the Bears won the Super Bowl. He gave them an identity for a long time—he was really all they had, either offensively or defensively, for a lot of losing seasons. Then (Mike) Ditka was a great personality who came into the organization and (Jim) McMahon made just enough plays as a quarterback, and then they put together one of the most ferocious defenses ever, maybe the most intimidating defense in the history of the league, and easily won the Super Bowl, losing only one game along the way.

He certainly is in the elite class of players I've seen since following football, at least in the top ten players and among the top three running backs just because of the many things he could do. He was a receiver, a great leader, had a tremendous work ethic, and just refused to be denied despite how bad the team was he was playing on. Walter Payton always rose above those things.

◇

MIKE ADAMLE played only two seasons with the Bears (1975–76), but he has remained in Chicago much of his post-football career as a television sportscaster and is a lifelong member of the fraternity known as former Bears players:

I think one of the things Walter wanted his former teammates to take away with them from all that has happened this weekend is that we belong to the greatest fraternity in the world, and that we also belong to the greatest football family in the world, the Chicago Bears football family. And that it shouldn't take a public memorial service in his honor to bring us all back together again. And it shouldn't be twenty-five years or ten years. So all of us

talking in the locker room today and yesterday's ceremony have made a vow that we will reach out to each other, we will stay in touch with each other, we will love each other for the rest of our days here on this earth because that's the way Walter would want it.[1]

◇

TOM THAYER played eight seasons for the Bears as a guard, giving him three seasons of overlap with Payton's career. Thayer played college ball at Notre Dame and then put in a stint in the World Football League before joining the Bears in 1985, where he was suddenly a teammate of his idol. Thayer was in the eighth grade in Joliet, Illinois, just outside Chicago, when Payton was drafted in 1975:

I was in a unique position in regard to Walter Payton. I went through three stages of my own Walter Payton era. When he was drafted by the Bears in 1975, I was in the eighth grade, growing up in Joliet, which is in the Chicago area. Football is Joliet. No matter how bad the Bears were in those early years, Walter was great, and he became a hero to me. The four years when I was in high school, we won the state championships, so you can imagine how much of a figure Walter Payton was for me growing up. Then I went to Notre Dame, still, being right in the vicinity, I was always a Bears fan. Then I got to know him as a teammate, a peer, and I got a chance to play with someone I had worshiped before I ever got a chance to meet him. Even after he retired, we remained friends. So there you have the three stages. He went from a hero to a peer and teammate to a friend.

I can remember the first day of practice with the Bears and looking across the huddle at Walter Payton while a play was being called and being in such awe. I couldn't believe I was standing there in the same huddle with him. I never looked at it as being the downside of his career. I never looked at him as an older player being on the downside of his career. I always saw

him as a player as enthusiastic as any of the players coming out of college.

I come from a close family in Joliet, and every Sunday afternoon my mom always cooks a big meal and all my nieces and nephews and brothers and sisters come over. One Sunday afternoon Walter shows up on his motorcycle, and he sat here with my family, and kids from the neighborhood were coming over, and they sat on his lap and sat on his motorcycle, and we had so much fun that day. The smile on his face is what I'll always remember, and these little kids didn't know at the time that here was one of the greatest football players in history. They just saw this guy showing up on his motorcycle, and they were laughing and giggling. That day was pretty awesome to me, the fact that he would take that time to show up and present himself like that.

◇

Many members of that Super Bowl Bears team of 1985 continued to stay in touch with each other over the years, and one of the lightning rods was the personable Payton, even after he became sick. **VAN HORNE** ran into Payton at a Bears game a year or two before Payton passed away, and they had a nice chat that included a promise to get together for dinner sometime. Little did Van Horne, or Payton for that matter, know that Payton's time for camaraderie was running perilously short:

I spoke with Matt Suhey a couple of weeks before Walter died and the word still was that Walter needed the transplant. At least, that's what most of us thought would do it—would turn him around. But we didn't know about the cancer, too. He didn't want anybody to know about it. And that's what I mean about his pride. I don't think he wanted the media involved with all the strain on his family and all the stress and worrying. And so he kind of always kept it to himself, his family, and his real close friends. Matt knew what was up when I was talking to him two

weeks earlier, but he didn't let on. Matt already knew then that Walter was dying, and that's a credit to Matt.

Three weeks later I was home watching TV, and it comes on that he had died. And that was quite a shock. It tore a lot of people up and caught most people by surprise because we all thought he would pull through it. He was the last guy, I'm serious, he's the last guy on that team that anybody thought would leave us at such a young age. He had more energy than anybody. It was sad. He had a great game face.

SWEETNESS

PAYTON'S CB HANDLE WAS MISSISSIPPI Maniac, a perfect moniker for anyone who ever saw him whiz by in a sports car or sat terror-stricken in the passenger seat praying to God with all sincerity. In his youth, Payton called himself Spider Man, a reference presumably to his favorite comic book hero, even though it's unlikely that Payton ever climbed a skyscraper. But he will forever be known as Sweetness, which is appropriate in one sense, considering that one of his favorite childhood pals was Edward "Sugar Man" Moses. Payton turned out to be the more famous of the two sugar men, apparently earning his nickname-for-perpetuity while playing at Jackson State and making moves around and through would-be tacklers that drew incredulous laughter. He tickled in the way he couldn't be tackled.

"Sweetness" may also have had something to do with his familiar high-pitched voice, although it was an apt description of his selflessness and humility. Payton was as accessible as he was affable, exuding a combination of those qualities that won over people of all ages, genders, and races. Being Sweetness was don-

ning bell bottoms and a half-shirt, shaking his groove thing as a national finalist in a Soul Train contest. Being Sweetness was when he went the motivational-speech route, moving grown men to tears and twice being called on by Seattle Supersonics coach George Karl to give his team a pep talk prior to an NBA game. Being Sweetness was giving the Bears' receptionist a break and playing telephone operator to unsuspecting callers-in. Being Sweetness was taking time out from practice to spend fifteen minutes speaking to and comforting a boy dying of cancer.

Sweetness was somebody special.

DAN JIGGETTS played seven seasons for the Bears as an offensive tackle and has established himself as one of Chicago's most prominent and popular sportscasters in the city. Once he starts reminiscing about Payton, he starts laughing—sometimes out of humor, other times out of sheer amazement at what Payton could accomplish:

His life was about enjoying himself and his teammates and having a lot of fun. He always had a positive outlook on life, and that was something to behold. When things get tough for a lot of people, they tend to go into a shell. He was just the opposite. While working with him in radio the last two or three years of his life, I got to see the whole range of Walter. I remember when he was given the Lamborghini. He was living in Arlington Heights at the time, and he called me, saying, "C'mon over, check it out." So I went over to take a look at the thing, and I go, "Walter, I'm a lineman. I can't fit into that thing, it's like a teacup." And he said, "I wasn't going to let you ride anyway, because you might hurt the suspension."

His life was always about having a good time with his friends and making sure he shared those good times. He was one of those rare individuals who enjoyed seeing other people around him enjoy all the attention that came with what he accomplished.

Most people in that position are not good about sharing the spot-light. When we did radio together, it wasn't hard for him because he would never stop. The things he would do when we were off the air are the same things he would do while we were on the air—always pinching you and prodding you and just generally bothering you. He would hide your keys and leave them with the maitre d' or whatever. As soon as you realized that something was missing, you would go, "Oh, Walter's got it."

He was extremely comfortable broadcasting. He was working right up close to the end, and as we were approaching this last season (1999), I figured it would be tough for him to come back and do the show. Until February, he kept it up. The day that he made the announcement about his illness, and it was on the radio show, we were sitting in the back of the restaurant and shed a few tears. You knew there was some serious trouble ahead for him. We had some one-on-one interviews for him to go do, and I'm rubbing him on the back and hands on his shoulders, saying "C'mon, Champ, let's go get 'em." So I pat him on the back, and he goes, "Hey, man, you hit me on my liver." And I said, "You don't even know where your liver is." Without looking back, he reaches back and hits me right in that area where you don't want to be hit. He was just nonstop.

◇

Payton was one grown man unafraid to cry, and there were times his selfless actions would make other people cry, such as the time Bears director of administration **BILL MAGRANE** got misty-eyed watching Payton take time out from practice once to visit with a high school student terminally ill with cancer:

The kid was from Barrington, which, ironically, is where Walter lived years ago. And they brought this kid to watch the practice one day, nice-looking young kid. And he wanted to meet Walter, and so I arranged it and Walter came out early for practice that

day. It was during training camp in August in Lake Forest. As he came out of the locker room, of course, people started to surge toward him to get an autograph and he was very stern as he said, "No, not now. I've got to see Pat (or whatever this kid's name was)." And he said, "I'll give you an autograph after practice." And he went over to where this kid was. Walter introduced himself and said, "C'mon," and he took the kid, and the two of them went clear down to the other end of the field where no others were around. This was before practice. Then there was a blocking dummy lying on the ground, and so Walter sat down on the dummy and the kid sat down facing him. And Walter real, real quickly snatched this kid up and snapped a baseball cap off this kid's head and put his helmet on him. And then he put the cap on. And they talked for fifteen minutes or so, and that was that. And the kid died in the fall, his parents had called and told us. And I told Walter, he said, "It's okay, it's okay. We talked, and he was okay with this." I remember things like that about him.

◇

Placekicker **BOB THOMAS** joined the Bears in that memorable 1975 draft that also brought in the likes of Payton and Roland Harper. Thomas ended up kicking for the Bears most or all of ten seasons before finishing his twelve-year career with the New York Giants in 1986. Thomas got to know Payton almost as well as any of his other teammates, finding the superstar running back as someone who cared about each of his teammates in a personal way that sometimes was hard to understand if you didn't know him. At best, placekickers usually are regarding by their real-football-playing teammates as necessary nuisances, although Payton wasn't like that, as Thomas, now an Illinois appellate judge, recalls:

One of my best memories of Walter actually concerned a time when I was playing for the Detroit Lions for a few games. This was 1982, Mike Ditka's first year with the Chicago Bears. I had been injured at the end of '81 and came back thinking there

wasn't much doubt that I was going to be the placekicker in 1982. They had a guy filling in for me at the end of the year by the name of John Roveto, and (head Bears coach) Neill Armstrong had made it very clear that I'd be the kicker in 1982. Well, Neill Armstrong was not retained. Ditka came in, and he decided to go with Roveto. Eddie Murray was the kicker for Detroit at the time, and, consequently, Eddie walked out on a contract dispute just days before the first game, which happened to be the Lions against the Bears. The Lions signed me to fill in for Murray, so I ended up kicking against the Bears. I kicked a field goal right before the half, and we went on to win the game. Then came the strike, which lasted nine weeks. Murray came back after the strike, and later that year I was picked off again by the Bears and played another three years with Walter in Chicago.

That Detroit game against the Bears was sort of surreal for me in the first place, as there I was watching all these guys I had played with, but I was wearing a Lions uniform. After the game ended, I was going up the tunnel and Walter came over—we really didn't even talk—he just came over and hugged me, and we stood there in the tunnel just hugging one another probably for thirty seconds, but it seemed like two or three minutes. That was really kind of a foreshadowing of what was going to happen when I was released from the Bears for good in 1985, which was right after I had had my best year in 1984.

In the '85 draft they picked Kevin Butler with their fourth-round pick. Ditka called me into his office on a hot, steamy day in August and told me that they were going to go with the younger guy, Butler, and he went on to do a great job and played another decade or so with the Bears. Unlike what had happened in 1982, with my playing for a while with the Lions, by this time I had played ten years and knew that my time with the Bears was over for good. I was a lot more devastated as a result of that. I left Ditka's office knowing there was a team meeting at nine o'clock in the morning, but I didn't want to go down and say my good-byes at this time because I wanted to have a few days to compose

myself and then go see my friends. So I went to see Ken Valdiserri, who at the time was the Bears' public relations man. Kenny was misty-eyed himself as well because here's Bob Thomas, a Notre Dame graduate, like Kenny, and he also recognized the fact that I wasn't going to be with the Bears anymore. As I was sitting there, I wanted to wait for a period of time so the team would be in a meeting. And I sat up there about a half hour just talking to Kenny, and then he left and I figured 9:30 even the stragglers would be in the meeting. So I walked down into the locker room, figuring it would be empty, to gather my personal things and my shoes and whatnot. I walked in and there wasn't even an equipment manager around, and you could hear a pin drop in that locker room. As I walked to my locker, I was startled to see Walter Payton in there, sitting in my locker on top of my shoes. And I said, "Walter, what are you doing here?" He took me outside and walked with me and buried my head into his chest, and I was at this point more than misty-eyed; I was crying like a baby, and here's the greatest football player, in my opinion, of all time, talking to a kicker at the end of his career and telling me what it had meant for him to play with me for ten years.

One of the things Ken told me was that Walter had been there before the offices opened that morning or at least right when they were opening. And Walter went right into Ken's office, figuring he knew something since he was the public relations man and certainly would have a press release written as far as the cuts were concerned. He demanded to know whether or not I had made the team. And Ken said, "I can't tell you anything," and Walter said, "Well, you've just told me everything." So he had gotten there early to find out, and that's why he was there at my locker—he was aware that it wasn't going to go my way, and that's how he ended up planning to sit there and be with me, knowing how I'd feel. So it was really a moving time for me.

◇

NFL Commissioner **PAUL TAGLIABUE,** giving a eulogy at Payton's memorial service at Soldier Field:

In celebrating Sweetness this week, a lot has been said. It is understandable because his impact on so many people was so extraordinary. . . . For thirteen seasons, he was your warrior, your warrior here in Chicago. He followed in a Bears tradition that began with George Halas and included so many people. Red Grange, Sid Luckman, Dick Butkus, the Monsters of the Midway, Gale Sayers, and then Walter Payton. In a way, he synthesized it all and underscored what it all meant. He was your neighbor, not just a warrior, but a neighbor. Jarrett (Payton) said it earlier this week, that the family's greatest thanks goes to you, the people of Chicago. You gave Walter Payton a home, and he moved in next door. He became your neighbor, constantly helping people in Chicagoland, and you pay tribute to him today by coming here with joy and by signing up for donor transplants. And you can continue to remember and honor Walter Payton by being great neighbors to each other as he was to you and as you were to him.

For fans all across America, Walter Payton was something else. He was a friend. He was open, accessible, easy. He was in many ways what we don't expect a superstar to be: open, accessible, genuine, down to earth, a unifier, and a binder. Never divisive . . . Walter Payton was a binder and a peacemaker. He made people see what bound them together, not what might divide them. I am tempted to call him a brother, but I reserve that for Eddie and for Pamela. So I'll just call him a friend who was Sweetness.[1]

◇

Defensive end **DAN HAMPTON** offered one of the most emotional eulogies at Payton's Soldier Field memorial service:

I'm very happy that the Chicago Bears team of 1999 is here today because you have to understand how special it is to be a Chicago

Bear. Walter Payton would say it, too. And if he could say one thing about going up to Green Bay, I know what it would be. Because he used to tell us that every week. So, excuse me, play your [butts] off. That's all he ever wanted from us. . . . We know what he was as a man. As good as you will ever find on the face of the planet. We know that he is now a great, great man, and we know the incredible legacy that he leaves behind and his family, Connie and the kids. But I've got to tell you something. You know, I remember this guy playing on this field and leaving it on this field time after time. I've got a little girl, she's four years old. Ten years from now, when she asks me about the Chicago Bears, I'll tell her about a championship, and I'll tell her about great teams and great teammates and great coaches, and how great it was to be a part of it. But the first thing I'd tell her about is Walter Payton.[2]

◇

Payton was playing drums in high school before he got around to playing football, and his love for percussions never wavered, as writer **BEN WOODS** recalls in the column he wrote following Payton's death, which is reprinted here with Woods's permission:

The late Walter Payton has been called the greatest football player by some, the greatest running back by others, even the greatest humanitarian in athletics.

Now, Billy Lowes, seventy, of Owensboro (Kentucky) would like to add another to the list—greatest athlete who could play the drums.

Lowes, originally from Marion, Indiana, lived in Chicago and played the drums in bands there for eighteen years. While playing in clubs as many as seven nights a week, he also worked at Ludwig Drum Company. During the day, Lowes took visitors on plant tours, then gave a demonstration on his drums.

One day in 1979, William Ludwig Jr., president of the com-

pany, told Lowes that Payton was going to visit and that they were to hold a drum duet.

Lowes was ecstatic Payton would be visiting. But he was unsure of the man's drumming talents.

"I thought he was just going to hammer around," Lowes said.

But Sweetness surprised Lowes. They played together for about ninety minutes. Lowes told Payton he didn't even know he played drums. Payton wanted to start his own rock band, so Ludwig Drum gave him a new drum set.

As a Chicago Bears fan, Lowes followed Payton's career. He watched a lot of the games on television because he was working whenever they played. Lowes even remembers the game in which Payton broke Jim Brown's career rushing record—October 7, 1984, against the New Orleans Saints at Chicago's Soldier Field.

The news of Payton's death November 1 (1999) hit Lowes just as hard as anyone who knew the man.

"Everybody was shocked," Lowes said. "He was so young. He was the sweetest talker."

But Lowes is still going. He moved to Owensboro ten years ago and still plays in two local bands, playing in Central City and Drakesboro. Of course, things are different from Chicago— things are slower here, and the pay's not nearly as good. But Lowes has enjoyed his time and will continue to play as long as he can.

Lowes also followed the Bulls and the Cubs—he was never into hockey much—but still considers the Bears his main sporting love. Although Walter Payton's main sporting love was football, Lowes believes Sweetness would have wanted others to know about his love of music as well.

"He would appreciate it," Lowes said. "Only a few people know he even had a rock band."

Who those few are, I'm not sure, but there is the Walter Payton's Roadhouse in Aurora, Illinois, which features live music, mainly jazz and blues. According to the Chicago Bears' Web site, Payton once said he would brag about his cymbal-playing abili-

ties. And he also once made it to the national finals in a dance competition on Soul Train.

Of course, there's always the "Super Bowl Shuffle."

If you're not familiar with the song, the Bears, on their way to winning Super Bowl XX, made a hit as ten players sang verses. The first was sung by Payton. A small sampling follows:

"Well, they call me Sweetness,

"And I like to dance.

"Runnin' the ball is like makin' romance . . ."

Music was always a part of Payton, usually left out because of his other great talents. Sweetness often ran as if he were moving to music, and that's how he'll be remembered. Billy Lowes, on the other hand, was one of the few who got to make music alongside one of the greatest athletes to ever live.[3]

◇

FRED CAITO was the Chicago Bears trainer for many years, during which time he developed a strong friendship with Payton, a friendship that continued long after both had left the Bears. In fact, not long before his death, Payton had been discussing with Caito the possibility of opening a fitness center near O'Hare Airport that would cater to executives. With the Bears, Caito had been part of the behind-the-scenes team that helped keep Payton shipshape enough to miss only one game in thirteen years, although there were plenty of scary bumps and bruises along the way:

He was unique as an individual—a very loyal, very caring person. He cared a great deal about the little guy, and while the public perceived that, that's exactly how he came across to me in private. Everyone knows that he was a prankster, but there was a serious part to him, too. I think I probably saw the serious more than a lot of other people because I had to deal with him and his injuries, and, believe me, he had injuries. He played the game with broken ribs, a separated shoulder, severely sprained ankle, and bad knees the whole second half of his career. He would fight

through those things and get his treatments, and that's where his uniqueness was. I don't know of any other athlete I've ever worked with who could have done what he did in dealing with his injuries and playing with them. He hurt and he suffered, and he paid for it. But he needed to be at the level he wanted to be, and he knew that he had to pay that price.

Walter's injuries were never of the nature where he wasn't functional. Now with football players in general, there are situations where the doctor will step in and make the recommendation that you can't play even when you want to and think you can. But as long as you had function, you could play. Walter could go out and play with a broken rib, where with other players, you didn't get that far. They say, "I can't play." "It hurts." "I can't do this." And if they can't run and they can't twist and turn, obviously then there is a risk in playing. But with Walter, all of a sudden on Sunday everything would be functional. Even though that rib was broken, he could play with it. He could twist and turn with bandages. That made him a rare, rare individual.

We were fortunate in this city, we saw with Michael Jordan, and we saw with Walter Payton, their longevity. By that I don't mean they just hung around for a lot of years—they didn't miss games. They played, and they played. I know that Michael Jordan played sick and hurt, and there were many times that he was able to come back out and play. Walter had turf toe in Tampa so bad once that the toe was quite swollen. Normally, turf toe knocks anyone out. Turf toe is tender to the touch, and 80 percent of your body weight is on your large toe. And he just went out in that game and scored a touchdown on an eight-yard run. It was one of the greatest runs covering eight yards I've ever seen—on his toes, and he had to dance on the sidelines to get to the end zone, and I know that hurt.

◇

Many people got to know Payton at a superficial level, and a number to the degree that they considered him a buddy, but precious few broke Payton's inner circle that included his wife, Connie, and former teammate Matt Suhey. **JOE KANE** was among those who had a spot in the second circle around Payton, and that status afforded him a view of some of Payton's different sides:

I think I got to know him pretty well. When he had a bad day or a bad game, you could see the moods that he was in. I would have dinner with him the Monday after the game or whatever, days when he couldn't raise his right arm up even to drink a cup of coffee, and he would be doing everything left-handed. He could sit and talk about how bad it was the last week or about whatever reasons they had lost the game, such as the time he got thrown out for bumping into the ref in the end zone, which was really a bogus call as far as anybody who saw it on TV.

Walter had a lucky pair of pants. The same pair of pants he wore for something like his first six seasons. It was one of those black-and-blue games against Detroit or Green Bay, I think, when he carried the ball up the middle, and sure enough he got hit again and split his pants right up the middle. He was on the ground and wouldn't get up. Someone asked, "Are you hurt?" and he said, "No, but I'm not getting up. Go and get the equipment manager."

"Are you hurt?"

"No! Get the equipment manager in here."

So the equipment manager came out, then came back to the bench, got a big towel, took it out to Walter. Finally, he came off the field with a big towel wrapped around him, and he changed his pants.

Another time, we had him, Doug Plank, and George Halas speak at a Hilton regional general managers' meeting in Chicago. Walter of course talked about offense, Doug talked about defense, and George talked about teamwork. There were some guys there that we used to like to kid by taking potshots at them. One

Englishman there was named Arthur Jensen, and Arthur was one of these people you either called "Ahhh-thuhh" or "Mr. Jensen." You never called him just "Jensen." I told Walter before it was time for him to speak, "Pick on this guy a little bit, would ya?" So Walter got up there and says, "Who's this Gib-son guy, anyway?" So you can imagine this proper Britisher getting red in the face. This guy ran a Hilton up in the Detroit area where the Bears would stay when they went up there to play the Lions. Walter checked in the next game after that, and Arthur put him into a room with no furniture. Walter just laughs and says, "I'll get back at him." Walter calls the whole team together, gave them the guy's name and the spelling of his name, and every restaurant check they signed from that time forward during their stay had the general manager's name on it. He was always doing something like that.

◇

ED WERDER has been one of the most astute NFL reporters for more than a decade, most recently with ESPN, and one of his most vivid memories of Payton occurred off the football field, long after his 1987 retirement from the Bears:

When the Dallas Cowboys opened the 1996 season on *Monday Night Football* against the Bears, Emmitt Smith hurt his neck at the end of the game diving over the top for a touchdown. It looked like a very serious injury, and Emmitt was attended to on the field for a very long time. He was then taken back to the dressing room to be transported to the hospital. He had some numbness in his extremities, so a cervical collar was placed on him and they actually cut his uniform off of him. Payton came into the room as he was being taken to the hospital and actually stayed with Smith to the hospital. Walter left the game in the ambulance with Emmitt, and before he left he wrote his personal home and cellular phone numbers down on the back of Cowboys

PR director Rich Dalrymple's pass and told him if he could be of
any further assistance with Emmitt that he would gladly do so.
That was something that speaks to what kind of humanitarian he
was, because Emmitt was a guy, and still is a guy, that many per-
ceive of being in close pursuit of Walter's career rushing record,
yet Walter cared more for him as a person than as someone who
might break his record.

◇

Not only was Payton a great player, he also was great at being playful,
even while on the air for a broadcast as was the case during Pro Bowl
week after the 1987 season. Bears radio broadcaster **HUB ARKUSH**
had the chore this time of trying to make it through a show without
letting Walter get to him:

In those years, the Bears were sending eight, nine, ten guys out to
the Pro Bowl, and the radio station had an arrangement where
they sent me and our play-by-play guy. We would do a live, two-
hour roundtable Pro Bowl talk show with players the day before

Now it's 1983 and the
Bears are starting to
turn the corner, thanks
still in large part to
Payton and the arrival
of new quarterback
Jim McMahon
(Number 9, in the
background). Few
ballcarriers could get
away with the one-
handed carry the way
Payton did.

the game. Walter retired in '87, and we were sitting out on the veranda by the second-floor pool, looking out over Waikiki Beach and set up with a crowd of a couple hundred people there. We had Walter and Ronnie Lott, Dave Waymer, Dave Duerson, and one other player. We were sitting on these bar stools. They had had these special shorts made up for us and they looked kind of goofy.

We go to start the show, and the producer gave me the cue to start, and Walter, sitting next to me, decides right then to pluck a hair out of my leg. Walter was famous for his physical contact. Every time during that two hours when he saw the producer give me the cue to start back in out of a commercial, Walter would yank a hair and I'd jump or screech or something. It was a typical Walter Payton moment, but you couldn't get mad at him. Walter was enjoying himself, and he thought it was the funniest thing ever.

◇

Behind that high-pitched voice and thousand-watt smile, Payton had a tough streak that *Chicago Sun-Times* reporter **BRIAN HEWITT** said made Payton even more like that other Chicago sports icon, Michael Jordan:

I think that high-pitched, almost squeaky voice is part of where the name "Sweetness" came from, because on the football field there was nothing sweet about him. He really was a nasty SOB. I compare him that way to Michael Jordan. I mean Michael has this wonderful smile and he's a Madison Avenue dream, but Michael Jordan was really a (no-nonsense guy) not only on the court against other teams but in practice against his own team. Walter, certainly on Sundays, would freakin' knock your face off if it wasn't protected. But there was a public image and there are a lot of athletes who have figured out they can be one way talking to a print reporter and be another way when the microphone or camera is going. In golf, Lee Trevino and Raymond Floyd are examples of guys who are like that. But I respected Walter and didn't

think he was a bad guy, but people would come up to me all the time and ask me what Walter Payton was like, and they sort of didn't want to hear the warts. They just wanted to hear that he was the greatest.

The irony is that Walter really was a good guy as opposed to an O. J. Simpson, who on the other hand was a writer's dream. I think O. J. in his own way was every bit the runner that Walter was—allowing for different styles, sure, they were two of the best five that ever lived. O. J., from a writer's standpoint, would suffer fools gladly. He would stay there after games and accommodate writers in waves, staying there until the last one was done. With Walter, it was like pulling teeth. That doesn't make Walter a bad guy because he didn't have a great rapport with writers—and O. J.'s rapport with writers doesn't make him a good guy.

◇

RALPH CIANCIARULO was another of Payton's off-field cronies, an avid hunting buddy, who saw Payton at his best when doing things for other people, such as making charitable appearances at which he gave 100 percent:

One year when doing the Halas/Payton Foundation event for all the inner-city kids, we had a thing at the McCormick Place with all the Bears. Walter asked me if we could set up a free kids' archery range. We probably ended up with something like eight hundred to a thousand kids shooting, which was cool. And I remember watching him with the kids. Just unbelievable.

The sad part is that a lot of people didn't know what he was all about. Maybe all they knew about him was seeing him play football on TV or his name on a lot of businesses. If I could say anything about him, it's that he was real. The trick was getting him away from the cell phones and the beepers. I would threaten him that "you're not bringing the cell phone into the tree stand.

No way you're bringing that damn phone up there." He loved the outdoors. He had a stack of bows. He just loved it.

◇

GREG MILLER, executive sports producer for Fox TV's affiliate in Chicago, had a hand in polishing Payton's media skills when Payton did some work producing features for the Fox station in the late nineties:

He was like a reporter for us. It was all his ideas, too—stuff that he wanted to do. One of the things he wanted to do was something funny on offensive linemen, like, What would you have the quarterback buy you for protecting him? It was a fantasy kind of thing. So we ran around all that week shooting this ridiculous stuff. In one of these instances, he had offensive lineman James "Big Cat" Williams at a jewelry store, showing him all these rings while we were shooting all this stuff. It's funny how Walter

The eyes have it as Payton cuts upfield in a 1984 game against the Tampa Bay Bucs.

seemed to know everybody in Chicago and was able to get this stuff arranged. He'd make a phone call and things would happen. He had arranged for three red Ferraris to be driven onto the practice field at the old Halas Hall, where these offensive-line guys stand in front of the Ferraris pretending that the quarterback had bought them for them. Of course, Walter hadn't told anybody with the Bears that he was doing this, and Dave Wannstedt was the coach at this time. So, you've got these guys from a Ferrari dealership driving these cars onto the practice field, where there's no road or anything. These three red Ferraris are then sitting on the practice field, and you could see Wannstedt looking out of his office with a look that said, "What in the hell is going on?" This was right before practice. And we're out there shooting this thing, and I'm like "Whatever. He does what he wants to." He was a spectacle.

He spent a lot of time arranging all this stuff. He was constantly on the phone. He had one of those cell phones that had the headset, like it was in his pocket or whatever, and he was constantly doing three things at once. We would go to a mall and he would know almost everybody there. He'd stop and talk to this person and would be on the phone at the same time. It was constant motion. It was exhausting for me because I wasn't used to it.

◇

BOB VERDI wrote a regular sports column for the *Chicago Tribune* for twenty years, until 1998, and still writes one column a week, and chances are that Payton was one of his regular readers, even if Payton would never have admitted it:

The last time I saw him was in O'Hare Airport, and he looked fine. I was running for a plane, and all of a sudden I hear, "Psssst. You! Verdi!" I turn around and there's Walter, holding a cigar. I smoke cigars, and he doesn't. He says, "This is for you." And I said, "Where did you get that?" And he said, "Someone gave it to

me. Now don't smoke it on the plane because I ain't coming to bail you out of jail." And that was that. That was the last time I saw him alive.

◈

Soon after he first got sick, Payton went around to tell his friends in a subtle way that he wasn't well. One of those to learn early about Payton's condition was his good hunting buddy **CIANCIARULO:**

At Thanksgiving (November 1998), he called me up and said, "Ralphie, are you going to be home? I'd like to come up." I said, "Good, because we're having turkey." And he said, "Oh, I hate turkey." I asked him if he had ever had it deep-fried, and he said, "No." But he said he would be there.

He pulls up. Mom and Dad, Vickie and I, and a good friend of ours were there celebrating Thanksgiving. Walter got out of the car, and he wasn't looking too good at all. He comes and gives all of us a big hug, then he turns to me and says, "I want to talk with you." Then he goes, teasing with me, "Man, you're getting stronger." And I said, "That's because you're getting too damn thin." And he just told me what's going on. It sucked. That's the bottom line. So many people out there who do so much crap in their life and nothing ever happens to them, and you wonder sometimes, "Lord, why?" And there's only one person that knows, and it's Him. You can't question it. It was bad. I was like, "Is there anything we can do," when obviously there wasn't. That evening when he left—and by the way he did try the turkey and he did like it—I had a horrible feeling because it just wasn't him.

◈

As outgoing as Payton was, he really wasn't an exuberantly vocal team leader among the Bears. He was moderately outspoken when circumstances called for it, and his hard play on every down for four quarters was an inspirational example, but when he spoke up, he

chose his moments carefully even while allowing few people to really get to know him, as offensive lineman **MARK BORTZ** could attest to:

He was a private person, but a straight, up-front guy with you, too. He didn't even have to say anything. He was the type of player who demanded respect without actually asking for it. People looking back at those great teams we had in the eighties will always say that we were what we were because of our great defense or because we finally got a quarterback, but the truth is that Walter himself had a lot to do with our success. He made everyone around him play better, and not just the players on offense.

Another thing you've got to remember about Walter is that he played in an era before the modern type of superstar emerged drawing these huge salaries you see nowadays. That's not to say Walter didn't make a very good salary. He did, probably somewhere around a million dollars a year. But compare that to today, which isn't so long after he retired, and I think now the average starter in the NFL is making something like $1.2 million a year. Even then, the money wouldn't have meant that much to Walter if he were still playing today. I know that he played for the love of the game and for the honor of going out there day after day and doing a good job. Sometimes it's enough just to be appreciated, and there's no doubt that everyone appreciated him.

◇

To know Walter Payton was to not really know him, not like you would a foxhole buddy or sorority brother. **MAGRANE** had a good open-door relationship with Payton, but there wasn't anything revelatory about that:

Yeah, he kept you out here. I don't feel like I got to know him well. But I felt a lot of times that I knew him pretty well. You know, he would say things; he would come in and talk—he loved to come in and visit. But know him well, no. I don't think any-

body did. And I think people who are really honest, his old team-
mates and so forth, would have to say the same thing. He only let
you get to know him to a certain extent, and that was that. I think
he let Matt (Suhey) get closer than anybody else. And Matt was
such a bulldog guy. You know the cartoons about the little dog
that gets hold of your trouser leg and you have to kick him off?
That's what Matt would do in his friendship. He wouldn't let go.
Connie (Walter's wife) said that Walter scared some people away
when he was sick because he was crappy and grouchy and pouty,
and Matt said, "I'm not going to let you do that. I'm your friend.
I'm going to be there."

THAT'S THE SPIRIT

As INCREDIBLE AS HIS CAREER rushing yardage record of 16,726 yards is, Payton's 3,838 total carries is perhaps even more remarkable. Unlike at-bats in baseball or field-goal attempts in basketball, carries in football are as much a mark of intestinal fortitude and perseverance as they are longevity. A carry in football carries with it all kinds of obstacles and risks, any of which can knock a player out for a game, a season, or even a career. And whereas a lifetime .240 banjo hitter can still get three or four at-bats a game six or seven times a week, a running back is only going to get the ball twenty times a game if he is consistently productive, in effect "batting .300 or better" season after season. History will show that Payton was practically injury-free over thirteen seasons, missing just one game (in his rookie season), but Payton often played seriously hurt with a variety of injuries, including knees that were rapidly deteriorating late in his career. He gutted it out for more than a decade. His inner spirit burned brightly.

There's another side to the spirit of Payton, and that was his spirituality: his walk with God, his profession of a life lived for

Jesus Christ. Many professional athletes claim to be born-again Christians, and they have the accompanying end-zone routines and other on-field rituals down to a T to prove it. Perhaps some or most of those public displays are genuine representations of an athlete's "twenty-four/seven" devotion to Christ, maybe not. Superstars have been known to practically profess Christ in one breath and snort coke in the other; the former does not exonerate the latter. Then again, celebrity athletes encounter temptations and opportunities that constitute most men's wildest fantasies, and remaining steadfastly virtuous while walking through those mine-fields requires a power beyond any one man's human capabilities.

Eddie Payton, Walter's older brother, said at Walter's memorial service at Soldier Field that his younger brother had always been a Christian believer, having been brought up in a home that nurtured prayer and regular attendance at church. Then again, is that enough? The Bible says that a man must leave and cleave, the first part of which refers to a man's leaving his birth family and going out into the world solely responsible for his personal salvation. A man's parents and siblings can pray for his salvation, but only he can acknowledge Jesus Christ and welcome the Lord into his heart. And that defines the difference in determining one man's faith. Payton did live an honorable, principled life, but his eternal salvation reportedly came on his deathbed, according to Bears teammate Mike Singletary, an ordained minister. In the Christian world, being principled and of high morals is expected, but it is not enough. One must acknowledge and accept Jesus Christ into his heart as his personal Savior, and Payton hit paydirt less than a month before he passed away.

◈

Perhaps even more amazing than his career total of 16,726 yards rushing was the fact that Payton carried the ball 3,838 times, an incredible record of endurance that likely will never be broken. Payton missed only one game during his thirteen-year career, which seems

almost superhuman considering that he was carrying the ball an average of between twenty to twenty-five times per game. Offensive lineman **MARK BORTZ** recalls Payton as a genuine iron man, while in turn Payton gave much of the credit back to the linemen in front of him:

He was durable. There were a number of games they didn't want him to play because of some injury or another, but Walter would want to play, and he would go out there and perform as best he could. That speaks highly of his mental toughness, too. He just wouldn't be denied, and there aren't too many people like that. A lot of players in his shoes, being banged up or whatever, would be more concerned about extending their careers and staying healthy in consideration of being a free agent in a few years, but not Walter. He gave you all he had at that moment. Not that he was reckless with his body or anything like that. He just wanted to play, and sometimes it meant playing a little bit hurt.

One time he gave shotguns to all of the offensive linemen because he knew that most of us liked to hunt. They were Brownings on which he had had inscribed the statement "Thanks for leading the way," as well as our names. Even though I'm a hunter, I still haven't fired mine yet, probably because it's just so nice. I don't want to break it in. I think he might have bought ones for Matt Suhey and Roland Harper, too.

◇

Football fans who watched Payton perform from a distance were often astounded by what he could do while carrying a football, catching a pass, or shedding a blocker. But there was more to the Payton phenomenon than what he did on the football field on Sunday afternoons or Monday nights, as attested to by former teammate **JEFF FISHER:**

Walter was an amazing person, and he could do some pretty incredible things. One thing he could do was stand at the forty-

yard line and throw football after football, consistently hitting one of the uprights in the end zone (fifty yards away). Other times he would walk on his hands all the way across the football field.

I remember one time going in to see our equipment man, Ray Earley, because I was always messing with my shoes to get them just right for my feet. I asked Ray for another pair of insoles for my shoes, and he immediately took me over to Walter's locker. "Here," he said while grabbing one of Walter's cleats, "put your hand inside this shoe and feel around." It was one of those old Spotbuilt shoes that had inch-long, screw-in cleats on the bottom. It was also a size eight and a half, which shows you just how small Walter's feet were. Anyway, I stuck my hand in the shoe and, literally, scratched my fingers. Walter had pulled out the insoles to his shoes so that, with his feet inside his shoes, he could actually feel the end of the screws from the other side that attached the cleats to the bottom of his shoes. Then he would wear only a single white sock over his feet. He did this so that he could always feel every cleat against the bottom of his feet, which he felt gave him great feel for maintaining traction while running on the turf. There were a lot of other hurts he played with that no one ever knew about.

◈

Quarterback **RUSTY LISCH** joined the Bears for one season, 1984, after being cut by the Cardinals, and he quickly got to
see just how relentlessly playful Payton was:

We had our summer camp in Platteville (Wisconsin) and would be going at it in the heat. Then when we got a water break, most of the guys would be sitting or lying down pouring ice water over themselves. Not Walter. He would run across the field to where there was a crowd watching and maybe grab a little kid out of the crowd and start running around the field with the kid, lifting him over his head as though he were lifting weights or

whatever. Other times during a break, he would walk across the field on his hands. It was obvious that he just enjoyed being a playful guy.

Everything with him was a contest. Who can punt the ball the farthest? Who can throw it the straightest? Stuff like that. Watching him show the sheer joy of playing football reminded me of what it had been like back in high school, where everything really was a game. But you realized after a while that all this entertaining was another way for him to train. He was working out the whole time, whether it was lifting a kid over his head, like in weight training, or just continuing to run while everyone else was resting up.

Just in that short time I played there, he could have left an impact on anybody. He had a different mindset than most players. I thought he had a great combination of playfulness and yet understanding his profession. He never lost sight of this being a game that you were brought up playing with your shirt sleeves cut off and going down to the lot and running around. He just had a real joy for the game you don't see at that level, where football becomes just a business. Every day, every drill, and every session he found a way to keep it a game. That is sometimes difficult to do day in, day out with all the mundane things that go with it—to find a way to keep it in perspective.

One time I'll never forget. Of course, I was a very average player. I didn't have a real professional attitude and didn't take the game to the level I needed to. I remember handing the ball off to him one time and him getting hit really hard. I was kind of following the play. He gets up, knowing he had gotten hit hard and that he had hit the other guy hard, and he never got up and taunted or whatever. He just turned around and walked back to the huddle saying, "Is he getting up, is he getting up?" But he wouldn't turn around to look or taunt. He wouldn't embarrass or showboat or turn around and make any kind of gestures. I don't know what his history is, but there must have been something going on with him in his upbringing with his work ethic and

developing a taste or passion for that. Something happened along the line that formulated inside him and made him what he was.

◇

JOHN DORSEY played with the Packers for six years, which gave him a dozen chances to go up against Payton in the black-and-blue games of the NFC Central Division. Dorsey also discovered that the intensity carried over to the basketball court as well:

I also played against Walter in some basketball games as well. You always talk about that Bears-Packers rivalry—not only does it extend to the football field, but every competitive field. A classic example of how intense the rivalry is occurred after the Bears won the Super Bowl. We had come down to Old Chicago Stadium to play the Bears in basketball after a Bulls game, in front of something like twenty thousand people. It was awesome. To Walter's credit, he was just as competitive on the basketball court as he was on the football field. He had really quick hands and played really good defense. He did everything in his power to drive that team to victory. But the Packers did win that game. I don't think he was as good a basketball player as he was a football player, but all those competitive attributes that you hear about—intestinal fortitude—come out in whatever he did. I wasn't quick enough to guard him. I was stuck down low guarding guys like Refrigerator Perry and Mark Bortz—the sluggoes. One time I was driving across the lane, and Walter hacked me. The ref didn't catch it because it was a homecourt ref. Jeez, he got away with everything.

As for football, I remember one time in particular. It was in '86 or '87. Mike Ditka and Forrest Gregg had this rivalry between the two organizations back into full swing. Walter took pride in being a Bear and exemplified everything about them. His name is synonymous with that organization. I'm not sure of the relation-

ship between him and Coach Ditka, but I guess it would be pretty good. Anyway, in the heat of the battle, Walter, of course, was running all over the Packers at Lambeau Field. He always seemed to get away with stuff. In one particular case, Mark Lee had run him out of bounds. It so happens they both wound up tugging and tossing on each other, and for some reason Walter had tugged a little too hard and kind of thrown Mark into the bench, and Mark Lee gets ejected, and Walter comes back and rushed for more yards.

◇

For the better part of ten years, **BOB THOMAS** was the undisputed placekicker for the Chicago Bears, although who's to say what would have happened to his job security had Payton decided to seriously pursue the kicking duties. Payton, you see, was not only a great runner with the ball and passer of the ball, he also was a talented kicker—a Walter of all trades, for sure, as Thomas points out:

I used to kid him and say I'm glad he chose not to be a place-kicker. But, you know, he wasn't bad. He kicked with his toe and had tremendous strength. He was a good punter as well. That was my joke with him, that I was glad he never chose to be a kicker. But we would go out there, and maybe he'd hit two and then miss a couple because he hadn't done it that much. We had these little contests. But usually he was smart enough to come out, hit just one and then walk away. If you're out there at the fifty and he hit his first one, he wasn't going to try a second one. He would just start making noises about how good he was and leave.

◇

Bears personnel guru **BILL TOBIN** lived near Payton for a number of years in a Chicago suburb, which meant he never knew when he might look into his rearview mirror and see No. 34 charging up from behind him in a sporty car:

Payton played through pain during much of his career, and his resilient spirit showed up even in workouts that included jumping rope. Despite a dislocated toe, here he is preparing for a 1986 game against Tampa Bay.

AP/WIDE WORLD PHOTOS, MARK ELIAS

Walter loved fast cars. After he broke Jim Brown's record, some company gave him a Lamborghini. I had never seen one before. Sometimes he would come up behind me as I was going to work early in the morning—and, of course, he would be going to work very early in the morning, too. He'd come up behind me and, almost like Indy 500, you'd be bumper to bumper and you'd look in the rearview mirror and there was Walter in a Lamborghini. He would see you look, then he would kick it outside and go around you and wave good-bye. He loved fast cars.

He was always approachable to sign whatever you wanted. He once signed a bunch of balls "Sweetness" for me, and all my children have one. Vince Tobin, my brother, put on a golf tournament for Saint Francis Hospital, where we grew up in northwest Missouri, and we've auctioned off a couple of Walter Payton balls

signed by him in his heyday—white balls with just one name on them—"Sweetness, Walter Payton," which he signed in '84 or '85.

◇

To know Walter Payton and to earn his respect, one had to have nerves of steel. For knowing Payton sometimes meant being a passenger in a vehicle driven to excessive speeds by the speedy running back. Business associate **JOE KANE** remembers what it was like to have Payton put the pedal to the metal:

I remember one day when he showed up driving an open-air jeep and said, "C'mon, get in. Strap yourself in because we're going for a ride." He ended up taking me to a construction site and jumping me over all these bumps of dirt while driving pretty fast. I was in a suit and tie and had come right out of the office to jump in the jeep with him. The construction area was right near the hotel, because we had ninety-some-odd acres we were developing for office buildings. He took it around there and said, "We're going to have some fun," and he started laughing and smiling. He always had this big grin about him when he was up to something. He starts running into these piles of dirt and flying over them. I wasn't exactly shaking in my boots, but I was a little concerned. But Walter just kept on going.

Walter loved speed. He loved his automobiles, and he loved to kick it. My wife, Frances, went back to Chicago for a visit after we had moved to Pittsburgh, and she had our youngest son with her. He was probably seventeen at the time. While they were there, they saw Walter, and Walter said to my son, "Would you like to go to the disco with me, because I need to check out the papers and everything at the disco." And my son said, "Sure, I'd love to go with you." So Walter took his Lamborghini and the back roads, and they came back from this place and they're kind of laughing. Frances said, "Okay, what happened? You've got something up your sleeve." And he said, "Well, Mum, Walter got

stopped by the police for speeding on one of the back roads."
And she said, "Speeding? How fast were you going?" And he said,
"He was going 130 when they stopped him." And she turns to
Walter and said, "You were going 130 with my baby in the
car!!??" Of course, he didn't get a ticket because he gave an auto-
graph.

◇

Putting Walter Payton into the proverbial driver's seat with a football
under his arm was a good move almost any time, but in the literal
sense, putting him behind the wheel of a vehicle with ample
horsepower involved questionable judgment, especially if you were
like **FISHER,** a former teammate familiar with Payton's *French
Connection*–like driving skills:

He was pretty good at weaving his way around those railroad
arms that come down to block traffic when a train was coming
through. If Walter got to the railroad crossing and didn't see a
train, he wasn't stopping.

◇

While most of his teammates were asleep on a long airplane ride
home after a game, Payton would often be wide awake contemplating
his next joke, as team trainer **FRED CAITO** saw on more than one
occasion:

He loved to fun with people. He was like that. One night on the
airplane—it was one of those four- or five-hour flights from the
West Coast—and people were sleeping. It was like three in the
morning, and he asked one of the flight attendants for her lip-
stick, and Walter went up and down the aisle. He would always
kiss and hug you, anyway, and then he was rubbing the lipstick
on everyone's shirts. So we all went home with lipstick on us.

◇

Even as Payton passed the ten-year mark as a Chicago Bear in 1984—
a milestone that few running backs ever reach in the first place—he
was the key to the Bears' offense, and his role hadn't changed. Bears
strength coach **CLYDE EMRICH** didn't see a player on the downslope
side of his professional life, but one who still carried a now-great team
on his shoulders:

I didn't see a change. I mean, maybe they used him less, obvi-
ously they knew his knees were aching and all that. But the
respect was there from day one to the last day. It was the same. I
didn't see any change. I don't know what the coaches were think-
ing, however, because I didn't discuss anything (in terms of team
strategy and players' roles) with them. But I mean, just his pres-
ence when he was on the field . . . I thought he could still play the
next year (1988). I was surprised he didn't, but I didn't know
how he felt. He never let you know how he felt. I hadn't seen him
deteriorate that much. His strength was always terrific. Even
recently, when he'd come to the game and he'd hug you, you
could just feel the solidness about him.

◇

Walter Payton wasn't just your typical jokester. To pull off a prank, he
rarely went for those that involved a complicated set-up and hours or
days of preparation. He was always playfully grabbing, pinching, pulling,
hugging, or wrestling anyone within arm's reach, just to be cute. When
you were around Payton, **BILL MAGRANE** observes, you had to be
ready for almost anything:

One thing that was truly Walter happened when we went to the
Super Bowl. I was on the same bus with him and Suhey, and
when you get into the Superdome, you had to walk from one end
of the field to the other to get to the locker room. And the way to
do it is just to walk down the field. And as I was walking along, I
noticed that Matt was a nervous wreck, so I was kind of talking
with him, nothing special, and all the time we were walking,

Walter was doing stuff to Matt, and by the time we got to the other end of the field Matt's shirttail was hanging out. Walter had taken his necktie off and gone through his pockets and taken stuff out of them. That was Walter. If he were here right now, in my office, he would be sitting here going through stuff on my desk and reading something with his feet up on the desk.

There was another time when my daughter, Katie, called the office one day and said, "Who's on the switchboard today? It sounds like Michael Jackson." It was Walter. He would come up on Wednesdays between meetings and fill in on the switchboard—he loved to run the switchboard. He was very good at it. He could handle it. I remember I walked in there once and he was talking to someone who was inquiring about Ditka making a speaking appearance. And Walter was explaining how he didn't do it during the season, but he should get in touch with him after the season, write a letter, and he gave them the address. He handled it very professionally.

◇

ROLAND HARPER, likewise a running back, was taken in the same draft as Walter, and they became close over the years:

You know, we could go on and on and tell you stories about Walter and how good he was and how many pranks he played. And everybody can laugh and joke about how he stepped over people, but you know this is a celebration, and it's for you guys to know that Walter wanted this to happen. We're not celebrating his death, we are celebrating his life, because we all want to get there. He's in heaven right now looking on us and saying, "Have fun, don't sit back and be mourning, groaning. Have fun." So I'd like for you all to stand up and show Walter you love him. This is what it's all about! Give us a piece of him, give him five! Beautiful! He's a great love, and let's keep his love alive![1]

◇

DAVE DUERSON, another former Bears teammate, remembers one time in particular when he experienced Payton's warmth:

My fondest memory is that Walter has this thing he does to first-time all-pros over at the Pro Bowl. And Jimbo, I'm sure, and Samuri (Mike Singletary), and everybody else can tell you about this. But, I was having just a wonderful day. We had just won the Super Bowl, and we had just flown over to Hawaii. You guys were here partying in the cold and the tickertape parade. And I was prancing out onto the practice field, so proud to be with all these great legends, on a wonderful warm afternoon in sunny Hawaii. After about three minutes, it started getting awful warm. Walter had put some unscented liquid heat in my jock. It was a very hot afternoon in warm, sunny Hawaii.[2]

◇

As an offensive tackle for the Bears, **KEITH VAN HORNE** spent a good portion of his days in the trenches blocking for the likes of Payton, although he would occasionally get freed up early enough as a play unfolded to watch Payton batter defenders to the turf, and it was fun to watch:

He would run a guy over and land on top of him. He'd just lower his shoulder and whack the guy, give him that forearm. He had a hell of a forearm. He would just lower his shoulder and give them the forearm, and they would just go flying. So it was a lot of fun to watch him. It was just quite an incredible honor to be able to play with him and for him. I just wish we could have got him a couple more rings.

◇

RICH WINGO played seven seasons for the Green Bay Packers as a linebacker, putting him in position when the Packers played the Bears twice a year to be on the lookout for Payton:

My rookie year, 1979, we were playing Chicago in Green Bay. It was cold, a typical Bear-Packer game. We had a losing record that year, but it really didn't matter because, as you know with the Black and Blue Division and this being a Bear-Packer game, it was going to be a battle. We were playing at Lambeau Field, which has that underground heating system. It was freezing. I mean, it was bitter. And it was rainy, so the field was real wet. The grass was tall, too, left uncut probably because Walter Payton was coming to town. I would have asked somebody about that, except I thought it better to remain a quiet rookie. I didn't ask any questions.

I don't remember what the halftime score was, but I think Walter was just kicking our butt. He was controlling the game. Well, we had an assistant coach—and I won't say who it was because I don't want to get him in trouble—who couldn't take this anymore. When we walked up the tunnel at halftime, we already knew which team was going to defend which goal in the second half. So this assistant coach, who knew right where all of the switches for controlling the field's underground heating system were, went in there and started flipping switches to shut down the heating system between like the twenty- and thirty-yard line in the Bears' end, and the ground turned hard as a rock. Walter had a hard time keeping his feet after that. Now, I didn't physically see the coach do this, but I heard some switches flipping in that room, and he was in there, all upset and complaining about what Payton was doing to us.

◇

BILL BATES played for the Dallas Cowboys as a nickelback on defense and a special-teams specialist, with about half of his career overlapping with Payton's. On the field Bates was privy to Payton's playful nature:

The first time I played against him was in my second year with the Cowboys, and it was in a game up there in Chicago. I tackled

him one time, got up, and as I turned around he pinched my butt. I turned around, and he just giggled. There were other times I played against the Bears, and he didn't do much talking on the field. You think he would be real intense and really focused to the game and intense, and you're not expecting something like his pinching your butt. His presence on the field was just amazing, and that was just my second year in the league.

During the other years that we played him in Dallas, we used to have a blitz, pretty much an all-out blitz, with two safeties hitting right up the middle, and we had other guys coming up the edge. The quarterback handed the ball off to Walter, at which time I'm right in the middle and hitting him head-on in the middle of the line. It's just me and Walter. I hit pretty hard and was known as a good tackler and those things. Well, he hit me with his forearm and I knew I hit him hard, but he hit me hard, right in the chest, right in the shoulder, and when he hit me he knocked me off of him and then gained about another twenty-five yards. And that was one of those amazing things about him. You always think of the defensive guys as the hitters, but for him to be the one actually initiating the hit was something very extraordinary from a running back.

◇

Early on in his hunting-buddy relationship with Payton, before he really got comfortable with him, **RALPH CIANCIARULO** sometimes didn't know what to expect from moment to moment, and there was a reason for this:

Any time you were with him, he would be grabbing your neck or manipulating an arm or leg where it wasn't supposed to go. One time we were taking a break from filming a video of us deer hunting, and we started wrestling, just screwing around, relaxing on the lodge floor, and I get him in a headlock. And his right hand picked me up—not both hands—his right hand lifted my body

off the floor, and at that time I weighed about 175 or 180 pounds. I knew right then, my dad didn't raise no fool, that I was going to die. I mean, if this guy with one hand can lift me up, and I thought I had a good grip, I knew it was all over. The next thing I knew, I think I had one leg over my head somewhere and my left arm was attached to my right side and I was yelling, "Uncle!" Lo and behold, he picked me up off the floor and says, "Let's go hunting." He was really cool.

◇

DON PIERSON, the *Chicago Tribune* sportswriter who has covered the Bears for almost thirty years, remembers one of the last in-depth interviews he had with Payton late in the Bear great's career:

This was right before the Pro Bowl before his last year, in Hawaii. It required twenty-two phone calls on my part to either him or his secretary, and I think Connie got involved. This was over a space of about two weeks to set up this time to talk to him, and that was only because I had known him for thirteen years that I was able to get it done relatively easily. Once you tied him down, he was okay, but he was a very mobile guy. That last interview was pretty memorable because it was one on one for a long period of time. He was away from home in Hawaii, so he really didn't have any place to go—he couldn't just jump in a car and run around. Another memorable interview I did with him was the one I did with him after he had that surgery on both knees—what he called his eleven-thousand-yard checkup. I went over to his house to do the interview there. He was lying down on the floor, and it was a good time to interview him because he had had the surgery and couldn't run around and get away from you.

◇

With the Bears' lopsided victory over New England in Super Bowl XX a foregone conclusion, the main plotline piquing interest in the game was whether Payton would get the chance to score a touchdown in his only Super Bowl appearance. He never got it, though, as Chicago Coach Mike Ditka opted to let defensive tackle William "Refrigerator" Perry get the short-yardage touchdown on a gimmick goal-line play that had worked a number of times during the regular season.

PIERSON remembers the aftermath:

I think that bothered him more than he admitted. He always said the reason he reacted like that initially was the whole thing seemed to be a letdown to him—Was this all there was? He didn't have to play as big a role. The TD would have been a token thing anyway—they didn't need the touchdown to win the thing. Still, I think Ditka regrets it. McMahon regrets it, too, for not changing the play and giving him the ball. I didn't realize until the later years that it was a bigger deal to him than he ever admitted publicly.

I talked to him on several occasions in the later years. He was always around, but it remained tough to get ahold of him. I did a ten-year anniversary thing in 1995 on that Super Bowl team and talked to him at length then. The one thing I remember, and the great regret of that team, was that they only won the Super Bowl once. When people ask me about it, I always simplify things and say it was because they didn't have a healthy quarterback. I have been accused of oversimplifying, and Payton had been foremost among those saying that. He said, "Bull(crap), it wasn't the quarterback at all." He wasn't trying to cover up for anybody. He thought it was the downfall of the whole team, that everybody got selfish. I don't necessarily agree with that, but he was very sincere in saying that it was a shortcoming of the whole team in terms of dedication and selfishness. If they had had McMahon all that time, I can't imagine them not winning at least one more. But he wanted nothing to do with that kind of theory.

◆

Former Bears kicker and Payton teammate **BOB THOMAS** is one of a number of professional and former professional athletes who have committed their lives to Jesus Christ as born-again Christians. Thomas wasn't one of Payton's closest friends, but they were good friends, enough so that Thomas believes he has a good feel for Payton the man as well as Payton the believer:

Over the ten years we were teammates, he let his guard down a few times with me. There were times he was struggling with faith issues, and there were a number of us on the team whose faith was very important to us—and it continues to be—and he would ask questions. When I ran for the Supreme Court, Mike Singletary did a commercial for me and he was at Walter's side at his deathbed, and he was telling me the story that Walter realized that at that point in time right before he died he needed to give his life over to Jesus, and Mike said he did—that Walter trusted Jesus for his salvation. I thought that was very touching and appropriate.

My faith is important to me. The image that came to me was, here's Walter dying and soon the Creator will again be with His created. As awesome as Walter was, he's still part of the creation, not the Creator. And those were the struggles that he had dealing with spiritual issues, because here's a guy who had everything that one could imagine—fortune and fame. And so he would ask questions of people like Bill Hybels, who was leading the team Bible study. We'd go to a Bible study, and Walter would ask questions of me, Singletary, Vince Evans, and other Christians on the team. So I did have the opportunity at the end to ask Singletary about Walter. I said, "Did he get it right?" and he said he did. I then think back to the image of my head buried in his chest, sobbing when I had been cut by the Bears, and his comforting me, and now here he is at the moment of salvation, probably with his head buried in his Savior's chest. Thankfully, he came to the Lord at the conclusion of his life, and that's reassuring.

In all of his years playing for the Dallas Cowboys, **BATES** never hid the fact that he was, and is, a Christian, which at times can seem counter to what it takes to play in the NFL. Faith also was an issue with Payton, and Bates can identify with the faith issues professional athletes deal with in a world filled on one side with organized brutality and on the other side with wayward temptations encountered by most celebrities in the public eye:

If you've accepted the Lord in your life, then you are going to heaven. He will strengthen you and help you get through the temptations and other things that happen. But my having been saved back when I was in high school really helped me. I know dreams and things have come true because of my faith in the Lord. But it's the strength that He gave me to just turn down temptation, to turn away from temptation, to fight it, which has only made me stronger. You know, just trust in the Lord with all your heart and lean not on your own understanding, and He'll make the path straight. That's Proverbs 3:5–6. The Lord made my path straight, and it is very comforting to know that Walter is in heaven right now. We'll someday have a good football game up there, that's for sure.

◈

REV. JEREMIAH WRIGHT, Trinity United Church of Christ, opened the Soldier Field memorial service for Payton with a prayer that included the following:

May we bow our heads in prayer. Eternal God, You have given us a gift of life. You have given us the gift of love. You have given us the gift of joy. You have given us the gift of laughter. You have given us the gift of beauty. You have given us the gift of movement, and You have given us the gift of grace, and for this, we thank You. But then You outdid Yourself, God. You combined the gifts of life, love, joy, laughter, beauty, movement, and grace, and You put them into one person. And You called him

Sweetness. And for this we thank You. You made him, God. You made him a man, You made him a son, You made him a husband, You made him a father, You made him an athlete. You made him a warm, loving human being whose smile could melt the hardest heart, and for this we thank You. You made him a special person whose spirit has touched all of our spirits and changed all of our lives, and for this we thank You. God, we ask Your blessings upon his family. . . . We ask Your blessings most of all upon his memory, . . . We did not know what only You and Sweetness knew, God, which was that You had a special whistle which only You and he knew, which would let him know when facing an opponent that You, his heavenly Father, were present. Thank You for that whistle You sounded last Monday to remind him that You were there. He faced his final opponent, but Your whistle reminded him that the victory was already his. Most of all, this day we thank You, and we ask for Your peace as Walter now rests in peace. In the name of Him, whom Walter claimed as Christ, our Lord, let the people of God forever say, Amen.[3]

◇

REV. JESSE JACKSON gave a profound eulogy at Payton's memorial service held at Soldier Field, excerpted as follows:

Today our hearts rejoice in pain as we celebrate. . . . All of us here and everywhere are trying to say something. We all want to express ourselves. So all of you who are sitting here, let's just give Walter "Sweetness" Payton a great, loving round of applause. On your feet and express yourself. . . . Express yourself for Walter. . . . Express yourself. For the yards, for the touchdowns, for the joy. . . . Express yourself . . . for No. 34. . . . Express yourself. . . . Express yourself! The power of the man. The teammate. For the good times. Express yourself. . . . What a joy, what a joy, what a joy. . . . One more time for Walter "Sweetness" Payton. . . . Give it up, give it up, give it up! . . .

We live life as if life was certain. And death is uncertain. The fact is that death is certain and life is uncertain, and when Walter's remains are taken to his final resting place, you will see in the city of the dead a birth date and a death date on each tombstone. Between these two numbers is a dash. You don't control or determine the birth date. You don't know when or to whom you are born. You don't control the death date. But on that dash is where you make your life's statement. The length of a dash is determined by forces beyond our control. All of us feel that when an infant dies, it's painful that an infant never knew the beauty of the challenges of life, and we accept the death of an infant with a measure of understanding. But when a very old person dies, there is reasonable anticipation and you count the years and the opportunities and you accept it. But when the dash is cut short, when the sun is eclipsed, we feel cheated. The length of a dash is uncertain: Jesus, thirty-three; Dr. King, thirty-nine; Walter, forty-five; Methuselah, nine hundred. He lived nine hundred years about nothing. There will be no schools or streets named after Methuselah. No one wants to wear his jersey or spend any time with him. . . . You cannot determine the length of a dash, but you can determine the depth and the height. Jesus was born in the slum, the slum was not born in Him. He became King of kings. The length of that dash, your achievements, the miles covered, Walter flew like an eagle. He flew high. He looked the sun bold in the eye and just soared and soared and soared. His depth was measured by his discipline, his commitment, his dedication. The Bible asked, "Have you seen the man diligent in his own business? His death was driven by his discipline."

Walter made the most of the span of his dash. The bad news, Connie, fate is uncertain. The good news, Mom, is faith is certain. Fate may be a killer cancer or an Egypt Air crash. You can't determine fate, but faith is a certain weapon. Faith is the substance of things hoped for, the evidence of things unseen. There's a mystery of faith because you cannot prove it immediately. I've seen a lot in my life. I've been blessed with travel from

one corner of the earth to another many times. I've seen the sun rise over the Pacific Ocean. I've seen mountains rising out of the mists of Europe. But one thing I've never seen is the righteous forsaken. Dr. King's father said to me one day, "I lost my son, Martin, at thirty-nine. I loved him so much. I mourned his loss as if I had lost everything. Before I could adjust mourning over the loss of Martin Luther King, my son A. T. was found drowned in a swimming pool. Before I could adjust, my wife was killed while playing the organ by a crazed man one Sunday morning. But through it all, I'm not going to give up on God. I'm going to thank God for what's left." We have a lot of Sweetness, but there is a lot of Sweetness left. Let him rest. A bright light burned out quickly, but, oh, how bright it was when it glowed. We're here today because the light did not go out. It was taken out and put into another socket. It is now screwed in a silver socket in glory. Behold a new heaven and a new earth. Mine eyes have seen the glory and the coming of the Lord. This light called Sweetness now belongs to heaven and to the ages. Thank God for Sweetness.[4]

◈

MIKE ADAMLE, Payton's backfield teammate in 1975 and 1976, offered this at Payton's memorial service:

When it comes to faith in God and faith in Jesus Christ and tremendous courage and dignity in times of adversity, no one can hold a candle to the Payton family.[5]

◈

EDDIE PAYTON, Walter's older brother, gives this take on his brother's life, death, and spirituality:

My mother, as we said during all the former players being introduced, she kind of broke down, and being the oldest in

the family, I was trying to comfort her. I said, "Why are you crying? I mean, this is good. All these fans, this is what he wants. He'd want all his friends to be a part of this. Why are you crying?" She said, "I wish the guy would stop announcing them because I figure as soon as he announces the last one, Walter's going to run out on this field, and I know it's not going to happen." She also wanted everyone here to know, there was a lot said last week about Walter accepting Christ in his last moments on this earth. That's great, but that's not exactly true, guys. In the Payton family, you learn to say your prayers before you learn to say your ABCs. Walter accepted Christ long before he was Sweetness, and he kept that with him until he was not Sweetness anymore.

To the current Bear who came up and said I'll play for Walter and dedicate this season to Walter, let me give you some advice from someone who's kind of stood in his shadow for a number of years. Whenever you measure what you do in regard to how well you do it against true greatness, you're always going to come up short of what you did. Don't measure what you do against what Walter did. Try to do it better than anyone else, and everybody and Walter will be proud of you. And for all of the young Sweetnesses out there watching TV or watching old clips, if Walter was here, I think he would want you to remember what will make you as good or better than he ever was. Play the game, every play in the game, like it's the last play that you'll ever play. You love it. Make every play count.[6]

◇

Payton's business manager, **GINNY QUIRK,** remembers back to that dark day in May 1999 when Payton went from believing his liver transplant was imminent to learning that he now had liver cancer:

He thought he was going home with a beeper to wait for the call and a new liver. Instead he got the news that he had cancer. It

devastated him. But he wanted to keep the fact that he had cancer quiet. He didn't want people to feel sorry for him.[7]

◇

GREGORY DICKOW, pastor of Life Changers International Church in Barrington, Illinois, eulogized Payton in a private memorial service:

He made his greatest gain on Monday when he died. He gained heaven. This is a celebration because this man, Walter Payton, is with his Lord Jesus Christ.[8]

WALTER PAYTON, SPORTSMAN

AS MUCH AS WALTER PAYTON loved football, he could not play it year-round. The sport simply isn't structured to be played that way, and neither is the body, not even a chassis as gloriously constructed as Payton's. So what's a guy with the level of energy that Payton exuded to do? Find other sporting activities, such as camping, hunting, and auto racing. Payton discovered the joy of all those activities at one time or another in his life. As a youth, he often went camping with his buddies, and those outdoors skills came in handy later in life when he went on hunting trips, a sidelight that also allowed him to develop his skills with a rifle and a bow. The hankering for racing autos also had been long ingrained, for Payton loved fast cars, and he loved to drive them fast, and faster. But his most enduring off-season form of recreation probably was hunting, and his basic instincts in that area served him well.

◇

Payton made many friends off the football field as well, friends who were afforded quality time with the man known as "Sweetness." One of those off-field buddies was **RALPH CIANCIARULO,** an expert hunter who, among other things, makes bow-hunting videos and goes around the country giving hunting seminars:

I met him in 1984. Some friends from the Chicago Cubs, like Keith Moreland and Jody Davis, had told me that Walter shot a bow a little bit and that's my forte. At that time I owned Archer's Choice, a large archery pro shop outside Chicago. I had a bunch of the athletes come in, and we'd end up talking and then we'd go hunting, the whole nine yards. Walter called me up one day, and I was like, "Oh, yeah, this is Walter Payton, sure." He was always a kidder, and he's going, "No, I am, but I think you don't believe me." And then he started telling me about how guys like Keith and Jody had told him to call me, so I was like, "This might be possible." So we arranged a meeting. We met and talked about nothing else but hunting. That's the way it was with all of these guys. They have enough going on with their sports. They don't need a bunch of questions or answers or anything else. It's nice for them to have a release like that. Hunting doesn't involve that same kind of pressure.

We hunted a little bit at first, but the problem was Walter was still playing, so we couldn't really connect. One of the things that brought us closer together is that I wasn't after anything with Walter, and he sort of knew that, and he wasn't after anything with me except, "Let's just go hunting." We had that common ground. After he retired, I remember going to the office, and one of the things I really cherished is Connie, his wife, taking some pictures during his last game, and he gave me one of them. It was like, Wow, I couldn't believe it. All the time I was growing up I had watched him play, so that was pretty cool.

We started bow hunting. After he retired, we set up a hunt to be filmed for a video: *The Caribou Epic,* with Walter Payton and myself. We went up to Quebec to go bow hunting for caribou.

When Walter bagged his caribou, he was all pumped up because it was the biggest animal he had ever shot with a bow. There was also some unbelievable fishing. It was really relaxing, and the bond from that trip on was just really incredible. Any chance he had, we would try to do some type of hunting, and we traveled a whole bunch. We would go to Ohio and also did a bunch of stuff in Illinois, like trying to get some deer with the bow. It was a great time, and I've been honored to be able to call him a friend.

I had gotten married in 1993 and he would call up Vickie because Vickie didn't really know him at the time, and in his high-pitched voice he goes, "Is Ralph there?" And Vicky is like, "Who's this?" And he would go, "Is Ralph there?" And again, she would go, "Who is this?" Then he would say, "If he ain't there, would you please tell him for me that he left his underwear here?" Just crazy stuff like that. That was Walter, always kidding around, but when it was time to get serious, boy did he. I've taken a lot of athletes hunting, and he's one of the strongest individuals I've ever met in my life. One time, it was between a morning hunt and an afternoon hunt, and he had this Nerf football and we were just taking a break from sitting in the stand where we had shot for a while. He threw it at me and I threw it back, and he said, "C'mon, try to get past me." And I'm like, "No way, I'm not trying. So you try to get past me." Here I am, little guy I am, I have Walter Payton running right at me, and I figure I'm going to tackle this guy? What a dumb idea that was. Reality, what a concept. All I remember is that right before I tried to wrap my arms around him, he had flung his hips right in to between my right shoulder and my neck, and I was looking up at the sky in midday and I saw stars, and he's sitting there laughing. That was the kind of stuff that went on constantly. I played sports in high school, but nothing like this. When he threw his hip into me, I don't care what kind of pads you had on, try to stop a man like him when he was serious? No thanks. I've tried to chase a lot of bears in my life, and Walter is the toughest that I've ever had to go after.

This was in early September, the first year after he retired. He

was all pumped up. We flew up there and ended up in a town called Shefferville, population ninety-nine, I think. We're sitting in this little restaurant, and lo and behold—I don't think they even had too many TVs up there—and this older woman and a young child come up, and she says, "Are you Walter Payton?" At that moment, it hit me how well known Walter was. Not well known just for football, but for being who he was as a person. I think he signed a napkin for the little guy. I mean here we are in Shefferville, with nothing around but some critters and maybe some Indians. It was unbelievable. From there we flew into a tent camp and set up, and we hunted off the river with Arthur Tallion, our outfitter who took us up there. I learned something else on that trip. Walter loved fires. Oh, man. In the tent we had these little wood-burning stoves, and if you keep it stoked just a little bit decent, it will keep you warm and dry. It rained a lot up there. Walter went back to camp a little early one day, and when I came back up a little later, I was walking up from the river and I see this tent glowing orange. And I'm like, "What in the heck is that?" When I got in there, I thought it was a sauna, but there he is inside sweeping the floor, throwing every piece of wood in this fire. The pipe was bright orange, which tells you how hot this fire was. And he just loved it. He was in seventh heaven, saying, "Hey, how do you like it in here." And I say, "It's freakin' hot, man. Open a door." And there he was listening to his little stereo, a Walkman, and I think it was James Brown he was listening to. We were sitting alongside this river on a big rocky shore—the bugs were bad—mosquitoes and black flies—so we had these head nets on and everything, and all of a sudden with the wireless mike the film crew was filming us. You could hear him listening to the music, then he puts on his sunglasses and starts dancing right on the rocks. That was him: spontaneous reactions to life. Just raring to go every time.

One day we were going down the rapids in a canoe. I was sitting in front and he was sitting in the back, and the outfitters were sitting in the middle, paddling. He had his Presidential Rolex on one wrist and a diamond bracelet on the other. As we

hit the rapids, water comes splashing up over the boat, and he grabs me by the shoulder and—you know his strength—so it was like "Ouch." He goes, "If we flip, I'm taking you with me." And I say, "Let me tell you something; if we flip, don't stick your hands up out of the water, because if you do, I'll take off the jewelry, let you go down the river, and retire on that stuff."

◇

Tennessee Titans head coach **JEFF FISHER** was another of Payton's Bears teammates who went hunting with him at least once, and once might have been enough:

I went hunting with him a couple of times. He loved it, and he was an excellent shot. He had a firing range built underneath his house. It was all tapered, beveled, and cemented. One hunting trip was a thing for guests being held at a pheasant club, with four or five of us guys going. I remember being a little leery because some of the guys in our group had never hunted before. At one point a bird went up into the air behind Walter, and one of the other guys started tracking the bird and then fired at it as it flew right behind Walter. He barely missed getting shot. Well, Walter dropped his gun and was in the guy's face, knocking the gun out of his hand almost before the rest of us realized what had happened. It was a quick course in gun safety.

◇

Payton would go almost anywhere, anytime when the invitation came to go hunting and/or camping with a buddy, such as when former Jackson State teammate **VERNON PERRY,** now the head golf coach at Prairie View A&M, would invite Payton back home to Mississippi for some all-night deer hunting:

Walter would come back down to Mississippi at times, and we would go hunting. We went to my grandmama's place, and

Walter brought this thirty-aught-six. He said, "Go ahead and shoot this thing just one time." I said okay, and put the scope up to my eye, and Walter is standing behind me showing me how to do it. I shot that gun. It knocked me and Walter off the porch, and put a cut across my eye.

Walter was fascinated with guns at that time. He loved to deer hunt. One time he took me deer hunting, and it was black dark up in these woods. We were in a deer stand, and Walter left me to go to another deer stand. Talk about being afraid. I was so glad to see Payton coming back down the road to get me. We would stay out all night and deer hunt, staying at the places of these guys who had homes in the woods up near Vicksburg, Mississippi. I didn't shoot anything, but Walter would always shoot a deer. I don't think we ever kept one. He would just give it to the person whose home we had used. He just wanted to go hunt deer.

◇

Payton's recreational pursuits off the field included hunting, and there were times he would ask teammates, such as offensive lineman **MARK BORTZ,** to join him. Said Bortz:

I went hunting with Walter one time. It was a team kind of thing in which we went hunting for pheasant at a hunting club outside Chicago and near the Wisconsin border. Actually, it was kind of scary because some of the guys had side arms (pistols), and there were a few guys with shotguns doing a bit of drinking, too. It looked kind of like a scene out of the movie North Dallas Forty.

◇

Hunting for caribou in Quebec was more than just waiting around for prey, scoping it out, and pulling the trigger. It was real sport, especially when the American sportsman is Walter Payton, as **CIANCIARULO** remembers so clearly and fondly:

Caribou hunting in the late eighties and early nineties was really rocking. You had the big herds migrating, going for the lichen, which is what they feed on in the tundras. So what you do is use the water thoroughfares with boats and motors, and try to intercept them as they cross the water. We would go upriver and downriver for hours to see if you could see any herds moving or what. When they started to move, you would try to intercept them on some very well-used trails. If you've ever flown over that country, all it looks like is one big road map from hundreds of thousand of years on these trails. We would try to get positioned above them on these banks because first of all you have the rocky shoreline, then you hit the alders; from the alders you come up to these pine ridges of black spruce. If you stayed above the caribou on the black spruce, we had mobility.

We would be running up and down through the black spruce trying to intercept them. Walter had the natural ability to shoot. He shot Apache style, which was three fingers under the arrow. At that time we had him shooting a bow set at over one hundred pounds. He draws back like we would draw back a sixty-five- or seventy-pound bow. In camp one day one of the old cooks was watching Walter and me shoot, and then he said, "Let me try," and Walter handed him his bow. This poor guy, I'm surprised if he can still cook, because he tried to draw it and he wasn't going to let no one show him up, you know what I mean. But he about hurt himself. Walter didn't shoot with sights; he shot instinctive, which is a little bit tougher to do. If you took one hundred bow hunters in a room and asked them how many shot without a sight, you might find six or fewer who said they shot instinctive.

WALTER PAYTON, SUPERSTAR

IF YOU START WITH THE thirteen-season, record-setting career in the National Football League, highlighted by a Super Bowl triumph and a spot in the Hall of Fame, and add in the collegiate records broken at Jackson State, thinking of Payton as a can't-miss superstar seems like a foregone conclusion. But it really wasn't that easy, and it never was "in the bag." Not only did Payton have to overcome playing in obscurity at Columbia High School—his second high school, at that—he had to start over and go through the same thing at Jackson State, which isn't exactly the capital of Major College Football, U.S.A. Then there was the drawback of going to the Windy City to join a team synonymous with hapless; a team furthermore that was in mild disarray, with a defense that didn't like the offense, and an offense with an aversion for the end zone.

This story, of course, had a happy ending, and Payton emerged as, arguably, the most popular and genuine superstar the city of Chicago had ever known. That's saying something, considering the other candidates, starting with Michael Jordan and con-

tinuing through the likes of Ernie Banks, Gale Sayers, Dick Butkus, and Bobby Hull. Before Payton came along and set numerous NFL records, including the one in which he eclipsed Jim Brown as the league's all-time leading rusher, most baby-boomer arguments about who the best running back was centered on Brown and Sayers. Then came the Brown-Payton debates as well as the Sayers-Payton comparisons, to be followed by the Payton-Jordan argument about who was, or is, Chicago's greatest superstar of all time. Payton, obviously, came a long way in his playing career, and in Chicago it all started with earning some respect.

◇

Payton didn't come on gangbusters as a Bears rookie, although he gained a credible 675 yards in thirteen games for a 4-10 team. Linebacker **DOUG BUFFONE** was on the downside of his long career with the Bears, but watching Payton come on after his rookie season helped get his juices flowing once again:

Walter was always full steam. He was a well-conditioned athlete. You know about the hill and all that. He was mentally strong, too, and that was the difference between him and a lot of other players—physical players who aren't mentally strong. One of the first things you consider when thinking about players is endurance. Look at him, the longevity. I hold the record on the Bears for the most years played, at fourteen. Here he is a running back and he played thirteen, which is only one less than me. This is a guy that going into every game everyone was gunning for you. It's not like he was back there with some other guy who's going to get the ball a lot, too. There's no question he was going to get the football when the game started.

The most amazing thing to me was the Minnesota game in which he set the single-game rushing record. I knew he was running well, but it never added up until the fourth quarter when I

was thinking, You need to get this guy out of here—how many times is he going to run this football? I had no idea at the time how many yards he had rushed for. Teams don't come up with 275 yards rushing, let alone one person. It was the most amazing thing. Someone said how good the defense was playing, and I said, "It's not the defense—Minnesota just can't get the ball. That's why." What they're doing, they know he's getting the ball, but could not stop him, and it only got worse in the fourth quarter, and that to me is the most amazing thing he has ever done. And he was sick that day, and it wasn't a very good day, either. He just kept pounding the ball and pounding the ball.

◇

LARRY MCCARRON, now a sports broadcaster in the Green Bay area, played twelve seasons with the Green Bay Packers, which gave him the opportunity to share a field with Payton and the Bears more times perhaps than he would have liked:

My impressions of Payton aren't so much specific games as they are cumulative from playing against him so many times over the years, with the Bears being in the same division as us. Insofar as Walter's effect on our team, it was devastating in the sense that he was one of the few guys I ever saw—and I would put Earl Campbell in this class during my era, too—who could actually, individually wear a team down. So often, when we played them, it seemed like after three quarters, Walter would have something like forty-eight or fifty-two yards, and the defense would be thinking about how we had done such a great job of containing him. And then in the fourth quarter, he explodes for a hundred and a half. I mean, he was that type of runner where he just individually wore down a team, a whole team of defenders that had spent the week in practice and then a tremendous amount of energy in the game trying to stop him. They could do it for three quarters, but Walter was irrepressible.

I also had the privilege of playing in the Pro Bowl with him, and the thing that really struck me there was that he was just one of those guys. Walter was one of the very best of the best. And yet he was one of the hardest-working guys out there that week. That tells me there is justice, that there is a football god, because here's a guy who's got as much ability or more than anybody, and yet he works the hardest. Here we were getting ready for an All-Star game, and Walter's running every play out—plays twenty, thirty yards down the field like he was a rookie trying to make the team. And he was a guy that had been there umpteen times already, who was headed toward the Hall of Fame. He didn't have to prove a thing to anybody, but he practiced like he did.

I got to talk to him a little bit. Obviously, Walter was a big guy and there were a lot of demands on him, but he was always very pleasant. I know a couple of times I needed an autograph— this was after I retired—no problem. I did an interview with him several months before he died. As you might have guessed, Walter just didn't look like Walter then. Still talked like him, though. I had a good-sized cameraman with me, and he had an affinity for linemen, so he kind of joked around with him, because he always liked the big guys and that kind of thing. There was a never-give-up fight in him. If there was ever a guy that could lick something if it was lickable, it was Walter Payton.

◇

Former Chicago Bears great **JOHNNY MORRIS,** who played alongside Sayers and then covered Payton's entire career as a Chicago TV sportscaster, offers his give-and-take on the Payton-Sayers comparisons:

Sayers was probably the quickest running back I ever saw in my life, like greased lightning. He could make a cut in mid-air. But he was not the well-rounded football player that Payton was. He didn't have the power, and so he got hurt. Actually, it's hard to

judge now. Sayers got hurt in his fourth year and never played much after that, and that really kind of limited him in terms of getting the chance to go down in history as gaining a lot of yardage and stuff like that. But even though he played, basically, only four or five years, he still goes down as one of the greatest who ever played. Look at the game in which he scored six touchdowns against the 49ers. He did that in the mud.

Most guys when they cut, the natural thing is to plant a foot and push off—if you're going to cut right, for example, you make a little head fake to the left, then plant your left foot and push off to the right. And Sayers did all of those things, cutting and pushing off, but he also had the uncanny ability to change his direction in midair, and then he would come down at a forty-five-degree angle or cut to the right. Now, most guys can't cut unless they plant the foot first. Sayers could whip his left leg over to the right and cross his legs in midair, and then he would change direction coming down. You'll notice that the next time you see him in the highlight films running. Nobody else could do that, at least nobody I ever saw, and I saw a lot.

Jim Brown was more of a power-type runner, but a great running back. There's no question about it that he was in the top three or four. But to me, like I said, if I wanted somebody for one play, I'd take Sayers, because he was the greatest and the quickest and much faster than Jim Brown. That's just something of a God-given talent there. That's one thing about a running back—there is so much natural ability. You can take a running back, a good running back, and he doesn't have to have a hell of a lot of training. You can throw them on that football field and if you've got it, you've got it.

◇

O. J. SIMPSON on the Sayers-Payton comparisons:

Gale is the only runner who made moves that I wonder if I could have done. Maybe he had only five full seasons and didn't have

great statistics, but all you had to do was see him. But all this ranking stuff doesn't really matter. All that great runners leave with us, anyway, are memories. Sayers may have been the best pure runner, but twenty years from now, when I think of Walter Payton, I'll feel good. And nobody can change that.[1]

◇

MIKE DITKA on rating running backs Jim Brown, Gale Sayers, and O. J. Simpson while stacking them up against his own Walter Payton:

As a pure running back, Jim Brown was something special. They said he didn't block. He used to say he didn't need to block because wherever he went, someone went with him and it had the same effect as blocking. He was wrong. It wasn't one guy; it was two or three. Jim Brown could do whatever he wanted to do. I thought Gale Sayers, no question, was the best broken-field runner, the best cutback runner I've ever seen. There are a lot of great football players. Johnny Unitas wasn't bad. A guy who never got credit as a team player was Paul Hornung. He kicked it, threw it, ran it, blocked it. I still don't know how they kept him out of the Hall of Fame for so long. . . . There are a lot of great running backs, but Payton is a great citizen as well. I think he's a good person. I think he gives as much back to the game as he takes out of it. Those qualities alone would make him something special. . . . I am not an O. J. Simpson fan. Why? Because he doesn't take the time to study the game the way he should, so I don't respect his expert opinion. I don't think he likes me either, so we're even.[2]

◇

Linebacker **DOUG BUFFONE** was one of the few Bears who played alongside both Sayers and Payton:

Walter was more outgoing, more rambunctious. He would do crazy things. One time we were in the dorm rooms. This was dur-

ing training camp, and I had the only air conditioner around. It was about twelve-thirty. Walter came around and said, "Let's go." And I said, "Where?" and he says, "Down to (trainer) Fred Caito's room." He had a couple of those big firecrackers with him, those M-80s. I don't think he ever went anywhere without those things. I boosted him up to the windowsills, where he could light the M-80s, and then we ran like hell. They blow up and set off the fire alarm. Gale, on the other hand, very quiet and very much a competitor, too. He had the same kind of desire Payton had, but a little more reserved. Piccolo was good for Gale because Piccolo would bust his chops all the time or make fun of him and laugh, loosening Gale up.

◇

Trainer **FRED CAITO** joined the Bears staff in 1967 and spent the next twenty years of his life monitoring and mending perhaps the greatest running backs in the game at any given time—first, Gale Sayers, and second, Walter Payton. Caito had a unique view when it came to comparing and contrasting Sayers and Payton:

They were two different eras of two great football players. If you have to break it down, Walter was more powerful, a stronger runner. Gale may have had more grace and fluidity to his running. There were games I saw Gale Sayers play in which he could have been in a tuxedo. Nobody touched him. I mean, he was so elusive and fluid, like a ghost. One second he was there, the next he was gone. He'd come back to the sideline after a series and wouldn't have any dirt on him. Walter was completely different in that respect: He was a banger, and he saw it coming and he'd take the head and deliver the blow. But it was a different game, too. So it's hard to compare them. They're both in the Hall of Fame, so what can you say? I was fortunate to work with Gale Sayers, and then I was fortunate to work with Walter Payton, and they both had their elements of greatness. And I know they had a mutual

respect for each other. But greatness is measured in longevity, and that's where Walter Payton is a step ahead of all of the great running backs.

◇

Comparing Payton to Jordan offers an interesting dichotomy of star styles, and the comparisons don't stop there. When it comes to rating great running backs, Payton also gets put alongside former Bears running back Gale Sayers, who had arrived in the NFL a decade before Payton. And, again, the differences between two men in similar positions are telling, as *Tribune* sportswriter **DON PIERSON** details here:

For one thing, Sayers played sixty-eight games, and Payton played something like two hundred—three times what Sayers did. Sayers's style was twenty-first-century, but his media was so Stone Age that people didn't even really know his personality. He did a commercial once, but it was a joke. This was such a Neanderthal time in commercials that they made him look like a fool, even though he's a well-spoken guy. They only know something about Sayers's personality because of *Brian's Song,* the Brian Piccolo angle.

I grew up in Cleveland and saw most of Jim Brown's games. I still think Brown was the best running back I ever saw, but Payton by far was the best football player I ever saw, and that was because he could do everything. He was just a phenomenal player, and he played so hard every play, every week, every year, and he was just phenomenal in practice. He could kick, pass, catch balls with one hand, and then walk on his hands fifty yards down the field. It was like a circus act. Showtime. And he was really a cutup and a prank without being a showboat. He never did that stuff for the benefit of the fans or the cameras, like any of those end-zone dances or jumping up after making a run to make someone look bad. But in practice and stuff he was as crazy as any of these guys today who are doing it only for the camera. If he

had taken any of that stuff from practice to the camera, he would have made Deion Sanders look like a wallflower. He had that kind of personality. But he respected the game enough that he never wanted to put himself above it.

The guys down in the trenches get a kick out of what kind of guy he was (such as untying refs' shoelaces from the bottom of a pile). He did this for the benefit of teammates, not the cameras. I remember another time where he went into a meeting after putting some sugar on his mustache and saying, "Ain't no cocaine on this team." No one else knew about it at the time. Ditka paid him a compliment as the guy who really kept that whole team together.

◇

As a football observer for several decades, journalist **HUB ARKUSH** has seen and compared enough great players to know which one he considers the best ever:

I always felt he was probably the greatest football player to ever play the game. He could do more things. In the running-back argument, I've always said that Jim Brown was certainly the toughest runner ever, that Barry Sanders was the greatest breakaway threat, but that Walter Payton was the greatest football player ever to play running back. I suspect that people still don't realize that the guy threw eight touchdown passes and that he was the Bears' backup punter and kicker. He actually played quarterback, too, and he was the best blocker I ever saw. I go back to that one drive at San Francisco in 1985. How many football players have you ever seen who could literally take over a football game all by themselves? A Jerry Rice or a Randy Moss still needs someone to throw the football to them. A quarterback needs someone to throw the ball to. Walter could just take over the game. I think it was Dick Butkus who once said to me, "You could have the argument all you want, but there never was a bet-

ter player than Walter Payton." Where does he rank among all-time players? Forget the rushing record—I think Barry Sanders would have gotten it, or will get it (if he returns to play)—but look at the number of carries, and the feat of missing only one game in thirteen seasons. It's incredible to consider how he had to take the pounding and still had the durability to show up every week with such a work ethic and commitment to the game. I'm sure if he could tell us, his greatest disappointment was never getting to own an NFL team. The game was his entire life.

◇

BRIAN HEWITT of the *Chicago Sun-Times* offers his take on the Payton-Jordan and Payton-Sayers comparisons:

If you took a poll of the fans and media, I think you would get a consensus, even factoring in Wrigley Field, that Chicago was always a Bears town. You've got two baseball teams, a popular hockey team, and a latecomer in the Bulls, yet Chicago in most people's eyes is a Bears town, and Payton is probably the greatest Bear player who ever lived. Walter certainly was an icon, but he was never as smooth as Jordan. Chicago might have turned into a Bulls town by the time they won their sixth NBA title. Walter was a smart guy, but he was not an articulate guy in that the language and syntax didn't just roll off his tongue. He occasionally would try to do some TV, and it wasn't very good, although Michael could sometimes fracture the language, too.

As for Payton and Sayers, I've lived in Chicago since I was twelve years old. When I was thirteen years old in 1963, I watched the Giants play the Bears in the NFL Championship game. I watched it on a Milwaukee station, where the reception was really snowy because it was blacked out in Chicago. One time I talked to Sayers when Walter was getting close to Jim Brown's career rushing record, and we were talking about the number of yards, and Sayers was commenting on that. Then I

said, "You know, you can make an argument that even more impressive than the yards was the number of carries he had," and when I told him the number of times that Walter had carried the ball (3,838), Sayers just started laughing, sort of an incredulous laugh. Here was a guy, Sayers, who didn't get a lot of carries because of his injuries, and he said something to the effect that when you consider the way Payton runs and the punishment he gives out and takes every time he carries the ball, and that number of carries in a career—Sayers was more impressed with that than he was the total number of yards.

Comparing them stylewise, I watched Gale Sayers run a lot. He eluded guys in such a smooth way. I'm not sure how to describe this with Sayers, but he'd be moving along the line of scrimmage, and then there would be this opening and he would just go. Nothing tricky about it, but his shoulders would be going straight north and his legs would be going east, and both would be going at full speed. It was almost like an optical illusion. He was just really cool to watch, and I've never seen anyone run like him since then. Walter was powerful, indefatigable. He was nasty. He was just a lot of things, but he was never smooth like Gale Sayers, nor did he have that pure speed. Some of his three-yard runs were the best three-yard runs you've ever seen. The thing that would take my breath away was the running back, who, when he broke clear, you knew it was over. Dorsett was that way for most of his career, although I remember Darrell Green once running him down from behind. O. J. had been on that world-record relay team at Southern Cal, and he was a legitimate sprinter. Dorsett wasn't far behind.

From a popularity standpoint, I think people liked Sayers and respected him, but he was pretty withdrawn as a player, although some of that got debunked when the movie Brian's Song came out. That whole NFL culture in the sixties wasn't what it became in the eighties and nineties. (Dick) Butkus was pretty big back then, and while everybody knew how good Sayers was, Butkus was the Chicago hero. Walter was that way,

too. Chicago, the city of broad shoulders, prides itself on being a tough guy's town, a blue-collar town as much as anything. In a town that loved the Bears, and particularly the Bears defense. They loved Walter because he was a great offensive player with a defensive player's mentality. There was the whole thing with Franco Harris—he would run wide, and when he knew he couldn't get any more yards, he would just run out of bounds. Walter wouldn't do that. He would turn up, and he'd punish somebody.

◇

Veteran Chicago sports columnist **BOB VERDI** remains one of the most highly regarded writers in the country, and he certainly had Payton's attention when it came time for the latter to consider doing his autobiography. It turns out, however, that Verdi had company in that regard:

I was "selected" to do his autobiography years ago and since found out that he went through a lot of us. I would go to his house and tape for ten minutes. But he just couldn't sit down, so he would go out to the fishing hole or go shoot baskets or say, "Let's go for a ride." He took me once in a Lamborghini, I think, and he must have been driving 115 on the side streets through Barrington. He looks over at me and says, "You're scared, aren't you?" And I said, "Heck, yeah, I'm scared." I still have Walter Payton tapes here for the book I never wrote. You might say I was designated as his autobiography writer, but I say that loosely because there were probably a dozen of us, although I guess one guy from *Sports Illustrated* (Don Yaeger) is actually doing a book. Good for him. He got him to sit down. I couldn't get him to do that.

I don't think Walter liked talking about himself. It was fun, though. I would call him and ask "?" and he'd say, "Sure, come on over. I'd be glad to see you." And he was glad to see me, except he just didn't want to sit down and talk. However, I don't think I was

Payton loved taking photos as much as his fans loved taking photos of him. This time he's outside Buckingham Palace in London in 1986 during the Bears' stopover in England to play an exhibition game there.

close to him by any means. I don't think he was particularly close with anyone in the media, but he was fine to deal with.

◇

Payton played thirteen seasons in the NFL, averaging three hundred carries a year, and yet he missed only one game, that coming in his rookie season and against his will. Leave it to **BUFFONE,** himself a fourteen-year veteran, to explain what it takes to survive so long in the NFL wars, when one serious injury is all it takes to end a career in the blink of an eye:

Part of my longevity came from luck and the other part from being physically ready to play, with all the off-season stuff.

Another part is football knowledge. There are ways of protecting yourself out there. Walter was one of those type of guys, someone who knew how to do all the fundamentals correctly, such as how to block and utilize the proper running style. Even when he was hit, he really wasn't taking the shots, he was delivering them. Same thing with me. There's a way of playing. Unfortunately with Butkus, it was a knee. There's nothing you can do about that. Same thing with Gale Sayers. Walter and I didn't have any of that, really. We were injury-free for most of our careers. I was with (Bears trainer Clyde) Emrich, and he started us doing off-season conditioning way ahead of everyone else. He wasn't even with the Bears then—we would go down to the Y to work out under him.

◇

Payton didn't spend near the time in the weight room that his teammates did, but he was probably in better shape than any of them, and part of the reason for that was his devotion to running a steep hill near his suburban Chicago home. Somewhere, somehow, Payton maintained peak physical condition, which pleased Bears trainer **FRED CAITO** to no end:

We've all read and heard about the hill, and it's true. He conditioned and trained exceptionally hard and well. But he understood that that's what you had to do to do what he had to do. And it all shows up in the fourth quarter. Walter worked very hard with his weight training—especially his legs. He had great upperbody strength, but he focused on the legs and the back for help. He wanted to do it in the fourth quarter—"Give me the ball," he would say. And he'd wear the other team down. You know, it's hard for a layman, even myself, to stand there on the sideline and understand how he could dish out as much punishment as he took. And he'd wear you out. And then he had that fourth gear, and in the fourth quarter, he used it.

Any resemblance to Michael Jackson is purely in the garb. Payton is dressed the part of the singer as he rests during rehearsal for an appearance on *Saturday Night Live* in 1987.

AP/WIDE WORLD PHOTOS, DAVID BOOKSTAVER

He was always honest with me about his condition game to game and what kind of shape he was in for playing that week. He would sometimes come out and say, "I need a break," or "I need a play," or "I need a series." And I'd say, "Fine." And then when he was ready to go back in, he'd come back over and say so. I could tell if he was BS-ing me and he never did—he was totally honest. There were games when he had some doubt about whether he was going to be able to function, such as when he cracked a rib one year. That was painful. We tried every pad in the world to put on him, because we knew he was going to get a hit. He didn't like this one. He'd take that one off. He didn't like this one. One good hit in some of those games, and you might be out. And then all of a sudden the game would get going, and he would just get into

the flow and he would come off, and I'd say, "Are you all right?" and he'd say, "Yeah, okay."

◇

One legacy and lesson Payton left for budding football players was the importance of serious, year-round training to stay durable. Bears strength and conditioning coach **CLYDE EMRICH** said when it came to preparation, nobody did it better than Payton:

There's absolutely no question about it that his fitness regimen played a major part in his durability and longevity. I mean he was built like a rock. He'd be the first to say it, there's no question that his training made the difference. He pushed it; he worked himself real hard. And he had great strength. I mean, he could dead-lift six and a quarter (625 pounds). Strength is not a substitute for skill; strength enhances skill. But very often it will be the measure that will take you over the top of some players that maybe have just a minimal talent. There's no question in today's climate that in almost every venue of sport that weight training is going to improve your abilities. And you get certain inherited pluses in sports, speed being one, your reflexes, eye-hand coordination, and that, and to enhance that, you need muscle development and especially in strength sports, be it track and field, football, wrestling, boxing, things like that. Almost every sport to a degree, even basketball—look at the sizes of those guys playing basketball nowadays. It helps to reduce injuries because your last line of defense are your ligaments as far as body structure. So if your muscle strength can't absorb the stress that's put on it, then the force is going to go through your ligament structure and you've got torn ligaments.

◇

Even with the changes in the Bears coaching staffs and other high-echelon management during the seventies and eighties, two of the

team's personnel who were mainstays were Caito and Emrich. Together, they helped bring the Bears out of the Stone Age of NFL health and fitness and into a modern era where workouts, nutrition, and medical practice are light-years ahead of where they were thirty years ago. **EMRICH** joined the Bears in the early seventies and had already been with the team several years when Payton arrived on the scene in 1975. Emrich, who could pass for Jack LaLanne's nephew, knows a thing or two about fitness, physiques, strength, and weight training. He had won U.S. championships and set world records as a weightlifter years earlier:

When I first met Walter, I was impressed with his physique; he was very muscular. But through all the years that I knew him, he was always so good-natured, too, always a prankster. And when he was on the football field, you just knew something was going to happen. You just had that confidence that he was going to do something, he just had such great ability. If he got hurt on the field, he'd always make it a point to get up fast. He didn't want anybody to know that he was hurt. But then he'd come over to Freddie Caito and he'd say, "Fred, give me the Darvon." Fred would go to the bag, and Fred would walk by him and slip it into his hand and no show was made of it that he had a problem. One time he had a slight hamstring pull and I had gone out of the weight room for a little while for something and I came back in and there is Walter doing dead lifts with 525 pounds. And I said, "Walter, what the hell are you doing? That affects your hamstrings." "Well," he says, "I'm fine. Don't bother me." And he did like three or four reps. And I said, "God almighty, this guy is just something." Another time he was sitting on the bench and you know Walter's always just kind of looking to do something, so he looks down and there's a dumbbell there, so he picks it up and starts pressing it. It was a one-hundred-pound dumbbell. He didn't train in the weight room often because he wanted to be on his own. He knew more about how to train himself than anybody I knew. He just seemed to know what he needed, and he pushed himself. But he would always come to me when nobody was

around, ask me to come see him, and we would go into the weight room.

One thing he and I used to do all the time, usually when we had our first minicamp, we would shake hands, and we'd squeeze and we'd squeeze and we'd squeeze and we would squeeze. Back then it had been just a few years after I got out of competition, and I had the strength of being able to outlast him, but as I got older, he started taking over and I said, "All right, Walter, you've got me now. Uncle. I'm cool." But it was fun. You just felt good in his presence.

◇

Running back **TONY DORSETT** came out of college two years later than Payton did, with a Heisman Trophy in tow and a spot on the roster of the Dallas Cowboys assured. Dorsett had been a big-time player at the University of Pittsburgh, where he sealed his collegiate marquee status by rushing for more than three hundred yards in a Panthers victory over Notre Dame. Pittsburgh also won a national title thanks to Dorsett, crowning his collegiate career in a way that was a stark contrast to the near-anonymity in which Payton had labored at Jackson State. The great equalizer was a new start in the NFL, and for more than a decade Dorsett and Payton stood out as two of the marquee running backs in the NFL. Dorsett was well aware of his rushing "rival" one NFC division away:

Walter was a real genuine, sincere person, and the other side of him has always been delightful. We exchanged helmets and other stuff once at a Pro Bowl, and I wish I still had that helmet.

The only similarities that Walter and I had as professional football players was that we played the same position. Walter was more of an attack-type runner, whereas I was more of an elusive-type of runner, and I think a lot of that had to do with our physical stature. Walter was about my height, but he was bigger boned and a lot thicker than I was. He weighed over two hundred pounds while I was 185. And so I was 185 and ran about a 4.2

forty where Walter ran about a 4.25 or 4.3, I don't know what it was. But I could appreciate his style. I liked his style. I liked to watch Walter run. He was always a guy that laid it on the line, all the time. Instead of taking the punishment, he was delivering the punishment in a lot of cases, and that I admired. I'd always wished as a runner that I had that kind of size where I could have attacked people in certain situations like Walter did, but I understood what my limitations were. It was my size, and I wouldn't have been around in the National Football League very long if I had tried to attack. My deal was I always tried to negotiate and outrun and just make them miss. One of my biggest assets as a runner was seeing things and being able to react to what I saw. I also had a lot of speed. I could be at full speed in almost two steps, and that was one of the things that I think helped me survive in the National Football League.

Running backs usually keep track of what other running backs on other teams are doing. I know I did. Somewhere along the line, watching Walter and Earl Campbell and Eric Dickerson and those guys indirectly had a lot to do with my being inducted into the Pro Football Hall of Fame. I would look at the box scores and see what Walter did, what Earl did, what Eric did, etc., etc., etc. It was a competition. It was a healthy competition between us all. We all wanted to pretty much outdo the others, and that kept us all playing at a pretty high level.

We all know that Walter is in a better place and playing football on God's team right there. He was not only a great athlete, he was a godsend.

◇

Former Green Bay linebacker **RICH WINGO** played against most, if not all, of the premier running backs of the Payton era. He kept mental notes on all of them and rates them according to his own observations:

Walter, in my opinion, was the best, although I wouldn't say by far. One reason was because, at least in the first half of his career, he didn't have a Miami Dolphin offensive line in front of him. He didn't have a Los Angeles Ram offensive line in front of him like (Eric) Dickerson did. He didn't have a Dallas Cowboy offensive line like (Tony) Dorsett did. And Earl (Campbell) was right there, too. Earl was one of the best running backs I'd ever played against, but Earl couldn't stay healthy because he didn't have the men in front. But Walter, he stayed healthy, even though he took some pounding.

◇

WINGO went up against Payton and the Bears about a dozen times. It all started with an encounter during Wingo's rookie season that showed it wasn't enough for a tackler just to hit Payton to make the great running back go down:

The only times Walter and I ever met were on the field. And as a middle linebacker and a tailback, we met many, many times over seven years, twice a year. We were playing Chicago in Chicago at Soldier's Field and this just always sticks in my mind as to what a competitor he was. It was fourth down and three. We were beating Chicago, and they had the ball on about the thirty-five. They needed this touchdown to win the game. And so they had to get this first down, and they went for it. We lined up, a gap opened, and I shot the gap. It wasn't a blitz, but it just opened up. Right up the middle came Walter, just like they'd done so many times, and with a lead fullback.

For some reason, the fullback either tripped and fell or was taken out by somebody else. I remember hitting Walter in his backfield after he had taken that fake step to the one side, so he was still in the backfield a pretty good distance, three or four yards deep. I had a clean hit. And I hit him, three yards deep, and probably knocked him back even more when I hit him. I

wrapped him up around the waist and leg. Just by sheer desire Walter kept going and kept going, and he missed the first down by maybe a yard or a yard and a half. It was just a phenomenal effort, and he was carrying some other guys, too, not just me.

One other thing about Walter that I can't prove but which I believe to be true is that he sprayed his uniform down with silicon before the game because sometimes you would go to hit him or grab him and his uniform would be really slippery. Again, I don't know for a fact that he did this, but it sure felt like it.

◇

Quarterback **BOB AVELLINI** ended up playing ten seasons with the Bears, giving him ample opportunity to study Payton and his moves, and make comparisons to the rest of the league's players:

Was Walter quicker than any other running back? Well, yeah. But it's not only quickness—it's also size and strength. Walter had it all. I'm sure there are guys just as quick, but they are thirty pounds lighter, or there are guys who are just as strong but they are fifty pounds heavier and much slower. The biggest thing I can remember is turning around and handing the ball to him, and just watching him as a fan would. Everyone should have the vantage point I had in seeing him jump through a crack or a hole big enough for a little cat to get through, but he would bust it, and then normally just one guy couldn't bring him down. He was one of those who attacked the tackler when he ran. If a guy was coming at him, he would throw that forearm at him and dish out a lot of punishment. You see some of these highlight runs where he would put his head down and sort of explode into the tackler. A lot of times he would end up running over that tackler.

Comparing running backs to Walter is a tough subject. There were a lot of great football players, and they weren't just running backs. He could block well, catch the ball well, and even throw the ball well, and obviously he ran the ball well. But I can name a

defensive back like Ronnie Lott who was a pretty good football player, too, and could do everything you ask of a safety. Maybe I'm a little more cerebral, thinking more about things before I say them. Do I think he was a great football player? Absolutely. One of the greatest running backs ever, too. That's an accurate statement. Honestly, though, the running back who was the most dominant for a short period of time was Earl Campbell. He was unbelievable. And then a guy who looked like he was going for a touchdown every time he touched the ball was Eric Dickerson. Another guy like that is Barry Sanders. Now, what do you want out of a running back? Look back at when I came to the Bears. Bobby Douglass, the quarterback, had run for something like a thousand yards, and you've got to ask yourself, "What do I really want out of a quarterback?" Do you want him running for a thousand yards, or do you want him to throw it for three thousand?

◇

Like Don Pierson, **HUB ARKUSH** is a veteran Chicago sports journalist who had the privilege of seeing both Payton and Jordan up close for a number of years. Ditto when you bring Sayers into the equation of great Chicago sports heroes:

I wouldn't be surprised if somebody actually did a poll or survey and found that Walter Payton came out more identified with Chicago than Michael Jordan. There's no question that Chicago loves Michael, but Michael is almost a national icon, a universal icon. He kind of belongs to the world more than he belongs to Chicago. If you asked Chicagoans, there's no doubt in my mind that the three names they would come up with would be Walter Payton, Dick Butkus, and Ernie Banks—you might throw Gale Sayers in there. I think Michael is viewed more as being bigger than the city.

I saw Sayers's entire career. In fact, I was at the game at Wrigley Field when he scored six TDs in the mud against the

49ers. Gale Sayers was probably the greatest open-field runner of all time. I know you can classify running backs in a lot of different ways, but I've never seen a running back who could make people miss the way Sayers could—not even Barry Sanders. Sanders was more of a pinball guy bouncing around. It would have been interesting to see what Gale could have been had he played ten or fifteen years later, when medical science was so much better with knee operations and the rehab part of it.

Also, Gale wasn't the great guy that Walter was. Walter was more than happy to be a possession of the city of Chicago and their fans. Gale didn't have that quality. He was distant, almost cold, and bitter over the injuries that he suffered, and so he didn't have nearly the impact on Bears fans that Payton had. He didn't give himself to the city the way Walter did. I think he admired the hell out of Walter. Gale has gotten better in the last three to five years, and has come out of it a little bit. But for a long time he was a pretty bitter, difficult guy. He was at the funeral, and I know he had great respect for Walter.

◈

LARRY McCARRON played against dozens of All-Pro running backs in his career, which gave him great credibility when it came to rating running backs:

He was not a finesse runner. He was a powerful runner. I mean, he was a physical runner. He wasn't a guy that played the fringes and then needed a lot of room. If it wasn't there, he'd take it, he'd make it. But when people talk about the guys who gained all kinds of yards, Walter didn't do it because nobody could touch him; he did it because he broke their tackles. Tony Dorsett was a guy who could run away from people, and that's how he gained all those yards, where Walter was just a much more powerful runner, and a more physical-type running back. I put Earl Campbell into that category, too, because of the way he could

wear you down in a game and actually take over as the game wore on.

◇

As an NFL player personnel expert with about forty years' experience, **GIL BRANDT** has seen about every running back known to man, and he enjoys comparing and contrasting running backs from over the years, starting with the Bears pair of Payton and Gale Sayers:

I don't know if anybody knows just what kind of a player Sayers could have been had he not gotten hurt. But he, too, was an unbelievable player and an unbelievable person. Then there's Tony Dorsett, who we drafted two years after Walter came along, in 1977. Dorsett had as good a running ability as anybody that you'll ever see. And by that I mean he could make a two-yard run into something sensational. It's a shame that (Eric) Dickerson had his career cut short by wanting to be traded from the Rams because the Rams were such a good running team.

When you talk about Dickerson, Dorsett, Sayers, and Payton, you're just saying, "What would you rather have, two half dollars or four quarters or ten dimes?" Those are all great players. I mean, there's just little or nothing to show between the difference of them. Now, what happens is, is that you may need an inside running game. And if you're an inside running team, Campbell and Dickerson are better players for you. If you're a team with a philosophy of spreading the field and having running backs who can catch the ball, then Dorsett, Payton, and Sayers are better running backs for you. Dorsett could have gained a lot more yards. The hardest thing to explain to Dorsett when he came in to the league was that he was running and carrying the ball (only) seventeen or eighteen times, because on our team we had extra wide-receivers, plus in those days you had the two-back offense. We also had (Robert) Newhouse and (Walt) Garrison involved in the offense, so our offense was more spread out as far as guys catching balls,

with the receivers and the tight ends. With Payton, you know he was productive and durable. Now I'm not sure that Dorsett would have been as durable as Payton was, although he never did get hurt.

When you talk about Payton and his durability, it's not only the amount of carries he had that is significant. The other thing is how often he had to play in inclement weather like you do in Green Bay, Chicago, and Minnesota before they got the dome. Playing in inclement weather like that is a lot harder. I think it's a lot harder from the fifteenth of November to the end of the season playing in Chicago than it is in someplace like Dallas.

◇

Buffone was already a Bears veteran linebacker when Payton arrived in 1975 and was still in Chicago in 1999 when Payton passed away, and in between **BUFFONE** liked what he saw as Payton went from shy rookie to worldly superstar:

What happens with a lot of players takes place between the first year and the second year, which is when the light goes on. You're a totally different guy in your second year because you know everybody and you're more confident. You understand what's expected of you, and you know how to play. Walter went along and got better and better and better. There was one guy, Walter Payton, carrying that offense, but he never complained. He just did his job over and over and over. As he got older, he not only got very good with the team but also outside the team in terms of speaking, the media, and working with people. He used to have his restaurant, and I used to do some functions there with him. I'd see him at golf tournaments—he was a very good golfer. I did see him one time when he didn't say anything, but I could notice an appreciable loss of weight. A lot of times guys would do that on purpose, working out and doing certain things. Walter and I would do our show on Score (radio). He was our Monday-morning analyst, so he would call in

every Monday morning, even when he was sick. A lot of people didn't know what was going on, but I sort of had an idea. We would go over the game played on Sunday, and he would go right through it. Didn't see him much after that.

◇

Hall of Fame linebacker **JACK HAM,** who played with the Pittsburgh Steelers, on Payton's unique versatility:

I played against him in many pro Bowls. You usually play against a running back who might be a great runner, but not a great pass catcher, such as Earl Campbell. Then you could get a guy who was a great runner, but not a great blocker. Very rarely, if ever, do you get a running back who combines running, blocking, and catching the ball. He took as much pride in his blocking as anything, even in a Pro Bowl. We're playing in Hawaii; it's a pretty low-key atmosphere. We're not hitting all that hard. He would still take some linebacker's head off. I was just glad he was in the other conference during the year.[3]

◇

USA Today sportswriter **TOM WEIR,** in 1984, a year before the Bears would go on to win the Super Bowl, writing on one of Payton's possible legacies as a sports hero:

Sadly, Payton might join the Cubs as a Chicago symbol of sports futility. He is a 1980s version of Mister Cub, Ernie Banks—a great player who never wore a World Series ring. There is a little of Roger Maris in Payton, too. Just as Maris had to wear an asterisk beside his name for hitting his (61) homers in 162 games, instead of 154 like Babe Ruth, statisticians are already sullying Payton's (career rushing) record because Brown amassed his 12,312 yards in eighteen fewer games.[4]

◇

MAGRANE often was in awe of Walter Payton the football player, but he also knew Walter Payton the person, and the star running back showed himself to be more human than superman, as was the case after the 1986 Super Bowl game:

He was vain and he was humble, he was kind and he was petty. He was all these things. He had a temper. He was furious after the Super Bowl game because he hadn't scored. (Matt) Suhey had an interesting take on that. He said Walter really had a pretty good game. He said the Patriots set their defense up to stop Walter. And they just beat the (heck) out of him, they really did. They put some really big hits on him. But what they did then was free up everybody else. Willie Gault went nuts and (Jim) McMahon went nuts, and Matt (Suhey) scored the first touchdown. And they (the New England Patriots) sacrificed everything else just to hold Walter. So in a sense, Walter did what he needed to do. I think he was hurt when Fridge scored and he didn't. And Ditka said afterwards that "if I had it to do over again I wouldn't have done that." McMahon was furious. Walter wasn't going to go on TV, he was all bent out of shape. They wanted him on television, and Ken Valdiserri and I spent about fifteen minutes with him back in some cubbyhole in the back of the dressing room talking, trying to talk him into going on TV. He was hot. But he went and said all the right things. He did what he was supposed to do.

◇

MIKE SINGLETARY, speaking after Walter's death on November 1, 1999:

Walter was a fourth-quarter player. When everybody was down and out, you could always look for Walter to make the block, make the run, make the catch. All great players are fourth-quarter players, and in the fourth quarter he was at his finest."[5]

◇

Every now and then an athlete comes along who transcends his or her sport, someone with special skills and charisma that go far beyond the stadium or arena. When it comes to comparing Payton to another athlete of similar lofty-icon status, **MAGRANE** compares the Payton phenomenon to that being experienced in recent years by another superstar athlete:

Tiger Woods. Every once in a while we'd have people come along in sports who transcend their sport, I certainly think ability is a huge part of it. But there's got to be something in that person, too, that makes them special. And you see it in all fields. Walter was one of those rare people. Just like we're seeing now in Tiger Woods. These guys, they have terrific ability, but that wasn't enough for them. They wouldn't settle for anything less than being the absolute best there was.

◇

Every major sports city has had its share of special superstars over the years, but no U.S. city can top the one-two punch formed in Chicago by, first, Walter Payton, and then Michael Jordan. With a year or two of overlap of their respective careers, Payton and Jordan gave the Windy City almost a quarter-century of continual superstardom. *Chicago Tribune* sportswriter **DON PIERSON** compares and contrasts the two great Chicago icons:

I see Payton and Jordan as like the dividing line between the twentieth and twenty-first centuries. Payton was right on the cusp of media explosion, sort of pre-celebrity lifestyle, pre-ESPN highlight shows sort of thing. He was more the workmanlike guy who personifies that hardworking, blue-collar Chicago guy and will always be the icon to those people. Jordan is like in another level—the cartoon character. Jordan is twenty-first-century stuff, where the media plays such a role. They overlapped only something like two or three years. It was like a perfect dividing line. You really can't compare one to another—and you can't pit one

against the other. They were so different in their eras and in their auras as well. Both were hard workers, for sure, but I call Payton the down-to-earth guy and Jordan was above the rim. But then, you don't have to limit your legacy to one athlete in this town. I think Payton pushed a whole lot of guys before him into the background, guys like Ernie Banks. Then Jordan set a whole new standard. Payton was the last of the Bobby Hull era, those kind of stars.

◇

Even though Michael Jordan and Walter Payton each had their run of Chicago in their own ways, they did it with style and class, and each had his own distinctive way of doing it, as veteran Chicago sportswriter **BOB VERDI** explains:

Walter was his own category—almost like a saint. Michael was more visible. You never associated Walter with all these marketing people—he never came across as Walter Payton Incorporated, if you know what I mean. I don't mean that in a bad way, it's just a product of the times. Walter actually was pre-ESPN. I want to say the day that he broke Jim Brown's record the building was not sold out. It might not even have been televised locally, as hard as it is to believe that. It was the same afternoon that the Cubs were trying to win a pennant at San Diego. I was out there, and I'm quite sure Soldier Field wasn't sold out.

◇

Former Bear and veteran Chicago sports personality **DAN JIGGETTS** has this to say about the Payton-Jordan phenomenon:

Michael is a worldwide icon. Walter had some of that because of the nature of who he was and his personality, but Walter was more of a people's superstar because he had a wonderful common touch. It goes back to what I said about superstars being willing

to share the spotlight. He was one of those guys who could walk through a lobby and go up to a doorman at the hotel or talk to the maid. His personality was that everyone is important, not just executives and people like that. Michael is a little more aloof, I think, in that he came through in an era where you needed things like bodyguards and all that kind of thing. Walter was one of those guys who just relished going wherever the heck he wanted to, doing stuff with the other guys, whatever. He was one of those guys always out there in the public.

◈

BUFFONE has spent most of his adult life in Chicago as a popular sports figure, and he discussed Payton's brand of sports celebrity status in a city that worshiped him:

All those guys (such as Michael Jordan, Bobby Hull, Gale Sayers, and Ernie Banks) left something in Chicago. I think Walt was more touchable than any of these other guys—more accessible. He'd be a guy where you'd say all of a sudden, "Oh my God, I saw Payton buying a pair of jeans," or "I saw Payton putting gas in his car," and then if you went up to Walter it was like he had known you forever because you were a Bear fan. He didn't run away from people. If there were people around and he liked what they did, he was always there signing autographs and saying thank you. People want to feel like "We're all in this together, in your city, you fans." I know it's hard to do because when you go out you're constantly around people. I can't imagine what it was like for him. He became more of a recluse because he was sick and didn't want people to see how he looked. What he left in this town was that he was just a part of this town, just one of you guys. People accepted him that way.

◈

Longtime Bears kicker and Payton teammate **BOB THOMAS** remained a resident of the Chicago area after his retirement, meaning he has been around long enough to compare his former teammate to basketball superstar Michael Jordan in terms of what made each special in the city:

In one sense they are very similar in that, in both cases, people feel as if they know them. They're approachable in the sense they both had/have the engaging smile, the quip, what have you. The other similarity is that, in this day of free agency where people are in one city one minute and another city the next, they both will always be known as Chicago. People say this is a Bear town, but we had the greatest basketball player of all time, and a guy who I feel is the greatest football player of all time, playing just for one city. That makes it special as well.

I remember someone saying that Jordan belonged to the world, for he is, like, all-universe, where Payton clearly belonged to Chicago. You look at their careers as far as the entertainment dollars go, and you see Jordan with all the commercials and the movies that did make him more of a world figure, almost like a Muhammad Ali–type of figure. With Walter, there weren't many endorsement and entertainment opportunities and the like in that day.

◈

Payton's death in November 1999 was a reality check for former Bears teammates, such as quarterback **BOB AVELLINI:**

The biggest thing people should remember is that you never know. When you'd see this guy walk by with one of the greatest bodies you'd ever see, and then to lose him at such an early age. When we all came back for his funeral, it was probably the biggest reunion of Bears at any time. I saw guys from the forties and fifties as well as guys who played in the nineties. As we sat

there at the funeral, I think we all thought of our own mortality, and that if it could happen to a guy like Walter Payton, it could happen to anybody. In the end it wasn't so much Walter Payton the football player I was thinking about, it was the human being and that we're not here for all that long a time.

WALTER PAYTON:
DOLLARS AND SENSE

WALTER PAYTON WAS A MAN of many talents and insights coolly hidden behind the spectacular runs, stiff-arms, practical jokes, pedal-to-the-metal drives, memorable public appearances, and unprecedented public access. He also had a nose for business, which, while it didn't manifest itself in number crunching and business-plan authorship, went well beyond the typical superstar scenario of a big-bucks superstar lending one's name to an endeavor, then sitting back to collect dividends and other payments. Also, Payton didn't treat his business associates as tolerated nuisances but as friendly acquaintances with whom he could enjoy life as much as they enjoyed success.

One of Payton's legacies he left behind is the Walter Payton Foundation, an organization that annually benefits tens of thousands of abused and neglected children in the greater Chicago area. Another enduring establishment of his is the Roundhouse restaurant in Aurora, Illinois. From boards of banks to kids in the inner city, Payton was often there to serve and to help, and he did it with a smile and a lot of heart.

◇

Chicago-area businessman **MICHAEL SILVERMAN** knew Payton for
about twenty-five years, having first met Sweetness soon after he was
drafted by the Bears. Silverman was a part-time associate of the Bears
for almost twenty years, doing some photography work for them and
occasionally traveling with the team. He would sit in the coaches'
booth at games and help chart plays. He also did some photography
work for the Bears. It didn't take long for Silverman not only to
befriend Payton but also to discover that the running back had a good
nose for the business world, certainly more than most celebrity
athletes who lend their name to businesses do. Silverman found
Payton to be a truly active business partner:

Walter was a very bright individual with good business sense.
Sometimes you'd be surprised at some of the concepts he would
come up with. Our relationship grew as friends before it was a
business relationship, and I was never involved in any of his
other business ventures. The bank grew substantially because of
his involvement. He had good business acumen. He was young
compared to a lot of other directors after he committed to coming
as a director in 1994. There were a lot of things he helped out
with at the bank in developing policies and developing some
strategy to move forward, what kind of bank we would become
and what our role in the community would be. He was not a
banker, so what he offered was from a personal point of view as
well as a business point of view. He was a people person. He did a
lot of things to help us in the grand opening, such as meeting
with customers and shareholders.

I met Walter at the College All-Star Game. He had been
drafted by the Bears, and I was helping some people working at
the All-Star Game. I got to meet him again after he got to the
Bears, and we had several discussions. I was rehabbing a knee
after surgery at that time, and I even played basketball with
Walter and did different things with the team. After the season
began and I began to see him more often, we began having some

more conversations. And ultimately, when I was opening up a bank with some other partners, I asked Walter if he wanted to be involved. Ultimately, he did. After lots of discussions and a lot of background checking, things like that, Walter was one of the five organizers of the First Northwest Bank, along with myself and three other people.

Periodically, we'd do different things. I'd go over to his house, or he would do things for me. He participated in an event at one of my kids' school, a function in which he showed up as a celebrity guest. He lived in the same neighborhood. We had this good relationship almost right away, as soon as we began talking. I wasn't a real close personal friend of his, but we would see each other often. I introduced him to some people at Hilton Hotels, and he became an area representative for Hilton.

Let's face it. Walter had a great reputation as a humanitarian and as an individual who was involved with his businesses. The real issue with Walter was that he was unlike a lot of athletes who lend their names to something but don't take an active role in it. He was a participant. Until he got sick, he was very active. The last time I saw him we had promised we would get together and that there was something he needed to tell me. We had a meeting at his office and had a long conversation. He told me that he was sick, but he didn't tell me everything. But I knew that there was a problem. I asked him what information he still wanted to receive from the board and things like that, and we continued to send him all the information, although I don't know if he ever read it all.

◇

Another of Payton's longtime business associates was **JOE KANE,** who knew Walter the last twenty years of Payton's life. Kane for many years hosted a luncheon for the Bears every Tuesday during football season and also pulled many of the Bears together for events, such as the time he opened a new disco:

The new disco was called the Cinderella Rockefella. We had five different opening nights for the disco. Doug Plank, then playing with the Bears, was one of the guys helping me with all this. Walter shows up one time and says to me, "Show me your discotheque; I'd like to see it." It was a really big place with large dance floors and something like fifty thousand lights. Walter really liked that music and the sound. He asked me if there was anything I needed and then asked if I had any celebrities to represent me and the discotheque. He then said he was available. Now this was still when he was pretty early in his career with the Bears. So I talked to his agent, who told me that Walter wasn't looking for money; he was looking for exposure. So he started making some appearances on behalf of the disco and doing some speaking engagements. We ended up having some great times together over the years.

It was an old theater, so you can imagine the stage in the center with all the seats around it. What we did was use the center stage as a dance floor, and it had large booths around it. We could sit about sixteen people in each of these booths, so you could put nice parties together. Then we built up the one side that had this one bar that overlooked it, and it was just covered with this shiny, glitzy material. A circular bar high overlooked all the action on the dance floor. On the other side was a quiet bar that was glass and also overlooked the dance floor. The place held about twelve hundred people. Lights would come down over the floor while you were dancing. It had confetti guns—all the fast-moving disco things you can remember from those days. And I can remember Walter being a great dancer. He used to get out there and do the air guitar, a lot and things of that nature.

One year we had the Bears Christmas party at the disco. It was a Sunday night, and what we did was just close it to everyone else. One of the defensive players loved to hear his country and western music. This guy went up to the disc jockey and wanted his music on, and he became upset when she (the deejay) said to him, "You know, after this set is over, I'll put some country music

on, but I need to finish this set up first." The player became irate and threw a beer bottle across the floor. It bounced in the seating area, and Walter and Connie were there. Ted Albrecht and his wife were there, too, as was my wife, Frances. I was somewhere else. Two of the ladies, Connie and Ted's wife, were both pregnant at the time, and that's why Teddy was especially upset about the bottle being thrown across the room. He wanted to go after him and Walter said, "No, no, no. We'll take care of it." So Walter came to me and said, "You go talk to this defensive end and calm him down, and tell him he can't be doing this stuff." Now I'm five-foot-eight, and I'm up there telling this six-foot-six, 270-pounder to cool it while all these football players were standing around watching me. Bob Avellini, the quarterback, later told me, "Joe, you handled it well. We were all behind you." The guy settled down, and everything went well from that point forward, even though Teddy Albrecht wanted to punch him out.

◇

As the Bears radio broadcaster for many years, **HUB ARKUSH** had plenty of opportunities to rub elbows with the post-retirement Payton, who always managed to find the energy to participate in fundraisers and the like, even when he was dying. Arkush remembers Payton as the dutiful businessman who accepted responsibility as a role model to the nth degree:

Walter was an extremely successful businessman. And he understood that one of the ways to enhance that success was to always make sure to give a little back. He was always involved in various projects. And he stayed very close to the Bears, and that was a neat thing.

Under Papa Bear (Halas), the Bears had had a reputation for turning away its stars out of frugality or cheapness. But Walter was immediately put on the board of directors after he retired, so he stayed very close to the team. I remember attending a function

for the Better Boys Foundation of Chicago. He would get into private charitable work, always showing up. For the team's seventy-fifth-anniversary book, I did the interviews. I set up an interview with him in his office, even though he wasn't giving any interviews at the time. I didn't realize why, but he had agreed to do this for the team. We were sitting there in the office, and he asked me how bad I thought his eyes looked, and I said, "What are you talking about?" and he said, "Can't you tell? They're all yellow and red." I hadn't really noticed. He was a race-car driver at the time—he eventually became an owner—and he had had an accident. His car had caught on fire. I don't think he had been burned too badly, but whatever they use to put out the fire had gotten into his eyes.

The strongest memories I have of Walter go back to the year before he was diagnosed, during the preseason of 1998. He had done the color commentary on Bears preseason games. He had never really done any broadcasting and hadn't really wanted to. We had talked a few times leading up to those games. He was doing TV, and I was doing radio. Normally we traveled with the team, but during preseason we didn't, and we ended up sitting next to each other on the plane. It was a coincidence. We spent a long time visiting about the team. Dave Wannstedt was in his last season, and he expressed a lot of concern about whether there was any hope of turning things around. What was remarkable to me about it was looking at him and thinking that he could still be playing. He was in incredible shape. He had gotten a little bit of gray maybe, but didn't look like he had aged a day. He was vital and as fit as ever.

◇

Payton might have been the greatest running back of all time, and likewise he had few peers when it came to making public appearances for a good cause. To him, it wasn't just a matter of showing up and signing autographs. Payton enjoyed meeting strangers and often had

genuine words of wisdom to pass along to his audience, as friend **JOE KANE** can attest:

After I had left Chicago and moved to Pittsburgh (in 1984), I was on the YMCA board there. They had a banquet once a year for high school seniors to honor them not only for what they had done in sports but also in academia. They honored about 100 to 130 kids. They were looking for a sports celebrity to speak, and I said, "Well, maybe I can get Walter Payton to come in and speak." They just went gaga. So I talked to Walter about it and, sure enough, he said he would come. We announced Walter Payton's name in promoting the banquet, and in the next five days it went from a thousand to eighteen hundred people. Then Walter came in and was doing interviews with the press, so he walked in a little late and went up on this four-tier dais that included all these kids. Then they announced Walter, and I looked around and suddenly I couldn't find him. While everyone was having dinner, he went to every one of these 130 high school seniors, met them, asked them what their sport was, what their grade point average was, and what they were planning to do with the rest of their lives. Then when he finished with this and dinner was over—he had wolfed down a cheeseburger while everyone else had their roast beef—he got up and gave a fifteen-minute speech on why academia was more important than sports and why these kids should spend their time studying when they went to college. It was the type of thing that Walter was really good at.

There was another occasion when he invited me to meet him in New York. He was being presented with a Black Athlete of the Year Award. We were to meet on a Sunday night in New York. We were both staying at a New York Hilton, and we had plans to have dinner at Tavern on the Green at seven o'clock. So I arrived at the hotel and checked in, and Walter wasn't in yet. I checked again later, and he still wasn't there. Finally, at around nine o'clock my phone rang, and it was another gentleman that I didn't know, and he said he was with Walter and had just arrived at the hotel, and

they apologized for being late. The reason why Walter was late was because he was in Iowa that afternoon meeting with a kid through the Make-a-Wish Foundation, and he was so entranced by this young person and the battle he was putting up for his life that Walter just overstayed the time and got to New York three or four hours later than planned. You know, he gave a lot to the people around him, mostly the children.

On another occasion, Walter and I were having lunch in the coffee shop of an open-air restaurant in Chicago. While we were having lunch, a friend of mine came walking through the lobby with his twelve-year-old son, and he waved. The kid looked up to where his dad was waving and saw Walter Payton there. So suddenly his father is motioning to me, and I said to Walter, "You wouldn't mind giving an autograph for this young man, would you?" And he said, "Of course not." I called them all over, and while Walter was signing an autograph for the young man, Stan Musial walked over to our table and said to me, "Joe, I wanted to thank you for a great stay, and I look forward to seeing you again." All of a sudden the father sees that it's Stan Musial, and all of a sudden he starts to go gaga. He wants an autograph from Stan, and I said to Stan, "Stan, you wouldn't mind signing an autograph, would you?" Stan said, "Of course not." He signed the autograph, and then he left. Well, the boy looked at his dad and said, "Dad, who was that?" And the father said, "Son, that was Stan the Man." The son said "Who?" and he said, "Stan Musial, the greatest baseball player who ever lived." And the kid said, "Never heard of him." So I then turned to Walter and said, "Walter, remember this day. Someday you will be forgotten as well. That's the way it works." There were some wonderful times.

◆

Payton played hard every play for all four quarters of a game, but it was not reckless abandon, even when he was banging into would-be

tacklers with an ironlike stiff-arm or a shoulder straight into the other guy's helmet. It was further testimony to the effectiveness of his dedicated training habits as occasionally monitored by longtime Bears strength coach **CLYDE EMRICH:**

He, (former Bears trainer) Freddie Caito, and I were up in his office on two or three occasions. He had some business and he was trying to get it ready to promote, and he wanted our input on some training centers that he was going to develop for CEOs. And he brought that about because often when he'd travel and would go to work out somewhere, the people—not that he didn't like it—but all the attention would interfere with his training. And he heard that from pro basketball players and other people that he knew. And so he thought it would probably be a good idea maybe to open up a place specifically for these people, these traveling CEOs, so when they went to the site, the idea was for them to have a physical, so it could be recommended what type of program they should follow, what type of diet they should follow. And it'd be like a twelve-room hotel, so if they're going through, they could stop, stay overnight, and then get on the plane and continue to where they're going— plus have this workout.

It was a good idea. And so Freddie and I organized the equipment that we thought he should buy for it. Freddie was making the plans for the layout and the training facility itself, the weight rooms, the saunas, and all that kind of stuff. The conversation was devoted to the kind of instruction you'd need, the quality of them, and the medical people you'd have on standby. But it was a good idea. The idea was to have it somewhere near an airport. And he had already gone out and looked at some property. So it was moving along, and then all of this came along. The long-term plan was to franchise this. Many people travel all over. And he would get advertising in the airline magazines where people would see that, these travelers, professional travelers. He had good business sense. He had a

good head on his shoulder, no question in my mind. He was alert and he was energetic, and you never met a man like him.

◇

After Payton announced early in 1999 that he was sick, officials with his charitable Walter Payton Foundation assumed that he would want to put their annual holiday toy drive for needy children on hold. Payton would have none of that and instead called on his foundation to add fifteen thousand names to its list of needy kids, and the collection goal was raised from $3.5 million worth of toys to $5 million, a show of determination that pleased foundation executive director **KIM TUCKER:**

I suggested that the toy drive is a lot of work, and maybe we should wait this year, and Walter said, "No way." He knew these children depend on us, and he made me promise that we would not stop the toy drive.[1]

SHORT (AND SWEET) TAKES

Jackson State teammate **VERNON PERRY** on Payton's appetite for friendship:

I used to have bite prints on my shoulder from the times Walter would walk up behind me and bite me.

◇

Longtime Minnesota Vikings head coach **BUD GRANT** on respecting Payton:

In our film sessions, our defense actually applauded when they saw Payton make some of his runs.[1]

◇

If someone on offense missed an assignment such as a block that led to Payton's being "prematurely" tackled, Payton would let them know about it, but in a quiet way, as offensive lineman **KEITH VAN HORNE** discovered on a number of occasions over the years:

It's just a stare. If you got the stare, you knew you did something wrong or you better do something right. But he wasn't a real rah-rah guy.

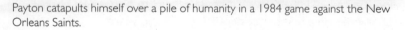

JIM McMAHON, the Bears'"punky QB" who helped lead his team to victory in the Super Bowl, capping an 18-1 season in 1985, called Payton totally unselfish:

How many times did he save my butt picking up a blitz before I was blown up? A lot. Never once did he say in the huddle, "Hey, give me the ball!" Whatever we called, he ran. Football has had very few like him.[2]

Payton catapults himself over a pile of humanity in a 1984 game against the New Orleans Saints.

MIKE DITKA, the last of three Bears head coaches Payton played for, said his best memory of a Payton play was one in which Sweetness did not touch the ball:

People ask me about the play he was involved in that I remember most, and it's probably a block he threw. There's no question he was one of the best blocking backs ever.[3]

◇

Fullback **MATT SUHEY** on Payton's mental state going into the 1984 Cowboys game with Jim Brown's career rushing record in his sights. As it turned out, Payton needed one more game to get there:

He was nervous. He talked about the record, saying there's all that pressure on him. He said, "I realize it's there, but we've got to win the game." Then he shook his head and said, "The pressure is unbelievable."[4]

◇

MIKE SINGLETARY on Payton's versatility and toughness:

He's the first running back I ever saw who I thought could be a defensive player.[5]

◇

DAN JIGGETTS on Payton's caring attitude for other people:

The thing that was impressive to me were the thousands of stories about how Walter did things for people he didn't even know.[6]

◇

Defensive lineman **DAN HAMPTON** on Payton's indefatigable attitude, even after ten brutal years playing in the NFL:

Walter still plays like he's trying to be the best tailback in tenth grade. He still has the same enthusiasm.[7]

◇

Veteran pro-football sportswriter **PAUL ZIMMERMAN** of *Sports Illustrated* once wrote that he interviewed Payton one time at twilight and got a feeling that there was a glow around Payton, almost like he was "giving off sparks":

Life was the thing that defined him, great, passionate bursts of life. He played football in a frenzy, attacking tacklers with a fury that almost seemed personal. He got stronger as the game went on. Defenses tired, he attacked them.[8]

◇

Dallas Cowboys running back **EMMITT SMITH**, who entered the 2000 season fewer than three thousand yards away from Payton's career rushing record, long ago tabbed Payton as his childhood idol. He dedicated the Cowboys' November 8, 1999, game against Minnesota to Payton. Smith ended up rushing for two touchdowns and 140 yards in less than a half before he had to leave the game with a broken hand:

I lost an individual that I had looked at his personal accomplishments in life as well as in the game of football. I think any player who cares anything about the game of football understands who he was, what he stood for, and what he did for the game.[9]

◇

Bears strength coach **CLYDE EMRICH** on Payton's fulfilled life:

He was given ninety years, and he lived them all in forty-five.[10]

◇

Former Bears assistant coach **Fred O'Connor** on Payton's physical package:

God must have taken a chisel and said, "I'm going to make me a halfback."[11]

◇

Ditka on Payton's last few months alive:

I think Walter thought it was a matter of him getting a liver transplant and being Walter again. A lot of people believed that, including me. He was going to be Walter all over again.[12]

◇

Jay Hilgenberg, one of Payton's former Bears teammates, on the shock of Payton's death at such a young age (forty-five):

You look at the roster of our Super Bowl team, and who would you think would be the first guy to pass away? He'd be your last choice. Tomorrow is not promised to anybody.[13]

◇

Richard Dent, the Bears' All-Pro defensive end and a teammate of Payton's during the Bears' golden years in the mid-eighties, on Payton's example:

He's been a great person to me in teaching you how to be the best you can be at anything.[14]

◇

Former career rushing leader **JIM BROWN** on Payton's worthiness to break his record ahead of the likes of Franco Harris:

Where are the gladiators now? Where are the football players who take the risks? Football is about survival, but they don't take chances anymore. Walter Payton takes risks. Walter is a gladiator. He follows the code.[15]

◇

In his book *One Knee Equals Two Feet,* television football color commentator **JOHN MADDEN** gave some of his highest praise of any individual to Payton:

As a runner, pass catcher, passer, blocker, durability, as well as kickoff and punt returner early in his career, occasional punter and quarterback if called on—any way you look at him, Walter Payton is the best ever.

◇

Running-back great **O. J. SIMPSON** on Payton's running ability compared to his:

His strength is unusual. In fact, it's amazing. He gets hit a lot—I mean really tagged—but the next thing you know, he's off and running. I broke my share of tackles, but I was never in Walter's league.[16]

◇

GALE SAYERS, another great Chicago Bear running back, on a running back's role when it comes to blocking as well as running with the ball:

Most backs, myself included, feel that if they're going to run the ball twenty-five times or more in a game, why put a lot of effort into blocking? But Walter didn't think that way. That's what set

him head and shoulders above other running backs—the maximum effort he put into other phases of the game.[17]

◇

Wide receiver **BRIAN BASCHNAGEL,** a former Bears teammate, on Payton's incredible throwing ability:

He could play any position, but he might have been limited at offensive tackle. He's only five-foot-ten. What amazed me, here's a running back, and I once saw him throw a football eighty yards, just kidding around. The most incredible thing I ever saw him do was the time he threw me a fifty-eight-yard touchdown pass. He was going down, two big linemen on him, and he not only had the strength to whip the ball that far sidearm, but also the presence of mind to realize he could do it.[18]

◇

Legendary Dallas Cowboys coach **TOM LANDRY** on Payton's assets as a running back:

Walter has two qualities you don't ordinarily find in a running back—great speed and great strength. Add great balance to that, and you have the best in the business. He always presents a special problem because you not only have to plug the hole once, you have to plug it twice because Walter keeps coming.[19]

◇

Payton's first high school head football coach, **CHARLES BOSTON,** on what he saw in store for the teenage sensation:

I'm not saying I knew back then he was going to be as great as he turned out, but I knew he was going to be something real special, and I'd been right before.[20]

◇

Defensive back **GARY FENCIK** on Payton's seemingly endless energy:

He's a man-child, a grown-up kid. He's always out there throwing and kicking and shooting his bow and arrow and a dozen other things. I've never known anyone who likes to play outdoors so much. It's not even football. I used to worry that he'd get hurt. I used to pray every night. But he's got a frame that just seems invincible.[21]

◇

MATT SUHEY on Payton's ability to laugh off mistakes:

I don't think people realize what a great sense of humor Walter has, an ability to say or do something funny at the right time. I dropped a pass against the Colts, and on the way back to the huddle he said to me, "You can always get a paper route or join the army." And he's a good mimic. He does a great Ditka and a great Buckwheat from the Little Rascals.[22]

◇

Bears quarterback **JIM MCMAHON** on Payton's career, spoken in the immediate aftermath of Payton's final game, a 21-17 playoff loss to Washington in January 1988:

I'm gonna miss him in the backfield. I'm gonna miss him in the locker room. I'm gonna miss being around the guy. The day he walks out of football is the day he should walk into the Hall of Fame. The hell with that (bleeping) waiting five years.[23]

◇

DITKA on his preconceived notions about Payton when taking over the Bears' head-coaching job in 1982:

I thought Walter Payton was one heck of a tough football player before I came to the Bears. I had great admiration for him because of the way he always gave something extra when he was about to be tackled. I like that. Then when I came here, I saw what an athlete he was. You see his strength, but you can't believe it. Nobody ever realizes how big he is under there. He plays like he weighs 230. He's the very best football player I've ever seen, period. At any position, period.[24]

◇

Former Bears quarterback **VINCE EVANS** on Payton's pranksterish ways:

The guy was a huge joker. Your head constantly had to be on a swivel. You'd be in a meeting, and he'd be flicking the lights on and off. He'd hit you upside the head with a rubber band and then look at you with a straight face, like, "What are you looking at me for?"[25]

◇

MIKE SINGLETARY on being at bedside for the last few hours of Payton's life:

There was no tense look on his face, just peace—a look of peace.[26]

◇

WALTER PAYTON, IN HIS OWN WORDS

On being in great shape:

I'm always fearful I'm not in the best shape I can be in. My goal is to be able to play all out for sixty minutes every game. Since you might have the ball only thirty minutes, I figure I've got enough left to go all out on every play.[27]

On his February 2, 1999, announcement that he was ill with a liver disease:

To some of you, I don't look healthy. I still am. Most of you guys I can still take.[28]

On humility:

I don't perceive myself as being better than anyone. I shovel my driveway. I go to the grocery store. I pump my own gas. Some athletes don't do that.[29]

On his missing only one game in his thirteen-year career, that coming in his rookie season when he was involuntarily held out of a game by the coaches:

Excuse me, an ankle? I played once after getting my ankle taped three times. Taped the skin without prewrap because they said it would hold better. Put on my sock and taped it again. Then I put on my shoe and had it spatted. Gained a hundred-something yards, scored a couple of touchdowns. . . . I'm going to set the record straight. If you're ready to play and the coach won't let you, is that a missed game?[30]

On setting an example:

I'm not a role model. I'm just Walter Payton. If kids see some good in me they can utilize and emulate and make their lives better, that's well and good. But they have to realize I'm human just like anybody else. I'm capable of making mistakes. I'm capable of

making the wrong decision. They should realize that. Nobody's perfect. Please don't put that on me, because I'm not perfect.[31]

On breaking Jim Brown's career rushing record:

Once my career's over, whatever happens, it's God's will. I have no control over it. As far as anyone coming along and breaking that record, I have no quarrels about it. Just as long as it's my son.[32]

On being physically aggressive with would-be tacklers:

It's not a matter of pride. It's a matter of survival, because if you let those guys beat up on you, you won't be in there too long, so what you have to do instead of being on offense, you have to take the defensive approach sometimes.[33]

Describing his running style to an inquiring reporter:

I'm not feeling a thing when I'm running and cutting on the field. I don't even know what I'm doing. My aggression fuels my burning desire. I block out everything. I'm an artiste! Everything I do is spontaneous and creative.[34]

In the book *Sweetness,* Payton was quoted in looking back over his first three seasons as a pro running back, a stretch that included his career single-season best of 1,852 yards:

I did start faster than Sayers and threatened some of his records and broke others in a shorter playing career—so far. I suppose the comparisons are valid. But back then they were pure speculation and put a lot of pressure on me. And you can't tell me the writers knew I was going to be a record-setting back. That kind of thing starts with every high draft pick. Three months later— when they discover the guy's a bust—he's looking for an assistant coaching job at his old high school, and the writers pretend they never predicted anything.[35]

On winning a championship, spoken before the Bears' 1985 season:

It's like icing on the cake with even a cherry stuck on top. To win, that's what it's all about. To be chasing a record, that's one of those things. But to win, that means a little bit more because everyone gets to share in it.[36]

On having a can-do attitude:

I don't like people telling me I can't do something.[37]

On comparisons:

Whatever you do, don't compare me to Gale Sayers. I don't want to make anybody forget anybody.[38]

His verse from the "Super Bowl Shuffle," released in 1985:

> Well, they call me Sweetness,
> And I like to dance.
> Runnin' the ball is like makin' romance.
> We've had the goal since training camp,
> To give Chicago a Super Bowl champ.
> And we're not doin' this,
> Because we're greedy.
> The Bears are doin' it to feed the needy.
> We didn't come here to look for trouble,
> We just came to do
> The Super Bowl Shuffle.[39]

On seeing the end of his career at hand only a year after the Bears had used a high draft pick to take running back Neal Anderson:

People won't say it to my face, but you hear mumblings. I remember times when it wasn't me they were on. It was other players, and it was unjust. . . . I'm not a good judge of myself. Everybody wants to think they're as good as when they first came in. You might be slowing down in areas and might not see it, but other people do.

The realization is sinking in that Payton has just played his last game, January 1988.

When even fans suggest that you retire, it hurts, but what can you do? . . . I know you can't maintain what you have forever. I work hard. I'm happy to be where I am, even to be competing with young guys like that and holding my own. It's a thrill to hear people argue, "I think Neal should be playing," or "I think Walter should be playing." I've been here twelve years. I'm an old man.[40]

Reminiscing to reporters immediately after he had played his last game, a 21-17 playoff loss to the Washington Redskins in January 1988:

The last thirteen years there were a lot of good moments and a lot of bad moments. There were times when you didn't want to quit and times when you could see quitting in sight. Over all, it's been

a lot of fun. When you take away the fun, it's time to leave. That's why it's so hard to leave now. It's still fun. God's been very good to me. I'm truly blessed.[41]

On being a Bear:

Searching my mind and soul for the words to express my feelings about being a "Bear," I keep coming back to the famous farewell speech of Lou Gehrig. He was reflecting upon being a Yankee, and I, too, share the same sentiments—I am the luckiest man alive. I am truly blessed.[42]

On living a dream:

I am living proof there is hope for a little boy born in Columbia, Mississippi, to get an opportunity and fulfill his fondest dream.[43]

On life and death:

It's just like football. You never know when or what your last play is going to be. You just play it, and play it because you love it. Same way with life. You live life because you love it. If you can't love it, you just give up hope.[44]

10

WALTER PAYTON: HIS FANS

YOU CAN COUNT ON ONE hand the number of athletes remembered in a book such as this who would warrant a chapter like this, but Walter Payton wasn't an ordinary superstar. He touched thousands of people's lives up close and personal, and some of their heartfelt stories are told here.

◇

My daughter Jill had the happy knack of bumping into Walter Payton from time to time, going back to when she was a pre-teen girl and Walter was still playing for the Bears. One time Jill was buying some cosmetics at a local store in the northwest Chicago suburbs. As Jill was about to pay for the merchandise, a hand reached over her shoulder with the necessary funds to pay the bill. When Jill turned around to see who it was, attached to this rather powerful arm was none other than Walter.

A few years later Jill met and fell in love with a wonderful guy named Michael. Michael was a fanatic Walter Payton fan; he kept

mementos such as a helmet and No. 34 Bears jersey. During Jill and Michael's courtship, Jill saw Walter again. Knowing how much Mike revered Walter, Jill walked over to Walter and asked him to do her a big favor—call Mike at home and say that it's Walter Payton on the phone. Walter being Walter, of course, agreed. Mike answered the phone, heard this guy claiming to be Walter Payton, and reacted as most people would—with total disbelief. Walter didn't give up trying to convince Mike, and, finally, Mike recognized the voice—no one could imitate Walter's voice—and they had a nice chat. Michael never did get to meet Walter in person, but he cherishes the memory of that call. Who else but Walter would do such a thing?

I saw Mr. Payton in a deli near our offices shortly before he got sick and reminded him of the phone call. He remembered, of course, and was delighted to hear how thrilled Mike had been to speak to him. Jill and Michael were married on April 29, 2000, high up in the Sears Tower overlooking Soldier Field. Thoughts of Walter certainly crossed our minds on that beautiful Saturday afternoon.

—*Joseph Weintraub; Hoffman Estates, Illinois*

◇

Being a lifelong Bears fan, I had the privilege of meeting Walter Payton when he was a guest speaker at a golf tournament in which I was playing. I had found a Bears Super Bowl XX poster at Montgomery Inn in Cincinnati, Ohio, that showed him carrying the ball. I asked him to sign it and some pictures for my kids. He signed everything I had. After the autograph session and his speech, he singled me out to talk about my college basketball career. We had gotten on that subject when he was signing my autographs. Little did I know that one of his sincere passions was to play basketball. It absolutely amazed me that someone of his

stature would take time to talk to me, whom he had just met, for over two hours. During the whole time he accommodated each and every person that came up to talk or for an autograph. He always will be the greatest.

—*Michael Gorney; Miami Township, Ohio*

◇

My greatest Walter Payton moment was the day that I was fortunate enough to actually meet Walter Payton. I have been an autograph collector for more than five years, but I've been a Bears fan all my life. I heard on a local radio station that Walter, my hero from childhood, was going to be signing autographs at the grand opening of a hardware store in Springfield, Illinois. I went there the day he was to appear. I waited in line for an hour, but during that time I watched him meet and greet his fans. He was talking to everyone, laughing, and was just having a great time. When I finally got up to the table where he was signing, I handed him a football, which he signed for me. The moment I'll never ever forget is when he handed the football back to me. He shook my hand, looked right at me, and said, "Wow, you're a pretty big boy. Want to arm wrestle?" I was speechless and in total awe of what he had just asked me. Walter was sitting there with his arm on the table trying to get me to wrestle him. He was smiling and saying things like, "C'mon" and "I can take you." I replied, "No, sir, I'd be afraid you'd rip my arm off." He laughed. Walter was so great to his fans that day. He truly is the hero I've always known him to be. The few seconds that I spent with him have made a positive, lifelong impression on me. I will miss him always.

—*Chris Witte; Arenzville, Illinois*

◇

My wife, Marcia, and I were at the races at Road America in Elkhart Lake, Wisconsin, and we heard that Walter Payton would be racing that day. We decided to walk around and try to locate Walter so we could get an autograph or a quick picture. When we located his pit area, we saw Walter behind the gate. We approached him and said hello. To our surprise he welcomed us to come into the "drivers only" area where his car was parked. He chatted with us for the longest time, and then we asked if we could take pictures with him. First I took a picture of my wife with Walter, then I got in position to get in a picture with Walter. Just as my wife took the picture, Walter pinched me in the butt! As you can see from the attached picture, I kind of got a funny look on my face. After the picture was taken, Walter told me that I just looked a little too nervous and serious, so he decided to loosen me up and make me laugh. If my wife wasn't there, nobody would believe that "Hall of Famer" Walter would do this.

Patrick Blackburn, another Payton fan, had just gotten pinched in the behind by Payton when this photo was snapped. Blackburn had plenty of company in that regard over the years.

When Walter passed away, it was a very sad day for me. Tears flowed all day. I was listening to all of the tributes to Walter that day on radio and TV, and then I heard some of the Bears say something that made me feel kind of special. They said that Walter was known as a practical joker and that when he was around someone that he felt comfortable with, he would "goose" them to make them laugh. Just knowing that Walter wanted to spend some time with me and make me laugh will forever remain in my mind, heart, and photo album.

Walter Payton touched many people in small and big ways. He will always be remembered!

—*Patrick Blackburn; Berkeley, Illinois*

◈

This was before records were broken and Super Bowls won. It was more about me than him in some ways. He was a young man with his whole life ahead of him. I was just some guy in the crowd at an auto show in Chicago who never went anywhere without a football in his hands. I have made lifelong friends by asking a guy if he wants to pass the ball around for a bit. You kind of click with someone who touches your life in such a pure and innocent game. He could have been standing at the bus station or in line at a movie. What mattered most to me at that car show was just playing catch, even if just for a couple passes. He was twenty-eight. I passed him the ball up to the stage after he had said I could throw it to him. Catching it, he replies, "Can I keep it?" Now, I had given money to charity and to poor people on the streets and Moonies in airports. I could afford to buy another ball, but that one was special. I should have known that even when I took it out of the box it had greatness already written on it. I would think about that years later when I still had that ball. I would tell people I am

passing a ball that he signed. I think that putting it away would have made it sad. I remember the last time I played catch with it, the strings were all torn and half replaced with a shoelace. You could still see a faded signature of someone who had put it there at one time. I had put my name on it also. It was like me and Walter.

I have since bought many footballs. Most have been the rubber type with the sure grip. There are no names on them. The manufacturer and the amount of pressure needed to inflate is about it. I still pass a nice tight spiral. I do it cause I love to watch it fly. To meet a new friend or pass a few minutes with an old one. It keeps my memory of him with me. And all I did was play catch with it.

—*Leroy Leroy Brown (no joke); Plymouth, Indiana*

◇

I have been a big Bears fan since I was little, watching the games with my dad every Sunday. I met Walter Payton several years ago. Three of my friends and I decided to go to 34's, a dance club in Schaumburg, Illinois, owned by Walter. They were celebrating their fifth anniversary, and Walter was going to be there. When he arrived, he went behind the deejay booth and signed autographs. Of course the booth was surrounded; we couldn't get anywhere near it. My friend John was a police officer in Schaumburg, so I told him that I didn't just want to get Walter's autograph, I wanted to meet him and get my picture taken with him. So I dared John to set it up, and he did.

We went with the manager to an office upstairs, and when we walked in, there stood Walter Payton. He smiled and said, "Hey, guys, come on in. " He was so nice, and when we asked him if we could take pictures of us with him he said, "Sure as long as they don't end up in the Enquirer." We must have taken at least fifteen

Nancy Kriz was one of many Bears and Payton fans who got to meet the man, in some cases, such as hers, more than once.

pictures, one of each of us alone, then two and two, etc. All the while he laughed and joked with us, making us feel so at home. He then offered to autograph them for us if we wanted. Like we would say no! He suggested that we blow them up, put names on the pictures so he could personalize them, and bring them to his office. We spent about forty-five minutes to an hour with Walter, and he never once made us feel that we were imposing on him. He acted like he could spend the whole evening with us.

John did drop off the pictures at Walter's office and a few weeks later I went with him to pick them up. When we asked the receptionist about them, she excused herself and a few minutes later Walter came out into the waiting area to bring us the pictures himself. He asked us if it was OK how he signed them. Wow, like I was going to complain about it!! And once again he was happy and joking with us. John had his police uniform on, and Walter joked with him about arresting and handcuffing him. He talked with us a few more minutes and then excused himself and went back to work.

We were so impressed both times, for as great an athlete as he was and such an important celebrity in Chicago, how down to earth Walter was, how he always seemed to have plenty of time to

talk to us. He was such a wonderful person and role model for young children. He will be missed and always remembered.

Nancy Kriz

◇

I was a summer assistant trainer to Fred Caito at the 1975 summer camp. Walter Payton was late getting to camp because he had played in the College All-Star game. He reported to camp with an injured ankle and forearm. I provided treatment to him when he first arrived. Trainers and players talk about a lot of different things during treatment. He began talking about his best play at Jackson State. He told a story about how he was hit in the legs and did a complete somersault and landed on his feet and went on to score a touchdown. He wasn't bragging. He was just remembering his favorite run. Everybody in the training room began to laugh and said, "Rookie, do you expect us to believe that BS?" Well, as it turns out, we all know that Walter was truly capable of doing just about anything that a running back could imagine. Walter was the perfect football player and a super athlete. Walter treated the trainers as his teammates and nothing less. God bless him for what he and his family gave the Chicago Bears, Chicago fans, and the city of Chicago.

—*Lou Pasquesi; Chicago, Illinois*

◇

I am a former employee of Walter Payton's Roundhouse in Aurora. I only worked there for a short time but was lucky enough to meet Walter. It was on a very busy weekend night that he came to hang out at the restaurant. He went from table to table socializing with the customers. He gave out autographs, played

with the kids, and joked around with everyone. I was new at the time and really wanted to be introduced to him but was too busy to stop to say hi. To my surprise, he made an effort to meet me! Throughout the night he kept tapping me on the shoulder, and every time I turned around he was gone. Finally I caught him! He said to me "You're new. What's you're name?" I told him "Nadene." Then all of a sudden he gave me a huge bear hug and said "Nice to meet you." I was so excited! Walter Payton hugged me! For the short time that I worked there Walter stopped in a few times on the weekends just to say hi to everyone and to make a round through the restaurant entertaining the guests. I thought it was great, and so did everyone else that ever got to meet him at the Roundhouse. I feel very privileged to have met him and will never forget the effect he had on everyone that was in his presence. He was a wonderful person with a great sense of humor. It's a great shame to see him go! We love you, Walter.

—*Nadene Lundmark; Glen Ellyn, Illinois*

◇

Two years in a row my Morton College buddy and me sat beside each other in the National Restaurant Convention Keynote Speech. The first keynote speech was where I embarrassed my buddy. Astronaut Jim Lovell is one of my heroes, but my buddy had to poke me in the ribs because I started snoring loudly during his speech. The next year was Aurora restaurateur Walter Payton's keynote speech. We got into the conference room as soon as the door opened and had an hour to kill. I did most of the talking. My buddy is a Bears fan like my father was. I was a Packers fan. So naturally, I talked about the good old days before Coach Ditka and Sweetness.

Sweetness gave a great speech, yet took very little time behind the podium. One child asked Sweetness to autograph his

program. Many others were asking for the football player's autograph also. Sweetness started walking up and down every aisle as he delivered his speech. Every time Sweetness changed locations, the audience would turn to watch him. The last aisle Sweetness worked was the one on which my aisle seat was located. As Sweetness walked to the back of the aisle behind my chair, I thought, That is Walter Payton. I do not have to watch my back with him behind me. As Sweetness was finishing his speech and moving back to the podium, all of a sudden I felt the strength of Sweetness as he made certain that I did not fall out of my chair as he gave me a Bearhug. No Packer fan failed to be punished around Sweetness. He must have been behind the curtain most of the time I had been telling my buddy about Bear football in the sixties. The last time I felt power like that around my shoulders was when my Bear fan father was very angry at my teenager self. God in heaven must have told my dad to watch the end of Sweetness giving his keynote speech. My daddy is going around heaven saying, "Sweetness hugged my kid!" God takes the good humans way too soon. Watch your pranks in heaven.

—*Robert John Byanski Jr.; Chicago, Illinois*

◇

I had the privilege of meeting Walter Payton in 1985. I was returning to Chicago from an air force reserves duty assignment in Florida. Our flight stopped in Atlanta, and Walter was one of the first passengers to get on. After we departed Atlanta, I asked the flight attendant to see if he would mind if I came up and met him. She went up to first class, where he was the only passenger, and relayed my request. To my delight, Walter turned around with a big smile and motioned for me to come up. I went up to him and introduced myself and told him what an honor it was to meet him. He asked if I would like to sit and talk with him for a

while. I was more than thrilled to accommodate his request. We spent the next half hour or so talking about the Bears and football in general. The thing he seemed to really like was when I asked him about the new Lamborghini that Kangaroo Shoes had given him for breaking the all-time NFL rushing record. He had the delight of a child with a new toy talking about the car, and how fun it was to drive.

I thanked him for taking the time to talk with me, shook his hand, and returned to my seat. For the duration of the flight, I thought of how nervous I was to be meeting such a great athlete, and how he took the time to make me feel comfortable. I left the airport that day and realized I had met a man whom I had regarded as a sports hero, but now had a newfound respect for him. Walter was not only one of the greatest athletes of our time, but also one of the greatest human beings of all time. Thank you, Walter.

—*Jim Fulmer; Portage, Michigan*

◇

In August of 1996 my dad and I went to Payton's Roundhouse in Aurora for Dad's birthday. While we were waiting on our food, we were talking about Walter being seen there all the time. About then I saw Walter come out from the back room and start washing glasses behind the bar. I walked up to him, shook his hand, and asked if he would give my dad his autograph. I told Walter my dad was in a wheelchair and pointed him out. He signed the coaster I handed him, and I said thanks and went back to the table. Our food came, and we ate. While we were deciding on dessert, Walter came over to our table and shook hands with my dad and wished him a happy birthday. All of us talked like we were college buddies. The whole time I kept saying to myself, This is the greatest football player Chicago has ever seen. As he

was leaving our table he told me to "take care of Pops." What a great man. My dad will never forget it. I raise my glass to you, Walter, for the thrills you gave us on the field; more importantly, for being a nice, down-to-earth person that gave my dad a special birthday. Walter, when you see "Pops," tell him hello for me.

—*Kevin Friel; Sandwich, Illinois*

◇

I cried when I met him, and I cried when he left us. I met Walter Payton when I was just graduating from navy boot camp, and me and two of my fellow sailors went to a Bears-Bucs game. We had fifty-yard-line seats and VIP passes to go to a special room and get food and drinks. When we were down in this room, we were approached by a man who told us he used to be in the navy. We were all in uniform. He asked if we wanted to go down to the field for a little tour. When we were down there, I saw so many people that I had never thought I would see in person. Then I saw Walter. I told my buddies I had to meet him. So the man who took us down there introduced us. I mean this was my hero—a very big inspiration for everything I wanted to be, and I was meeting him. I couldn't speak. He thanked us for what we did for our country, and then we got a picture with him and that was it. I started to get teary-eyed. My friends were like, "What's wrong?" I told them I just got to do what men and women all over the world want to do. After we left, I couldn't wait to tell my family. Of course they didn't believe me. But that didn't matter. Now I'm stationed in Okinawa, Japan. I was sitting in my room when they broke to the show we were watching and said the man had passed away. I was heartbroken. I was in a state of shock. I thought men like that lived forever.

—*HN (FMF) Nicholas A. Hanetho; Danville, Illinois;*
stationed in Okinawa, Japan

◈

I was invited to play in a fundraising basketball game against some high school teachers in Rolling Meadows, Illinois, following my rookie season with the L.A. Lakers. I was to play with some Chicago Bears in the game, and it sounded like fun. I go into the locker room and am sitting there getting ready when Walter Payton walks in and sits down next to me and introduces himself to me (like I didn't know who he was!). He was very cordial and made me feel really comfortable right away. He seemed excited to play in the game and seemed to enjoy the opportunity to "get away from his normal workout routine" and play some basketball. The one thing I noticed about Walter in the locker room was his size. He wasn't very tall, but he was as physically fit as anyone I had ever seen. As the game progressed, I couldn't help but watch him play, being the Bears fan that I am and a huge fan of Walter Payton's. He was all over the floor. He would be guarding one guy and follow the pass from one guy to the next.

His quickness was incredible. When he had the ball, he penetrated and tried to go by his man. When he didn't have the ball, he was slashing around and cutting to the basket. He was very active on the floor. The highlight of the game was when he stole the ball at midcourt and went in and dunked it. I could not believe how high he got up and the power that he showed on that play. He was the kind of guy you wanted on your team. He wasn't a great shooter, but he was very competitive, even though it was just a fundraising game. After the game Walter asked me where I worked out during the off-season and gave me his home phone number to give him a call to work out some time. Unfortunately, I did not spend much time in the Chicago area that summer and never got the chance to call him. I am sure that if I had the chance to work out with him, it would have been intimidating. His workout routines are legendary, and I think I would have had a hard time getting through it. When Walter passed away, my

mother called me and reminded me about how I had put Walter's phone number on the fridge when I got home from that game. It stayed on the fridge until they moved three years later! Even though I did not have the chance to know him better, my one night of basketball with him is a great memory that I cherish.

—*Kevin McKenna; an assistant basketball coach at*
Creighton University in Omaha, Nebraska,
who grew up in Palatine, Illinois

◈

Walter Payton is my single most-motivational factor when it comes to just about anything I don't feel like doing. I think back to the day when I saw some guy running up and down this hill near my home on a miserable March afternoon. I was only eleven or twelve and didn't realize who he was at the time. It was raining and cold and six months away from preseason, but that man ran up and down that hill as if his life depended on it. It was probably 1977 and Walter Payton was known around Chicago, but he wasn't as well known as he is today. If somebody would have told me that was Walter Payton running up and down that hill over there, I probably would have gone over and talked to him. But my friend and I didn't realize who he was. We just watched him for a little while and thought, That guy must be nuts, it's miserable out here. We thought he was going to kill himself. A few weeks later a local sportscaster did a short segment on Walter Payton and some of his exercise routine. They showed him running that hill, and I realized who we saw that miserable day. He was out there all by himself; there was no coach yelling at him, no photographers taking photographs of him, no other teammates to motivate him, and no fans asking for autographs from him. I'm sure there's many other things Walter Payton could have done that cold rainy day. I can't tell you how many times I haven't felt

like doing something and I think back to that day—what a glorious vision Walter Payton was that miserable day.

—*Tom Borst*

◇

I remember being in Woodfield Mall in Schaumburg, Illinois, with my wife on the Friday before a Mother's Day when we noticed a well-dressed man with a striking outfit entering a store with a little girl perhaps eight or nine years of age. I looked again and exclaimed to my wife, "Hey, that's Walter Payton"! She said to me "Are you sure?" I stated that I was certain and proceeded to enter the same store to satisfy my curiosity. Well, it was Walter all right. He was standing off to one side watching while the young girl was browsing the aisles. Walter looked splendid in black slacks, a black shirt, a bright yellow sportcoat and a black and yellow tie to match (an outfit only Walter could get away with wearing). I approached Walter with a greeting and introduced myself, shook his hand and introduced him to my wife, Diane. Walter was extremely cordial and explained to us that he was merely escorting his daughter because she wanted to pick out a Mother's Day gift. My wife mentioned to Walter that I was truly a "die-hard" Bears fan and a longtime season ticket holder—a very vocal one at that. She stated, "I bet you could even hear him on the field." Walter asked me where my seats were, and after I told him, he replied, "You know . . . I think I did hear you," and he laughed. We laughed, and I talked about some great Bear "memories" I had about him. I know at one point I mentioned to him that my license plate was URSA FAN, and that *ursa,* a Latin word, means "bear." He thought that my plates were pretty clever, but that I probably had to do a lot of explaining to most average people—like him—then he laughed out loud at his comment with that huge grin that could light up a room. I then began to compli-

ment him on his outfit—when he stopped me with a laugh and said, "I guess I'm not exactly incognito, am I?" We laughed and agreed with him. Soon some young boys and older teenagers noticed Walter was there and a crowd was forming, so I thanked Walter for his time and wished him well. He said that it was a pleasure talking to us, but felt he should check on his daughter. Walter was talking to the group around him and signing autographs as we exited the store. It was one small non-event in his life I'm sure, but a lasting memory in mine.

—*Bill Walenda; Addison, Illinois*

◇

About two years ago I flew to Las Vegas to meet my sister Bonnie and her husband, Mike, for a day of sightseeing and gambling. We spent the afternoon mingling and casino hopping when we happened to stumble into Caesars Palace. As we toured this grand casino, we stopped at a bank of slot machines, where suddenly Mike shouted, "There's Walter Payton!" Sure enough, I looked over to see none other than the great Walter himself just standing there in the middle of the casino. Well, I had no idea how to approach the famous figure. With a little persuasion from Mike, I took a deep breath and sauntered over to him. Without having anything prepared, I just blurted out, "Mr. Payton, my name is Scott. I am from Chicago, and I am a big fan!" As I held out my hand, he grabbed it, pulled me close, and said, "Please call me Walter!" As I gushed in his presence, I rambled on about his records and if he was concerned about Barry Sanders breaking them. He then put an arm around me, gave me a shot in the ribs, and said, "All records are bound to be broken!" We soon parted, but as I turned to leave I felt a great deal of pride for having met a truly class act.

—*Scott Heiden; Chicago, Illinois*

◇

Walter has a restaurant in downtown Aurora, Illinois, and in combination with the Fox Valley Park District, he sponsored the Sweetness Run, which was a 5K-10K race that included wheelchair racers. I am a police sergeant for Aurora and was in charge of security for the race. One of the agreements we had was that when Walter was out among the public and inside his restaurant, an officer was to be with him the entire time. I really didn't have any officers to spare, so I did it.

Some professional athletes have a "too good" attitude and find people somewhat annoying. He never gave that impression. He spent time talking to all of us, veterans or rookies, in a professional, friendly manner—never belittling us. We would walk around the restaurant, and he was equally as friendly to all his employees and never backed off from the public. He would pick up kids and carry them around. He never seemed to get tired or bored or bothered and made everyone feel special.

There was a young girl in the race that I knew and who got sick after the run. Walter sat with her and told her that it was good to get sick because now she knows her limits and where to improve. This was good advice from someone who knew.

When we had taken him out to the pace car to lead the race, he had asked to be handcuffed. We obliged, and he gave quite a comical performance as we walked into the crowd. It was obvious he genuinely enjoys being with people of all ages. As we drove the course, he would carry on a conversation with me, my daughter, and a nephew who rode along, as if we knew him all our lives.

I was totally impressed with his mannerism, demeanor, and genuine realism. He had to be somewhere after the race, and his partner kept reminding him to get going, but he chose to spend a few extra minutes with the other officers and myself, laughing and joking with us, never using his celebrity

status as a power trip. I gave him a hard time about his singing voice at Wrigley Field, and he jokingly warned me to be careful.

Patrick Rolison; Aurora, Illinois

◇

Back in the late seventies, I was the engineering manager for the company that manufactured Walter's football helmet. As an avid Bears fan, I made it a point to see as many games as I could. Even though he had only been playing a couple of years, it was clear that Walter was emerging as a superstar.

During the course of one televised game, the broadcaster excitedly announced that Walter was playing with a helmet that had cracked in back. I was alarmed. That was absolutely not supposed to happen.

Back in those days, we had an agreement with the NFL—any helmet damaged during the course of a game was to be on my desk Monday morning for evaluation. But Walter was superstitious and wouldn't part with the helmet that had been given him during his rookie year. After several discussions with the Bears equipment manager, Walter agreed to let me look at the helmet, but only if he brought it in personally.

The next day he came into my office cradling his helmet. After we shook hands, he sat down and placed his helmet on my desk. In my job, I was well aware of the superstitious nature of many sports figures. Even so, I couldn't help noticing that even as he sat and we spoke our first words, Walter held on to his helmet with his fingers wrapped tightly around the facemask. He wasn't about to let it go.

After introductions were made, I explained that our concern about the cracked helmet was that thousands of high school kids were playing with the exact same helmet. For their safety, it was imperative that we find out why it had failed. Walter understood

immediately and became as concerned as I was. He agreed to let me have the helmet on the conditions that we would do only nondestructive testing on it, and that he could have it back when we were through. I agreed, with the understanding he could never play in that helmet again—which he wanted to do.

When our business was through, we spent the next thirty minutes chatting about football in general and safety issues in particular. His soft-spoken, polite, and respectful manner had already impressed me, but it was during that time I discovered his great sense of humor. He was quick to laugh and just as quick with a one-liner. When our meeting was over, I felt like I had known him for years.

Three days later, I reported to the equipment manager that they had used the wrong paint on Walter's helmet. The paint had "attacked" and crystallized the plastic, reducing the helmet's impact resistance—hence the crack. I asked that Walter be told of the test results and told them that his helmet would be returned the next day. Later that afternoon he called me. I'll never forget his question to me. "Are you sure," he asked, "that the kids will be safe?"

In that one-hour meeting with him, I learned that his nickname—"Sweetness"—was as real as it gets, that he had an enormous concern for the youngsters playing the game of football, and that he had a wonderful, genuine sense of humor. The last I heard, by the way, his cracked helmet was in the Football Hall of Fame.

—*Unsigned*

◈

I was born and raised in the Chicago suburb of Skokie. When I was growing up, the only football team my father and I followed was the Chicago Bears—through the good and not-so-good years,

we followed them and their progress, never giving up on our team. The first game I ever saw was a Bears-Packers game. What impressed me the most, though, about Walter Payton was his soft-spokenness and his unselfishness. He would go out every play and do what he had to, to help the Bears try to get a win. I played Little League baseball. At the end of every season, the league held a banquet for all teams in the league, from the youngest up to the oldest group of kids that played ball. At the banquet, there would be a guest speaker, usually an athlete from one of Chicago's six sports teams. I believe the year was 1978, when Walter came and spoke. He told the crowd about his experiences in football with the Bears, and how he could not imagine playing for any other team. He talked about the training camps, what it was like to play week in and week out, the dreaded Chicago winters, and being able to play against some of the best football players of the day. I think what really stuck in my mind was when he talked about his work ethic. He always did more than the other person, just to stay on top of his game, and be the best. He mentioned how important it was for us as youngsters to always strive to do our best, and work hard. But the most important aspect of playing sports is to enjoy what you are doing, because without enjoyment it takes the fun out of playing.

After he spoke, the kids then had a chance to meet him and have him sign a team pennant for us. Upon learning about his death, I went into my garage and found the old pennant—it was rolled up and in a plastic bag. I unrolled it, and the pennant did not roll back up (much to my surprise). The pennant was personalized, and autographed by him with his number. After twenty-two years, the pennant is in great shape.

—*David Berkson; Arcola, Illinois*

◆

I met him at a picnic in Schaumburg, where he and my aunt had offices in the same building. My aunt invited me to the company picnic because she said Walter would be there. He played games with the rest of us, and I even played him in a putting contest. He was unbelievable, talking and kidding like he was just a normal guy. After the games he did pictures and autographs, never once turning anyone away. I was more impressed with his human spirit than the fact that I just got the autograph of one of the greatest football players of all time. I think I figured out where the "Sweetness" thing came from.

—*Roger Sakinsky; McHenry, Illinois*

◇

My family has been Bears season-ticket holders since 1959, when the Bears used to play at Wrigley Field. (As an aside, on the day that Gale Sayers broke his leg, as he was being carried off the field, my dad told my mom that it was just a "thigh bruise.") My father was a Sayers man, until Walter came along.

When Walter first joined the Bears, I was pumped. I went to all the games. There is a tunnel that leads to the Bears locker room that I would visit after the player warm-ups before the game. During his rookie season, Walter walked past me and stopped where I was standing to smile, extended his hand, and asked my name. I shook his hand, wished him well, and ran back up to my seat by my parents to tell them what happened.

What happened the next year is unbelievable. During the first game of the year and almost a year after I met him in the tunnel, Walter walked past me and said, "Hi, Bill. How ya doin'?" Wow!!!! Walter Payton, my boyhood hero, remembered my name!!!!!! I again ran up the stairs to tell my parents, who were equally impressed with his memory and genuine caring. You see, Walter was one of very few sources of joy for me in my boyhood. I wasn't

very popular or athletic. Walter brought so many good Sunday memories during a rough time of my life and it was greatly needed and appreciated. His remembering my name meant the world to me!!!!!

Later the next year, on a cold and blustery November afternoon, I went down the tunnel as I had done before and sought out Walter. Finally, he came out of the locker room, but he looked feverish with beads of sweat on his forehead, above his lips, and basically all over. His nose was running. He reached out to shake my hand, and I noticed that the strongest handshake I had ever felt had been reduced to nothing. His hand fell into mine with no strength. I looked at his weak condition and asked, "You OK?" He looked at me and just said, "Just a little flu, Bill, I'll be all right." I was not convinced, so I went back up to my parents' seats and said, "Walter looks sick, he doesn't look like he'll do real well today."

He rushed forty times for 275 yards to set the NFL record while sick as a dog. My father looked at me and said, "Sick, huh?"

—*Bill Sibert; Lake Zurich, Illinois*

◇

P.S. Here's a side story:

I went to a game one time against the Raiders and had stolen my dad's vodka bottle, poured out the vodka (I did not like vodka) and substituted some bourbon. A friend and I had gone down to see the players before the game, and while we were waiting, we decided to take a swig or two. Upon my first sip, a very large Chicago policeman guarding the Bears locker room door saw us, came over, and said, "You know you are not supposed to have bottles here at Soldier Field. Give me that." He confiscated the bottle and told us to get lost. Walter had witnessed the whole thing, and

as I was getting tossed from the area, he gave me the "shame/shame" finger gesture and was laughing pretty hard. He laughed even harder when we came back at halftime and saw that cop crocked on our whiskey. The guy was red-faced, obviously drunk, and slurring his words. Walter thought that was hysterical.

—*Bill Sider*

◇

I first met Walter at his annual Halas Hall/Walter Payton Foundation Golf Tournament in Oak Brook, Illinois, in the early nineties. My many duties at the tournament included working Casino Night at his then-nightclub, the Pacific Club. I was playing hostess at the "Money Wheel" and assisted another former Bear, Curtiss Gentry, at the blackjack table. Walter was being his usual self, greeting people and hosting the event. He made everyone feel welcome by meeting each and every person at his fundraiser and taking the time to pose for pictures.

My purpose at the tournament was hospitality and media. At the hospitality center, Walter took the time out to get to know me and thanked me for volunteering for his event in which I thought was very nice of him. Little did I know, Walter had something up his sleeve. As the media person, it was my job to assist the photographer and any media crew for photo opportunities and interviews. Walter made it a point to be available and ham it up for the photographer and any media personnel that were around.

During his hamming sessions and throughout the tournament, Walter would drive his golf cart wildly on the course, playing golf polo while going between holes or fencing with other celebs on the course. Of course, Walter would play his practical jokes on the participants and volunteers. During one of his escapades, Walter got me reeeeal good. I did not realize what was going on since I was so tuned in to what I was doing for the event. Suddenly, Walter was grabbing his side as if in pain, so I

began to assist him to his cart and asked if he was all right. His
reply was, "Me lady, I hath been wounded." I realized then, he
was clowning around. Then, the jokester offered me a ride in the
cart but moved it as I tried to get in!

I saw Walter years later after another event, and he still
remembered me.

—*Sophia L. McGrew; Waukegan, Illinois*

◈

I remember as a little girl watching Walter Payton when the Bears
played the Detroit Lions. I lived in Detroit and was a big fan of all
of the Detroit teams, except for the Lions. For some reason, I
never liked the Lions, and after seeing Walter play a few games, I
decided to give up the hometown team in favor of a team that had
the greatest player to take the field—Walter Payton. I went to col-
lege outside of Chicago (Wheaton College) and was there the year
the Bears won the Super Bowl.

My greatest memory of Walter was getting to meet him on
the *Oprah Winfrey Show.* She had a show where people got to
meet their sports heroes, and I was fortunate enough to be cho-
sen to meet Walter. It was in meeting Walter that I realized the
reason he had the nickname "Sweetness"; it's because he is the
sweetest guy you'd ever want to meet. He made me feel like I
was the important one as he stayed after the taping to sign some
items for me and just talk for a little while. He could have just
cut out like the other sports celebrities did that day, but he
didn't; he stayed and took the time to give me just a little bit
extra. Years after that meeting, I had the thrill of being at the
Hall of Fame when he was inducted, and I was moved by his
speech of how we are all role models and how we can take
something good from every person we meet. These weren't just
words—Walter Payton lived them. He was the role model's role

model. Like most fans of his it broke my heart to see him look so weak when he first announced his illness, but I was also proud of the way he fought it to the end and became an advocate for organ donation. I can picture his last days and think about him reading Scripture and praying with Mike Singletary, and I find peace in knowing that the greatest football player to ever play the game is in heaven. I have many things to keep his memory alive, including a dog named after him, but the best will always be the memory of standing at the *Oprah* show as he shook my hand and his saying, "Nice to meet you, Shelley, I'm Walter Payton." (Like he had to tell me!)

—*Shelley Dodson; Liberty, Indiana*

◇

I had a chance to see Walter Payton not only at Soldier Field while I was sitting in the stands watching the game but also at the Mike Singletary Invitational Eight Ball Tournament that was played at Navy Pier several years back for a children's charity. I was able to actually meet Walter and talk with him and have my picture taken with him. This is a moment that I will always treasure. He talked and teased me as if I had known him for years, when actually it was the first time I met him. Another reason I had admired him was because there were people walking around with briefcases filled with his pictures and wanted him to sign them. He refused to do so knowing that they would take those pictures and sell them out on the street. This was a children's benefit we were at, and he knew that what these people were trying to do was wrong. Watching him that day play pool and have fun with the other athletes and audience truly showed how much he enjoyed fun and life.

—*Pat Witt; Lombard, Illinois*

I had the pleasure of meeting Walter Payton prior to the 1995 running of the Indianapolis 500. The Payton-Koyne team was preparing their car for a qualification attempt.

Since I am in charge of a golf outing to benefit the Keenan-Stahl Girls and Boys Club, I am always interested in finding sports memorabilia and autographs for the charity auction connected with the outing. I have worked at the Speedway for more than fifteen years and had heard that Walter Payton would be there in person on the Friday before qualifications. Knowing this, I purchased two footballs with the hope of simply getting a famous football player's autograph. Little did I know that I would come away with so much more!

In my position at the track, I am used to talking to race-car drivers and celebrities that visit the garage area. But I must admit that when I first saw Walter Payton standing alone in the corner of their team garage, my heart started racing (no pun intended!). I somehow gathered the courage to approach him and began stammering my request. To my amazement, he began asking me questions about the club and was genuinely interested. After talking for about fifteen minutes, Walter signed both of my footballs.

It is difficult even today to think of Walter Payton without a smile on my face and a tear in my eye. Maybe someday when the dictionary is rewritten and someone looks up the word class, Walter Payton will be listed as a synonym.

—*Jim Keenan; Greenwood, Indiana*

During a Monday morning staff meeting in 1983, about fifteen coworkers and I decided to visit Studebaker's in Schaumburg after work that evening. I believe that was Walter Payton's first

restaurant/bar. Throughout the day, I kept kidding a fellow female worker, Karen, that I knew Walter and would introduce her if he was at the bar that evening. Of course, I didn't know Mr. Payton, but I never expected him to be there either.

As luck would have it, Walter was at Studebaker's that evening. I was fortunate enough to speak with him in the back of the club and asked if he could come and greet our group. I mentioned how Karen was one of his biggest fans. On the way to the group, he casually asked me my name. Upon reaching the group, he introduced himself as my friend and asked for Karen. Then he bought the entire group a round of drinks and signed autographs for all of us. Karen was ecstatic, and the entire group was in awe, believing that I actually knew Walter Payton. The most amazing fact is that I never mentioned to Walter about my false bragging of knowing him. I believe that he just sensed something and played along with it.

My second encounter with Walter Payton was in February 1988 at the Pro Bowl in Hawaii. My wife and I were vacationing at the Hilton Hawaii Village. Unbeknown to us, the players were staying at the same hotel. Although Walter was not in the Pro Bowl that year, he was there supporting several teammates. My wife and I ran into him on the hotel grounds one early evening on our way to a booze cruise. I could not resist mentioning our previous encounter five years earlier. While I am sure Walter did not really remember, he claimed to recall the meeting and stated how he was pleased to meet me again.

It was with both great sadness and joy that I attended the memorial service for Walter Payton on November 6, 1999. Those memories will forever be with me, along with the thousand others that I have from watching every Bear game during his career. I think my most cherished memory is that I was so fortunate to have slightly grazed the life of one of the most dedicated and special people to walk the face of the earth.

—*Rick Alcala; Bridgeview, Illinois*

NOTES

CHAPTER 1: OUT OF MISSISSIPPI
1. *New York Times,* November 2, 1999.
2. Mark Sufrin, *Payton* (New York: Charles Scribner's Sons, 1988), p. 87.
3. WFLD Fox Television, Chicago, coverage of Soldier Field Memorial Service for Walter Payton.

CHAPTER 3: THE GOLDEN BEARS
1. WFLD Fox Television, Chicago, coverage of Soldier Field Memorial Service for Walter Payton.

CHAPTER 4: SWEETNESS
1. WFLD Fox Television, Chicago, coverage of Soldier Field Memorial Service for Walter Payton.
2. Ibid.
3. Ben Woods ,reprinted by permission.

CHAPTER 5: THAT'S THE SPIRIT
1. WFLD Fox Television, Chicago, coverage of Soldier Field Memorial Service for Walter Payton.
2. Ibid.
3. Ibid.

4. Ibid.
5. Ibid.
6. Ibid.
7. *Sports Illustrated,* November 8, 1999.
8. *Jet* magazine, November 22, 1999.

Chapter 7: Walter Payton, Superstar

1. Sufrin, *Payton,* p. 30.
2. Mike Ditka, with Don Pierson, *Ditka: An Autobiography.* (Chicago: Bonus Books, 1986), pp. 218, 220.
3. *Football Digest,* February 2000.
4. Sufrin, *Payton,* p. 108.
5. WFLD Fox Television, Chicago, coverage of Soldier Field Memorial Service for Walter Payton.

Chapter 8: Walter Payton: Dollars and Sense

1. *Chicago Tribune,* November 30, 1999.

Chapter 9: Short (and Sweet) Takes

1. *Football Digest,* February 2000.
2. *Sports Illustrated,* November 8, 1999.
3. Ibid.
4. Sufrin, *Payton,* p. 1.
5. *Football Digest,* February 2000.
6. Ibid.
7. Ibid.
8. *Sports Illustrated,* November 8, 1999.
9. Associated Press wire story, January 6, 2000.
10. *Chicago Tribune,* November 5, 1999.
11. *Chicago Tribune,* November 2, 1999.
12. Ibid.
13. Ibid.
14. Ibid.
15. Sufrin, *Payton,* p. 8.
16. Ibid., p. 12.

17. Ibid., p. 15.
18. Ibid., p. 17.
19. Ibid., p. 32.
20. Ibid., p. 43.
21. Ibid., pp. 84–85.
22. Ibid., p. 110.
23. Ibid., p. 139.
24. Ditka and Pierson, *Ditka*, p. 217.
25. *Football Digest*, February 2000.
26. *People* magazine, November 15, 1999.
27. *The Sporting News*, November 15, 1999.
28. *Chicago Tribune*, November 2, 1999.
29. Ibid.
30. Ibid.
31. Ibid.
32. Ibid.
33. Ibid.
34. Sufrin, *Payton*, p. 33.
35. Ibid., p. 64.
36. *Chicago Tribune*, November 2, 1999.
37. Ibid.
38. Ibid.
39. "Super Bowl Shuffle," Red Label Records, 1985. Lyrics by R. Meyer and M. Owens.
40. Sufrin, *Payton*, p. 115.
41. Ibid., p. 139.
42. Richard Whittingham, *The Bears: A 75-Year Celebration* (Dallas: Taylor Publishing, 1994), p. xi.
43. Ibid.
44. *Chicago Tribune*, November 2, 1999.

APPENDIX:
WALTER PAYTON BY THE NUMBERS

REGULAR-SEASON, GAME-BY-GAME RUSHING STATS AND SEASON TOTALS FOR RUSHING AND RECEIVING

1975

Opponent	Result	Score	Carries	Yards
Baltimore Colts	L	7-35	8	0
Philadelphia Eagles	W	15-13	21	95
at Minnesota Vikings	L	3-28	18	61
at Detroit Lions	L	7-27	10	0
at Pittsburgh Steelers	L	3-34	DNP	
Minnesota Vikings	L	9-13	10	44
Miami Dolphins	L	13-46	7	26
Green Bay Packers	W	27-14	14	49
at San Francisco 49ers	L	3-31	23	105
at Los Angeles Rams	L	10-38	4	2
at Green Bay Packers	L	7-28	12	40
Detroit Lions	W	25-21	27	65
St. Louis Cardinals	L	20-34	17	58
at New Orleans Saints	W	42-17	25	134

Season Totals:
196 carries, 679 yards, 7 TDs
33 receptions, 213 yards, 0 TDs

1976

Opponent	Result	Score	Carries	Yards
Detroit Lions	W	10-3	25	70
at San Francisco 49ers	W	19-12	28	148
Atlanta Falcons	L	0-10	23	86
Washington Redskins	W	33-7	18	104
at Minnesota Vikings	L	19-20	19	141
at Los Angeles Rams	L	12-20	27	145
at Dallas Cowboys	L	21-31	17	41
Minnesota Vikings	W	14-13	15	67
Oakland Raiders	L	27-28	36	97
Green Bay Packers	W	24-13	18	109
at Detroit Lions	L	10-14	17	40
at Green Bay Packers	W	16-10	27	110
at Seattle Seahawks	W	34-7	27	183
Denver Broncos	L	14-28	14	49

Season Totals:
311 carries, 1,390 yards, 13 TDs
15 receptions, 149 yards, 0 TDs

1977

Opponent	Result	Score	Carries	Yards
Detroit Lions	W	30-20	23	160
at St. Louis Cardinals	L	13-16	11	36
New Orleans Saints	L	24-42	19	140
Los Angeles Rams	W	24-23	24	126
at Minnesota Vikings	L	16-22	24	122
Atlanta Falcons	L	10-16	24	69
at Green Bay Packers	W	26-0	23	205
at Houston Oilers	L	0-47	18	79
Kansas City Chiefs	W	28-27	33	192
Minnesota Vikings	W	10-7	40	275
at Detroit Lions	W	31-14	20	137
at Tampa Bay Bucs	W	10-0	33	101

Green Bay Packers	W	21-10	32	163
at New York Giants	W	12-9	15	47

Season Totals:
39 carries, 1,852 yards, 14 TDs
27 receptions, 269 yards, 2 TDs

1978

Opponent	Result	Score	Carries	Yards
St. Louis Cardinals	W	17-10	26	101
at San Francisco 49ers	W	16-13	21	62
at Detroit Lions	W	19-0	22	77
Minnesota Vikings	L	20-24	24	58
Oakland Raiders	L	19-25	27	123
at Green Bay Packers	L	14-24	19	82
at Denver Broncos	L	7-16	22	157
at Tampa Bay Bucs	L	19-33	15	34
Detroit Lions	L	17-21	18	89
Seattle Seahawks	L	29-31	18	109
at Minnesota Vikings	L	14-17	23	127
Atlanta Falcons	W	13-7	20	34
Tampa Bay Bucs	W	14-3	27	105
at San Diego Chargers	L	7-40	17	50
Green Bay Packers	W	14-0	18	97
at Washington Redskins	W	14-10	16	90

Season Totals:
333 carries, 1,395 yards, 11 TDs
50 receptions, 480 yards, 0 TDs

1979

Opponent	Result	Score	Carries	Yards
Green Bay Packers	W	6-3	36	125
Minnesota Vikings	W	26-7	23	182
at Dallas Cowboys	L	20-24	22	134
at Miami Dolphins	L	16-31	15	43

Tampa Bay Bucs	L	13-17	15	46
at Buffalo Bills	W	7-0	39	155
New England Patriots	L	7-27	15	42
at Minnesota Vikings	L	27-30	23	111
at San Francisco 49ers	W	28-27	23	162
Detroit Lions	W	35-7	22	113
Los Angeles Rams	W	27-23	18	41
New York Jets	W	23-13	20	53
at Detroit Lions	L	0-20	18	54
at Tampa Bay Bucs	W	14-0	22	77
at Green Bay Packers	W	15-14	25	115
St. Louis Cardinals	W	42-6	33	157

Season Totals:
369 carries, 1,610 yards, 14 TDs
31 receptions, 313 yards, 2 TDs

1980

Opponent	Result	Score	Carries	Yards
at Green Bay Packers	L	6-12	31	65
New Orleans Saints	W	22-3	18	183
Minnesota Vikings	L	14-34	16	39
at Pittsburgh Steelers	L	3-38	12	60
Tampa Bay Bucs	W	23-0	28	183
at Minnesota Vikings	L	7-13	23	102
Detroit Lions	W	24-7	27	101
at Philadelphia Eagles	L	14-17	17	79
at Cleveland Browns	L	21-27	11	30
Washington Redskins	W	35-21	17	107
Houston Oilers	L	6-10	18	60
at Atlanta Falcons	L	17-28	12	40
at Detroit Lions	W	23-17	18	123
Green Bay Packers	W	61-7	22	130
Cincinnati Bengals	L	14-17	18	78
at Tampa Bay Bucs	W	14-13	29	130

Season Totals:
317 carries, 1,460 yards, 6 TDs
46 receptions, 367 yards, 1 TD

1981

Opponent	Result	Score	Carries	Yards
Green Bay Packers	L	9-16	19	81
at San Francisco 49ers	L	17-28	27	97
Tampa Bay Bucs	W	28-17	21	64
Los Angeles Rams	L	7-24	17	45
at Minnesota Vikings	L	21-24	20	49
Washington Redskins	L	7-24	5	5
at Detroit Lions	L	17-48	19	89
San Diego Chargers	W	20-17	36	107
at Tampa Bay Bucs	L	10-20	22	92
at Kansas City Chiefs	W	16-13	21	70
at Green Bay Packers	L	17-21	22	105
Detroit Lions	L	7-23	13	37
at Dallas Cowboys	L	9-10	38	179
Minnesota Vikings	W	10-9	33	112
at Oakland Raiders	W	23-6	7	28
Denver Broncos	W	35-24	19	62

Season Totals:
339 carries, 1,222 yards, 6 TDs
41 receptions, 379 yards, 2 TDs

1982

Opponent	Result	Score	Carries	Yards
at Detroit Lions	L	10-17	14	26
New Orleans Saints	L	0-10	8	20
Detroit Lions	W	20-17	21	87
at Minnesota Vikings	L	7-35	12	67
New England Patriots	W	26-13	13	70
at Seattle Seahawks	L	14-20	14	40
St. Louis Cardinals	L	7-10	20	73

at Los Angeles Rams	W	34-26	20	104
at Tampa Bay Bucs	L	23-26	26	109

Season Totals:
148 carries, 596 yards, 1 TD
32 receptions, 311 yards, 0 TDs
(Note: Strike-shortened season)

1983

Opponent	Result	Score	Carries	Yards
Atlanta Falcons	L	17-20	20	103
Tampa Bay Bucs	W	17-10	17	45
at New Orleans Saints	L	31-34	28	161
at Baltimore Colts	L	19-22	3	4
Denver Broncos	W	31-14	23	91
Minnesota Vikings	L	14-23	20	102
at Detroit Lions	L	17-31	15	86
at Philadelphia Eagles	W	7-6	30	82
Detroit Lions	L	17-38	20	80
at Los Angeles Rams	L	14-21	14	62
Philadelphia Eagles	W	17-14	23	131
at Tampa Bay Bucs	W	27-0	22	106
San Francisco 49ers	W	13-3	16	68
at Green Bay Packers	L	28-31	16	58
at Minnesota Vikings	W	19-13	17	94
Green Bay Packers	W	23-21	30	148

Season Totals:
314 carries, 1,421 yards, 6 TDs
53 receptions, 607 yards, 2 TDs

1984

Opponent	Result	Score	Carries	Yards
Tampa Bay Bucs	W	34-14	16	61
Denver Broncos	W	27-0	20	179
at Green Bay Packers	W	9-7	27	110

at Seattle Seahawks	L	9-38	24	116
Dallas Cowboys	L	14-23	25	155
New Orleans Saints	W	20-7	32	154
at St. Louis Cardinals	L	21-38	23	100
at Tampa Bay Bucs	W	44-9	20	72
Minnesota Vikings	W	16-7	22	54
Los Angeles Raiders	W	17-6	27	111
at Los Angeles Rams	L	13-29	13	60
Detroit Lions	W	16-14	29	66
at Minnesota Vikings	W	34-3	23	117
at San Diego Chargers	L	7-20	23	92
Green Bay Packers	L	14-20	35	175
at Detroit Lions	W	30-13	22	62

Season Totals:
381 carries, 1,684 yards, 11 TDs
45 receptions, 368 yards, 0 TDs

1985

Opponent	Result	Score	Carries	Yards
Tampa Bay Bucs	W	38-28	17	120
New England Patriots	W	20-7	11	39
at Minnesota Vikings	W	33-24	15	62
Washington Redskins	W	45-10	7	6
at Tampa Bay Bucs	W	27-19	16	63
at San Francisco 49ers	W	26-10	24	132
Green Bay Packers	W	23-7	25	112
Minnesota Vikings	W	27-9	19	118
at Green Bay Packers	W	16-10	28	192
Detroit Lions	W	24-3	26	107
at Dallas Cowboys	W	44-0	22	132
Atlanta Falcons	W	36-0	20	102
at Miami Dolphins	L	24-38	23	121
Indianapolis Colts	W	17-10	26	111
at New York Jets	W	19-6	28	53
at Detroit Lions	W	37-17	17	81

Season Totals:
324 carries, 1,551 yards, 9 TDs
49 receptions, 483 yards, 1 TD

1986

Opponent	Result	Score	Carries	Yards
Cleveland Browns	W	41-31	22	113
Philadelphia Eagles	W	13-10	34	177
at Green Bay Packers	W	25-12	18	57
at Cincinnati Bengals	W	44-7	10	51
Minnesota Vikings	W	23-0	28	108
at Houston Oilers	W	20-7	22	76
at Minnesota Vikings	L	7-23	9	28
Detroit Lions	W	13-7	21	67
Los Angeles Rams	L	17-20	19	61
at Tampa Bay Bucs	W	23-3	20	139
at Atlanta Falcons	W	13-10	20	69
Green Bay Packers	W	12-10	17	85
Pittsburgh Steelers	W	13-10	31	90
Tampa Bay Bucs	W	48-14	20	78
at Detroit Lions	W	16-13	19	83
at Dallas Cowboys	W	24-10	13	51

Season Totals:
321 carries, 1,333 yards, 8 TDs
37 receptions, 382 yards, 1 TD

1987

Opponent	Result	Score	Carries	Yards
New York Giants	W	34-19	18	42
Tampa Bay Bucs	W	20-3	15	24
at Tampa Bay Bucs	W	27-26	6	30
Kansas City Chiefs	W	31-28	8	15
at Green Bay Packers	W	26-24	8	22
at Denver Broncos	L	29-31	12	73
Detroit Lions	W	30-10	13	60

Green Bay Packers	W	23-10	8	22
at Minnesota Vikings	W	30-24	10	39
at San Francisco 49ers	L	0-41	7	18
Seattle Seahawks	L	21-34	17	79
at Los Angeles Raiders	W	6-3	20	82

Season Totals:
146 carries, 533 yards, 4 TDs
33 receptions, 217 yards, 1 TD
(Note: Includes only games in which Payton played. One 1987 game canceled by players' strike and three games played with replacement players.)

CAREER TOTALS (REGULAR SEASON):

Rushing:	3,838 carries
	16,726 yards
	110 TDs
Receiving:	492 receptions
	4,538 yards
	15 TDs
Kickoff returns:	17 returns
	539 yards (31.9 ave.)
	0 TDs
Passing:	34 attempts
	11 completions
	331 yards
	8 TDs, 5 INTs

CAREER PLAYOFF GAME STATS

	Result	Score	Carries	Yards
1977				
at Dallas Cowboys	L	7-37	19	60
1979				
at Philadelphia Eagles	L	17-27	16	67

1984

at Washington Redskins	W	23-19	24	104
at San Francisco 49ers	L	0-23	22	92

1985

New York Giants	W	21-0	27	93
Los Angeles Rams	W	24-0	18	32
New England Patriots	W	46-10	22	61

(Super Bowl)

1986

Washington Redskins	L	13-27	14	38

1987

Washington Redskins	L	17-21	18	85

Playoff Totals:
180 carries, 632 yards, 2 TDs
22 receptions, 178 yards, 0 TDs

(Source: Chicago Tribune *special section, "The Greatest Bear,"*
November 7, 1999)

INDEX

ABOUT THE AUTHOR

Mike Towle is a veteran writer and author who has written about sports for more than thirty years. As a sports reporter, he covered the National Football League, among other beats, for the *Fort Worth Star-Telegram* and *The National*. His previous books include *I Remember Ben Hogan, I Ain't Never Been Anything But a Winner, Roger Staubach, I Remember Vince Lombardi,* and many more. The president of Towle House Books, he lives in Nashville, Tennessee.